Outsta... ...
Michael Curt...

THE LAST KING

"Michael Curtis Ford's love for the ancient world emanates from every page: in his magical settings and spectacular re-creation of monuments and landscapes, in his bold portraits of the protagonists, and in his intriguing and swiftly-moving plot."

—Valerio Massimo Manfredi,
author of the "Alexander Trilogy" and *Spartan*

"Ford captures the Roman first century B.C. from a novel perspective, viewing it through the prism of one of Rome's most formidable enemies. Battle scenes are described with great skill . . . the book demonstrates the author's ability to imagine the Roman world from its periphery and shows the same mastery of military history as his first novel, *The Ten Thousand*."

—*Publishers Weekly*

"*The Ten Thousand* and *Gods and Legions* were so detailed that they seemed real. Now Ford has done it again. Brutal, straightforward, exciting and informative, *The Last King* is a hair-trigger ride on ancient sands and hills. This is Ford's best so far, and only those who have read his first two know just how good that makes this book."

—*The Statesman Journal* (Salem, OR)

"Powerful telling of historical drama. Michael Curtis Ford brings the Roman Empire to life. *The Last King* is complete with battle scenes and powerful storytelling about one of history's most feared warriors."

—*The Oregonian*

MORE...

"Ford has crafted a fascinating fictional biography of King Mithridates the Great. Eloquently narrated by Pharnaces, the illegitimate son of Mithridates and one of his favorite concubines, this rousing saga also provides an illuminating glimpse into the often vast divide that separated Eastern and Western warfare, culture, and philosophy during antiquity."
—*Booklist*

"A swashbuckling account of the exploits of Mithridates the Great. Solid fun: a good, old-fashioned adventure tale with plenty of action."
—*Kirkus Reviews*

GODS AND LEGIONS

"Powerful and passionate. A truly compelling story—one not just of gods and legions but of men."
—*Library Journal*, starred review

"A powerful, moving, exciting and altogether fascinating novel. The frenzy of ancient battlefields leaps off the pages with an almost palpable power."
—*The Statesman Journal* (Salem, OR)

"Stirring and adventurous tragedy of the first rank, written with all the gusto of a master pulp stylist."
—*Kirkus Reviews*

"Ford has crafted another magnificent piece of historical fiction."
—*Booklist*

"Thanks to the author's excellent research of both his subject and era, the reader experiences this great man's transformation step by determined step. Highly recommended."
—*The Historical Novels Review*

THE TEN THOUSAND

"[Ford] combines historical accuracy with eloquent story-telling to create an epic story that will capture the imagination of anyone interested in the history of ancient Greece. A worthy successor to Steven Pressfield's *Gates of Fire*."
—*Library Journal*, starred review

"The descriptive language throughout is heroic, at times echoing the *Iliad*. Ford brings an interesting, fictively personal outlook to one of the classics. Inspired and highly informed, *The Ten Thousand* may lead many readers back to the original [*Anabasis* by Xenophon]."
—*Kirkus Reviews*

"While *The Ten Thousand* has swift pace, a solid story and realistic characters, it is the fact that the book drops you into the reality of the times, dirt, grit, blood, passion and all, that gives it its strength . . . it is a book that makes the reader feel the story has been lived, not merely read."
—*The Statesman Journal* (Salem, OR)

"The Greek mercenaries of the time of Socrates lost a war to the Persians but gained immortality. Thrilling, eloquent, illuminated by scholarship comes this retelling of the epic running battle of the Ten Thousand from Babylon to the sea."
—James Brady, author of the bestselling *Warning of War*

ST. MARTIN'S PAPERBACKS TITLES
by MICHAEL CURTIS FORD

The Ten Thousand

Gods and Legions

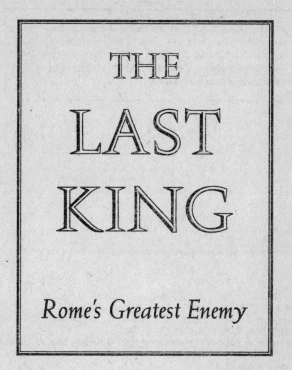

THE
LAST
KING

Rome's Greatest Enemy

MICHAEL CURTIS FORD

St. Martin's Paperbacks

THE LAST KING

Copyright © 2004 by Michael Curtis Ford.
Excerpt from *The Sword of Attila* copyright © 2005 by Michael Curtis Ford.

Map by Jackie Aher.

ISBN: 0-312-93615-X
EAN: 80312-93615-0

Printed in the United States of America

St. Martin's Press hardcover edition / March 2004
St. Martin's Paperbacks edition / April 2005

St. Martin's Paperbacks are published by St. Martin's Press, 175 Fifth Avenue, New York, NY 10010.

10 9 8 7 6 5 4 3 2 1

For Eamon, Isabel, and Marie-Amandine

THE
LAST
KING

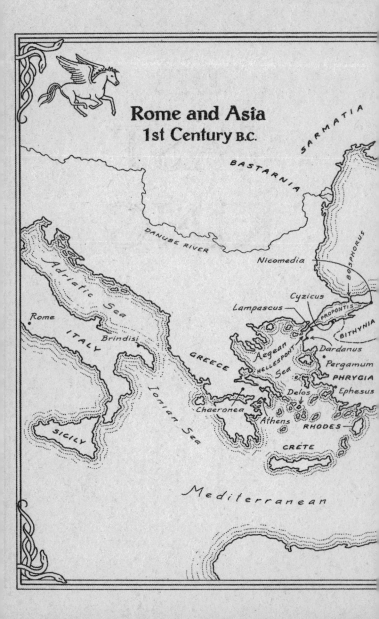

Rome and Asia
1st Century B.C.

SARMATIA

BASTARNIA

DANUBE RIVER

Nicomedia

BOSPHORUS

Adriatic Sea

Cyzicus

Lampascus

PROPONTIS

BITHYNIA

Rome

ITALY

Brindisi

GREECE

Aegean Sea

HELLESPONT

Dardanus

Pergamum

PHRYGIA

Ionian Sea

Delos

Ephesus

Chaeronea

Athens

RHODES

SICILY

CRETE

Mediterranean

HISTORICAL NOTE

The greatest and most feared of all of Rome's enemies was not the mighty Hannibal, whose mid-winter march over the Alps has captured the imagination of generations; nor the wily African king Jugurtha, who so capably exploited Roman political rivalries; nor even the Germanic hordes, who during a particularly vulnerable period in Rome's history poured over the Alps and nearly sacked the entire Italian peninsula. To the Romans of antiquity, no foreign enemy elicited as much fear as one monarch of a small eastern kingdom virtually unknown before his reign, who was able to defy the might of Rome and its most illustrious generals for almost four decades—Mithridates Eupator VI of Pontus.

Unlike many Asian rulers, Mithridates never assumed for himself the epithet of "the Great"; this was a title granted him by his enemies themselves. So intense was Rome's fear of him that the announcement of his death in 63 B.C. was like a deliverance from a forty-year nightmare: The Roman patrician Pompey leaped onto a pile of army saddle blankets, troops burst into rapturous celebration, and people in the street donned holiday garb, rejoicing "as if ten thousand enemies had died in his person." Yet though Rome's joy at his death was, in effect, a backhanded salute to his greatness, the city also honored him overtly in what by any standards was an extraordinary display of magnanimity: Pompey granted Mithridates a lavish burial, "like the most valiant prince of his time," and Cicero publicly hailed Mithridates as the greatest of all the kings against whom

Rome had waged war and the most powerful monarch since Alexander. Certainly only Mithridates' death, and the resulting assurance of Rome's survival, could give the victors the confidence to so generously praise their former enemy.

Although Mithridates was Persian by blood, religion, and military training, nevertheless he was Greek in his language, tastes, and love for urban culture and civilization. In his heritage and upbringing he combined these two great civilizations, Greek and Persian, which for centuries had disputed control of the eastern Mediterranean. Alexander the Great had been the first to attempt to reconcile these ancient adversaries and meld them into a higher form of coexistence; it was an ingenious idea, and it is impossible to say what the results might have been had he not suffered a premature death. Two centuries later, Mithridates revived Alexander's magnificent vision, which he made his own by birthright.

Mithridates was extremely conscious of his historical entitlement to this legacy. Indeed, long before Achilles battled the champions of Troy, centuries before Rome was more than a muddy herders' village, Mithridates' ancestors were crafting fine bronze weapons, ruling a large and prosperous peasant class, and practicing a sophisticated system of religion combining the familiar Greek deities with many of the more exotic Eastern gods. Mithridates' goal, therefore, from youth to old age, was to reestablish a vast Hellenistic realm that would include all the countries of Europe and Asia where Greek had been the language of the ruling classes and Greek culture the vehicle of progress. He sought to reclaim his ancestral heritage, but more than that— he sought to reclaim his ancestral *potential*.

This dream he pursued relentlessly, with an intensity and single-mindedness astonishing to our modern way of thinking, bound as we are by the benefits and constrictions of a rule of law. Mithridates suffered no such inhibitions—he *was* the law, and he was determined to advance his rule as far as his strength and resources would take him. He was unhampered by doubts, knowing for a certainty that to the extent he succeeded, to the degree that he extended his conquests and restored the influence of ancient Greek culture, the world would be a better, more secure place. He would go down in history as the savior of civilization, against the chaos and threats of barbarity.

Yet in doing this, he inevitably clashed with the growing ambitions of his rival—for Rome's objectives included quite the same regions as Mithridates was targeting. And the rivalry was not merely geographic, but philosophical, indeed personal. Rome's whole attitude toward life—what Greeks viewed as a crudeness of culture, an unnecessary cruelty to slaves and conquered peoples, and an overweening desire for money and advancement to the detriment of the higher values—was downright abhorrent to Mithridates. He may not have been a sophisticated philosopher or political theorist, but he knew in his deepest instincts that the Roman way of life was incompatible with his own, and that the two could never coexist. Indeed, the very notion of coexisting with such a repugnant neighbor was impossible to imagine—for both sides.

Three of Rome's greatest generals and mightiest armies were sent to quash the danger Mithridates posed to its growing empire. Though none were truly able to conquer him, Mithridates, in the end, went the way of all previous threats to Rome, the way of Spartacus, of Sertorius, of so many others. It remains a matter of conjecture precisely which qualities allowed Rome to prevail over so many perils, to dominate so many civilizations, to survive for so many centuries. Scholars may debate the merits of its military innovations, its superior political organization, the vast wealth it was able to accrue from profitable trade in slaves and other goods. History, as they say, is written by the victors, so our knowledge of Rome's adversaries is sometimes rather sketchy. Yet despite all of Rome's strengths, it was never invincible, and on occasion it verged on complete disintegration. In fact, there were individuals who, had circumstances been only slightly different, might have stopped Rome dead in her tracks, with incalculable consequences for our lives today.

Mithridates was one such individual, and his story deserves to be told.

BOOK ONE

THE MAKING OF A KING

Quod cibus est aliis, aliis est venenum.
One man's meat is another man's poison.

—Lucretius

1

The hawk circled silently and broodingly over the desert sands, so high he was a mere speck against the cloudless blue sky, peering down at the scene below.

The Persian army marched in stately procession, just as it had for a hundred leagues or more, raising a dust cloud that could be seen by Alexandria's garrison from a distance of two days' march. The fierce, leathery Arabs of the camel corps, robes billowing behind them, were followed in close order by the lumbering beasts of the elephant brigade, each bearing a platform carrying five armored lancers. Five thousand elite Parthian archers rode next, mounted on identical white stallions and bearing saddle quivers containing a hundred barbed reed missiles fashioned by the most skilled weapons makers of the Mesopotamian armories; they were succeeded by another five thousand Armenian horse troops, whose skills with the bow, less developed than those of the Parthians, were supplemented by heavier, ashwood shafts and poison-tipped barbs.

Fifty thousand regular infantry marched implacably behind in the dust and filth of the enormous bestiary. These men were resigned to the wretched road over which they traveled, inured to the suffocating heat and dust by seven years of campaigning, from the Persian Gulf to the Aegean Sea, from the frigid Caucasus to the Syrian desert. Fresh from a monumental victory at Pydna, the men were laden with plunder and cocksure in their strength. Their general was no mere tribal headman of roaming Bedouins, nor even a royal satrap of ancient noble family. Leading the massive invasion force was none other than Antiochus IV Epiphanes, King of Kings and Brother of the Planets, descendant of Darius the Great, heir to the vast Seleucid Empire and monarch of Lesser and Greater Armenia. Only forty-seven years of age, he was in the prime of life, ruler of a domain that extended to the distant birthplace of the rising sun and the frigid shadows of the Scythian north. And Antiochus was leading his men to the greatest prize of all, the opulent city of Alexandria, the seat of Egypt's boy-king Ptolemy, whose agents had for days been accosting the Great King on the march, pleading for mercy. Each soldier's share of the plunder from this one city alone would allow him to retire with incalculable wealth, households filled with slaves, and the silks and artworks of generations.

Antiochus encountered no opposing army as his forces entered the fertile Nile delta. Even at several hours' distance from his objective he could see that the entire population of the floodplain had retreated behind Alexandria's walls, its portals sealed tight, even the forward trenches and defensive works abandoned. *A pity to besiege it,* the King thought to himself. *With elephants and engines the gates will fall within hours. Siege merely increases the men's thirst for plunder, limits their restraint once the walls finally crumble. The boy Ptolemy deserves his fate, for employing such incompetent advisors.*

In the final miles before arriving at the city, the men's excitement grew visibly, and the army's lumbering pace picked up. Even the King felt the glow of anticipation at the thought of this additional jewel in his crown. Brushing off the chattering and importuning of his captains and advisors, who were already pressing him with plans for the coming siege, he galloped forward to be alone with his thoughts, to savor a few moments of calm. Peering far ahead, he spied three mounted figures just visible down the deserted road. Although they were too distant to be recognizable, Antiochus could still guess who they were, and he sighed in exasperation at the thought of being forced once again to listen to the disgraceful begging and fawning of Ptolemy's ambassadors. He glanced back at his corps of camel drivers, their eyes glittering fiercely behind the swaths of wrappings masking their faces. The restless Bedouins had been uncharacteristically patient on the long, uneventful march. He would give them a chance to stretch their legs.

Spurring his horse forward into a sprint, he loosed the shrill war cry of the Arabs. Instantly the lead camel drivers began furiously whipping their mounts, sending them into ungainly runs, all knobby knees and flailing heads, and then the entire corps followed suit. The furious sprint of the thousand beasts straining to catch the King's lead set up a deafening thunder as they approached the trio of figures. Smiling to himself, the King spurred his horse again and pounded even more furiously, the hot wind in his face raising water in his eyes, making it difficult to distinguish the three riders he was rapidly approaching. *Not to worry,* he thought. *After I catch them I shall permit the Arabs to chase them down with their lances. Let them play a round of that barbarous game with which they amuse themselves in camp—that foul sport with the headless carcass and the goalposts . . .*

Looking up, the King spied the hawk circling lazily overhead—an opportunistic creature, waiting for a sign of weakness or exposure among small life, for death to occur on which he might feed. The King smiled. *Best reserve your place in line at Alexandria, evil bird,* he thought. *The pickings there will be much more to your liking than a mere three skinny diplomats, even if there is anything left after the Arabs have their sport.* He pushed away thoughts of the hawk and focused on the trio ahead. Something was amiss—he was approaching them far too quickly. The King knew his horse was the fastest steed in the army, yet it would be impossible to catch up with mounted quarry this quickly. Still sprinting, he wiped his eyes with his sleeve and peered again at the men. Oddly, they were not fleeing. They stood as still as mileposts, facing him calmly. The lead man was not even armed and wore only a white ceremonial robe, although the two flanking him were handsomely equipped with newly polished bronze cavalry shields and bore beautifully cast breastplates and helmets, with lances butted into the leather holsters in the vertical rest position. One of the men had a pennant draped dispiritedly from the point of his lance. The king squinted at the dusty fabric of the banner as it hung limply in the oppressive air, and he swore under his breath. An eagle.

A Roman eagle.

The exasperated King skidded to a stop only steps from the motionless riders, and the camel corps behind him did the same, though not as smoothly. The evil-tempered beasts reared and bellowed, angry at being made to run in the first place, even angrier at being forced to stop. The King's horse skittered and danced, eyes rolling nervously at the snorting and spitting animals towering over its rear, and the King struggled to control his mount. The three smaller Roman ponies facing him stood as motionless as their riders, staring in seeming disdain at the undisciplined display before them.

With not a little trouble the King forced his horse to stand, and he glared for a moment at the trio of silent Romans, considering what to make of this incongruous welcome. Resolving to force the encounter, he held up his right hand in the universal gesture of welcome and boldly announced himself.

"Greetings, Romans!" he intoned in measured Greek, the common language of the civilized lands of the eastern Mediterranean. "Behold the conquering army of Antiochus IV Epiphanes, King of Kings and ruler of these lands. Welcome to all men of good intent. State your business."

For a long moment the lead Roman, the one in robes, remained staring in silence. He was tanned and somewhat tired-looking, or perhaps merely world-weary, just approaching the paunchiness of prosperous middle age, but with the steely gaze and erect bearing of a military man. He neglected even to remove his own hand from the reins—a grave insult to the King, who had offered his peace first. Without a word, the Roman slowly dismounted and strode imperiously forward to a spot precisely between his own pony and Antiochus' white charger, where he stopped, looked into the King's eyes, and pulled out a papyrus scroll he had been carrying under his arm.

The enormous army had by this time caught up to their position and rumbled to a puzzled halt, and the cloud of dust wafted stiflingly over the King and the three Romans. The Persian generals eyed the Romans contemptuously, and the camels continued to bray fiercely, spoiling to continue with the march to the city they could see and smell in the distance. Still the three Romans did not budge, and the King realized that in order to continue, he would have either to read the scroll or physically remove these men from his path. The sound of swords sliding from leather holsters behind him told him the opinion of his officers. Incredibly, the two Roman soldiers drew their own short cavalry swords from their holsters in response. *By the gods!* the King thought. *Do they intend to take on my whole army?* Still, a voice inside him warned him to be prudent.

The man identified himself. "Gaius Popilius Laenas," he declared in brazen, monotone Latin, which, although the King spoke it well, he received as a second insult, as a failure to recognize his status by speaking to him in the common language of these parts. "My rank is senator of Rome. I bear a senatorial decree, which I request you read. Your response thereto will determine how I, and the Roman Senate, will reciprocate your greeting, and whether we are to consider you friend or foe." With that, he pursed his lips, held out the scroll, and fell silent.

A murmur of outrage could be heard behind the King. He glanced behind at his captains, affixing a confident smile on his face and lifting his chin, as if to tell them to humor him in this jest. They glared, but the King nodded amiably and they retreated several paces on their mounts. Then swinging his leg over his horse's haunches, he dropped athletically to the ground, strode to where Popilius stood waiting for him, and seized the scroll, feigning an amused expression. Upon reading it, however, he was unable to disguise his astonishment and outrage.

"How dare you present me with this, insolent jackals!" he sputtered, his face reddening. " 'Forgo the attack on Alexandria and depart Egypt?' By what right do you order this, by what authority—!"

"Your response, if you please, Majesty," Popilius interrupted him, his expression cold, his gray eyes burning into the King's. "Alexandria is under the protection of Rome. The Senate awaits your response."

Antiochus stared at his adversary for a moment and then burst out laughing. "The Senate awaits my response? Your Senate is three weeks' sail across the Mediterranean! It sends a junior senator and two tribunes here to insult my army and demand my response? I haven't time for this nonsense, but I am not so ill-bred as to insult your illustrious Senate with the same rudeness as you have shown me. My counselors will draft something appropriate—"

But Popilius interrupted Antiochus by calmly turning his back, and the King's speech faded into astonished silence. The

Senator strode to the lead tribune, seized the lance bearing the pennant, and returned, holding it vertically before him. The restless Arabs tensed and edged forward, but the King nodded them off. Popilius planted the butt-end of the lance in the dirt, the eagle fluttering lightly over his head, and then calmly, deliberately, paced one revolution around the King, tracing a circle in the dirt that enclosed the monarch. He then stepped back outside the circle, handed the lance back to the tribune, and crossed his arms.

"No," Popilius said simply. "Your counselors will do nothing of the sort. You yourself will give me your response before you step out of the ring."

Antiochus caught his breath. He stared at the determined Roman, then down at the line in the sand, and back up at the Roman. The entire army of beasts and men, sixty thousand strong, stood at his back. A defenseless city, bursting with wealth, stood within his very sight. The King was an intelligent man and knew how to weigh his gains against his risks.

And he knew he had been beaten.

"I shall accede to the Senate's request," he said quietly.

With that, the Roman stepped into the ring and gravely shook the King's hand. He then turned and mounted his horse, and without a single look back, the three riders trotted calmly back to the city walls.

Antiochus returned with his enormous army to Syria and, to the end of his life, never overcame the disgrace of this display of cowardice. Indeed his shame and his resulting hatred for Rome were passed on, like a disease or a curse, to his own daughter Laodice, who herself swore she would never be put in a position to be so humiliated. And so she wasn't, though her methods of avoiding such compromise were ineffectual and controversial at best. In reality, it was left to her own eldest son, King Mithridates, to regain the family honor for the scandalous treatment received at Rome's hands. But that is a matter not to be discussed quickly, nor dismissed lightly.

All this detail, for an event that occurred over a century ago. How would I know such things? Because I have studied Polybius' history of Rome to understand my enemy; I have paced the deserted battlefields like a conscientious commander; I have analyzed Roman speeches and Roman foreign policy like a competent administrator. But more important: Because I am Pharnaces, son of King Mithridates the Great of Pontus, who was the grandson of that disgraced monarch Antiochus. Because my father was Rome's most fearsome enemy, scourge of its greatest generals and destroyer of countless legions, a dagger in Rome's side for forty years, a terror who was beaten in battle but never defeated in spirit.

And because like his grandfather, Mithridates was also driven by a desire to conquer and unify, to create a magnificent empire of all the Hellenistic lands; and like his mother, Laodice, Mithridates was cursed by a fatal fear and a hatred for Rome. It was a hatred that would confine him and encompass him, much like that circle drawn in the sand years before, a hatred that would shape his very destiny—and mine, as well.

There are distinct advantages to being the son of a mere con- cubine, which not even a true prince, born of a legitimate queen, possesses. Chief among these is the trust of the King, who need not fear that son's ambitions. Such fear, of course, extends even to queens, as exhibited by Nysa, a recent queen- regent of the neighboring kingdom of Cappadocia, who a few years back assassinated each of her five sons in succession be- fore they came of age to take power from her; or Cleopatra, widow of Demetrius II of Syria, who killed one of her sons with a skillful arrow shot from a window, while watching the other die from the cup of poison she had tricked him into drink- ing. There was never any doubt in my mind that the women in my family showed signs of belonging to this same paranoid race of females; hence my gratitude to the gods for allowing me to have been born of bloodlines that fell outside their suspicion.

But other advantages accrue to sons of concubines as well. When defeated in war, they are not subjected to the same penal- ties as are genuine princes. To a Roman general, leading a con- quered king's illegitimate son by a slave-ring through the foreskin does not have the same impact as parading an actual heir to the throne; there are simply too many of us worthless urchins to make an impression on skeptical Roman citizens. In defeat, if a concubine's son has learned well his lessons in flat- tery, he is more often simply ignored by the victors, at best given a minor city to govern, at worst sold into soft servitude tutoring the spoiled children of a Roman merchant. In defeat, a lack of prestige is a considerable advantage.

But hold, I can justify even further my youthful contentment at my lowly lot. A concubine's life, and by extension that of her children, is one of luxury and ease, lacking in the tiresome royal duties of protocol. Not for me the interminable state banquets, the tedious opening ceremonies for the new sewage lines of decrepit little towns, the lengthy receptions for minor state functionaries. My half brother in the palace, poor Machares, was forced kicking and spitting to attend such events, as lessons in future rule. Of course he was born to the job as eldest son of the King *and* the Queen. I, however, little Pharnaces, the snotnosed ruffian, was unpresentable in polite company, royal bastard that I was. Nevertheless, I enjoyed a full measure of my father's love and attention, as well as living quarters only slightly less luxurious than those afforded the King's family itself. *Pity for him,* I often thought, as Machares was dragged from his play by the servants of the wardrobe to meet some obscure ambassador, while I raced to the royal stables alone, to ride my pick of the King's thoroughbreds.

Reading back on what I have written, I see these are not actual advantages at all but rather the limiting of disadvantages. The one true benefit to lacking a birthright, however, is this: If one is ambitious and competent, if one truly has brains in the skull rather than the sawdust that often passes for them among the offspring of royalty, then the son of a king's concubine may have precisely the same opportunities to excel, the same chances to advance and succeed, in fact the same likelihood of becoming king as a true prince. But without the cost.

Could underestimated little Pharnaces ask for anything more?

From our very earliest age Machares and I were allowed to travel on Father's campaigns almost as mascots, beloved of his officers and indulged by his soldiers. To my great joy I, especially, was even ignored by my assigned eunuchs and tutors, whose complaints at my behavior Father laughed off, as his early expectations for me were so low in any case. Why hunch over my wax tablet for hours on end, memorizing the exploits of obscure Greek heroes in the *Iliad,* when I had my very own Greek hero directly at hand? I followed Father around camp like a lapdog, clinging close to his thigh as he made the rounds among his rough Scythian and Thracian mercenaries, roared out his approval at their bawdy jokes, and boldly seized shield and blunt sword to strike down the brawniest drill sergeant in the training exercises. Father was not merely a hero—he was a colossus, a god. So immense was his stature, so dazzling his broad smile, so awe-inspiring the gold-plated armor that covered his massive frame, of such a weight that a normal-sized man could not even lift it without staggering, that he and the royal priests were sometimes hard pressed to keep the populace from worshiping him as the earthly embodiment of Zeus himself. But I knew other than to think of him as a mere human, for the man was a god to me—and I the unrecognized son of a god.

I have a memory of attending a state dinner with him—not one of those tense, protocol-laden affairs to which the princes in the city were constantly being dragged but rather a manly, bawdy function in the field in the midst of a campaign, with the troops' spirits high in anticipation of achieving yet another of their overwhelming victories. I had been born in Father's thirty-fifth year, making him perhaps forty-three years of age at the time of this event, myself a mere eight, Machares twelve. A large tent had been set up in the middle of camp, to host a dinner for several dozen foreign ambassadors who had been invited to witness the morrow's slaughter and to contribute forces to the King's coalition. The canvas sides of the structure had been rolled up to invite a breeze on the hot night, and all around us in the gathering darkness, advancing up the sides of the surrounding hills for what seemed like miles, were winking orange lights—the campfires of the fifty thousand troops the King would be leading into battle the next day.

Father strode to the tent, fashionably late as always, after skipping the preliminary entertainment of dancing girls, fire swallowers, and musicians that had kept the guests in thrall until our arrival. I trotted on his left, struggling to keep up with his long legs, while Machares walked easily on his right, nodding confidently at the officers, who greeted him with the deep bows reserved only for the most senior leaders, though he was still a boy. Generals Archelaus and Neoptolemus flanked us in turn. The gigantic ivory-clad bow that Father was never without slapped softly against his back and I could see the faint outline of the curved dagger strapped to his hip under the baggy trousers. He was as robust and energetic as an Olympic athlete. Men cheered and shouted as he passed, and he bellowed hearty greetings to all, his huge hand cupping the top of my head as if it were an egg. The air fairly crackled with excitement, my limbs almost tingled in anticipation of viewing my first battle the next day, and I felt I would almost burst from pride. This was my education, *this* was what I had been born for, and I knew even then that one day I, too, would command armies, I, too, would attain victories. Of what value was it to rule a kingdom, as Machares was destined to do? Let him have it. Leading soldiers was *my* lot, the greatest lot of all for the King's bastard.

Entering the tent, Father interrupted the herald's formal Greek introduction with a shout of welcome to his guests and then made his way slowly around the waxed and polished beechwood trestle table, grasping hands and slapping backs, exchanging impossibly fluent greetings in a dozen languages. Finally arriving at his place at the head, he sat down heavily and motioned for me to stand nearby, in a place reserved for a steward. On his right, in a place of honor, sat Machares, the acknowledged heir and future king of Pontus. With a nod of Father's head, all the other guests stepped over their own benches and also sat down, and the scullery slaves entered, bearing enormous platters of well-scrubbed copper. The diners nodded appreciatively at the rustic yet elegant presentation of the main course: garlic-rubbed sow bear, roasted on green pomegranate-wood spits and marinated in sauce of wild chives and gorse flower, its fat paunch laid open and the umbles tastefully arranged on the sides, alternating with servings of stewed dormouse, snipe, and other small game. Along the length and breadth of the table were mounds of simple yet exquisitely prepared fare: butter-dipped asparagus, barley bread soaked in olive oil, sea-fowl eggs pickled in samphire brine, vast bowls of plump, yellow sun-dried grapes, rounds of robust sheep cheeses, plates of roasted filberts rolled in garlic salt, delicate honey cakes scented of wild thyme and inlaid with intricate designs of sliced pine nuts, and conical lumps of soft figbread soaked in the fermented juice of wild blackberry. All this was well complemented with wrought gold cups of century-old wine flavored with the bitter resin of Stychian pine trees, which skilled slaves carefully decanted from enormous earthenware jars propped in the corners, each standing as high as a man. The scents wafting through the tent were heavenly, overpowering.

An enormous wooden camp trencher of steaming meat and lentils was placed before Father, and dipping his hand into a nearby bowl of white, garlicky seasoning flecked with gray, he sprinkled it liberally over the food, rubbing it in generously with his dagger. Just before tucking in, with a hunk of bread in one hand and a dripping joint of meat in the other, he stopped and suddenly stood. The entire room fell silent. Fifty hungry men stared at him, some with food already approaching their lips, their eyes watering from the scent.

For a moment he stood staring silently from face to face, a half-smile on his lips at the impatience of his guests. Then he spoke, in a voice as cultured as a high priest's, but in a tone as rumbling and commanding as that of the bear he was about to eat.

"The food must first be tasted," he intoned.

The men stared at him blankly.

In a patient tone, he explained. "As king, I cannot risk my health on rancid meat—or worse. Even on campaign. I require a taster."

As if on cue, two guards suddenly emerged from the rear of the tent, dragging a resigned-looking prisoner whom I recognized as a Bithynian enemy scout bagged earlier that day when he had ventured too close to our outposts. Father looked at him closely.

"He looks healthy—and hungry. He'll do."

The guards released the man's arms and he slumped momentarily but immediately straightened himself and stared defiantly down the table at the expectant guests. Father laughed at the man's audacity, and carving a generous slab of meat off the joint he had been about to bite, he dipped it liberally into the bowl of grainy seasoning and held it out to the prisoner on the point of his knife.

"Join our feast," Father said heartily, in the Bithynian tongue.

The prisoner glared at him disdainfully at first, but then glancing down at the pink, steaming flesh, he seized it in his right hand, greedily stuffed it into his mouth, and began chewing. He gulped the fragrant meat, a trickle of juice dripping from the corner of his mouth, and then swallowed, licking his lips noisily, though out of pride and obstinacy he maintained a scowl to disguise his obvious delight.

The foreigners at the table watched the man enviously. However, just as Father nodded in satisfaction and was about to sit down, the Bithynian's eyes bulged in their sockets and his face flushed crimson. Choking and gasping, he clutched at his belly, and the juice trickling from the side of his mouth turned to blood. He collapsed to the ground, writhing and moaning in pain, and the two guards seized him by the armpits and dragged him, retching, out the door. The ambassadors observed this in shocked silence, their eyes flitting between the wretched prisoner and their unperturbed host, who himself maintained the most steadfast calm, sporting the same half-smile on his lips.

"I believe the meat is done just right," Father said, and then to the horror of his guests he resumed his seat and began contentedly munching the same joint of meat from which he had just fed the prisoner.

Outraged at what he had just witnessed, the Rhodian dignitary to Father's left mumbled something in Dorian Greek to his companion on the other side, but he did not speak sufficiently softly and Father heard. His face darkened, and the table fell silent upon seeing his expression, though he did not respond immediately to the Rhodian's comment. Rather, he carefully set down his knife and bread, wiped his fingers with a soft linen proffered by the steward, and then turned slowly and deliberately to the Rhodian.

"Did I hear you correctly, Ambassador," he said in refined Dorian, "that I 'couldn't pay you to eat this slop'? This is how you compliment your host while sitting at his table, when served food killed by his own hands?"

The Rhodian blanched.

Father continued. "I'll wager I can pay my men to eat it."

Reaching into the voluminous folds of his pants, he pulled out a small silken bag, shook it several times so all could hear the jingling of the gold inside, and dropped it unceremoniously beside the plate of Archelaus. The general looked disdainfully down at the bag, tossed it back to his host, and without further delay began heartily scoffing the meat from his own plate. Father did the same to the next Pontic officer, who also returned the bag, and he and his two companions began wolfing their own food without hesitation. The foreign ambassadors stared. If the King's men were unharmed by the meat, then clearly the poison must be in the saltlike seasoning that lay in small bowls beside each setting.

Laughing heartily, Father sat down and again began devouring the meat, chatting cheerfully with Machares. The foreign diners stirred the food nervously around their plates, eyeing the seasoning bowls suspiciously. The King loudly announced the meat needed more flavoring and sprinkled another handful of the stuff onto his plate, flicking a hearty pinch into his wine goblet for good measure.

"Eat!" he commanded with his mouth full, his lips smiling but his eyes taking on a menacing glint. His officers continued to do so with relish, but the ambassadors looked up at him helplessly. Father dropped his knife loudly onto his plate and slammed his fist onto the table, making all the utensils bounce into the air.

"*Eat!*" he roared, his smile gone now, and the foreigners stared at him, some in horror, the bravest of them in outright defiance.

Pushing back his bench, Father stood up, throwing out his great, bearlike chest and pulling himself up to his full height, an entire head above Archelaus and his officers, who had also stood and were not small men themselves.

"By the *gods*!" Father bellowed, seizing the end of the table and lifting it into the air before turning it sideways and spilling the entire steaming, dripping contents into the laps of the luckless ambassadors sitting on that side.

"I'll be *damned* if I will enter into treaty with men who do not trust me!"

Nodding angrily to the royal guards who lined the outside of the pavilion, he stepped back from the terrible commotion, stretching out his hand and again placing it like an oversized caul on the top of my head, drawing me in close to his leg. The guards moved forward as one man, seized the astonished ambassadors, and dragged them bodily away from the table, their linen robes stained with food and drink. From here they were lifted bodily onto their horses, their baggage having already been rudely packed while they were at dinner, and sent away in disgrace, accompanied only by the meanest of military escorts.

As they were led by the guards away from the upturned table, the Rhodian nearest to me sputtered in fury to the taciturn Archelaus.

"What was in that wretched seasoning?"

"In yours? Sea salt and powdered garlic," Archelaus replied, calmly observing the furious ambassador as he departed.

Father nodded, his eyes still flashing fire, as he contributed to his general's response.

"Mine was arsenic," he said.

He turned away from the chaos within the dining tent, staring past the Pontic guards standing their watch only a few feet away, out to the hillside flickering with the lights of thousands of campfires. These men were his, and he demanded absolute trust, absolute loyalty, in the venture he was about to undertake. Usually he was not disappointed. Nevertheless, he felt a constant need to test, to probe, to prove to himself that the men surrounding him were committed to him with their whole being. Every man, whether general, ally, or common soldier, every man must harbor complete devotion to his cause. Every man must demonstrate utter confidence, with every muscle he flexed, every breath he drew—every bite he swallowed. At stake was the very future of his kingdom, his plans for empire, his New Greece, his destiny. There was no room for mistrust. Mistrust led to halfheartedness and fear, and that, in turn, to betrayal. Extraordinary measures were required.

I looked up at him. The smile had disappeared, and an almost wistful expression passed over his face, and then he turned back to the scene of the ruined banquet.

"Arsenic," he repeated. He paused, shaking his head, and then almost as an afterthought, he spoke softly, under his breath. "The usual dose."

3

I spy him standing alone, framed by a window, peering calmly at the swaying, chanting throng below. I am so far away I can barely identify him, and he is standing almost at the edge of my view, as if overwhelmed by the great space all around, as if retreating from my vision before the immensity of the sky. Nevertheless, I see him, I do see him, in my mind's eye now perhaps even clearer than I did then—the profile illuminated by a light from behind, fading in and out of view as men step into my line of vision. I cannot make out his expression, though he moves away for a moment and then returns to my view, this time holding something in his hand, something golden—a weapon, a goblet? He so loved shiny objects, things of value and beauty, but it is impossible to tell.

A crash of thunder rolls toward me from behind him, washing over the crowd like breakers on the beach. There is a momentary pause among the men shouting around me and then a blinding flash and fire, black smoke billowing in a menacing column toward the sky, partially obscuring my view of Father. The earth shakes and rumbles, and angry war chargers thunder through the crowd, eyes rolling fiercely, tongues lolling in their effort, as they storm toward Father, who still stands motionless, watching the scene.

I hold up my hand, as much to signal my men and force my

way through the crowd as to attract his attention. It's not far—if I can simply shoulder my way through, I can be there in an instant. This is no worse than all the other times.

I'm coming, Father.

4

The large wagon had been drawn up across from us, separated from the location of our seats by the long ditch, still filled with glowing coals, over which the sides of kid had been roasted earlier that evening. The wagon was covered by a dingy canvas tarpaulin, stretched tightly over four iron hoops that extended up from the sides, hiding the mysterious contents from our eyes but not from our ears—for there drifted out the most exquisitely terrifying snorts, groans, and growls a boy could possibly imagine.

I snuggled closer under Father's enormous arm and he tousled my head with his other hand. Across the roaring bonfire, Archelaus laughed at some private joke and elbowed his twin brother, Neoptolemus, both of them generals under Father's command. Machares sat quietly apart, studying a tablet on which his tutor had written a philosophy assignment. Not for the future king to neglect his studies while on campaign! The outer circle of firelight was a buzz of activity, with couriers coming and going and passing discreet salutes, conferring with Father's advisors hovering behind us. Only occasionally did an officer edge forward for a quick word with Father, who would merely nod or shake his head impatiently. The brightness of the fire was the haven of privacy, the hearth, the family, around which only the chosen few were permitted to gather. All lesser mortals were confined to the darkness beyond, and at this hour Father only reluctantly permitted any to advance beyond their station into the glow of his light. But no matter. The army had been ground and lubricated like a finely honed blade, cut and polished like a gemstone, and for all but the greatest of decisions it could run on its own. On some nights, the King could hang up his crown and simply be a father.

My attention was focused on the strangely growling wagon that had been drawn up in front of us. At the sound of a loud gong from within, the otherworldly groaning suddenly ceased, and a most extraordinary personage pulled aside the canvas flap and hopped down to the ground.

He was not a dwarf—for many such men and women I had seen in the streets of Sinope and several were even employed in the palace—but rather a perfectly proportioned man who, though of middle age, was completely bald and no larger than a four-year-old child. His face was brown, his skin of an ageless, tanned-leather quality, and he sported not a single tooth in his bony head, which gave his cheeks a drawn, sunken look, skull-like in the flickering shadows of the torches planted in the ground before him. He swaggered to the front of the packed-earth "stage" he had earlier stamped out in front of the wagon, and bowed to us with a deep flourish.

"Gentlemen!" he shouted, far louder than necessary for the thirty or so onlookers before him. Horses whinnied in the distance at the volume of his cry.

"You're not in the amphitheater of Corinth," Father complained. "Keep your voice down or the guards will be upon you."

The tiny man nodded but scarcely broke his stride. I quivered with excitement.

"O Great King Mithridates, Esteemed Generals and Advisors: Freshly arrived from our triumphal appearances before the pharaohs of Egypt, having astonished the satraps of Arabia and the Great King of Parthia himself, I, the Amazing Otus of Armenia, present the world's greatest spectacle: The Wild Beasts of Africa!"

With a flourish, the entire caravan tarp was lifted and thrown back with the aid of unseen ropes and pulleys, and a quartet of huge, furry creatures leaped down from the sides and began parading solemnly around the circle of the makeshift stage as Otus stood proudly in the middle. The scene was astonishing: An enormous lion, shaking his mane in relief like a dandy just wakened from his nap who wishes to freshen his hair; a large brown bear who stumbled along on his hind legs, looking from side to side and blinking in the suddenly bright illumination of the torchlights; an ape of some sort, who screeched in delight at being released from the wagon and knuckle-walked around behind his fellows, swatting playfully at the tuft on the lion's tail; and a large gray wolf, who trotted taciturnly around the circle, bearing on its back an exact image of Otus—though considerably smaller and perhaps five years old. It was a tiny bald boy, sitting on a miniature saddle and clutching the beast's fur, dressed in leather military finery, looking for all the world like a miniature cavalry officer.

The men roared in appreciation as Otus put the animals through their paces. The ape was dressed to resemble a tax collector and engaged in a playful fight with his trainer; a tiny chariot was produced, and the wolf, dutifully snarling, was set to hauling the young boy, who was also named Otus, in a mock charge against the infinitely patient bear; and a live rabbit was produced and made to race past the lion, who bounded after it, caught it, and released it unharmed back into Otus the Elder's hands. Undoubtedly the beast was as toothless as his owner. To close the show, the midget father, son, and four animals lined up in a row and bowed simultaneously. All stood up on command, with the exception of the ape, who was busily scribbling in the sand before him with a fingertip. Otus pretended to reprimand him until the beast finally joined his fellows in standing up and parading serenely back into the now re-covered wagon, at which point the Greek word *XAIPE!*—Greetings!—was seen to have been traced into the dirt. Father marveled that the ape's penmanship was better than mine.

Father tossed Otus a small purse of silver in appreciation for the entertainment, and the family of midgets bowed liberally, vowing to perform again for us the following year, as they had done every year for as long as anyone's memory served. I was agog, and as the wagon rolled out of the camp into the night, bound for its next distant destination, I could not stop chattering. My ambition to become a prince or a general had completely flown—when I grew up, I would be an animal trainer! I couldn't wait to begin practicing with Machares the next day, but my half brother, a jaded adolescent, had already seen Otus' performance several times before, during the midget's earlier swings through Pontus, and now he couldn't be bothered to care about such trivialities. He feigned a yawn and returned to his studies.

Big Bituitus the Gaul, Father's chief guard, chewing on the remains of a bone from dinner, gazed at me thoughtfully from across the fire. His enormous shaggy head of russet hair was in stark contrast to the swarthiness of the other men around us, Greeks and Persians, Cappadocians and Armenians. His skin, burnt a reddish bronze from campaigning, glowed almost golden, and the sinews in his huge arms stretched and rolled tautly in the flickering light. If Father was Zeus, this man was surely Apollo, though lacking in the quick wit and eloquent speech of that glib-tongued deity. Bituitus' palms rested on his knees, and I stared at the missing little finger of his right hand, long a source of fascination to me, and a running joke between us.

"Bituitus," I asked for the hundredth time, "how'd you lose your finger?"

The big Gaul glanced down at his hand. "This?" he said in his thick barbarian accent. "Well . . ." He paused, as if trying to think. "Some time ago old King Oeneus invited me to rid him of the giant boar that had been tearing up his fields. It was a huge beast, which had developed a taste for man flesh. I had the monster cornered up against some rocks when—"

"Liar. That's from an old Greek myth. Anyway, last time you said it was a bear."

"Bear, boar, what's the difference? They're both edible."

"I'm with Pharnaces," Father broke in. "You can't even keep your lies straight. I heard you lost your finger to the teeth of a sacred prostitute in the temple of Conama, who was angry because you had—"

"I said that?" Bituitus hastily interrupted, glancing down at me ruefully. He looked suddenly confused as he struggled to remember. "That must have been the wine talking. Far as I can remember, she only broke my nose, and it was an honest misunderstanding about the size of my offering."

"The size of your offering!" The men roared at poor Bituitus' excuse. "You should be glad she only bit off your finger!"

The big Gaul blinked into the fire in more bewilderment than ever. The men often took pleasure in tormenting Father's thickheaded bodyguard, knowing that, as they say, his mills ground slowly. He decided to change the subject.

"You know, young Pharnaces," he said, working a hunk of gristle like a dog, then tossing it into the flames, "your father wasn't much older than you when he left home to claim his kingship. Fact is, you remind me of him in some ways."

I smiled and settled back. Of all the stories Bituitus told, and he could easily go on for months without repeating himself, this was the one I enjoyed most.

"Bah, the Gaul's going to bend our ears again with lies about his adventures in the woods," Archelaus groaned mockingly. "Careful what you tell the boy. We were there, too. We'll keep you on the straight and narrow. No sacred prostitutes this time."

Bituitus snorted, wiped his greasy hands in the sand at his feet, and with a grunt heaved Father's enormous shield from where it had been leaning behind him out into the light. He commenced polishing the intricately carved bronze designs with a pumice stone.

"Right, you do just that," he said thickly, "but I don't see any of you attending to the boy's education, as I do. Not even his own father—" And he looked pointedly and fearlessly at the King, who merely smiled in silence. "The boy follows us on campaign like a pup, missing his lessons for months at a time. Least we can do is pass on our own schooling. You don't spend seven years roaming among the goats without learning something. . . ."

"Bituitus," Father growled, "Pharnaces *is* learning. He's only ten and he's already got a better head for strategy than most of my officers. At this rate, by the time he's fifteen he'll be ordering *you* into battle. You blather. Just get on with the tale."

The Gaul nodded and commenced his storytelling in his thick, halting barbarian accent. That night it was his turn. The next night it would be Archelaus' or Father's. Machares had no patience for such unstructured boasting and family fables, as he called them, and would amble off to his cot to read assignments given him by his tutors. I would remain still and silent at Father's feet, hoping not to be noticed, to be allowed to pass the night by the warm fire in the company of the men, remaining as long as I could before being shooed off to bed. Even then, though my half brother would fall asleep almost instantly, I would lie in the darkness, listening to the men's raucous laughter until far into the night.

From stories over the campfire I learned the history of Pontus, the tales of my ancestors, the story of Father's life, the roots of his ambitions for empire. Machares' education was on tablets and scrolls. Mine was on wood smoke and shadows.

5

Young Prince Mithridates was scarcely fourteen years of age when he left home—he, the twins Archelaus and Neoptolemus, Bituitus, and several others. They were a band of hooting, punching, high-spirited boys, all roughly the same age, raised together in the palace as the sons of noblemen. Together they departed Pontus' capital city of Sinope on what the young prince said would be merely one of their weekly hunting excursions. Except in this case, they never returned.

Even at that age, Mithridates was as large as a boxer and twice as strong, towering over the rest of his comrades, with the exception of ruddy-faced Bituitus, who was every bit his match in weight and strength and in fact resembled him so closely in everything, including his posture and gestures, that from a distance people often confused them. Mithridates had stature and strength to impress the Asiatics and beauty to seduce the Greeks, useful attributes in a kingdom that embraced both races. He was handsome as a god and clever as a stoat, admitting neither error nor regret. He wore his wavy chestnut hair long and loose, past his shoulders, in the manner of Alexander as depicted on the ancient coins in his father's treasury; and his flashing, winning smile was already legendary throughout the kingdom. With merely a glance from his laughing gray eyes young girls would feel their thighs tremble and even ancient grandmothers would have to sit to calm the fluttering of their hearts.

Nor did Mithridates mind being such a center of attention—in fact, he rather cultivated it, if one can be said to cultivate an appearance that, even by nature, was almost superhuman. Though born in the palace of the Greek seaport of Sinope, nursed on Homer and speaking Greek in the home, he never forgot that by descent he was far more than the mere spawn of one of Alexander's highborn Macedonian generals, as so many of his comrades boasted of themselves. Mithridates was in a direct line of the *Achaemenids,* the Persian royal family, a scion of the greatest empire in the world, and he never let his peers forget this fact. Even while walking through the crowded *agora* of sun-drenched Sinope or offering sacrifice to Apollo at its white-marbled temple, surrounded by loose-robed Greeks chatting of the latest political scandals of far-off Athens, Mithridates strode like a conquering barbarian, wearing the traditional attire of Persian noblemen. The long-sleeved tunics hemmed with the gaudiest of silk needlework, the baggy linen trousers caught at the ankles—and if these were not enough to draw the crowd's gaze to his eccentric dress, he carried in his wide belt an enormous curved and bejeweled dagger and slung over his shoulder a bow as large as Odysseus', as if he were just returning from battle. It was enough to set even the most cultured tongues wagging in astonishment.

He was only twelve years of age when his father, King Mithridates Euergetes V, died of poisoning. The murderer was never found, though circumstantial evidence pointed to his wife, for before her husband's body was even cold she produced a hitherto unknown will, leaving total control of Pontus to her, as queen-regent until Mithridates came of age nine years hence. For a time, this situation suited both mother and son well, for after the Prince overcame his initial grief, he found he was quite satisfyingly left to his own devices, particularly the pursuit of his education and the hunt, his two great passions. As for the Queen—she sought above all to spare herself the humiliation that had been visited upon her own father by the Romans in the Egyptian desert, though in a way unlike that which a stronger ruler might have chosen. For she devoted every resource not to defying Rome but rather to ingratiating herself with it, seeking at all costs to avoid its lethal attention. She had no desire to end her days as a debased trophy in a Roman Triumph and every incentive to retain her title as queen-regent for as long as possible.

To this end, once she assumed command, she reversed the entire foreign policy of regional dominance her husband had so painstakingly laid. To her, the key to peace with Rome was total obscurity and Pontus' complete withdrawal from its earlier conquests. Pontic garrisons were brought home; ambassadors were recalled; and our trade routes to the Mediterranean were allowed to wither, to avoid even a semblance of competition with Rome. Even Pontus' coinage was changed: The Queen ordered the removal of the Mithridatic coat of arms, and minted coins displaying only her name and profile. All in all, her policy was akin to indentured servitude to Rome, one devised to maintain her lifestyle while assuring the Roman authorities of her benign intentions.

Even at his young age, Prince Mithridates could not help but note with dismay that his mother's policies would leave him with precious little to rule over when he finally came of age. It would be a far cry from the true power wielded by his mighty Persian ancestors, once he assumed control. *If* he assumed control.

For there was also the matter of the lack of maternal instinct among the female members of his clan. Of late, he had started to notice an unusual taste in his food, followed by an unpleasant burning sensation in his stomach after he ate. Nothing to be alarmed about, of course—the feeling was so mild as to be barely noticeable. But the sheer number of occasions this occurred, night after night, was enough to make any heir to a throne feel ill at ease. He was never sure whether his perceptions were correct or he was simply suffering from an overactive imagination, brought on by the knowledge of his mother's love of rule and that her authority would be lost when Mithridates finally came to power in a few years.

As a precaution, he secretly consulted a most extraordinary personage he had inherited from his father, an elderly yet spry Scythian of the Agari tribe, far to the north on the Maeotian Sea. This tribe had long been famous for its use of the venom of serpents as remedies, and Papias the herbalist was known for being among the most skilled in the art of serpent milking.

Though he was probably no older than middle-aged when I first knew him, he seemed at the time to be the wisest, most ancient being I had ever met. His appearance was striking enough, with his blue-tattooed face and the chip of amber inlaid in his one remaining, yellowed front tooth. Yet his looks were no rival, in matters of strangeness, to his obscure knowledge and skills. Papias could predict the weather days in advance, sense when plants were at their peak medicinal potency, and even, it was said, communicate with animals and the dead.

When Papias was told of the symptoms Mithridates was experiencing, he shared the Prince's concerns and after some experimentation devised a compound of secret proportions, which from that day forth the boy drank every morning upon rising, before his first taste of water or wine, as a certain remedy against any poison. The ingredients with which it was concocted were known to none but the healer and Mithridates and, years later, me. Rumor gave rise to all sorts of foul and magical elements supposedly included in this daily libation; certainly the Prince did not discourage such talk, for it only added to his growing legend. It was a brave boy who would swallow such a potion on a daily basis, but desperation is the mother of determination, and concern for one's life can induce extreme measures.

Nor was poisoning the only method of assassination the young prince had cause to fear. On several occasions, during target practice with the military instructors hired by his mother, arrows had whizzed by uncomfortably close to his head. Such an incident can easily be dismissed as a mere accident, and this he did the first time, graciously laughing off his tutors' profuse apologies. As a sensible precaution, however, he assigned them to other students and arranged for new archery instructors. Nevertheless, during subsequent rounds of training, sometimes even weeks or months later, the same thing happened again, and then yet a third time. Either he was being targeted for assassination or the instructors had execrable aim, and either case would be grounds for dismissal, if not outright execution. So as not to create tensions in the court, however, he held his tongue.

The final straw, however, was the matter of the horses. Several times, when he had started off happily on his jaunts into the surrounding hills, he had been told at the royal stables that his usual steed was lamed and a replacement would be found for him. To his dismay, however, on every such occasion the grooms somehow neglected to tell him the horse had not been trained to follow the usual command for "stop"; or it had a nervous tendency, almost as if bred into it, to react to the sight of a bear by throwing its rider directly into the beast's path, or the oats it had been fed that morning had apparently fermented or perhaps been mixed with the mad-horse herb hippomanes, leaving the animal colicky and writhing on the ground in pain ten miles out from the city. On one occasion, a stallion he had just mounted bolted through the low door of the stable building, knocking him senseless and nearly killing him when he slammed into the stone archway above it. These events were more than a mere embarrassment to the Prince, though they were that as well, for he was considered to be the finest horseman among his peers, if not the entire kingdom. The Prince was growing weary of close escapes. He had long suspected they were no accidents and finally concluded that if he was to survive the next seven years before he came into manhood and his inheritance, he would need to take more extreme measures than a daily vial of medicine.

Just shy of his fourteenth birthday, Mithridates gathered together a small party of his closest friends and set out on a hunt. There was nothing unusual about this trip, beyond the fact that they planned to be away longer than normal, in this case several days rather than the customary one or two. Consequently, they carried a small supply of military rations, lightweight canvas tents, and a double supply of arrows and brought with them an extra horse apiece, in case any should be lamed in the wooded, rocky hills of inland Pontus. Mithridates also stuffed a pannier full of scrolls and philosophical and scientific texts he had raided from his father's unused library. This, however, surprised no one, for the boy often brought texts and studies along with him on his journeys, with which to while away the heat of the afternoon or the pre-dawn hours, while his comrades slept.

But to the genuine surprise of Queen Laodice, and the despair of the other boys' parents, the hunting party never returned. Weeks passed and then months with no sign of the boys, nor even word from the rustic inland inhabitants of their passing. Search parties were sent out, rewards announced, but no sign was heard from them again.

Of course, from the Prince's point of view, this was all quite according to plan. The boys were not lost; they simply had decided not to return.

For seven years they lived like bandits in the rugged forests and mountains of inner Pontus, changing locations every night, eating only game they had killed with their own arrows and javelins. They traveled secret goat paths known only to the herders who had lived in these lands for centuries, watering at tiny springs and holes untouched by any but nymphs and nyads. They spurned cities and markets, took circuitous paths, and avoided roads. This despite the fact that Mithridates was ruler by right over every valley and river they traversed.

The band of youths ranged from the high steppes of Cappadocia to the jagged peaks of Lesser Armenia, appearing like ghosts on the steps of the craggy castles of the Prince's vassal lords whenever they needed to replace a lamed horse or acquire new clothes. They hunted deer, feral goat, and bear, picked wild berries in season, and gathered the seeds of grasses to pound into meal on lazy summer days, in the coolness of their mountain caves. Wild honey they procured for the mere sport of it—hives were discovered by observing individual bees laden with pollen as they flew off to their homes. The bees' paths were staked out with sticks, and since bees always fly straight when traveling hive-ward, the nest could always be found at the intersection of the various bee-lines.

It was a fine life for boys, one that required little outside contact with civilization. Yet despite their seclusion, or perhaps because of it, it was during this time that Mithridates' legend first became established among the proud Pontic nobles of the mountains. These haughty families of ancient Persian stock had for generations paid their tribute to the Greek-loving kings on the hot and decadent coast but had in truth cared little or nothing for them, and especially not for the weak-spined queen-regent, whom they viewed as lolling in useless splendor in her coastal palaces.

The situation was altogether changed, however, when this strange Greek-speaking youth dressed in antiquated Persian finery descended upon their secluded mountain fifes, claiming kinship with the Achaemenids, like them, and speaking of restoring the glory of their ancestors and the empire of Alexander. To these battle-loving nobles, descendants of mighty Persian warriors who had conquered these lands generations earlier, Mithridates seemed the very reincarnation of the ancient heroes of the past. Strong and commanding, mysterious in his comings and goings, slipping easily into the languages and dialects of all the remote provinces through which he traveled, from Highland Armenian to coarse Troglodyte, he seemed the very embodiment of the leader they craved, one who would be worthy of the allegiance of highborn mountain horsemen; and for seven years they kept their knowledge of his very existence secret from the diminishing numbers of search parties sent out from the decadent coast.

These stories of Father's boyhood wanderings were my favorite, and the eccentric renderings of the adventures as told over the campfire always made them better still.

"How did you live on your own for seven years?" I once asked, seeking to stretch out the "history lesson" by peppering him with questions before he could send me off to bed.

Father chuckled. "Well, sometimes we did cheat a bit. Ever notice how Bituitus looks a bit like me?"

"Yes—you're both big like a Cyclops!"

Machares snorted at my childish response, and I glared at him.

"True enough, boy," Father said, smiling, "though I prefer to compare us to Greek heroes, like Castor and Pollux. For people who had never seen me, who had only heard a description of me, old Bituitus here was just as good as the real thing. Those highland chieftains, who spoke only Persian anyway, didn't even notice Bituitus' Gallic accent—figured it was a result of poor education in Sinope, that he could only speak Greek."

"But his Greek is *terrible*!" I objected. The men laughed and Bituitus grinned sheepishly.

"Well," Father continued, "he communicated with those nobles like a born herald. Sometimes he would go to one estate, pretending to be me and asking for food and a change of clothes for us all, while I went to another estate, asking the same thing there. Everyone was only too happy to provide a service for their prince, and we'd end up with double rations! Life wasn't as hard as Bituitus makes it out to be."

"Your memory is selective," Neoptolemus broke in gruffly. "We were once beaten to within an inch of our lives."

Father tensed, and his face turned suddenly grim. "No, I haven't forgotten."

"What happened?" Machares and I asked together.

Father looked at our expectant faces. "That first autumn, we traveled to a remote shrine to the goddess Ma, who watches over Pontus. Her cult was brought here from Persia. It is said that Alexander himself stopped at the little shrine two centuries ago and left a bronze helmet as an offering, though where it is now is a mystery.

"When we arrived, the shrine was overgrown. In fact, the one local priest had died shortly before we arrived, and the place was practically abandoned. It was still beautiful, however—a tiny temple of limestone columns with open walls, and a single small altar in the middle for the priest's daily sacrifice. There was a spring of sweet-tasting water nearby and we decided to camp awhile, restore the shrine, and curry favor with the goddess."

He paused, and the other men shook their heads. "A terrible mistake," muttered Bituitus.

"They came that night as we were sleeping," Father continued. "A band of horsemen sent by an estate owner nearby who coveted the shrine's land and spring for his own use."

"A Roman," Neoptolemus spat.

"Yes, a Roman, a retired tribune who had been granted the land for his service. For years he had waited for the local cult to die out, and with the priest now gone he felt it was finally his. When he heard of our arrival as new worshipers, prepared to restore the shrine, he called his lackeys and set them upon us in the dark."

"He couldn't have known who you were!" Machares remonstrated. "He never would have dared, had he known!"

"Oh, he knew enough. He knew we were *Pontics* and he was a Roman, and that entitled him to beat us with staves and send us fleeing into the canyon without our horses. Said we were cattle thieves worshiping a barbarian deity on his land. When we passed by again a year later, the shrine had been dismantled and the stones carted away for outbuildings."

I was aghast. "How could they do such a thing?"

"Because Rome owned Pontus. Simple as that. When my father died, control of the kingdom was lost and Rome filled the empty space. But it won't happen again. I swore that very night, as I was nursing my bruises, that I would be avenged. Alexander suffered defeats but each time came back stronger. I swore, even then, to punish the occupiers."

There was a long silence as the men stared defiantly into the fire. Suddenly Archelaus chuckled and looked up.

"Have Bituitus tell us about the golden horse," he said.

"Oh—the horse. Is that necessary?" Father protested, though looking up into his face I could see that his good humor had returned.

"Of course," rejoined Bituitus. "Pharnaces, here, is a future general. We can't fail to educate him in such a famous incident, which has become so well known that even my family in Gaul has heard it told—"

"By you!" Father rejoined.

"Naturally," Bituitus responded, unperturbed. "How else to account for your fame across all Europe, even among the wild tribes of the Danube and the Rhine?"

"All Europe," Father muttered. "All Europe, and all Asia, will soon have other reasons for knowing the name Mithridates."

One fine spring day, in Mithridates' twenty-first year, a thousand Pontic horsemen arrayed head to toe in dusty leather and full, unpolished battle armor emerged in perfect formation out of the forested hills behind the coast. They galloped along the peninsula of Lepte jutting out from the great promontory of Syrias, past the rich and sprawling vineyards clustered in estates along the isthmus, and around the edge of the sprawling fish market outside Sinope's city walls, where the mullet and tuna traders stopped their crowlike haggling and fell into silent amazement at the sight of the armored troops thundering past their stalls. The army cantered almost to the very gates of Sinope before the alarm was sounded—so lax had the city garrison and outposts become under the reign of Queen Laodice. The city's heavy bronze doors swung shut in the very faces of the horsemen, who, far from being dismayed, simply stood in quiet formation beneath the walls as the garrison troops hastily gathered on the battlements above, shouldering past the thousands of common citizens who thronged to the best vantage points, to view the spectacle beneath them.

"Tis pothen eis andron?—Who are you, whence do you come?" cried the city's governor, in the ancient Homeric demand for identification.

In response, a voice boomed out in cultured, formal Greek from a source unnoticed until now, in the midst of the horsemen. At the signal, the troops in the front parted, the crowds on the wall above fell to a hushed silence, and a most extraordinary being slowly walked his horse forward.

The beast immediately caught one's attention. It was a beautiful stallion, of the type bred in the wild mountain estates of the interior, who are left to run wild through the craggy canyons for the first years of their life before being caught and expertly trained for the hunt or for war. The steed was of enormous size, even for his breed, and every care had been taken in his appearance: the long, uncut mane had been braided into a hundred fine rows of tresses that hung to either side of his neck, each tied off with a tiny golden bell; the bit was of solid gold and the bejeweled bridle of newly polished leather; even the tail had been carefully arrayed, like the mane, in long braids with tinkling bells. The horse pranced as if on parade, head high and eyes rolling excitedly at his drab cavalry counterparts as he passed. Most extraordinary of all was his color—for it was gold, as shiny golden as the sun itself, of the exact color as the bit he champed. Like a statue, every inch of the animal had been covered with a layer of pure gold, painted on or brushed into his fur, and the people stared in wonder as if the animal had descended from heaven itself.

As their eyes traveled up the height of the amazing creature, they settled upon the rider, who was no less extraordinary. Though the man was seated on his animal, it was apparent he was godlike in size. Every muscle in his broad frame was taut as a bowstring and as clearly defined as if carved of wood. Even the tendons and fibers in his massive shoulders stood out, his oiled, olive skin in stark contrast to the polished black leather straps over his collar, cinching the glistening golden breastplate to his chest. His thighs, though partially obscured in the white linen of the baggy Persian trousers he was wearing, were huge, the girth of a normal man's waist, his calves the size of another man's thighs. His hair was pulled back to his shoulders and tied with a simple leather thong in an unaffected style, and unlike the thousand fierce horsemen who surrounded him, he wore no helmet. A faint murmur of recognition began to be heard from the walls above, and if there were any doubts they were soon shattered when he looked up into the faces of his fellow citizens of Pontus and flashed the broadest, whitest grin they had seen in seven years.

A roar rose from the crowd above, and as the news was passed down both sides of the long lines of spectators, the sound deepened and spread until every man and woman, every soldier, along the entire length of the wall for a hundred paces in each direction, was cheering, waving joyfully at the lost prince. Mithridates sat below them on his golden horse, lacking only wings to fly to his weeping admirers on the walls. He continued to grin, acknowledging the adulation with dignified nods of his head as he paced his horse a few steps in each direction—then he looked straight forward at the massive gates and gestured impatiently.

As if on cue, the huge doors swung open, squeaking on their long-unused hinges, and Mithridates rode into the city, the first city he had entered in seven years, followed by his boyhood companions and the thousand horsemen. They rode down the flagstoned principal street and past the Milesian gymnasium, and then turned down the Street of Temples, which ran in a small half-circle around the center of the town. Here were countless shrines to the deities whose benevolence had blessed Pontus: not merely the expected Olympian pantheon of Poseidon, Apollo, Athena, and the Dioscuri but eastern gods as well, Serapis, Isis, and Ahura Mazda. Even the Argonauts, who had passed that way with Jason a thousand years before and who some said had founded the city, were honored as gods with their own marble-walled temples painted in blue and ocher. Priests and temple servants rushed in ceremonial dress from the sanctuaries, anxious to determine the source of the commotion outside, and were astonished to see a golden god in their very midst. In a mixture of joy and consternation they, too, joined the cheering throng following the strangely clad young prince and his fierce warriors.

They arrived finally at the very center of the town, the Acropolis upon which stood the chief temple to Zeus, the city's treasury, and, looming over all, the ancient royal palace, gloomy and foreboding in its sheer massive stoniness. The fortresslike structure was entirely lacking in windows to a height of forty feet or more, at which point the thick walls were finally broken with wide, airy columns and verandas opening onto the royal living quarters. In the large courtyard fronting the palace a series of military exercises had been prepared for the benefit of visiting dignitaries. Hanging from a beam and flapping in the wind in front of the stone wall was a small straw effigy of a man, used for the archery demonstrations. Spying the swaying figure, the young prince seized the bow from his back and, in a single, fluid motion, fitted an arrow and let it fly, straight into the throat of the swinging doll. The crowd behind him gasped and fell silent at this extraordinary display of marksmanship.

Just at that moment raucous cheers broke forth from the soldiers in his band, who were quickly joined by the crowd that had gathered. On the uppermost balcony of the palace above stood the Queen Mother of Pontus, Laodice, watching the proceedings below in disdainful coldness, her mouth set in silent fury.

"Citizens!" Mithridates shouted, walking his horse up the very steps of the palace, directly below the Queen, without dismounting. After a few moments of furious hushing by those in the crowd nearest where he stood, a silence descended over all. Mithridates smiled.

"Citizens," he continued. "Seven years ago, my companions and I left Sinope for the harsh mountains and canyons of the interior. There we lived by our strength and our wits, overcoming bandits and wild animals, suffering hunger and blizzards. I have traveled every step of this kingdom. I have seen and explored every castle and hidden fortress of its canyons. I have learned the language of every tribe and clan in every valley. I have discovered the ancient homes of the Amazons, the caves and altars of our ancestors, and the dwelling places of the gods themselves!"

A cheer of approval rose from the crowd, augmented by

clanging shields of the mounted horsemen. Holding his hand up before him, he called again for silence and continued.

"But during my long absence not a night passed that I did not look up at the stars and think of my beloved Sinope; not a day went by that I did not feel the vitality and strength of the Pontic people and their greatest city. And on this day, citizens . . ."

The murmur began to rise again in anticipation of what was coming. The Queen turned in a whirl of silks and stalked back into the palace.

"On this day, citizens, I come of age and return to you, as your true king!"

A deafening bellow drowned his remaining words and the crowd surged forward, up the steps to their smiling monarch, who now raised a bejeweled sword triumphantly into the air. Laughing, he swung his leg over the neck of the horse and leaped down from that enormous height, landing as lightly and gracefully as a mountain cat. He stepped forward to greet the crowd, towering over them, receiving their adulation, beaming at the thousands of ecstatic faces.

The horse, meanwhile, that golden horse of the gods, now relieved of his mighty burden, was suffering from the heat of the day, covered as he was in a thick and irritating coating of gold dust. As a result, he did what any animal would be expected to do on such an occasion, when no longer forced by his rider to stand still. He flexed his knees, looked around warily, and shook—a mighty shake, beginning with his head and passing unimpeded, like a wave, to his neck and shoulders, his tremendous flanks and huge haunches. And with each tremor of his skin, a cloud of gold, a fine mist of shining, frostlike particles, sprayed into the air and settled on the hair and skin of the surprised and delighted throng around him. With a flick of his ropelike tresses of tail, he shot a streak of gold dust across the stone wall of the palace behind him, and with a toss of his head he threw strings of gold-flecked saliva onto the heads of the women and children before him. After finally ridding himself of most of the itchy powder and feeling more at his ease, he happily dropped a load of manure on the steps behind him and then, almost as an afterthought, stamped his feet firmly where he stood, raising one last, low cloud of gold that settled lazily over the steaming mound, turning even the huge turd into a beautiful, glistening nugget.

Mithridates' first act as newly acclaimed king was to relieve his cursing mother of her title and place her into safe confinement where she could do no harm—a luxurious prison to be sure, with all the sumptuousness and amenities to which she was accustomed, but lacking her freedom and dignity as queen-regent. Attended by a small coterie of eunuchs, she lived thus in furious splendor, raging at the gods and her son every waking moment, before dying of pure vexation less than six months into Mithridates' rule. Of her fate and her legacy nothing more need be said.

BOOK TWO

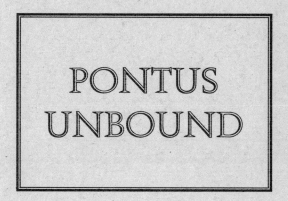

For myriad states that were once great have since become feeble; and those that are presently powerful were weak in times gone by.

—Herodotus

1

A new king's first order of business is to examine the state of the royal treasury, though this was somewhat more difficult than Mithridates had anticipated. Oh, finding the actual treasury *room* was no hard task—despite his seven years' absence from the palace, he knew precisely where to look, as he had often spent time there as a boy examining the collections of ancient coins and heirlooms. What he was not prepared to find upon taking power, however, was that the room was empty. Literally, figuratively, in all senses of the word—there was nothing there besides a few trifling bags of gold dust, which if carefully hoarded might be sufficient to pay the palace staff for a few weeks or months at most.

How had the Queen managed to pay the expenses of running a country?

Granted, she had no army to speak of, so military defense was not a burden. But what of the dozens of fortresses and strongholds scattered along the coast and the interior? What of the opulent furnishings of the palace at Sinope, and the battalions of diplomats and advisors she nourished to maintain her good graces with Rome? What of the new capital city she had been building from scratch on the cool and breezy shores of Lake Stiphanis, which she had ever so modestly named Laodicea? The Queen's financial advisors had fled when Mithridates came to power, and the ledgers had mysteriously disappeared, but he had an idea of the source of the funds, which was soon confirmed.

Within two weeks, a smiling Roman delegation—a junior

envoy from the proconsul at Pergamum and a coterie of
bankers—had arrived to congratulate him. Not that he meant
any great thing to Rome—political shifts in minor states on the
frontiers are of little concern, hence the low rank of the envoy—
but the change in government meant a great deal to the Roman
financiers.

For the Pontic royal house was in complete and utter hock.

Every sinecure, every government position, was paid through
loans from Rome. The Roman Senate itself held the bulk of the
promissory notes, largely against the Queen in Sinope, but
every city, town, and village in Pontus had its share of Italian
bankers, all of whom held leverage against the local municipal-
ity. Even local merchants, of second- or third-generation Roman stock, did a profitable sideline business lending seed
money to farmers against a share of their crops or indenturing
the sons and daughters of Pontic craftsmen for a share of their
production. The entire kingdom of Pontus was built on a tall,
crazily tipping tower of loans from Roman investors, most of
them at the highest legal rate permitted by the Senate, which
was fast driving all but the most profitable enterprises into ruin.

Mithridates emerged after hours of closed-door conference
with the bankers, red-faced and shaking with rage.

"They own everything!" he fumed to Bituitus. "Everything!
She's pawned it all to Rome."

He stalked out the door and down the beveled flagstones of
the principal arcade, where artfully arranged terra-cotta flower-
pots and fruit bushes alternated with tiny plots of manicured
grasses and mosaics. In silence he made his way to the palace's
central courtyard, where the fifty-jetted fountain played, supplied by crystalline water piped on aqueducts from a source in
the mountains twenty miles away. Servants were just setting out
the furniture and tables for the opulent banquet he would be
hosting that evening for his Roman guests. He picked up an intricately carved cedar chair, gold filigree carefully worked into
the delicate whorls and embellishments, upholstered in the
costliest of purple silk. Turning it upside down, he made a great
show of carefully examining the underside.

"This should have a label on it," he declared loudly "*PRO-
PRIETAS SPQR*—PROPERTY OF THE SENATE AND PEO-
PLE OF ROME."

"But it doesn't," Bituitus declared. "And I see no papers saying you owe anything."

"Ah, but the Romans have such papers," Mithridates hissed, heaving the chair against the plaster wall, shattering it to a flying spray of shards and torn fabric. "They have all the promissory notes signed by Mother and her treasurer. And they have the Roman legion in Cilicia to back them up, even if the notes are frauds. There is nothing to stop the Romans from acting at will, no counterweight, no balance. Once there was Carthage, before that Greece, even a great Hellenistic empire! But that is long gone. Now there is only Rome."

Bituitus was bewildered. "What do you mean? Of course there's Greece. Its capital is Athens. You speak Greek. I speak Greek. More or less."

"Wrong."

He paused and picked up a fragment of the shredded purple fabric, fingering it pensively.

"There is no Greece. Greece is only an idea, a myth. It existed long ago, when its traditions and laws were known from Attica to Egypt, when you could walk a thousand miles and still encounter men who shared your ideals and revered your philosophers. That is no more. Now Greece is a hundred cities, ruled by Roman proconsuls and bankers, each vying for favorable tax treatment, or for export rights, or for the honor of hosting the Consul's next foreign visit. Men trip over each other to learn Latin, to enlist in the legions, to become slaves serving Roman masters so that they in turn may enslave others. They are a hundred tiny rats against a single, lumbering bear and they could overwhelm and defeat the bear if they worked together, but instead they quarrel with each other, and the survivors seek only to curry favor with the enemy."

Bituitus listened wide-eyed to the outburst.

"Our Pontus is just a rat? And those skinny-armed bankers are the bear?"

Mithridates nodded. "So it seems."

"So what will you do? How will you pay your men, support your people? The country is bankrupt."

"I've been considering that for seven years. All that time we were in the mountains, I had more on my mind than just the next goat we were going to eat."

"It's no crime to think about eating. In fact, I'm thinking about it now."

"It doesn't pay the bills, Bituitus. But there are ways of raising funds. While my father was still alive, he had contacts. I know their names. It's just that . . ."

He paused, and Bituitus looked at him, puzzled. "It's just *what*?"

Mithridates glanced up sharply, still fingering the fabric. "Our Roman friends will not be pleased."

The second order of a new king's business is the continuation of the dynasty. The children of a king must be conceived by a female of royal blood, and herein lay a problem, as there were very few women in the world whose blood Mithridates considered worthy of the honor of mingling with his. No longer was there any Greek royal house with daughters of appropriate age or wealth; Syria was collapsing, a victim of political infighting and Arab incursions; and most neighboring states, such as Cappadocia and Pergamum, were mere vassal states of Rome and therefore beneath his dignity. Bituitus helpfully offered him a choice of his girl-cousins, who he claimed were princesses of the Aquitani tribe in Gaul, but Mithridates gracefully escaped the obscurity of that liaison by pleading ignorance of their language, an excuse unlikely to have worked for most potential suitors but which seemed to satisfy Bituitus.

With Greek prospects so paltry, Mithridates and his advisors despaired of ever finding a suitable wife and in the end were forced to resort to a less attractive alternative: his younger sister, Laodice.

This union, however, was ultimately as unsuccessful as one might expect. Though it yielded Machares and a trio of other offspring, the King and Queen were more like rivals, even enemies. Indeed, the fate of the marriage was sealed several years later, when Mithridates departed on one of his periodic tours of his domains. He returned after twelve months to find Laodice unaccountably cold to him, and even more unaccountably pregnant. At a loss with how to deal with her, Mithridates shut her up in bare apartments tended only by a handful of slave girls and courtiers, intending to keep her hidden until after the child was born.

Far from being grateful for this amazingly lenient treatment, however, Laodice was consumed with rage. Undaunted by her husband's daily ingestion of antidotes, she arranged to poison his food at a state banquet. In fact, the food did manage to kill two foreign ambassadors and sicken many others at the table before Mithridates understood what was happening. He himself, of course, had sensed nothing more than a queer taste in the meat. This time he did mete out the appropriate punishment. Needless to say, he never again married, preferring the relative safety, and considerable variety, of the harem.

And now no more of Laodice.

The King's third major concern was to reestablish the Pontic army, which had fallen into neglect since his father's assassination. This had been very much to his mother's liking, since Rome would have viewed with deep suspicion any signs that Pontus was attempting to establish a military force.

For Mithridates, therefore, the difficulty lay in restoring Pontic glory without openly provoking war with Rome. Yet although the problem was delicate, it was not insoluble. Rome's noble class, increasingly threatened at home by the Social Wars, thirsted for peace abroad. In its foreign policy, it subscribed to the ostrich's strategy of hiding its head in the sand to avoid danger. As long as Mithridates was not blatant about it, Rome would allow him considerable freedom to act.

But because he had very few raw materials to work with, he had to move very slowly. Money was an issue, though not insurmountable. The Roman moneylenders of Sinope were only too willing to extend further credit to the royal house. This could not be a permanent state of affairs, of course; the loans would eventually have to be repaid. But there would be time to ponder that later, once the kingdom's defenses had been shored and its trade routes reestablished.

Mithridates' first step was modest—like Asian monarchs in ages past he began by hiring a body of Greek mercenaries, in this case six thousand. The number was carefully calculated to be no more than a Roman legion, so as not to raise eyebrows. In any event, Romans considered Greeks to be much inferior in terms of military value. Yet what the Roman observers did not know was that these were not just any Greeks. Of the many mercenaries who had applied for Mithridates' forces, only a small proportion were chosen. His purposes required only those trained in a specific method of warfare, a battle technique that was all but invincible: the phalanx.

This was a solid block of soldiers four ranks deep or, even better, eight or sixteen, each man standing shoulder to shoulder with his comrades to the right and left. Every warrior carried a bronze shield mounted on the left arm, sheltering him and the man on his left; an eight-foot pike was held in the right hand. Those in the front ranks would aim their pikes horizontally at the approaching enemy; those in the middle or rear carried the weapon vertically, ready to be whipped down into thrusting position as soon as the front-rankers had been killed off or trampled. A trained phalanx would charge, with perfect precision and blind valor, into the very teeth of the enemy facing it, forming a solid block of grinding, slashing iron and bronze, overcoming all in its path. Once unleashed, the men in the phalanx had nowhere to go but forward, for the soldiers behind them fitted their shields into the backs of the men in the fore, forcing their comrades into the maw of battle, just as the men behind did to them. The phalanx would not cease its relentless charge until the last enemy had been trampled into the bloody mire or had fled into the hills. It was hard men such as these, trained in the mindless bravery of phalanx warfare, who comprised the solid core of Mithridates' army.

Meanwhile, as his boyhood companions from the mountains drilled the new troops, Mithridates dedicated himself to building a navy. Here he was on somewhat more solid footing with the suspicious Romans. Pontus had always been a seafaring nation, known for her fisheries and trade along all the ports of the Black Sea. It was only logical that a young king would seek protection against seagoing invaders by developing a powerful navy.

In this he was fortunate in that he already had an armada close at hand, manned by the finest seamen on the face of the earth—the vast fleet of Cilician pirates. Years before they had been friends of his father, who had provided them with safe harbors in exchange for a share of the plunder they captured from merchant vessels. No port on earth was safe from these fierce, hawk-eyed men of strange clothing and uncut hair. No ship in the sea, no matter how carefully it dodged from haven to haven along the shore, could avoid the pirates' beachside watchtowers and the speedy cutters that tore from their hiding places in tidal caves to seize cargo and hostages at their pleasure. No men lived such dangerous lives and none were wealthier than these feared pirates. And in reestablishing contact with them and restoring his father's earlier agreement, Mithridates not only acquired a ready-made navy, the largest on the Black Sea—but a source of considerable revenue besides.

All of which led to his next step: outright conquest.

As Rome sank into a cycle of violence between its two political parties, the *Optimates* and the *Populares,* Mithridates turned to regaining the territory and the prestige that were his by right of his king's blood. The lands to the north, across the Black Sea, were of no interest to Rome. The entire region was virgin territory. In fact, if Rome even noted what Mithridates might be up to in those wastelands, it could only be thankful a Greek-speaking king had taken it upon himself to spread civilization to those barbaric shores.

After two years of stiff fighting by Mithridates' Greek mercenaries and crack pirate navy, the entire northern coast of the Black Sea, including the lands of the Scythians and their vast grain fields, had been organized into the Pontic kingdom of Bosporus. The remote tribes of Colchis, at the far eastern end of the Black Sea, whence Jason had fetched the Golden Fleece, had declared their allegiance to Pontus as well. So, too, had allies been acquired among the neighboring barbarian tribes, and those wild men dwelling in the region of the Don and the Danube and around the Maeotian Sea. Over all this was King Mithridates.

Still he was not satisfied, though there were few other outlets available to him—until rumor made its way to Pontus of a great battle that had taken place in Gaul, in which an enormous host of Germanic warriors had destroyed an entire Roman army. The massacre at Orange sent a shock throughout all of Europe and beyond, and there were few rulers, who did not sit up and consider the implications of this sign of Roman vulnerability. Mithridates was no exception. He had a standing army of Greek mercenaries and a fleet manned by experienced sailors. Thousands of fierce mountain horsemen from the interior of Pontus and upland Cappadocia were at his command. He could call up as many battle-hungry troops from all corners of his domain as he could afford to pay—and with his pirates' tribute pouring in, he could afford to pay a great deal. The Romans' military affairs abroad were a shambles, and their political situation at home was explosive. Mithridates looked up questioningly at the gods in their lofty perch in the heavens.

And the gods looked down at him in return, and smiled.

2

In the very year after Rome suffered its disastrous setback in Gaul, Mithridates entered into an alliance with King Nicomedes II of Bithynia. Under normal circumstances this would have been of concern to Rome, but these were not normal times, and Rome had other worries. Mithridates ignored the proconsul's halfhearted protests and with Nicomedes quickly overran hapless Galatia to the south and Paphlagonia, the small territory separating Pontus from Bithynia. With these borders secured, Mithridates turned eastward to do the same to Lesser Armenia, stopping only at the Euphrates River. Here he entered into a treaty with the Armenian king Tigranes, to whom he gave his thirteen-year-old daughter, my half sister Cleopatra, in marriage as a sign of good faith. Mithridates would be father-in-law to a man who was considerably older than himself.

In Cappadocia, he stalked bigger game. Certain family tensions were also at play, as Mithridates' eldest sister was still queen there though her husband had died several years before. She was acting regent for her son Ariarathes, who was just coming of age but had not yet assumed power.

This queen, my aunt, had inherited her share of the family resourcefulness in military matters. Father often said he would hate to have faced her had she been a man. She made it tough enough on our invading allied army, though merely a woman.

"By the gods, Mithridates, she's your own sister!" King Nicomedes erupted after irregular enemy forces had destroyed an allied infantry column. "Can you not talk reason with her?

We outnumber her five to one, but she'll cut us to pieces in the mountains if we invade."

Mithridates snorted. "The bloodiest battles are fought between siblings."

"Still . . . there must be some common ties you can exploit . . . love for your father, anything!"

Mithridates shook his head. "I haven't seen the woman since I was ten years old, when she was sent away for marriage. She can't have heard many good things about me from our mother, either!" He laughed in exasperation.

Still, he sent envoys to Cappadocia requesting a truce for negotiations. To his surprise, the Queen agreed—on condition it not be she that he talk to but rather her son Ariarathes, the future king himself. In Mithridates' view, the discussion would be merely a formality in any case, preparation for either Cappadocia's surrender or defeat. He was indifferent between the two, provided that the territory ultimately fell into his hands.

The conference was arranged to take place on the open plain beneath the walls of the Cappadocian capital, Mazaca. There Mithridates and Nicomedes drew up at the head of their joint army, spearheaded by the six thousand mercenaries of Pontus' Greek legion. Three hundred paces away, just at the foot of the city's walls, the Cappadocian garrison stood waiting for them. Though the Cappadocians were clearly outnumbered, their display was cocky and confident. In full armor and regalia they had also fittingly decorated the defensive walls behind them, draped with massive banners and tapestries bearing the sword and serpent symbol of the Cappadocian royal house, glinting in the sun from the gold and silver thread used to embroider the brocade.

Mithridates, his generals Archelaus and Neoptolemus, and Bituitus began calmly riding forward toward the center of the plain as the army shifted into its ease position. The Cappadocian side did not reciprocate, however—there was only silence from their ranks for a long moment, until a single herald began trotting forward from their lines, bearing a flag of truce.

"Hear me, King Mithridates, as I convey to you the words of your nephew, King Ariarathes VII, Grand Ruler of Cappadocia."

"So he's of age then?" Mithridates asked Bituitus. "My sister actually let him survive to be king?"

Bituitus shrugged.

"King Ariarathes states that this conference concerns no one but himself and the King of Pontus, and therefore no other parties shall stand within one hundred paces of the center of this plain, where the two kings shall confer. Furthermore . . ."

Mithridates shifted impatiently on his horse. With his restless forces behind him Cappadocia was in no position to be making frivolous demands. Still, for the sake of his sister and nephew he bit his tongue and continued to listen quietly.

"Furthermore, each king shall be carefully searched for weapons by a chosen guard from the other side, before being allowed to approach the center of the plain."

"My reputation precedes me," Mithridates retorted. "My sister must have passed lies on to him from our mother, and now he fears treachery. The coward."

"You will speak with respect of the king on whose territory you stand," rejoined the herald, expressionless.

Mithridates shrugged, took off his great bow, quiver, and sword from where they hung on his body, and tossed them to his generals. "Search me for weapons—I have nothing to hide!" Waving his generals back to the Pontic lines, he lightly dismounted and stood expectantly. The herald, approaching on foot, looked up at him nervously, as the King towered over him like some huge tree. The small man carefully examined Mithridates' tunic and sleeves for hidden darts, ran his hand lightly down the length of his legs to ensure there were no daggers strapped to them beneath the baggy Persian trousers, and then nodded in satisfaction. Mounting his horse, he returned to the Cappadocian lines.

Immediately a commotion arose among the opposing forces, as with a blast of trumpet fanfare the newly crowned King of Cappadocia emerged from his surrounding soldiers, about to perform his first act as monarch, in full view of his army and the watching citizens atop the walls. He trotted calmly toward Mithridates' position, and then Bituitus dismounted and stepped forward to intercept him. Ariarathes descended haughtily from his mount and submitted to the same search—then Bituitus returned to his horse and cantered back to the Pontic lines as the young king sauntered the final few paces to where Mithridates stood waiting for him.

Ariarathes had inherited the size and bulk of the males in his clan but had a soft pudginess about him, in contrast to Mithridates' hard-muscled stance, developed from his years of campaigning and outdoor living. Ariarathes had waist-length black hair, oiled and braided in the ancient Spartan style his troops had adopted, and a stoop-shouldered, almost simian gait. His face was blank and stupid-looking from a distance, but up close his eyes glittered with calculating intelligence. Mithridates held out his hand in greeting, for it was the first time he had ever met his nephew. The welcoming gesture was fruitless, however, for the younger man rudely ignored it.

None of the conversation between the two kings could be heard by the generals, of course, as they stood a hundred paces behind their respective monarchs, with the eagerly watching troops even farther behind them. All could see, however, that the conversation was becoming increasingly animated, with hand gestures and vigorous shakes of the head. Suddenly Ariarathes reached behind his neck as if adjusting the knot in his hair, and as his hand reemerged, it bore the flashing blade of a knife that had been secreted in the braid.

In one swift movement he stepped forward and lunged at Mithridates, who neatly sidestepped the maneuver and simultaneously shot a glance back at his generals, not in fear or as if beseeching help, but with a knowing expression and a hand signal for them to stay back. Bituitus was hard pressed to hold, and kept edging forward as Neoptolemus seized him by the shoulder.

"Wait!" he hissed. "The King can hold his own. If you charge up there the soldiers behind will follow and we'll have a full-scale battle. Watch."

And then Mithridates did an amazing thing. He laughed.

He clasped his hands against his belly, rocked back on his heels, and let loose a laugh that would have awakened the drowsy gods on Olympus itself. Both armies fell into stunned silence. There was no movement anywhere, but for the grass softly blowing in the breeze and the shaking shoulders of the King in the distance as he roared out his defiant laughter, on and on. Then suddenly he, too, fell silent, straightened up, and peered at his adversary with a determined expression. Still, the echoing laughter hovered in the air and in the men's ears, like the endless humming of a bell that has just been struck and whose sound lingers in the air and in one's memory and imagination.

Snarling with rage, Ariarathes lunged at Mithridates, who this time caught the youth's wrist and gave it a quick jerk backward, eliciting a snap heard even by the hushed troops, sending the knife flying high in the air, to land with its point buried in the hard earth. Ariarathes stumbled to his knees, grimacing from the pain of his broken wrist, but managed to scramble to where the knife had landed. He seized it in his left hand and then turned in a crouching stance to face his tormenter, who in turn stood relaxed, his hands dangling limply at his sides.

Scattered cheers and applause broke from the Pontic soldiers behind as all watched their king. What happened next, however, would be fodder for legend for years to come.

As Ariarathes warily circled the King, waiting for the opportunity to leap in and consummate his treachery, Mithridates calmly and deliberately brought his hands to his waist and started untying the drawstring of his pants, without taking his eyes off the furious youth in front of him. This action caught Ariarathes off guard, for he straightened up slightly and relaxed his shoulders, as if wondering why a man about to die would be loosening his waistband.

Having untied the knot, Father then casually loosened the pants and plunged his right hand down the front of his trousers. Both armies fell stone silent at this display, and even Ariarathes seemed to forget his rage and throbbing wrist for a moment as he watched the strange behavior of the man before him.

It was the last thing he was to see. When Mithridates' hand emerged a moment later it, too, flashed in the sun from the glint of a blade. Lunging forward, he plunged it so swiftly into his nephew's throat the younger man did not even have time to step back or raise his hands in self-defense. He crumpled like a sack of wheat at Mithridates' feet, dead instantly, his half-severed head flopping to the side.

With his left hand, Mithridates still held tight to the drawstring to keep his pants from falling down.

The mood in camp that night was jubilant, for the next day, we knew, the army would march triumphantly through the streets of Mazaca and Mithridates would take possession of the Queen's palace.

"Easiest conquest I ever made!" he gloated as he and his comrades gathered at their nightly bull session around the fire. "There are few men in the world, or even horses for that matter, who could carry a knife like that strapped to their dicks!"

The men laughed at the outlandish boast, tossing out their own mock insults. Bituitus smiled but remained silent, his tongue too slow to joke effectively. Mithridates egged him on, determined to raise a reaction out of the big Gaul.

"It wasn't a small knife, either," he continued, grinning broadly. "No one complaining about the size of *my* offering!"

The men jeered and ribbed Bituitus, and the Gaul rolled his eyes in irritation. "By the gods!" he complained, though with a wry smile. "What a pack of braying donkeys. How big do you think that knife was? The way the King tells the story, it was a full-length Parthian scimitar. Hell, I've seen Archelaus' ugly mistress use one just like it to trim her nose hairs!"

The men hooted again, and Archelaus clutched his chest in mock pain at being the victim of such a jibe. "The Gaul has wit after all!" Mithridates cried, raising a wineskin to his friend. "Archelaus, he cut us both with a single stroke!" But then he winced as he sat down. "Oof!" he grunted ruefully. "I should have used a sheath today. Damn near made myself a eunuch when I drew that blade. I don't think I'll be sampling Ariarathes' harem for a week or two."

As it turned out, the day's flamboyant gesture was largely wasted, and the harem never did become Mithridates' to sample. The next morning, as he made his way through the silent streets of Mazaca to accept the Queen's surrender, he was met by Nicomedes on the steps of the palace.

"Welcome, brother-in-law!" the Bithynian shouted triumphantly.

Mithridates stared at him blankly. Brother-in-law?

"The Queen has accepted my offer of marriage!" old Nicomedes exulted.

Baffled and infuriated, Mithridates withdrew his army, leaving Cappadocia to his former ally. He had defeated the King of Cappadocia in fair or at least in equally *unfair* battle. The Queen had lost her regency. But she had now become queen-consort of both Cappadocia and Bithynia, and King Nicomedes was now ruler of both territories. The only loser in the outcome was Mithridates. He had been outmaneuvered, and though he shrugged it off as a temporary setback, it rankled him for years to come.

3

"Sight down the arrow carefully—like this." Father stood behind me and gripped the bow over my own hand, his massive paw completely engulfing my own. "Aim just over the duck's head, to allow for the arrow to drop during its flight, down to the bird's wing. Like so. . . ." Sighting over my shoulder, he guided me in drawing back the string and holding the oversized bow steady. Oddly, the goal was not to hit the bird's breast for a kill but rather the middle of its wing, using a special blunted arrowhead that would break the delicate bones but not penetrate the duck's body—the point being to cripple the bird without spilling its blood.

I released the arrow, but it flew wide, splashing into the water at the duck's tail.

"You overcompensated for the breeze," Father murmured. "These blunt arrows fly heavily; they are not easily deflected."

With the splash, the entire flock took flight in a panic, but Father smoothly pulled an arrow from his quiver and, in a single motion, fitted it, drew the bow, and loosed the missile. Far in the sky, a duck took the arrow in its wingtip, and it fluttered to earth, where it lay flopping in distress. Father strode calmly over to where it had landed, severed the head with a stroke of his blade, and inserted the neck stump quickly into the wide mouth of his unstoppered flask. Not a drop was spilled. Within moments the blood had been drained, the bottle recorked, and the body of the duck tied to a string loop he hung from his belt. Father's old herbalist, Papias, who always cooked his own food and ate alone, would enjoy it for dinner that night. We returned to the duck blind to retrieve our gear and then began walking back to the palace.

"Next time I won't aim so much to the tangent if the breeze is slight," I said thoughtfully.

"You analyze too much," Father said. "That's the sign of a beginner. Shoot a thousand or two arrows and you won't think like that."

"What do you mean?" I asked in surprise. "The weapons instructors always say brains win out over brawn."

"Of course they do. But instinct wins out over brains. Look at Bituitus—if he had to think every time he fought in battle he'd never make it past the door of his tent. But there's no other man I'd rather have beside me in a fight."

"But an archer—"

"All the more so for an archer. Look—a beginner uses reason. That's good and proper—you must know the fundamentals. You must experiment with the balance of the bow, the tension of the string, the weight of the arrow, the changing wind and shifting light. But that will only get you so far. If you do all those calculations before you shoot, the duck—or the man— will be gone. You must practice, practice until it becomes as natural to you as breathing, until you become possessed by the god. Invoke Apollo's name before you shoot; allow him to draw the string and loose the arrow; surrender yourself to the god's will."

We strode down the path in silence for a time while I thought on this, until I noticed him absentmindedly shaking the flask hanging at his waist, to prevent the blood from coagulating.

"Father, the duck's blood, the antidote—I don't understand. Why all this trouble? You're the *King*—who would want to kill you?"

At this, he stopped suddenly on the path, looked around, and then sat heavily on a boulder just outside the palace's rear gate. As he considered his words, he stroked the smooth wing feathers of the duck where they had become ruffled.

"Pharnaces, many people would want to kill a king. Especially those who themselves wish to be king. I have a son by Laodice, who is in line for the throne. Though he is my son, ambition often begets madness, and lust for blood can overwhelm ties of blood." He paused, not sure whether I understood his words. I did, but I felt nothing more than an enormous sadness.

"Machares is your heir—you mean you fear him?"

"Machares is a scholar. But he'll make a fine king in his time." Father shook his head and stood back up. "But this is not for you to be concerned about."

"But I'm your son, too. Do you fear me as well?"

He chuckled. "I think I would hardly be teaching you to make my antidote if I feared you, lad. Nor do you have cause to fear. You are of no threat to anyone. But of great help to me. We're finished here. Take the duck and bottle to Papias."

He passed through the gate and turned immediately toward the residential wing, to prepare for a state function to be held that evening. I walked slowly in the opposite direction, to Papias' quarters, in the most isolated, neglected wing of the palace, thinking over Father's words.

Papias received me without comment, for I had often visited him in his darkened, musty rooms and we were accustomed to each other's silent company. He accepted the body of the duck and dropped it casually, almost carelessly, into an empty bronze bowl on the corner of the table, to be plucked and cleaned later. I wondered briefly when he might get around to doing that. I had never seen him eat, did not know even if he *did* eat—he was so thin and wizened he seemed to subsist on air alone, perhaps flavored by the fragrance of the herbs and animal parts he stored in jars and flasks scattered about, filling every available shelf, nook, and cranny.

The old herbalist took the stoppered flask I offered him and immediately opened it. He held it to his nose and his eyes lit up, though his expression remained inscrutable.

"Fresh, is it?"

"Just before sunset. Father drained the bird while it was still alive."

This was important to Papias, for the bottle's contents comprised the base of the antidote he prepared for Father's daily draught. The ducks from which the blood was taken were raised in the preserve behind the palace and fed on a species of poisonous reed. This reed had much the same effect on humans as hemlock, the paralytic that had been used to kill Socrates. Papias had observed that ducks developed a remarkable tolerance to this plant—thereby supplying them with a unique blood that already contained an antidote for the poison. It was the perfect medium in which to mix all the other ingredients his *pharmacon* required.

Papias carefully decanted the liquid into a long-handled brass *calyx* and began heating it over the coals of a small fire while I wandered about the room, peering at the samples. I had little interest in the dusty claws, tusks, and bones resting in dishes on the shelves. Papias had long ago identified for me the beasts from which they had come and their medicinal uses when added to potions. I was much more interested in the botanical samples, which the herbalist spent most of his days procuring from the surrounding woods or trading for in the markets and herbariums. His finds constituted some of the most toxic, hallucinatory, and deadly ingredients known, which he added in various quantities to his vials of duck blood. I easily recognized dried and ground samples of deadly mushrooms and such poisons as belladonna and hemlock, but others were less familiar to me.

"Papias," I said, "what's this?"

He looked up distractedly and squinted at the plate I held, bearing long, knobby tubers.

"That, young prince? Mind thy fingers, that thou aren't nipped. 'Tis mandrake root."

I grinned at his archaic Greek dialect and peered more closely at the contents of the plate. "They look like little men."

"Indeed," he said, in all seriousness. "They struggle and shriek when pulled from the ground. Near to drives some harvesters mad."

I put the plate down gingerly. "And this?" I asked, pointing to a plain square box, a *pysix*, which I hadn't seen the last time I had been there.

"A rare one, lad. Wolfbane, it's called. From the spittle of the hellhound Cerberus, a very deadly poison. I'm told the Senate in Rome has banned it from the city. Too many assassinations involving the stuff. A Roman matron seeking to be a widow would pay a mint for the little box you hold in your hands. Don't breathe it."

I closed my mouth and put it back, then turned to watch him.

"How many ingredients does the mixture have?" I asked.

"Fifty-four, young prince."

I gasped. "Fifty-four!"

"Indeed." He nodded. "Thy father's mixture is nothing simple. Takes the better part of a day to mix it, and far longer to assemble the ingredients, though I try to procure in quantity. Knowest what this might be?" He sprinkled a grainy powder into the blood now steaming in the little pot.

"That's easy," I said. "Father sprinkles it on his food. It's arsenic."

"Correct, young master, straight from the copper smelter here in Sinope. Don't let me catch thee putting it on thy food, or I'll tan thy hide."

"Ha! If I ate that I wouldn't even be alive for you to give me a whipping!"

Papias peered at me through the steam. "I didn't say I'd give thee a whipping; I said I'd tan thy hide—like that one there," and he pointed to the wall where the tanned skin of a lion hung, moth-eaten and neglected, various talismans draped from its claws and teeth. I shuddered.

"But Papias," I asked, "Father needs antidotes. So why do you add *poisons* to his mixture?"

"Ahh," he chuckled, "the fairest question thou hast asked all evening. Two reasons, young prince. One is to test the effectiveness of the antidote in the mixture. If he starts feeling symptoms like those of wolfbane poisoning, then I know to increase the quantity of the wolfbane antidote."

"And what's the other reason?"

Here he lowered his voice. "To make thy father invincible!"

"What!?"

"Thou'st heard me, boy. Thou'st seen soldiers bathe in the frigid streams? Allows them to build a tolerance to cold, so they need not a cloak even in the bitterest of ice."

"I don't understand. . . ."

"So, too, does thy father take poison, to allow him to build strength against its effect. Every day he swallows enough arsenic to kill a horse thrice over, and twenty other poisons besides."

I was flabbergasted.

"But I still don't understand why! Father's not afraid of anyone, especially not Machares and me!"

"Not even Machares, eh?"

"No, he's just a scholar."

Papias chuckled. "So he is. But thou art the young warrior, I mark. Perhaps thy father should fear thee instead?"

"I'd never hurt Father. I'm going to be a general, not a king."

"So be it. But, Pharnaces, thy father—as a king—must fear *everyone*. His safety is the safety of the kingdom, and so must be his first concern. A king is never safe."

"Even from you?"

He eyed me over a jar of deadly nightshade he was measuring into the mix.

"Even from me."

4

At just over forty years of age, Mithridates was King of Pontus, Bosporus, and Colchis, the greatest ruler in Asia, and an energetic man. He was conversant in over twenty languages, as well as numerous dialects within each language. Indeed, he even knew the women's dialects, for in the traditional Persian villages of the remote interior the women were kept so separated from the men as to develop their own way of speaking. He was a patron of the arts and letters and a tremendous athlete who had won the admiration of both the common classes and the aristocracy. Moreover, he was a superb administrator: Pontus and his various new conquests had been consolidated, and Mithridates was now as powerful a ruler as it was possible to be and still remain independent of Rome.

And then came Manlius Aquilius. Accompanied by a train of abject-looking Germanic slaves, the newly appointed Roman governor of the neighboring capital of Pergamum arrived with all the pomp of a conquering monarch and immediately set about reorganizing the provincial government to better serve his own tastes. He eliminated civil advisors, promoted barbers and decorators, and razed courtrooms to provide space for more lavish baths. Summary punishments, such as amputation and even crucifixion, were instituted for even the most trivial crimes, and the city's ancient assembly was disbanded and replaced by an advisory council staffed by palace sycophants reporting solely to him. Rarely had the world seen as loutish and knavish a governor as Aquilius.

Yet beyond his manifest stupidity and cruelty, this man topped all comers for sheer avarice, even by the normal standards of Roman envoys. He quickly installed himself in an opulent estate, a true Roman *villa latifundia,* drafted a notice announcing his arrival and appointment, and sent copies of it by mounted courier to every king, prince, regent, tribal headman, and temple priest within five hundred miles, including Father. The couriers were instructed to make it exceedingly clear to the recipients that protection money was expected. He then sat back with a smile of satisfaction and waited for the funds to roll in.

After several months of sending out increasingly urgent letters with similar notices and implied threats if money did not arrive forthwith, Aquilius was in a murderous mood. Roman governors are expected to meet the expenses of their lifestyles through their own funds and are compensated by the wide latitude Rome allows them for developing their own local sources of revenue. Hence Aquilius' impatience, for while the cost of his lavish existence was excessive, his revenue was close to zero, and he had his own Roman moneylenders to contend with.

Most noticeably absent from Aquilius' list of paid-up "clients" was Pontus; indeed, Father had no intention of giving so much as a *denarius* to this crude jackal. Father was king for life, and Aquilius was in Pergamum for a three-year term only, unless recalled for incompetence even sooner. No Roman enjoys being labeled incompetent, and no Pontic king enjoys paying money needlessly to one. Aquilius continued to sit and stew until he came up with a plan.

He first did precisely what the Senate had mandated him to do: order Mithridates and Nicomedes to withdraw from their most recent conquests. Since the two kings had fallen out over the matter of Nicomedes' marriage to the Cappadocian queen, neither would support the other and therefore neither could stand up to Rome, even though Aquilius' threat was backed by only a single Roman legion. Both kings withdrew quickly, thereby disappointing Aquilius, who was denied the opportunity to take enforcement action and acquire valuable plunder.

Though compliant, Father inwardly seethed. By demanding his withdrawal, Rome had, in fact, set itself up as the protector of barbarians against a king who represented the cause of

Greek civilization! If there had been any doubt in his mind before, Father now was certain Rome had stepped beyond the bounds of all rationality.

A different opportunity soon presented itself to Aquilius, when Nicomedes suspended payment on his loans from Rome—claiming Cappadocia had been ravaged by Father's attack (disregarding the fact that Nicomedes had also been involved) and that the Bithynian coastline had been plundered recently by marauding pirates, also at the orders of Mithridates. Though Father had not, in fact, given such orders, there was no doubt that he had profited from the results. Thus the situation: Bithynia and Cappadocia defaulted on their loans. Their Roman financiers were furious and placing increasing pressure on Aquilius. And Aquilius had his own personal debts that were delinquent because of a lack of revenue—all attributable to Mithridates. Pontus, however, had not been invaded or plundered for a century or more, and its citizens were living high on the wealth of its neighbors, which by right belonged to Aquilius—or so Aquilius reasoned.

There could be only one solution.

We were sailing back from the land of the Maeotians on the northern Black Sea coast, where Father had been receiving additional Scythian recruits. We were still a day's sail north of Sinope when we were hailed by a Pontic squadron, led by Father's old comrade Neoptolemus, now admiral of the Pontic fleet. Father ordered his squadron to back water and his lead vessel to ship oars, allowing Neoptolemus' fast Pontic cutter to pull deftly alongside. The admiral swung to our deck on a rope tossed from an overhanging yardarm, not even waiting for planks to be laid between the two vessels. Like his twin brother, Archelaus, he was muscular and athletic, and though he stood a full head shorter than Father, his shoulders were at least as broad. He pushed quickly through the crowds of sailors gathering around him on deck and approached Father.

Father was puzzled at Neoptolemus' unexpected arrival but smiled nevertheless.

"Neoptolemus! Still a day out from port and you bring me a welcoming party! Or are you training a new crew? I'll have some new Scythian sailors for you soon, my friend."

The admiral's face was black with fury.

"This is no welcome, Your Majesty. And we will need those sailors in short order, I warrant. I bring bad tidings." He looked at the men crowding around him, unsure whether to continue.

"Speak, man. There are no secrets on a ship at sea."

"Nicomedes has attacked Pontus."

"What! When?"

"Two weeks ago, just after you left Sinope. Timed to occur when you would be out of communication. Sixty thousand Bithynian infantry. Our coastline was undefended. Nicomedes was unopposed. He plundered every city as far as Amastris."

For a moment Father was speechless, though the sailors surrounding us burst into an angry buzz, passing the news on to their colleagues behind. Finally he regained his voice.

"And what steps have you taken? The army—what did Archelaus do with the army?" he demanded, his face now only inches from the admiral's.

Neoptolemus stared his chief back in the eye without a flinch. "As soon as we received word, my brother marched half the army, including the phalanx, west to meet the Bithynians. The remainder, the greener troops, he left behind to defend Sinope. He hasn't yet returned, but couriers have brought news. Nicomedes retreated as soon as he heard we had sent out a force. Archelaus has halted, to await further orders from you."

Father paused a moment in thought, though his eyes still burned fiercely. "He was wise not to pursue them," he admitted. "Attacking a Roman ally on its own territory would have broken our treaty with Rome. This is to be handled first in the courts and the Senate. Our ambassadors have lodged a protest with Aquilius in Pergamum?"

"Indeed, sire. We demanded Nicomedes issue a formal apology and return all plunder."

"And? What is the response?"

"Useless," Neoptolemus replied. "Nicomedes simply claims the plundering was in retribution for previous raids by Pontic pirates. Word from our contacts in Pergamum is that Nicomedes actually did not *want* to attack us, but Aquilius threatened him with the Roman legion if he did not plunder our coast. Expect more soon. Aquilius will not be satisfied until the richer cities of the eastern side are plundered as well."

"Send an embassy to Aquilius immediately. From this day

forth, Pontus will defend against any attacks, even if that means attacking a Roman ally."

Neoptolemus lowered his voice so only those of us very close could hear, and dropped the formal tone he was required to adopt when addressing the King in public.

"A risky proposition, given the state of our armies."

"It's a risk I have to take. Showing weakness will only encourage Aquilius to greater outrages."

"He will commit them anyway. We must delay as long as possible, while we form our defenses."

"Then begin forming them immediately. The length of delay is entirely out of our hands."

That summer, Father came into his own, though none would have thought it possible at the time. From the west, Nicomedes was attacking again with fifty thousand troops. He was supported by Aquilius, who himself had gathered forty thousand mercenaries and local allies of Rome. And from the south marched the Roman proconsuls Cassius and Oppius, with another ninety thousand men spearheaded by two Roman legions. Father was faced with four armies, attacking simultaneously from different directions, totaling one hundred eighty thousand men.

Aquilius was about to receive what he was due.

BOOK THREE

RISE
TO
POWER

No man is so thoughtless as to choose war over peace, in which fathers bury their sons rather than sons their fathers. But the gods willed that this be so.

—**King Croesus of Lydia**

1

In the spring of the 173 Olympiad I was eleven, practically a grown man, at least in my own eyes, sufficiently mature as to make my own observations of the momentous events taking place in the world. No longer was I dependent upon blessed Bituitus' interpretation of history—for months I had been Father's constant companion in his military rounds, and I was now as familiar with the army's state of readiness as was he. Take then what follows with a smaller grain of salt than you ordinarily might from an old man recalling his memories as an eleven-year-old. I was no ordinary boy and King Mithridates no ordinary father.

The main body of Bithynians was marching east along the coast; they were expecting to lock horns with the Pontic army at any time. Yet a smaller unit of Nicomedes' troops had taken an inland route, aiming to circle behind us and capture Sinope. Father's tight network of allied mountain tribes had observed the maneuver, however, and sent word to us by smoke signal that an attack was imminent. Accordingly, Father sent a fast-moving detachment to meet them, ten thousand horse and a thousand light infantry, commanded by Archelaus and Neoptolemus.

Word first came to us of the battle early the next day, so early, in fact, that our Greek phalanx had not yet even started marching. A small squad of Archelaus' cavalry troopers thundered into camp, dirt-streaked and exhausted, several of their horses lamed—they had spent the night picking their way along the rocky mountain trails in the darkness, to bring the news.

"Sire!" shouted their leader, a squad captain named Rufinus, at the entrance to our compound. He slipped off his horse but collapsed, his feet and legs numbed by the hours of tense riding. Father and I raced out of the tent to see dozens of men standing over the haggard riders, shouting at them for news and wildly gesturing with hands and weapons.

"Rufinus! Get up!" Father bellowed upon arriving, lifting the exhausted man to his feet with one hand under his arm, supporting his weight as he stared into the soldier's face. "What is it? Out with it, man!"

Rufinus was still panting but soon regained his breath, and the shouting around us died.

"The Bithynians! We—we engaged, yesterday evening at nightfall! Took the hill in the middle of the plain—they outnumbered us, but our cavalry was stronger. Last night, though—the cavalry can't fight at night, sire, with no moon, can't see the ground to ride!"

Father's face darkened in anger, but he remained calm, urging the soldier on. "What happened last night—quickly now!"

Rufinus breathed deeply. "Bithynian infantry attacked—painted their bodies and armor black, we couldn't see them. Chased down our infantry and overran the cavalry. That's when Archelaus sent us to bring you news. The generals and men are retreating down into the valley, fighting every step, but don't know . . . don't know if they can hold. Archelaus is calling for the phalanx. Before he's surrounded . . ."

Father did not hesitate, even to set Rufinus down. He leaned the exhausted rider over the shoulder of the nearest guard and began racing to the paddock where his horse was kept, all the while bellowing to his chariot commander.

"Craterus!" he yelled as he ran. "Craterus!" And just as he arrived at the entrance to the small horse yard, the wiry little Persian appeared at his side, a crooked grin on his face.

"Craterus—ready your teams!" Father bellowed hoarsely, though the man was standing scarcely an arm's length away.

"I have already done so, sire," Craterus said calmly.

"Then move! The road south, into the mountains!"

Craterus sprinted away toward his unit. For months, he had been waiting for this moment. His corps of scythe chariots, each pulled by four horses and manned by a driver and an archer, had been honed to perfection. On level ground, Craterus claimed, chariots such as these, with four six-foot blades mounted on the rims of the wheels, could cut a deadly swath into the tightly packed forces of an enemy phalanx. Still, this exotic weapon had never been tested among the troops, and Father was skeptical. Now Craterus was about to have his day.

Meanwhile, Father readied his mount, not even waiting for the groom to arrive with his gear. Seizing the bridle, bit, and saddle blanket from one of the lamed scout horses that had just been brought to the paddock, he threw them onto his own gigantic warhorse and adjusted the reins in his hand. Just before kneeing his mount into action, he looked down, spied me racing up, and seemingly noticed me for the first time that morning. He paused for a moment in thought, and then a slight smile passed over his face.

"Well, Pharnaces," he said, "are you coming?" And leaning far down on his horse, so far he had to grip the animal's back with his heel in the manner of the Huns, he seized me firmly by the upper arm and swung me up behind him in a single motion, dropping me hard onto the horse's bare haunches. I had just enough time to grab the leather shoulder straps of his jerkin before he spurred the horse sharply and the animal leaped forward, scattering the milling crowds of soldiers as they rushed to formation. We raced then onto the dusty mountain road, as Bituitus and a half-dozen of the King's guards who had also seized horses thundered after us.

We were not the first to leave. Craterus, perhaps foreseeing his role that morning, had placed his forces' encampment on the leading side of the army's position, and thus they had been able to depart at a moment's notice. For a time, we galloped headlong through a blinding cloud of dust, unable to even bring the horses to a run because of the choking air. I coughed and wiped my streaming eyes, and Father did the same, all the while cursing Craterus and urging on his mount until finally, at the top of a low rise, a breeze sprang up and cleared the dust cloud from before us.

We were met with a magnificent sight. Just below us, several hundred paces ahead, Craterus' chariots thundered in a long line down the road, wheels bouncing madly along the rocky ruts, as the four matching white stallions of each vehicle strained at their tethers. Even from this distance we could hear the frantic shouts of the drivers, the snapping of the whips as they urged the horses on to greater speed, and the clang of metal as the sharp scythes, disassembled and secured by stout leather straps, slapped against the sides of the carts. Father did not take the luxury of pausing to enjoy the view, however.

"Zeus curse that jackal Nicomedes," he muttered, and he again heeled his horse sharply in the ribs.

"Pharnaces!" he shouted as we raced behind the chariots to catch up with Craterus. "Today you'll learn the art of war—and see whether I'm an artist or a grave digger!"

"Why a grave digger?" I shouted back.

"Because if I don't prove to be an artist at war, I'll be digging many graves, including yours, or you'll be digging mine."

I felt not an inkling of fear, so convinced was I of my immortality, and of Father's.

"I won't be digging yours," I shouted back. "No enemy holds the weapon that can kill you! Look—ahead!"

And peering where I pointed, he, too, could see it—rising from between the folds of the sharp hills and escarpments several miles before us. The thick brown cloud of dust had been rising for many hours, for the filth in the air had drifted and spread widely, now smudging the line of the rocky horizon. Archelaus' battle with the Bithynians! And it was a good sign, that his besieged troops still had the strength to raise that cloud!

The sight was not lost on the drivers, who whipped their horses to a frenzy as Father and I, along with Bituitus and the guards, thundered behind, hard-pressed to keep up with the frantically careening chariots. All conversation now was impossible, even by shouts—all my efforts were devoted to simply holding on, with fists and knees, for falling off my precarious perch on the horse's rear would have meant certain death under the sharp hooves of the massive war chargers thundering behind me. Within the space of time it takes a man to walk from the agora of Sinope to the strand and back, we came to the last bend in the road, the last one before arriving at the battle itself. So intense was the fighting that no scouts had even been posted—no one, Pontic or Bithynian, had detected our arrival.

Father sprinted to Craterus' side at the front of the armored column and ordered a halt, but Craterus had already issued the command. The horses were reined in and stood panting and frothing in the hot sun as Father leaped from his mount and ran ahead down the road, followed by Bituitus, crouching below the brush line, to see if he could spot any of the battle. Shouts drifted to our ears from the valley just ahead, and the ringing clash of metal on metal was unmistakable. The horses quivered in anticipation, and I could scarcely breathe, in my suspense.

Meanwhile, the chariot drivers had hardly stopped their vehicles before they leaped out, seizing the scythes from the racks inside. With practiced efficiency they tightly jammed the handles of the razor-edged blades, each as long as a man was tall, into the leather-lined sockets of the rims, four to each wheel. Each man then pulled out a large water skin, ripped the plug with his teeth, and doused the sockets. Within moments the leather had swelled, gripping the blades even more tightly, preventing them from being thrown off accidentally by the spinning of the wheels. By this time, Father and Bituitus had jogged back from their reconnaissance.

"We're on the enemy side, behind their lines," Father reported matter-of-factly to Craterus and the guards. "The enemy phalanx is intact, and advancing on our troops. I couldn't see the Pontics, or signal to them."

Craterus looked at him without expression. "And the ground?" he asked.

"It's good—slight downslope, gravel and grass plain. A dry creek bed cuts across between us and the phalanx. It's rocky, so tell your men to pick their routes carefully."

Craterus nodded.

"You show me these contraptions of yours are more than parade pieces," Father continued, "and you'll go to sleep tonight a general."

Craterus nodded again and turned to his men. Once he had arranged them in a column ten wide and six deep across either side of the road, they trotted in disciplined order around the bend where Father had just reconnoitered the terrain. Father and Bituitus remounted, and we followed behind.

As we emerged into the valley, a horrific sight met my eyes. The broad field had been churned to a wasteland. Where shrubs and tufts of grass had once stood, now all was trampled and crushed. For hours, since deep into the previous night, the combatants had ranged back and forth across this field in surges of destruction, impenetrable Bithynian phalanx against swift Pontic cavalry. The plain was littered with the carcasses of men and horses strewn about in impossible positions, some crawling weakly or flopping their limbs in agony, others lying still as stones, eyes glazed and dry in the harsh morning light. Where Bithynians lay, they lay in groups: Entire squads had been separated from their comrades by the charging Pontic horse and surrounded, heads and arms cut off by the slashing cavalry scimitars. Where Pontics lay, they lay alone where they had fallen off their horses, shot by Bithynian archers or snagged by the long pikes of the enemy hoplites and toppled to the ground, where they had been set upon by the enemy and stabbed to death.

We could see now that the Pontic troops were in rout. Cavalry can harass an army and destroy small units, chase down fleeing enemy and sow panic—but it cannot stand up to a well-trained phalanx. Our men were being backed against the steep nether wall of the valley, where they would be crushed and destroyed. Father wasted no time. With an earsplitting whistle he signaled the charge to the chariot corps. The eager, foaming horses leaped forward and tore across the field, chariots bouncing and careening behind, without regard for dead or wounded in their path, simply roaring over the top of every obstacle. The rumbling and shaking of the vehicles could be felt rather than heard—and it was this shaking, this trembling of the ground, that made the rear echelons of the enemy phalanx in front of us pause and look laboriously behind them in their helmets, to identify the source of the sound.

The charge was devastating. It was a mere sixty chariots, but the whizzing, whirring blades of death served their purpose with murderous efficiency. The front line of cars careened full into the rear of the Bithynian phalanx as the following lines veered off at the last moment and circled back to the sides. The enemy ranks shattered at the impact, as the chariots sliced their way through what had now degenerated into a terrified mob. I watched, transfixed, as a dozen Bithynian soldiers, unable to leap away from a chariot careening down upon them, dropped flat to the ground in a desperate attempt to duck under the whirring blades. The vehicle's iron-shod studded wheels slammed into their bodies, crushing armor and helmets like eggshells and lopping off limbs as effectively as the scythes themselves. One warrior, seeing no place to escape as a chariot bore down upon him, stood up straight and raised his spear, determined to dodge the horse and take out the armored driver. Mouth wide in a bellow of rage, he pulled back his arm to throw—just as a second chariot swiped by him from behind. The terrible blade sliced through his waist, toppling his two halves to the ground like the pieces of a sawn tree, leaving him still alive and screaming in agony at the site of his separated legs and pelvis.

The chariots raced through the enemy lines, leaving behind a trail of mangled victims, fragments of their bodies and armor still hanging in pieces on the scythes. After completing each pass, the drivers reined in their horses and turned back for another. The impact was immediate. Panic set in as they witnessed the mutilated arms and heads of their comrades flying through the air in the wake of the vehicles' passage. The phalanx's hold was broken, the game lost—our horse troops poured into the breach and the Bithynians' tight formation hampered them, preventing them from moving or fleeing.

Seizing the opportunity, Father raced forward while I hung tightly to his back, straight into the maw of the terrified enemy, who had no thought now but to escape the circling and marauding chariot drivers. Frantically signaling with a pennant he had seized from a courier, he caught the eye of Archelaus on the far end of the field, who immediately understood what was happening and reversed the retreat of his light infantry, driving a concerted attack at the Bithynians from the front, while Neoptolemus restored discipline among the beleaguered cavalry, rallied their forces, and circled around to the flanks.

The Bithynians could do nothing. Father spotted King Nicomedes himself on the left flank and bellowed for the cavalry to cut him off and seize him, but the Bithynian king managed to cut a way out and escape with a small body of guards. As he galloped westward, over half his panicked forces were slain; the rest surrendered. By evening, our own phalanx had arrived, and the Pontic army took three thousand prisoners. The entire enemy camp and baggage train was captured, as was its rich war chest, more plunder than any Pontic ruler had seen in generations.

I had witnessed my first battle, and my hunger was whetted for more.

Father needed no urging to push this victory vigorously: he must not allow the Romans time to shake off their astonishment and reunite the three remaining armies. He immediately sent one corps to Cappadocia to stop the Roman proconsul Oppius; the bulk of his army, two hundred thousand men strong, he drove by relentless forced marches west to attack Governor Aquilius.

As word of the Pontic victory spread, the demoralized Asiatic auxiliaries in the Roman armies deserted in droves. Father cleverly exploited the sentiments of the enemy by simply sending home every prisoner of war, without ransom and with even a small travel stipend. Thousands of released prisoners and enemy deserters reenlisted in the Pontic army. Nicomedes lost all heart and disbanded the rest of his army.

Within days, all of Bithynia, northern Phrygia, and Mysea had surrendered to Father, who rapidly passed through these provinces and absorbed their armies into his own forces. Still Rome's control continued to unravel. The Roman navy's powerful Bosphorus fleet, learning of the rout of the land armies, capitulated without battle and surrendered all its vessels—four hundred ships of war, transport vessels and fast cruisers. Father now commanded the Black Sea, the Bosphorus, the Propontis, and the Hellespont and threatened shipping and commerce in the Aegean as well. It was a stupendous victory for Pontus, a debacle for Rome.

Everywhere Rome turned, a Pontic army was there to meet it. Father seemed to have a sixth sense, to know precisely where the Roman generals would go next, anticipating their every move and speeding his troops there by relentless forced marches to confront the enemy when they arrived. The successive destruction of four Roman armies in a mere two weeks of fighting, and the capitulation of Rome's entire northern fleet, destroyed its authority utterly. Fortune may have played a part, but fortune is nothing more than favor from the gods, and those whom the gods love attract further favor from men and deities alike. With each new success, additional city-states declared their allegiance to Father, and before long most of Asia, even territories where the Pontic army had no presence, was in arms against the Roman overlords.

Upon arriving in Phrygia, Father established his staff head-quarters at an inn once occupied by Alexander the Great, believing it a happy sign to lodge in the very spot where the conqueror of Asia had once slept. In fact, due to some confusion of room assignments, it was I, rather than Father or Machares, who stayed in Alexander's actual room, as I was informed the next morning by an old slave woman who served us breakfast. Father showed his surprise when I told him this news.

"So it is you, Pharnaces, who are destined to be the next Alexander, not I!" he exclaimed.

Delighted at the omen, I could scarcely hide my pride. "Ah, but you can be his father, King Philip," I replied in mock consolation.

Father smiled teasingly. "The comparison isn't even close," he countered. "Philip was a thug and a plunderer. He had only one eye and was much stupider than his son. Besides, he was ugly as a Gorgon. I'm the exact opposite in every way."

"Maybe you're right," I conceded. "At least, you have two eyes. And how do I compare to Alexander?"

Father winked. "To start with," he said, "Alexander was a good student."

"He had Aristotle to teach him," I rejoined.

"And you have Mithridates!" Father laughed loudly, slapping me on the shoulder. "And that does make you worthy of Alexander!"

Father's former ally, Nicomedes, fled for Italy. Cassius sent his troops away and retreated to Rhodes. The proconsul Oppius held fast at Laodicea, but the city was taken by the Pontics within days, when Father promised impunity to the inhabitants if they would surrender the Roman general. They compelled him to march in full regalia of office, surrounded by his lictors, forcing him to declare his surrender with the pomp and ceremony of a Roman magistrate. Father made the most of this coup, while at the same time treating his captive with a studied generosity: he did not place him in irons but rather made him accompany our train as a prisoner of honor, displayed to the astonished peasants as the captive Roman proconsul of Cilicia, an adornment in his conqueror's cortege.

Meanwhile, Aquilius, the villain who had started it all, nearly escaped. No longer safe even in Pergamum, he again fled, this time to the small coastal city of Mytilene. There, separated from Italy only by the sea, he was forced to pause, wracked by a sudden illness. The locals, however, surrounded the house in which he had taken refuge, bound him in chains, and took him to their new ruler. All of Father's fury was discharged on this wretch. By taking command of an army, Aquilius had waived his privileges as ambassador; he was thus treated as a common prisoner of war. For weeks after his capture he rode through the cities of Asia tied to the back of an ass or attached by a chain to an enormous Bastarne who preceded him on horseback; he was forced, at the threat of beatings, to proclaim his name and his shame.

Finally, at the end of Father's triumphant tour through his newly captured territories, Aquilius was brought to Pergamum, until recently his own capital city. There, in a public ceremony in the agora attended by the city's entire population, the scoundrel was brought to trial for his crimes, as Father sat in judgment. Defiant to the end, Aquilius rejected all charges of bribery, extortion, and murder, and in fact claimed he was exercising the authority of a superior civilization over the barbarians under his control. Outraged, Father pronounced him guilty and sentenced him to receive—the sum of one hundred gold darics.

The man's eyes opened wide in astonishment and then narrowed in suspicion while the watching crowd fell silent in disbelief. A *hundred* gold darics for attacking the kingdom of Pontus? But the people soon understood, as Aquilius was seized and bound to the execution table. The hundred darics were brought out for his inspection—in the form of *molten* gold in a stone crucible. The furious governor's curses and threats were soon silenced as the glowing liquid was poured down his throat until he died, a token of the greed by which he had sinned.

2

In the audience room of the Roman prefect's palace, Father sat on an ancient and rickety throne, staring moodily into the crackling fire he had built in the chimney at one end of the hall. Machares and I lolled about on the floor nearby with a large hunting hound the prefect had left behind. Archelaus and Neoptolemus sat at a low table in a corner with a flagon of wine, discussing the next day's plans, while Bituitus dozed against the wall, away from the firelight. For months the Pontic army had been sweeping up the last Roman holdouts among the garrisons of Asia, and though most of the cities through which Father marched hailed him enthusiastically as the new champion of Greek civilization, a few still resisted. Even now, long after Aquilius' execution, Father's victories had not been entirely consolidated, and the tepid reception he received from some of the peoples he had liberated rankled him deeply.

We had arrived at a small and unremarkable fortress city north of Ephesus whose name now I cannot even recall. That afternoon the city elders had coldly opened the gate to Father, and the Pontic army was now encamped around the walls. The troops were prohibited from plundering a now allied city but were feeling in high spirits nevertheless. They reveled riotously and even convinced some daring young women from the town to join them—yet the atmosphere among the townspeople was subdued, and in the palace of the former Roman prefect, which Father and his generals had expropriated for their own use, the mood was positively black.

Suddenly Father slammed his fist down hard on the arm of the chair, splintering off a section of the old and rotten wood. Everyone in the room jumped, and Archelaus and Neoptolemus stopped talking and turned.

Father's face remained expressionless, but his voice was hard.

"I rid these people of a nightmare, of two generations of slavery to the Romans, but they are silent. They are Greeks here in this city—yet when I offer them the dream of a New Greece, they ignore me. When I unify all of Asia Minor, create a Hellenistic empire as large as any since Alexander's time, they fail to understand. When I build the first credible challenge to Rome, the first Greek navy to dominate the Mediterranean in four centuries, I get nothing but silence in the streets. What do these people want?"

The room was silent for a moment before Archelaus cleared his throat.

"Perhaps, my lord, they view you as just another conqueror, one no different from Rome, who in turn will be conquered soon afterwards. The people may be reluctant to commit to a ruler until he has consolidated his power."

"And installing myself in the prefect's palace, canceling all taxes and tributes, does this not demonstrate my power? Calling every city in Pontus, Bithynia, Paphlagonia, and Cappadocia my own does not consolidate my power?"

"There are still holdouts," Archelaus answered. This had been a topic of much discussion of late. The worst of the malingerers was Rhodes, the fortress island on the King's southeastern border, a crown jewel of military defensive works, which had boldly declared not simply its independence but also its outright opposition to Mithridates' rule—it was determined to maintain its alliance with Rome.

"Rhodes is a problem," Father conceded. "I fear it may be a symptom of a broader disease, which we must cure outright, while the world is watching. If we don't, its rebellion will spread quickly among our tepid new allies."

The generals turned their chairs toward Father, and even lethargic Bituitus woke up and took notice.

"So I ask you," Father continued. "How do we bind our allies to us, convince Rhodes and other waverers to place their bets with us?"

The men fell silent and stared into the fire.

"Do I scatter money, to buy them? Do I play like the Romans, and enslave them? Do I claim to be Alexander Reincarnate, appealing to their patriotism and sense of tradition?"

Father's eyes traveled from man to man until finally he cursed and stood up, stretching. The dog I was holding gave a low growl, then lay silent again under my hand.

"Do you think I am asking you rhetorically?" he challenged, his voice rising as he paced before the fire. "I ask for an answer! I don't employ you as lackeys, but as generals and advisors. Start earning your prodigious keep!"

"Buy them," Bituitus growled. "Use your purse."

The men nodded quiet assent. In fact, everyone knew the short and brutal war against Aquilius had made Father wealthy beyond all his dreams. Huge quantities of plunder had been taken from the Roman legions and the rulers of Bithynia and Paphlagonia. Yet Father shook his head in exasperation.

"Thank you, Bituitus. My bodyguard answers before my generals, and for that I applaud you."

Bituitus smiled and nodded modestly.

"Nevertheless," Father continued, "it is a policy I would expect from a bodyguard. Which is not to say it is wrong. In fact, I already implemented it several months ago, which you probably forgot, Bituitus. After Aquilius was captured we canceled all debts owed to the Pontic state and waived all taxes from Asian citizens for the next five years. I placed local supporters in all the high offices formerly held by Romans and tripled their stipends, to reduce corruption. Yet what has that bought me?"

"The support of the people," Neoptolemus answered quickly.

"No, General—the support of the *rich,* who are a damn sight fewer than 'the people.' The poor have no government debts to be waived. I don't begrudge buying the loyalty of a few ruling clans, but their support lasts only as long as the gold. What happens after the glow wears off—do they go the way of Rhodes? Does buying the loyalty of a few rich merchants and clan elders ensure a steady flow of soldiers into the army or provide a supply of grain and iron into the coffers? These all come from laborers and peasants. Paying their masters more money will not make the laborers work harder. What else? Bituitus has had his say."

"Sire," said Neoptolemus again, "if you wish to gain the loyalty of the common people, you must give them more power. Don't stop at restoring Greek temples and schools of grammar—that's merely cosmetic. You must strike at the heart of the Roman presence. Remove Roman slave traders and merchants, eliminate Roman constitutions in the cities and provinces, and implement true Greek democracy."

"Thank you, General; my faith in you has been restored. In a way, we've already started something of the sort—we've manumitted the slaves, released the peasants of the bonds to their overlords, and lifted servants of their indentures. We can do more—a complaint I hear during my audiences is that in the cities resident aliens are abused because they lack citizenship. It is impossible to acquire it without inheriting it. I spoke with a man whose family had lived in Pergamum for four generations, yet he was still denied citizenship and treated by the municipal authorities like a wandering garbage picker. I can order all the cities to enfranchise their resident aliens."

"Right—and that will create opposition by the rich." Archelaus spoke up. "They will have lost all their laborers and their source of income!"

"They will have also seen all their taxes and tributes repealed. They will be able to afford to hire back the slaves and servants at real wages. Does that solve our problems?"

Silence reigned in the room, as each man looked at the others.

"I ask you again," Father said more loudly. "Does that solve our problems? Will we now be secure in our conquests?"

"No." A thin, reedy voice piped up from the darkness at the far end of the room. Every man looked in that direction, startled, and Bituitus leaped to his feet, hand on dagger. None of us had been aware there was another person in the room.

"Papias?" Father spoke up cautiously. "Is that you? How long have you been with us?"

"Long enough to know thou hast need of new advisors," the old man sniffed, shuffling the length of the room to stand just outside the bright circle cast by the firelight. His rich olive skin glowed like finely tanned leather in the dim light, and the speck of amber in his tooth sparkled as he spoke.

"Have you no magic *pharmaca* to mix tonight?" Neoptolemus rumbled in irritation. "Speak your piece, healer, then be off."

Papias smiled, happy to ignore Neoptolemus and address Father only.

"Ha! So thou hast now eliminated the threats from the rich and the poor. Thou has begun to fulfill thy dreams, to create a New Greece, to launch a new cycle of legend with Mithridates as the hero, not Alexander or Achilles. Yet there remains one enemy to beware of."

"Rome," I piped up. The answer was obvious.

"Indeed, Prince. Thy father has done a most dangerous thing—humiliated the enemy, seizing its territories, conquering its leaders, reversing its policies of generations."

"Rome has its own problems," Neoptolemus scoffed. "It's in civil war; the Optimates and the Populares slaughter each other daily."

"Ah," said Papias, "so it is. But that will not last forever. Marius, the leader of the Populares, is old, and the young Optimate Sulla is vulnerable. One will lose, the other prevail. It does not matter which. The victor will then don armor and send the legions marching back to avenge Rome's defeat and regain its provinces. And when Rome returns in force, who then will the rich and the poor support? The legend? Or the reality?"

The men now looked at a complete loss. Papias scanned their faces one by one. His stare even rested on me for a moment, before I buried my face in the hound's long neck fur.

"Come with me," Papias said, and started for the small rear door of the Great Hall, which led to the private apartments. Shuffling slowly through the corridors, he was followed by the small group of men, two boys, and a hound. Occasional scornful remarks were heard as to the herbalist's waste of their time, until Father cut them off with a stony glance.

Arriving finally at a small, open courtyard bathed in moonlight, Papias stopped at a low stone altar built at the middle, just wide enough for a private sacrifice to the former owner's *lares*, his household gods. Laid out neatly on the flat altar stone was a flint ceremonial knife, a silver bowl, and a small jar of combustible lamp oil. A stack of dry yew wood had been placed carefully within arm's reach to the side. Tied to a stone boss affixed to a nearby pillar was a small kid goat. Papias had prepared in advance.

"In a question of magnitude, the gods must be addressed," he said simply.

Without hesitation he seized the kid and, holding it struggling against his chest, intoned a short prayer to the gods in the ancient Maeotian tongue. Then still muttering, he took the knife, slit the animal's throat, and held the creature over the altar, draining the blood into the silver bowl until its convulsions stopped. I was surprised at the old man's strength, yet none there stepped forward to assist. All were transfixed at the sight of the sacrifice, which was swiftly and efficiently accomplished in the silver moonlight.

After a moment, when the blood stopped pulsing, Papias laid the animal on the altar and with a practiced stroke inserted the blade and ran it from anus to jawbone, taking care not to pierce any organs. Parting the rib cage, he swiftly removed the liver, heart, and lungs and placed them to one side, still quivering with life. I inched closer to listen to the old man muttering to himself as he handled and examined each organ. He dipped his hands again into the body cavity and gently lifted the silvery entrails, separating the slippery loops between his fingers, dropping them back in and lifting them out again as he examined their consistency. After a moment he paused, picked up the organs he had set aside, and shoved them unceremoniously back into the body cavity. Then pouring the blood carefully into the trough at the side of the altar, he stepped back and slumped on a low bench at the edge of the courtyard, his face haggard and exhausted in the moonlight, his eyes glazed as if in silent trance or meditation.

Father and Archelaus moved forward, quickly stacking the sticks of wood around the carcass on the altar slab, splashing the oil onto the wood, and then lighting it with a spark struck from Father's steel dagger against the flint knife. Crackling flames rose quickly, and a plume of black smoke lifted into the air. The small offering was consumed to ashes in moments from the intense heat. As the roaring flames died down to spitting embers, Father and the men turned to the old herbalist, who still muttered and stared blankly into the middle distance. Gradually his focus cleared and he gazed serenely back at them.

"Thine enemy," he intoned in a voice that could scarcely be heard, "is not the rich or the poor, for they follow only strength. Thine enemy is not bureaucrats or merchants. Thine enemy is Rome."

Father's expression was unmoved.

"This is not news, old man. I have long known the legions want me dead."

"I am not speaking of the legions."

Father paused. "Tell me what the gods have said."

"Thy curse, thy blessing, thy hatred for Rome—this must be infused among the people. Only this can ensure their loyalty, to thee and to thy dream of Greece. A threat must be made to the people, an irresistible sacrifice offered to gain their allegiance. A deed that will etch thy name into their hearts and minds, that will write thy legend large for all to see. A deed that will forever bind every man to thy cause."

"A deed, old man? I know of a deed, but is it the same? Of which do the gods speak?"

"A deed of blood. Thou knowest the deed, and the gods as well, for thy desires are no secret to them. The enemy lives within thy lands; it burrows deep into the tissue of thy kingdom like maggots into a wound. Unless they are plucked out and thrown into the fire, the wound will never heal but only fester. Unless the maggots are destroyed, the body will die."

Father stared at him.

The Romans of Pontus.

Their roots and tentacles, their money lending and slave trading, reached into every level of Pontic society, strangling progress, defying Father's every attempt at empire, his every move to restore the ideals of ancient Greece. To achieve his goals, sacrifice was needed. And the sacrificial goat was obvious.

We looked at him questioningly. A deed of blood was needed.

Father shuddered and then nodded at Papias. "All of them?" he asked.

"Every one," the old man hissed.

He fell silent, and no further words would come.

The next morning Bituitus burst into the harem quarters, where slept the women and children of the royal compound, including the boys like myself who had not yet sprouted chin hair and been banished to the barracks. The women near the entrance vestibule, who spied him first, recoiled. They were unaccustomed to men entering the quarters, other than the King and a small coterie of palace eunuchs, and a man of Bituitus' size and uncouth appearance was particularly upsetting. I ran up to him joyfully.

"Bituitus! Looking for me? You should have just sent a messenger—"

But Bituitus' expression was distracted and his gaze passed right over me, as if I did not exist. Sweeping the area quickly with his glance, he strode into the next room, and then the next. Frightened women scurried out of his path like grouse before a hound. I trailed behind, wondering at his strange behavior. Finally, in the children's sleeping quarters he found her—my own nurse Felicia, an Etruscan girl whom I knew Bituitus occasionally saw when she was able to slip away from her duties.

She glanced up, startled, as he entered the room with a black look. Seizing her arm, he whispered something to her while fending off my curiosity with his flashing eyes. The girl turned ashen at Bituitus' words, quickly whispered a response, and pushed him away. He left the compound as wordlessly as he had appeared, ignoring me completely, as if I were nothing more than a stone by the side of the path.

Felicia, on the other hand, was a whirlwind of action. Quickly seizing some personal articles, she stuffed them into a small bag, slung it around her neck, and made to leave by a side door. I could tolerate Bituitus ignoring me. Felicia, my own nurse, I could not.

"Felicia!" I said, springing over to her side breathlessly. "What's happening? Why did Bituitus come here?"

She stopped and looked at me. "You were with your father last night, at the sacrifice, Pharnaces?" she asked, the Italian lilt quavery and her voice breaking.

I nodded, puzzled.

"Then you already know!" she sobbed. Tears streaming down her face, she gave me a quick embrace and hurried out the door. It was the last time I would see her in my life.

It was then that I recalled Papias' words. There was still one overlord in Asia to whom all were beholden, rich and poor alike. There was still one power that rivaled even Father's ability to strike fear into the hearts of the people, one power to whom the rich owed their estates, the farmers owed their seeds and oxen, and the poor the meager shelters over their heads, indeed the very sandals on their feet. And one power on whom the enemy relied for all its field intelligence, for all its counsel.

Converting all those Roman civilians in Pontus to allegiance to Father would be unlikely. Expelling them all would be impossible. The logistics seemed insurmountable, including even the most basic of questions: How to recognize a Roman in the first place? The task was not trivial. No plan to confront the Pontic Romans could be dragged into the miasma of submitting every foreigner to a public trial to determine his place of birth. A simpler solution was needed; a simpler solution had been found.

Every Italian in the kingdom could be recognized by his speech. In fact, under a recent decree, all Italians were Roman citizens; therefore, elimination of all Italians would accomplish the goal. Every man, woman, and child in Asia who spoke an Italian tongue must die.

All eighty thousand of them.

That morning, a secret order was issued throughout all of Father's domains. On a single day, one month hence, the magistrates of every town and city must eliminate every resident, traveler, and stranger who spoke an Italian tongue. Speech would be the only criterion; no consideration would be given to status. Even slaves and manual workers, if their native tongue was an Italian one, were to be put to death. Those who disobeyed, who gave refuge to Italians or concealed them, were themselves to be killed and their goods confiscated to the royal treasury. Asian slaves who killed or betrayed their masters were to be given freedom, and debtors who did the same to their creditors were to have half their debt remitted.

I shall not mince words in describing this terrifying policy, nor shall I excuse it, although even now, four decades after the fact, I see no feasible alternative. Father's comrades were appalled at the rigid brutality of this solution, at its very . . . un-*Greekness,* as Neoptolemus ungracefully put it.

"Foreigners and barbarians," he warned Father, "are to be pitied, perhaps despised for their ignorance; but ignorance is no grounds for death."

"And if that ignorance causes them to undermine my rule? To support Rome, the center of barbarism? To threaten the unity of our empire?" Father rejoined.

Neoptolemus sighed. "Sire—to hate a barbarian simply because he is barbarian is to give him too much importance, too much influence over the superiority of the Greek soul. You risk being swayed by another barbarism, the herbalist's barbarism, a worse kind of barbarism."

Yet Father, in his ambition and hatred for all things Roman, would have none of it. "From Papias," he said, "I receive both poison and its antidote. I receive death mixed with life, good mixed with evil. If that is barbarism, I accept it. From the Roman barbarians, however, I see nothing but evil."

He knew his people; he knew the contempt with which the indebted Pontic families of the interior held the Roman bankers in their midst. Popular instinct expected, nay, *clamored for* precisely this solution. This was no time for the faint of heart. Father was not devising a new policy—he was simply following the river's current where it led him. Elimination of the slavery that held his people in thrall was the last step to establishing complete unity among the inhabitants of his empire.

Yet even more important than vengeance was this: the loyalty of the people to Pontus, and against Rome, would now be ensured forever. Though the citizens of his new territories had changed sides in the past to save their fortunes, they would never do so again. With such a quantity of blood on their hands, Rome would never again trust or accept their services. By fulfilling Father's demands, they would be committing themselves to unconditional lifelong enmity with Rome.

It was this argument that most convinced him to undertake his bloody step.

When the time came to perform the deed, all Asia obeyed, not only willingly but enthusiastically—evidence of the hatred that years of Roman rule had engendered. It became known to history as the Night of the Vespers.

Asia was in turmoil. Papias' policy had been executed flawlessly. The deed of blood had been accomplished.

3

Rome exploded in rage, its citizens rioting in the streets. The Pontic emissaries representing our interests there were caught by surprise—they heard the news of the massacre at the same time as it hit the streets. They and their families were caught by the mob and murdered in retribution, their possessions ransacked, and their houses burned to the foundations. Pontic trading vessels in port along the Italian coast were seized, their crews put to death. The Roman Senate was outraged, calling Father a madman, baying for his head, pledging that Rome would not rest until Mithridates had been hunted down and brought to justice. Never had Rome experienced such a defeat, never had so many of its citizens, both soldiers and civilians, been destroyed at the hands of an enemy—not even Hannibal or the Gauls had struck such a terrible blow—and the city was devastated. After the initial shock, rumor even spread that Mithridates was on the march and would be attacking, putting all of Italy to the sword just as he had the Italians in Asia. From the Aegean to the Adriatic, panicked citizens erected barriers and walls, strengthened fortresses, laid moats and ditches, all in an effort to forestall the terrible might of Mithridates.

The legend grew, out of all proportion to Father's actual plans and actions. Countries and tribes we had never even heard of, Ethiopians and Picts, sought trade relations with us. Allies rushed to send us tribute and praise, while Rome's traditional enemies hastened to deliver effusive thanks. Itinerant poets and singers who passed through our lands had already composed long epics recounting Rome's final days, the fear and terror of its citizens, mothers putting their own children to the knife to spare them a lifetime of slavery under Mithridates the Conqueror. Father was compared to Alexander, Darius, and Xerxes, his kingdom hailed as the New Greece, the restoration of the ancient glory of Agamemnon. Only a few states, Rhodes and Delos and several other Roman loyalists, lodged cautious protests against Father's actions. But he cared little what others thought, or if he did care, he did not show it. Rather, he ignored them, and to further demonstrate his contempt, he celebrated his victories over Rome in high style.

State dinners by night, games by day. In Pergamum, the seat of his new royal court, Father engaged in a display of horsemanship that stunned the locals and put even the region's champions to shame. He decreed a new contest in the hippodrome, a series of chariot races involving not a mere eight horses per car, which had been the previous maximum size of a team, for the sake of safety; nor even twelve horses, which had occasionally been used for displays and stately ceremonial tours; but rather full, flat-out races, with an astonishing sixteen horses per chariot. People still speak in awe of his winning performance, of the fact that he himself drove a team of the frothing beasts—not some light-bodied boy jockey or stand-in, as other kings had used in the past to avoid endangering themselves, but forty-six-year-old, giant-muscled Mithridates himself, in a specially made iron car carefully fitted with red-gold plating, iron roll bars, and axles thick as a man's arm to support his huge weight. His team of matched white chargers each had a Gorgon riveted to the frontlet on its head and bells set to the reins, which—like the stories they tell of Pallas' war shield—made terrible music as they slapped upon the frantic animals' backs. A ceremonial *aspis,* golden engravings of Hercules aglow in the sunlight, hung upon his back, and the bouncing chassis of his vehicle as it caromed crazily around the arena was the terror of the other competitors and the delight of the onlookers.

Father's state dinners were attended by the most famous artists, politicians, and literary figures of Hellenistic society. The lively evenings often evolved into raucous drinking bouts, with the King himself accompanying his guests back to their lodgings at dawn, one time half-dragging a besotted visiting magistrate from Athens under one arm and a giggling bare-bottomed dancing girl under the other, whom he introduced to the astonished early-morning passersby as his "new team of advisors." On one memorable occasion, Father was issued a friendly challenge to an eating contest from a professional boxer, one Calamodrys of Cyzicus, during a dinner in the royal banqueting hall. Father laughed.

"Calamodrys!" he exclaimed. "You may be a fine athlete, but save your boasting for the arena. Eating well is a true skill in which you have not been tested."

Calamodrys scowled, unaccustomed to being made light of and no doubt emboldened by the considerable wine he had drunk that evening.

"With respect, sire," he said gruffly, standing up, "everyone knows that boxers in training are the world's greatest gluttons, and I am the greatest boxer. It follows, then, that I am the greatest glutton—and king or not, I challenge you to prove otherwise!" He sat down heavily, and the room fell silent as everyone stared at Father.

He remained silent for a moment, a half-smile on his face. I leaned over to him from my position behind his shoulder.

"Father—he's been waiting to challenge you. He's hardly touched his food all evening."

Father looked down at his own plate, which was now almost empty. He had already eaten a full meal. "Not to worry," he laughed. "That was just a warm-up."

He stood and raised his cup to the boxer. "My misguided friend—I think you've taken too many punches to the head. Surely it takes a king to be a true glutton. You're a bold man, or a drunk one. I accept your challenge."

The guests at the table cheered, and it was immediately suggested that such a momentous occasion be made public. Accordingly, the two contestants and the table were moved out onto a hastily set dais in the middle of the palace courtyard, where the event would be in full view of anyone in the city who cared to attend at that late hour of the night. Archelaus assumed the role of judge and bustled about busily, ordering the stewards to arrange platters of equal amounts of meat and flat bread before each contestant and to stand ready with a steady supply of wine cut with water, to quench the eaters' thirst.

"No throwing food on the floor," he intoned self-importantly before the growing crowd of jostling onlookers. "No hiding scraps in clothing. First contestant to lay down his knife ends the match. The meat remaining on each platter will then be weighed, and he with the smallest remainder will be declared the kingdom's greatest glutton. Begin!"

The original platters were not enough. After an hour of raucous shoveling and swilling of food, both men called for another platter, and then Calamodrys bellowed for a third. The crowd now filled the courtyard and even the square outside the wall, and self-styled bookmakers circulated through the cheering, milling throng, shouting their odds. Gazing out at the onlookers, I was delighted to see even the old showman Otus the Armenian and his wolf-riding son, both of whom were apparently in town for a performance and had convinced a pair of kind spectators to hoist them onto their shoulders so they might view the event. Perspiring servers fought their way through the close-packed crowd, bearing more plates of meat, flagons of wine, and pitchers of water. Calamodrys tore into his food with a frenzy, stuffing huge slices of venison into his mouth and alternating it with crushed wads of bread. Father's technique was more measured, slower, as he chewed each mouthful deliberately and, it seemed, with pleasure. He had fallen behind his challenger by a full half-platter but did not seem concerned.

Midway through his third plate, Calamodrys blanched, emitted a huge belch that set his prodigious jowls flapping, and slapped his palm on the table in a sign he was through. Father looked at his rival in surprise and, some spectators later swore, in disappointment, sprinkled some more arsenic on the bone he was gnawing, finished it handily, and then calmly called for his own third platter. The boxer's eyes bulged as he watched, and then his face drooped in disappointment as Father continued with his steady, methodical approach and handily finished the entire serving—it alone enough food for an entire meal under normal circumstances. He then stood, smiling. The King had not even loosened the waistband of his Persian pants, nor unstrapped the wide leather dagger belt from around his belly. As the bloated athlete looked on miserably, Father rapidly chugged an entire skin of wine to slake his thirst, tossed the empty bag onto the table, and then raised his hands to acknowledge the cheers of the spectators. The onlookers were ecstatic. After long cheering, Archelaus waved his arms to call for silence. This took some doing, but the raucous crowd finally settled, and Father's voice boomed out over the throng.

"All honor to my worthy competitor for his performance," he said as the bystanders tittered. "He lost, it is true, but he was at a disadvantage, challenging me to an event in which I am quite accomplished." The crowd laughed and he raised his hands again for silence.

"I have decided to allow worthy Calamodrys an opportunity to regain his lost honor, in a contest involving his own specialty." Calamodrys straightened out of his slump and peered with muted interest out of puffy, reddened eyes. "I challenge him to a boxing match!"

The crowd fell silent for a moment; then pandemonium erupted. Archelaus stepped forward to the front of the dais to take control. "Let us agree, then, on the date and the terms!" he shouted as the noise died down, and the onlookers listened in delight to the preparations for this wondrous event, their new king challenging a champion boxer to a match.

Father stepped forward, and Archelaus raised his voice in the grand manner of a master of ceremonies at the Olympic games. "And where shall this contest of the champions be held?" he called to Father, in a voice that carried across the entire courtyard.

Father looked around him, still holding a half-loaf of flat bread on which he continued to munch. "Why, right here on this dais," he announced in reply. "As good a place as any." The boxer nodded in assent.

"And when shall we hold this championship bout?"

Father now assumed an expression of puzzlement. "When? Right now, of course, as soon as I can unstrap this confounded belt and take off my weapon." He began to strip down to his loincloth, and the dense crowd of onlookers exploded in cheers. The boxer swayed sickly in his seat and looked at the King in ill-disguised astonishment.

The match went no further than that. When poor Calamodrys rose unsteadily to his feet to accept Father's challenge, he vomited and then fell off the edge of the platform in a swoon. He was carried away—across the shoulders of his smiling king—to the nearest shelter we could find, which happened to be the wagon of Otus the Armenian parked just outside the palace gates. Father strode up to the vehicle and deposited his burden inside the canvas, to the dismay of the animal trainer and his son, who had followed him out of the courtyard with the rest of the crowd. With an ample payment from the King, the two midgets were persuaded to let the soused wrestler regain his consciousness in their care, though when he awoke the next morning with a splitting headache to find a grinning ape and a she-wolf peering down at him, it is unlikely he ever fully recovered his sanity.

Yet Father did not fill his days with sports alone or with idle leisure. His new station afforded him access to the greatest minds of Greece and Asia and the time and resources to dedicate to studying their works. Countless hours were spent honing his skills in the many languages of his kingdom, learning new ones, and developing the eloquence and forcefulness of speech that would later prove such an effective tool to his leadership. The arts, and especially sculpture, became dear to him and he endowed magnificent grants on temples, attracting the most famous sculptors of the world. Even the ancient privileges of the temples, many of which had been revoked under Roman rule, were restored, to the great acclaim of the priests and the general populace.

Exiled and discredited politicians, thinkers, and soldiers from all parts of the world traveled to Pergamum with hopes of starting new lives, adding to the luster and renown of the already famous city. Smaller cities in the region, which had been heavily damaged by a recent earthquake, were rebuilt in their entirety at Father's expense. And while every measure was taken to override the bitter memories of the recent Roman domination of the province, Father continued to respect what he viewed as the few positive vestiges of the Roman presence, including the well-functioning judicial system, many harmless cults to Roman deities, and certain peace-loving schools of philosophy and rhetoric. These measures were cleverly designed to ensure the rapid transfer of the population's loyalties from their old masters to the new one.

Truly, a golden age had arrived for the Greek world.

Yet Father did not have to bear these duties alone, for he had recently acquired a new mate. Not a wife, for after his disastrous experience with his sister Laodice years ago he had vowed never to marry again. Yet not a mere harem wench, either, for of these he had dozens. This one was something else entirely.

During his triumphant march through his new domains, his path had taken him through the small regional capital of Stratonicea, a city that had remained a tepid Roman ally until the very day when Father appeared before its weakly defended walls with his army. After accepting the city's surrender he rode into the agora leading his troops, and while he was moodily wondering at the cool reception of the crowd, his eye was caught by a pretty face. This was often the case with Father, who rarely spent more than a night or two alone, even on campaign, and whose habit was simply to point his finger at any fortunate girl his gaze fell upon and gesture to her to join his train of courtiers. Invariably, of course, the girl would do so, most often joyfully, often nervously, but never reluctantly, for an invitation to join the King's harem was a pass to fortune and honor, as well as protection for the girl's family in the future, from predators and creditors alike.

This girl, however, was different from the other street wenches who answered to his summons—she was a stunning beauty, who stood out among the typically motley, greasy, gap-toothed city girls like a thornless rose among weeds. She could not have originated among the noble families, for her clothes were as grimy and threadbare as any in the throng; in any case, no nobles would have been caught dead standing in the filth of the street observing a conquering army. But her face—her face was the most sublime I had ever seen, with wide green eyes that stared unblinkingly at Father as he rode past, and shimmering jet hair that hung to her waist, roped in a long twist and bound back with a simple beaded band around her forehead. She had clear, pale skin, a lovely straight nose, and delicately pursed lips. Even to my eyes, the girl practically glowed light, and she made no effort to turn modestly or avert her eyes from the sidelong stares of the Pontic officers as they passed. Why should she? She was a goddess, an Aphrodite among peasants, and her proud, confident expression indicated that she knew her value and that she had stationed herself in that position for a purpose—for the eyes of Father. And Father had noticed.

Performing a quick double take as he rode past, he did not hesitate to point his finger at the girl as he was accustomed to doing—yet her reaction was not what he expected. The wench frowned visibly, then turned to a conversation she was having with an older man who appeared to be her father. A black look instantly passed over the King's brow.

"Go fetch that girl," he muttered to Bituitus, but the patient guard returned a few moments later empty-handed.

"My lord," the Gaul whispered to him as they continued their ceremonial march into the city. "Her name is a strange one—*Monime*—'all alone.' I do not like the omen. . . ."

Father glared at him. "Why should I care about her name? I told you to fetch her."

"She refuses to come. She says she is only seventeen years old, too young to leave her family unless she is married."

"Married!" Father exclaimed. He literally stopped in the street to stare at Bituitus, and the officers and troops behind bunched awkwardly, at a respectful distance, as their warrior-king openly argued with his guard. Behind the officers, a commotion had developed. Sliding off of my own horse, I slipped through the crowd to investigate.

Bituitus' offer to the girl Monime had obviously not been subtly put. Undoubtedly his thick Gallic accent had attracted the attention of bystanders and relatives surrounding the girl. Now a crowd of fifty cheering tradesmen and peasants approached, carrying Monime and her father upon their skinny shoulders, jostling their way through the ranks of bemused Pontic officers as they celebrated the good fortune that had befallen a girl of their own caste, through the King's offer of marriage. It took only moments for the laughing, shouting crew to catch up with where we stood.

Father stared gape-jawed at the crowd, listening to their congratulations.

"Marriage!?" he bellowed. "No one said a thing about marriage!"

"He did!" the girl's father called back accusingly, pointing at Bituitus. The bystanders snickered and Bituitus turned a deep shade of red.

"Sire, I said no such thing!" he stammered. "I issued an order for the girl to . . . to . . ."

"To what?" the girl's father shouted.

"To accompany the King!" Bituitus shouted back.

"And what does that mean, if not marriage?" the girl's rascally father retorted. "My girl is a virgin, a paragon of virtue. What would the King have her for, if not to marry her?" The men around him again set up their infernal yelling, accompanied this time by the celebratory ululating of certain women relatives in the girl's party, who had appeared from out of nowhere to catch up with their menfolk and, if anything, formed an even more formidable block shouldering through the Pontic officers.

Father was astonished and exasperated, never having meant for the procurement to escalate to such a level.

"The girl refuses to accompany her new king?" he said in a low but furious voice to Bituitus, who struggled to hear over the raucous shouts of the girl's clan. "She should be delighted to do her duty to the Crown! Seventeen years old—I was a man when I was seventeen! She should have been married three years ago, and if not, then she is now fair game for other uses. Send her to my quarters at once."

Bituitus shrugged, and nodded at the girl, who looked at him with a sly expression. With resounding cheers, the entire party of celebrants pushed into the ranks of the Pontic officers' horses and marched all the way to the governor's palace where we were lodging. There it was only with great difficulty that Bituitus was able to send the joyful crowd home in order to initiate talks and explanations with the father and daughter alone.

She drove a bargain that the Romans would have envied. In fact, her father, seeing the King's interest in acquiring his daughter's favors, did not even deign to talk up her beauty or her talents at spinning and weaving. "Praising her charms," he said unctuously, "would be like spreading honey on honeycomb."

Instead, the girl's father made all sorts of outlandish demands, to which Bituitus could only listen in astonishment and then seek to obtain the most reasonable terms possible for the vixen. After the scene in the street, Father could hardly allow himself to lose face among the citizens by sending her home without striking a bargain—that would make it seem as if she had asked a price the King could not afford, that her value was beyond the resources of even her conqueror, something Father's pride would not allow. It was an awkward situation, from which he tried to distance himself by withdrawing to his private quarters alone and allowing Bituitus to settle it.

In the end Monime did not attain the marriage and queenship she had demanded in the middle of the crowded street. But after a long night, consummated not by love but by a bewildering series of financial negotiations, she was the sudden and fortunate owner of fifteen thousand gold pieces and had been granted the right to wear the jeweled diadem and receive the public honors of a full consort. Furthermore, her hawk-eyed father, who claimed to be a cobbler but after close examination was found to be a clever-spoken Italian merchant who had somehow evaded the recent destruction of his countrymen, was not only spared his life; he was also promoted to the position of governor of the province of Ephesus. Nor did the sly bastard even properly express his gratitude. Rather, he acted as if the vast honor he had just received and the caskets of gold that came with it were simply his just reward for yielding up his daughter.

Monime, at least, had achieved her goal and was now entitled to recline at Father's side at all state functions, Queen of Asia in every respect except lawful marriage. Father, too, had achieved a goal of sorts, though at a price far beyond what he should have paid, had his pride and vanity not clouded his judgment.

For had he known what a thorn in his side this woman would be, he would have used the funds he paid her father to ship her to Rome, where she could annoy his enemies instead.

That fall, Father's realm continued to expand with almost no effort on his part, like an interest-bearing investment held by a Roman banker. On a routine Aegean cruise with the Pontic fleet, Admiral Archelaus found the Island Greeks as eager to throw off their Roman masters as had been their Asian brethren. Awakened early one morning on his ship of state, the admiral found his cabin besieged by a half-dozen ambassadors from various cities and islands, begging his acceptance of their allegiance to the new King of the Greeks, Mithridates. Before the week was through, Archelaus discovered he was master of every island east of the Greek mainland. Without loosing a single arrow or sinking a single enemy warship, he was now in complete control of all the shipping lanes from Crete to Thrace.

The only holdout was the tiny island of Delos, birthplace of

Apollo and Artemis, site of the great Roman slave market, and host to perhaps the most holy shrine in the Greek world, the temple to Delian Apollo, which was under Roman control. Here the Italian slave merchants who governed the island stubbornly resisted Archelaus' demands to surrender. In a fury, Archelaus loosed his fleet of pirates on the unwalled city, which was defended only by the sanctity of its temples. Within a day he had overwhelmed the inhabitants and freed thousands of slaves, including a troupe of African dwarves, whose ancestors had been brought from their homeland as captives centuries before and who had been forced to inbreed ever since, to provide a plentiful supply of dancers for an annual festival celebrating the defeat of the Pygmies by the cranes. The pirates burned the town and vast warehouse facilities fringing the south side of the port, up to the very edges of the temple precinct itself. Much to Father's chagrin when he found out, many priceless statues and works of art also perished, crushed in the pirates' artillery barrages or thrown drunkenly into the sea by the ignorant plunderers.

Still, the treasure of Delian Apollo was enormous: five centuries of tribute from every city in the Greek world, vast rooms filled floor to ceiling with bars of silver and bags of gold, precious artworks, rare marbles and statuary, a library filled with scrolls containing property deeds and loan titles, cases of precious jewels, golden goblets, fine silks from mysterious lands to the east—the island's treasure was the greatest trove in the world. But as Archelaus stood between the huge bronze doors to the treasury in the center of the temple precinct, viewing the smoking ruins of the razed city below and observing his sailors setting up camp on the very steps of the holy buildings before him, he scratched his head at his quandary. What does one do with such a stupendous quantity of captured wealth—wealth that belongs not to a defeated enemy but to a god, donated by countless city-states and kingdoms, some of which are no longer even in existence? Abandon the site to capture more territory, leaving those incalculable riches to be guarded by a garrison of . . . *pirates*? The idea was laughable. Return it to its original donors? A logistical nightmare. Empty the treasury and haul the entire lot back to Ephesus for the King? The risk of incurring the wrath of Apollo and the donor states was unthinkable.

The solution came from Father himself, in a routine dispatch that arrived a week later, congratulating Archelaus on his feat and thanking him for the consignment of Pygmies, who were delightfully rude to all, including the King. Upon hearing of the sack of Delos, Father had immediately recognized the difficulty of ensuring the safety of the shrine treasure. Unlike his admiral, however, he had not wasted even a moment agonizing. The solution he hit upon instead was to send the entire treasury to . . . Athens.

Archelaus must have been taken aback by this order—his brother, Neoptolemus, who had remained back at Pergamum, was appalled and protested as soon as Father informed him of the message he was to take to Archelaus.

"Sire!" he exclaimed. "Athens has been disarmed for over a century—no troops are levied from among its citizens; no Athenian has served in a phalanx or rowed a *trireme* for generations. How can Athens protect such a treasure?"

He was correct, of course. For well over a hundred years Athens had avoided conflict, an ancient city declining peacefully into genteel irrelevance in a Roman world. Still, its prestige remained immense, so much so that no Roman had ever even presumed to govern the city and no occupying Roman army had ever set foot within its walls, though it remained under Roman "protection" through the propraetor in Macedonia. Father looked at Neoptolemus slyly and nodded.

"Not all protection is by force of arms. Even without army or navy, Athens is the most valuable ally we could acquire. Why else would Rome treat it so delicately? The city's prestige is enormous—"

Neoptolemus interrupted impatiently. "But it is undefended! A single Roman legion could breach its gates at any time! And all that treasure—"

"Not completely undefended. The Acropolis and Piraeus are the strongest land and sea fortresses on the continent. They may be in ruins, but you can be sure that when Archelaus arrives with a treasure fleet, walls will be repaired."

Indeed, with the sack of Delos and Father's gift of the entire treasure to Athens, the world's balance of power shifted completely. The cheering of the Athenian people at the King's gesture of goodwill could be heard to the tip of the Italian peninsula. Father sent a vast fleet and army, both under Archelaus' command, to garrison Piraeus, to the enthusiastic acclaim of the Athenian people.

Pontic conquests continued to snowball, even beyond the hopes and expectations of the King himself. With Athens' declaration of loyalty, it was only days before ancient Sparta followed suit, and then powerful Thebes as well, both of which actually had significant armies to contribute to the Pontic alliance. All of Greece now proclaimed Mithridates savior and king.

And then all of Greece declared war on Rome.

Two victories during the course of a summer, over a Bithynian vassal king and a Roman governor, had been sufficient to make Father supreme ruler over a territory that rivaled that of Rome itself. He was the most feared man on earth—feared by all, that is, except the fierce Pygmy dancers and his consort Monime.

And the tiny island of Rhodes.

4

"Almighty Zeus," Father muttered as he stood on the bow of his flagship trireme, a fast war cruiser powered by three banks of oarsmen. He was leading a squadron of twenty-five such vessels—sturdy Chiot and Cretan ships—that made their way slowly out of Mandraki harbor below the fortress of Rhodes. We passed through the narrow channel the Colossus once straddled, the bronze remains of which could still be seen lying shimmering and desolate on the white sandy bottom. The ships then emerged into the strait separating Rhodes from the mainland, where the rest of the armada was awaiting the results of his war parley.

"I paid for half that city, the ingrates!"

Though blockaded by the largest navy in the Mediterranean, led by the newly acclaimed King of the Greeks, the little city of Rhodes refused even to reconsider its long-standing alliance with Rome. It was the sole holdout among all the Greek islands, but because of its strategic harbor just off the Asiatic coast, guarded by an impregnable fortress high on the rock, it was a thorn in the side of any mainland ruler desiring unfettered control of the trade routes to Asia.

Even more: the Roman proconsul, Cassius, had taken refuge there with his Rhodian allies, as had other survivors of the Night of the Vespers, and Cassius himself was leading the Rhodian resistance. Even from this distance, beyond the harbor mouth, we could see hundreds of laborers busily strengthening the city's walls and preparing the famous Rhodian warships and cruisers in their protected dry docks, deep in caves cut directly into the stone cliffs at the water's edge below the city. In truth, the Rhodians were not complete ingrates: since they were still making use of the magnificent public buildings constructed several years before from a donation by the King, they had at least had the tact to retain the enormous statue of him they had erected in the agora in his honor. Even from as far as the strait I could see this new "Colossus," its gold plate shining so brightly in the searing sunlight it hurt my eyes. Rhodes would be a tough nut to crack, I reflected; even at my own young age I could see its defenses were daunting. And the first thing to be toppled by our *ballistae* would be the statue of Mithridates.

"Neoptolemus!" Father shouted, and his old friend stepped quickly to his side from where he had been signaling orders to the captains of the other vessels. Though Father was a brilliant commander in his own right, he had little experience with sea warfare and had left all tactical command of the armada to Neoptolemus.

"We have some game to hunt. Look!"

Peering through the glittering spray of the prow and the blinding sparkles of the sunlit waves, Neoptolemus could see movement from one of the sea cliffs near the harbor entrance. Six Rhodian cruisers had emerged from a cave and were now rowing mightily, seeking to slip out through the Pontic blockade of the channel, most likely to obtain supplies in Crete. Our own twenty-five triremes were the nearest of the Pontic fleet to the harbor entrance, but the Rhodians clearly thought they could outrun us.

Neoptolemus grinned. "Like fish in a tub."

Shouting rapid orders to the ship's captain, he ordered Machares and me to take places at the stern, to be clear of the marines assembling on the deck amidships. I scrambled over the coils of rope, weapons, and spare oars as nimbly as a monkey, but Machares lagged. Though almost a grown man now, he had not proven himself a competent sailor on this voyage.

"I feel sick," he moaned as he caught up with me at the stern. I peered at him closely. His face was the color of Calamodrys the boxer's after the eating bout, and he was swaying dangerously. "I don't think I can stand here," he said, and then with a lurch and a hiccup he vomited over my feet.

"Sit here," I told him, spreading a canvas tarp over a thick coil of rope at the base of the mast. He sank into it gratefully and closed his eyes, trying to shut out the rocking of the ship. "I'll be right up here above you."

Clambering halfway up the mast, I seized a rope and swung onto the lookout platform, which the sailors also used for peering into the water for tuna and swordfish they could harpoon to freshen their diet. There I perched in comfort without obstruction from the furled sails, watching the action over the heads of the marines crowding the deck below.

The throbbing beat of mallets on wood blocks increased as the *keleustai,* the vessels' timekeepers, picked up their tempo and the sailors strained at their oars. The ship lurched forward as its speed increased. Unlike the Romans and their Rhodian allies, every ship in the Pontic fleet was rowed by fighting men, pirates and sailors all, who upon making contact with the enemy could wield weapons as handily as oars and do double duty. No wasted manpower here. More important, every last oar-humper among them was guaranteed a share of the plunder. Amazing how quickly that makes a man row.

Our ships shot through the frothing waves, rapidly closing in, with the wind fast astern. The six enemy vessels, though built in the characteristically streamlined Rhodian style, struggled to attain cruising speed—hampered perhaps by the cliffs at their side that denied them the advantage of the wind or by an unseen surface current crabbing the oars. Their stroke looked ragged and panicky, their timing inept, and their vessels were beginning to drift out of voice contact with one another. We were approaching the narrowest point of the channel at an angle, cutting off their escape, after which we could slow our pace and pick them off piecemeal as they tried to flee back to their cliffs or to the safety of Mandraki. We closed in, only a half-mile now from the narrows, then a quarter-mile. Every man could see the Rhodians had lost the race.

Father's smile broadened into a grin as he faced into the west, his long chestnut hair streaming behind him, chest rising and falling under the bronze corselet he had donned in anticipation of the coming battle. Though his flagship would be the last to enter into combat, he was prepared, and I saw his fingers eagerly grip the thick Persian bow he wore always at his side. Never was there a man like Father, I thought.

Only Neoptolemus seemed troubled. "Hold!" he shouted to the ship's captain, and initiated a series of rapid hand signals to the steersmen of the other ships in the Pontic squadron. The order was inexplicable. We would lose the enemy if we slowed now, now of all times!

"No!" Father roared, pushing through the bewildered sailors on the deck. "Cut them off! Neoptolemus, what in Hades' name are you doing? Push forward and cut them off!"

Neoptolemus remained silent, staring so hard at the captain of the nearest Rhodian cruiser that he leaned forward over the rail. I saw what he was looking at—despite the slowness of the enemy vessels, the Rhodian captain remained calm and unperturbed.

Neoptolemus suddenly glanced up at Father.

"Sire—there is something wrong about this. The enemy captain is Admiral Damagoras, commander of the entire Rhodian fleet. Why would he be leading a tiny squadron of six cruisers . . . ?"

"Because he's been demoted for incompetence," Father bellowed, "which is what I will do to you if you do not cut those bastards off! Now forward!"

Neoptolemus set his mouth in a grim line and continued to stare silently at the enemy captain. The Rhodian stood perfectly still beside the *kybernetes,* the craft's helmsman, shouting no orders and facing not the narrows, his squad's ostensible goal, but rather athwart his starboard side—directly at our own flying triremes. The two squadrons were now so close I could see his cold expression for myself, jaw jutting sternly forward as he gripped a stanchion for support, eyes seeming to bore directly into the hull of our vessel.

There was no way the Rhodians could make it into the narrows in time. They were aimed wrong, straight toward a spit of rocky outcrop protruding from the island, and would founder on it within moments. Their only recourse would be to stop, back-paddle to reorient their vessels, and then row back against the wind. Their forward progress was blocked, and when I glanced aft I saw half our squadron had already cagily spun off to starboard in anticipation of the Rhodians' turnabout, blocking their escape in that direction. They would be caught between pincers and captured or destroyed—depending upon whether or not they put up a fight.

The men on deck cheered, a lusty roar that carried easily over the water to the city we had just left and to the rest of our armada in the channel outside the harbor walls. Six ships' prows as trophies we would be bringing back to our comrades—not a bad haul for a simple diplomatic mission, and fair recompense for the insulting response to Father's demand for surrender. The city would pay for its stubbornness, and these blockade-runners would be the first to feel the King's wrath.

Still Neoptolemus was unhappy, and as the Rhodians slowed further, preparing to reverse direction, I could not understand why. He had surrounded the enemy, cornered them against the cliffs, cut off their escape—what choice did they have but to surrender? What choice but . . . ?

Without warning, without even a shout or signal from the Rhodian commander, all six enemy vessels suddenly fell into perfect alignment and wheeled left as one, like a flock of gulls hitting an air current, the port-side oars back-paddling in precise counterpoint to the now frantic tempo of their drum, the starboard oars doing the same in forward motion. Without breaking the hypnotic rhythm, the ships turned as if on an underwater wheel, not back to the cliffs but . . . directly toward us.

Our men's cheers died in their throats and the ship fell silent. This was suicide! Archers began fitting arrows and infantry unsheathed their swords, but we had no one to fight—there was not a man on the enemy's decks but for the admiral and each ship's helmsman standing behind protective ramparts at the sterns. No soldiers were on board the Rhodian cruisers, only sailors manning the oars, under the decks.

The Rhodian ships leaped toward us as if propelled from a catapult, the waters parting from their sleek, polished prows like flesh before a knife. Their belabored rowing of a few moments before had been a sham. These were seamen—born and bred to the oar, rowers and ship handlers like none in the world—and the deadly bronze-sheathed rams mounted on their prows were bearing down on us with furious speed. Our deck erupted in chaos.

"Disperse the squadron!" Neoptolemus yelled. "Don't give them a target!"

Back-paddling furiously, our cumbersome vessels struggled to wheel and change course, but it was fruitless—this was a maneuver for which we had not trained. Twelve of our triremes were still in a tight, compact formation and wheeling only made it worse—the long rows of oars in the sides clashed and became tangled with each other.

With a sharp crack, two of the Rhodian vessels plowed directly amidships into two of the much larger Pontic vessels, crushing and tearing through hull timber and penetrating deep into the decks. Furious shouts were heard as Pontic marines were thrown into the water at the impact or crushed between the bronze prows and the masts, which snapped and toppled into the sea. Both our ships were destroyed instantly, the hull spines crushed, and as they sank hundreds of men, many of whom could not swim, in full armor, leaped into the water where they splashed frantically, crying for help or searching for a timber on which to float.

The Rhodians sent no men onto their decks to engage the Pontic marines or even to pick off the survivors in the water with arrows. That was a luxury their undermanned craft could not afford. Rather, both attacking ships calmly back-paddled away from the carnage and wheeled about to regain formation with their four colleagues, which had sped through the midst of the frantically wheeling Pontic ranks without collision and had turned for a second pass.

Father was furious, and Neoptolemus bellowed again to scatter the squadron, while simultaneously maneuvering to pluck the survivors from the current before they drowned. It was an impossible task. Again the Rhodian vessels launched themselves like massive arrows directly into our midst, again the terrible crunch followed by the screams of men thrown to their deaths. Our ships wheeled and staggered at the fury of the bronze-prowed Rhodians, and if the enemy ships themselves were not sufficient menace, our own confused captains and rowers became one as well, as oars clashed and rudders snapped from collisions between our own vessels.

It was chaos, a mass of churning water, dotted with broken timbers and men splashing and sinking, screaming to be rescued. Half the marines on deck were taken out of fighting formation and ordered to fish out the drowning men, throwing ropes and floats overboard or even dangling from the sides of the decks themselves. Some were held at the ankles by the strong grips of their comrades as they reached into the water with spear shafts, oars, and broken yardarms to reach the floundering soldiers. The captain and Neoptolemus shouted contradictory orders to the helmsman, attempting to head the vessel toward the largest groups of swimmers, and neither could keep more than half an eye on the assaults of the enemy vessels—until it was too late.

At Father's enraged bellow, the steersman finally tore his gaze from the rescue scene below him and toward the onrushing Rhodian cruiser—as always, strangely silent and empty, like a ghost ship. It was not aimed at us but at one of the huge, lumbering Chiot vessels wallowing like a whale directly in front of us, its men doing the same as ours—desperately pulling drowning comrades from the water. At the King's roar, all eyes looked up and saw the deadly cruiser bearing down on the Chiot craft at full speed. For a moment, every man froze—and then all leaped into sudden, chaotic action. A dozen Chiots who could swim simply dove overboard, preferring to face fate in the water rather than risk death by being crushed under the bronzed prow of the cruiser or pinned beneath a toppled mast. Others rushed to the side of the vessel opposite the impending collision, forcing the ship to lean dangerously to that side, and sought railings and stanchions on which to secure their grip.

The Chiot captain was the bravest of the lot. With no sign of fear on his bearded face he himself seized the rudder alongside his helmsman, all the while bellowing orders to the rowers belowdecks. With a graceful roll, the huge ship heeled in a perfect arc to starboard just as the Rhodian cruiser shot by, so close it cleanly sheared off all the Chiot oars from the port side but otherwise caused no harm. All hands on the Chiot vessel cheered the successful maneuver, but their joy was short-lived, for the huge ship's off-center momentum carried it straight into our own path, slamming into our bow at an angle with a sickening crunch.

I hardly had time to see what had happened, for my next sensation was of gasping and choking, as water poured down my throat and into my lungs. Looking up, I could see the strangely serene surface, the sun shining dim and green through the water, the legs of swimming men above me looking oddly small and insectlike. The impact had thrown me off my perch on the yardarm, and wearing the oversized armor Father had fitted on me at the last moment, I sank like a stone. I felt no panic, not even fear—just a terrible surprise and shock at the cold, and the burning pain of the salt water in my lungs as I choked and struggled to cough. The light was getting dimmer and the legs above me tinier. . . .

Suddenly I felt an immense pressure on my chest and a surge of water past my face, as if I had hit bottom and was bouncing back up through to the surface, like a dwarf tossed in a blanket. I struggled to remain conscious as the surface approached like an onrushing mirror and the swimmers' legs grew larger and clearer. I broke through with a momentum that carried me waist-high into the air, and it was then, through my gasping and sputtering, that I realized how close I had come to death, that the pressure around my chest was Father's enormous arm, wrapped around me as tightly as a rope harness. He swam toward our nearby vessel with his remaining arm as nimbly as a dog clutching a bird in his mouth, and looking up I saw a dozen sailors dangling from the side of the ship by their ankles, reaching to lift me up. With their strong hands under my armpits, they pulled me onto the deck, where I lay crumpled and retching, blood-streaked water foaming from my burning throat.

Shouting men leaped over and around me, still struggling to disengage the Chiot vessel's mast from our yardarms. Machares pumped and pounded my chest, shouting my name repeatedly—"Pharnaces! Pharnaces!"—all traces of his nausea seemingly forgotten. Father clambered up over the rail, streaming water from his armor, and shot me a worried glance. Quickly confirming that I was in good hands, he turned back amidships to inspect the condition of the vessel. Neoptolemus, meanwhile, kept a wary eye out for the Rhodians' next pass.

It didn't come. All six Rhodian vessels slipped away and disappeared into the maze of coastal caves. We saw none of their sailors or soldiers, nor even any sign of life from the strange craft, save the occasional flash of a brown arm through the oar ports in the hull, or the wary glance of the helmsmen over the sides of the rudder barricades where they crouched when steering. Our loss was two complete ships and over fifty men drowned, their bodies never recovered. Another half-dozen vessels were so badly mauled as to require repairs on the mainland. The squadron limped sorrowfully east through the channel to rejoin the armada waiting outside the harbor entrance. They were in complete ignorance of the results, though Father's unremitting bellowing at the incompetence of the Chiots soon remedied that. It was an entire day before I could walk and weeks before I could breathe normally again without pain. Father's arm around my chest had broken several ribs. An inauspicious start to my military career.

If only Father had read the signs when the storm blew up several days later. Papias had warned him, after examining the calf's organs at the sacrifice, that the liver was cancerous, the omens foul. Nevertheless, he persisted in ordering the infantry transported across the narrow channel from the mainland to the north side of the island, a half-day's march west of the fortress city. It was an easy passage that should have taken the armada a single morning to accomplish under ordinary conditions. The error, however, was in trying to save time by conveying the entire army at once, rather than moving the troops in shifts. As a result, five hundred vessels were on the water simultaneously when the storm hit. The fierce winds scattered the vessels up and down the entire forty-mile length of the island's coastline—at least those of the vessels that survived.

The warships and triremes rode out the waves easily enough, with their greater maneuverability and draft and the stronger sailing skills of the pirates manning them. But for the flat-bottomed transport scows it was a different story entirely. Ten were lost forever beneath the waves, with over a thousand of the men they had been conveying; many others were rammed and sunk by Rhodian cruisers, who shot out from their rock caves like vultures on a wounded boar, even in the midst of the storm. Others were dashed up on the rocky, unprotected shoreline, where they and their crews were subjected to the attacks of local shepherds and hastily organized militia watching for just such an occurrence. Roman and Rhodian observers on the mountain ridge along the channel watched the entire fiasco and provided a constant flow of information to their rulers on the progress of the "surprise" attack on the city.

The skirmish outside Mandraki, and then the storm damage to the armada, had only confirmed the obvious: A victory over Rhodes would be next to impossible. The sea was not where Father's true strengths lay. He longed to be astride a rearing war charger; the weapons slapping at his back and the dagger swinging against his hip were constant reminders that they had not been used for weeks during his campaign with the fleet. His great size and agility were a hindrance in the small confines of ships, and the marines staffing his fleet, many of whom were horsemen and land warriors like himself, felt equally frustrated and out of place.

Father's strengths lay in the ancient clans of fierce Pontic warriors, the hordes of heavily armored fighters he could command to pour out of the mountains and ravines at a moment's notice. His advantages were the nimble mountain ponies on which his troops could storm across the high passes, and the pure, brute strength and fierceness of his Scythian mercenaries. In short, his advantage lay not with the fleet but with the army. At sea, the gods were not with us.

And when the Fates frown on your efforts and cast the evil eye in your direction, it is best to look elsewhere and wait for them to turn away.

5

Father returned furious to his court at Pergamum, leaving his admirals to maintain the siege that winter, which deteriorated to a desultory blockade. Although the Greek islands continued to declare allegiance to him and pay tribute, this was now at a much diminished rate. His failure at Rhodes was evidence to the skeptics that this new "King of the Greeks" was actually not invincible, as many had at first thought.

With campaigning suspended until spring, we found Monime in rare form, having turned the palace upside down while we were away. The treasury groaned with the strain of her absurd purchases, from garish and vulgar artworks to the latest Greek fashions in furniture and draperies, and our schedules were filled weeks in advance with banquets, receptions, embarrassments, and frivolities. Her effete friends were everywhere, seeming to pop out at us from every corner, decorating, advising, seeking favors, and otherwise boring Father nearly out of his mind. His comrades were made to feel awkward and unwelcome; indeed, Monime constantly humiliated poor Bituitus for his slowness of speech and bull-in-the-pottery-shop ways, though the Gaul was unfailingly polite to her. Even I, young as I was and raised my entire life in army encampments rather than in the rarefied atmosphere of the court, was often appalled at the crudeness of her manners and her lack of subtlety.

Did Father love her? I once contemplated this question but came to a quick conclusion. Of course he did not. Yet what in

the name of the twelve gods did he see in her, besides her kit-
tenish beauty, which could be had much more cheaply from a
street trollop? Why would he gamely endure her, defying his
closest friends, even neglecting his very kingdom, rather than
simply dismissing her? Because of a blind spot in his judgment,
a damnable stubbornness, a refusal to admit he had been played
the fool by Monime and her relatives. They had forced him in
the very streets of Stratonicea to publicly declare his desire for
her and to pay an absurdly high price for her favors. In Father's
mind, the only thing more foolish than continuing to put up
with her follies would be to actually dismiss her, thereby publicly admitting his error in judgment, calling into question his
administrative competence. And so he gritted his teeth, shut his
mouth, and put up with her.

Monime and the citizens of Pergamum tactfully overlooked
the Rhodian debacle, and to welcome the King back the city fathers organized a magnificent theatrical tribute. Monime, of
course, was the main instigator behind the event—I had over-
heard her planning it with the eunuchs for weeks. It would be
the ideal occasion to bolster her position in the minds of the
city's nobility, who had slighted her for her low birth ever since
her arrival three years before. The day she announced to him
that a great series of plays was to be held in the amphitheater in
his honor, Father inwardly groaned, since he enjoyed these
pompous displays even less than I did. Still, clever Monime had
made her announcement in full court, surrounded by a dozen of
her ladies, all cooing at the deep love she had shown for the
King by organizing such an event. There was little Father could
do but glare at her and assent.

The court flew into a frenzy of excitement, which grew pal-
pably with the approach of the great event. Not only was it the
first major production of the theatrical season, but it promised
to be the greatest spectacle of recent history. An entirely new
dramatic cycle had been composed for the occasion, with actors
imported from as far away as Athens and Antioch. An enormous choir had been engaged and practicing behind closed
doors for weeks, and the greatest singers of the world were
preparing to dazzle the King with their range and sonority.
Dozens of renowned set designers, painters, artists, carpenters,

and seamstresses had been shipped in from all the islands and from as far distant as Carthage and Crete to contribute their skills to the great enterprise.

The evening of the great show, Father sat enthroned in the upper-tier royal boxes of the opulent amphitheater of Pergamum, with Monime beside him at his right, radiant as a goddess in her silks and finery. Even I had grudgingly agreed to attend, despite the teasing of Machares, who knew how I normally shunned such functions and who himself had pleaded a headache. However, when I had appeared in Father's apartments just before our departure wearing only normal officer's attire, Monime had exclaimed in horror.

"My lord! Your son's clothes—I won't have him attending the theater like that. He'll look like a radish among jewels."

Father looked me critically up and down. "He's wearing his military ceremonial outfit. He looks as fine as any of my officers."

Monime flushed. "He's *not* one of your officers; he's a boy of twelve and the son of the King! You might as well bring that lout Bituitus along, for all the honor this boy will bring to you tonight, dressed as a . . . *soldier boy*!" She sniffed disdainfully.

Father stared at her a moment as I burned with humiliation that this girl, scarcely older than me, could speak in such a way in my presence, as if I were a pet dog. Yet Father, as he always did of late, thought better than to cross her whims. Looking at me, he shrugged and washed his hands of the affair. "Do as she wishes, boy," he said, and left the room.

At Monime's insistence, I was perfumed and dressed in a smaller version of Father's silken trousers and head-wrap for the occasion. In the theater, I sat sulkily beside him on his left as he draped one meaty hand over my shoulder, with the other resting stiffly on Monime's neck. Four thousand of the city's leading citizens and their wives were present, and the hall was abuzz with excitement at the magnificent spectacle to be played before them. Heads swiveled this way and that as the audience openly gawked at their neighbors, and no heads turned more than to us, the magnificent trio in the royal box. Monime maintained her icy, haughty demeanor, staring vacantly and somewhat impatiently at the closed curtains of the stage, while

Father affixed his customary broad grin, occasionally lifting one hand or the other to gesture to acquaintances in the crowd.

The spectacle was magnificent, surpassing all expectations. In fact, the splendid show is still talked about to this day, in hushed tones by old people, though not for the reasons Monime would have preferred. The huge choir, filling the stage from end to end, roared out Father's praises in unearthly harmonies so innovative and daring, so modern and moving, that it brought tears to the eyes of all. Great actors whose names everyone had heard for years but whom few had ever seen perform emerged from the *paradoi*, the stage wings, dressed as gods, declaiming in measured and majestic iambic trimeter the favors heaven would bestow upon the Liberator of the Hellenes. Others, dressed as allegorical figures or famous men of past ages, praised his virtues and declared their thanks for the benefits granted them by the great and generous king. Father sat back and actually seemed to enjoy the spectacle, while Monime positively glowed. The misery of the weeks on Rhodes and the humiliation suffered at the hands of the besieged Romans was finally beginning to fade.

The climax of the event was the magnificent descent of Nike, Goddess of Victory, from the night sky to crown the King with the royal diadem. At the very peak of the choir's majestic hymn of praise to their Savior, the actors onstage looked up, pointed, and then fell to their knees in awe at the magnificent sight. Slowly descending from above us was the golden goddess herself, in the form of a lovely young actress, nude but for her winged sandals. Her skin was painted entirely in gold dust from head to toe, a stunning image of a deity and a not-so-subtle tribute to the famous legend of his golden horse. Long golden tresses wound their way from her head over her breasts, like ivy creeping over a statue. Enormous gilded wings cunningly fastened to her shoulder blades with thin golden straps gently fanned the air. The girl was suspended by thin filaments, nearly invisible in the shadows, attached to a black-painted crane that had been silently rotated on its winches into position directly over our heads during the booming of the choir and that could scarcely be seen against the dark night sky. The polished mirrors of the spot lanterns were trained on the girl's glistening body, focusing on the splendid jeweled diadem she bore in her hands. As she was slowly lowered into position just over our box, her outstretched arms displaying the glorious crown destined for the King's head, the effect could not have been more magical. Father gawked in delight at the utter vulgarity of the spectacle. It was one that only Monime could have pulled off.

I was stunned. Never had I seen a nude woman so close before, hovering a mere arm's length before my very eyes, not to mention one whose body had been plucked completely hairless and then gilded. She drifted slowly past my face, in a kind of gentle choreographed flight to allow the audience to gaze upon her golden beauty for a few moments before the crowning of Victory's Beloved, the King. As she floated gracefully through the air before us, flecks of gold dust fell from her body in a gentle sprinkle, glittering in the lantern light like tiny showers of meteors and landing in our laps and hair.

It was both the most lurid and the most magnificent spectacle I had ever seen. I longed to reach out my hand as the winged goddess passed slowly by, to grasp a full golden breast as Paris had grasped the golden apple before gifting it to Aphrodite, to declare to all the world who was "the fairest," for indeed I had never seen as lovely and astonishing a sight in my life.

Monime, however, was livid. She impatiently brushed the specks of gold dust off her face and visibly tensed, her eyes narrowing at the hovering girl who seemed to bask rather unnecessarily long in the King's gaze, extending the moment when she was to deposit the crown on his head and then swiftly disappear from sight. As Monime leaned back on her cushion I could hear her loud whisper to the eunuch behind her.

"Nike is a *goddess,*" she seethed, "not a naked wood nymph! This is *not* what we rehearsed. Where are her robes, for the love of Zeus? Where did you come up with this . . . this lowborn *hireling*?"

I almost wet my trousers with mirth at Monime's mocking of the girl's parentage, though the eunuch was much dismayed at his mistress's anger.

"My lady, we meant to dress her as a goddess—but the gold dust would not adhere to the silk! Only to her skin! This was the best we could do—"

His words were interrupted by cheering from the crowd as the crane above guided Nike on a broad, swinging arc over the main floor, affording a closer view to the eager watchers below. The goddess gracefully acknowledged their applause with a delicate shimmy of her torso and a fan of her wings, sending a small cloud of glittering dust floating down upon the ecstatic crowd. Monime rolled her eyes and crossed her arms in disgust while Father watched transfixed, a delighted grin creasing his face.

The goddess completed her last teasing path around the balcony and the crane carefully returned her for the final hover over our box. She was just leaning forward to place the crown upon Father's head when I heard a faint *twang* and saw her right leg unaccountably jerk and then drop to an ungainly dangle from the horizontal position in which it had been suspended behind her. One of the thin guy lines had broken. An expression of horror passed across the girl's face and she froze. Then another *twang* and another jerk, and her left shoulder dropped. Yelping, she forgot all goddesslike decorum and spun in the air face up, seizing the remaining guy lines with one hand to secure herself, as the ungainly wings dropped down on us and slapped Monime full in the face, raising a thick cloud of dust that set her to coughing. The crowd froze and the choir fell silent. Another *twang*, this time heard by the entire theater, and with a scream the girl juggled the crown, dropped it, and then fell in a tangle of arms, hair, and broken wings directly across Father's and Monime's legs. A distant tinkle of shattered glass and precious stones could be heard from the marble floor far below.

Appalled, the King seized Nike under her golden armpit with one hand and effortlessly lifted her, as he would a spider that had suddenly fallen onto him. Then standing and pivoting, he dropped her unceremoniously and rather painfully onto my own surprised lap. He sprang to the edge of the balcony to watch where the crown had fallen onto the stone steps far below, the delicate gold filigree and crystal bursting upon impact and the jewels rolling under the feet of the stupefied guests nearby. One woman broke the silence with a loud wail and fell to the floor to gather the pieces in the outstretched fabric of her garment. The crowd came back to life in an outraged roar, and the girl, now terrified, clambered over me and fled the box in tears, leaving her crushed and wilted wings behind. Father,

Monime, and I, faces and clothes streaked with flaking gold dust, walked out past the guards to our waiting litters. Our cheeks were all aflame, though all for different reasons.

The next day Father began work early. He sent couriers from one end of his empire to the other, to inquire as to whether anything of importance had happened at that precise moment, whether any of his armies in Europe or Asia had suffered a defeat, whether any of his generals had been assassinated. The runners all trickled in over the next several weeks, informing him that nothing of importance had happened that day; he therefore ascribed the fall of Victory's crown simply to unfortunate coincidence and dismissed the matter. Monime was mortified, remaining cloistered in her apartments for days after the humiliating event. It would be only a matter of time, I estimated, before she would be discreetly sent into concubine exile, spending the rest of her life living in luxurious boredom in the remote mountain castle to which Father was accustomed to sending surplus females from the court—the sisters he had declined to marry, unwanted members of his harem—"for their protection," he always claimed.

And then the last courier straggled back to Pergamum, the last of those who had been sent out the day after the goddess's fall in the theater. The man had traveled in disguise as far as Rome itself, and upon his arrival back in Asia, his first action was to loudly and ostentatiously thank the gods for his safe return to King Mithridates' glorious realm. Father snorted impatiently at this protocol and puffery.

"Get to the point, courier. What did you learn?"

The man smiled and looked around him pompously at the courtiers hanging on his every word. "My lord," he continued, "as I was saying, never have I been so thankful to return to the land of my birth as I am now. The contrast between your peaceful and prosperous realm, and the ignorance and poverty of the lands to the west is scarcely to be imagined. Indeed, all those regions under your domain are basking in the glorious beneficence of your reign, while those under Roman control continue to suffer from chaos and barbarism. . . ."

Father rolled his eyes in exasperation at the courier's rambling. "Smooth-tongued Apollo is cursing me—even Bituitus speaks more fluidly than this specimen. Get to the *point*, courier!"

"My lord," the man began again, feigning not to have heard the interruption but speaking faster nonetheless, as beads of perspiration broke out on his brow, "omens occurred that, by common opinion of the skilled Etruscan haruspices I consulted, bode ill for Rome, though of course this is for your own sooth-sayers to ascertain. Fire, it is said, erupted spontaneously from the staffs of the heralds of the legions in Gaul, which was extin-guished only with great difficulty. Ravens landed in the Forum with their young and proceeded to eat them in the very sight of the people. Rats caught in traps gave birth and then, like the ravens, ate their young. And on one clear, cloudless day, a sharp sound as of trumpets rang through the air above Rome, fright-ening people nearly out of their wits."

Father snorted. "You can't be serious. You travel all the way to Rome, and this is the information you bring me?"

The courier's face fell in dismay at Father's skepticism. "But sire, these are *omens,* direct messages from the gods! Surely these are what you meant for me to seek out. Naturally, there were human actions and signs as well. . . ."

"Ah, now we're getting somewhere. Human actions? What kind of actions?"

"Sire, naturally you are aware—all of Rome is in chaos! Like the families of rats and ravens, Rome is being devoured from within. The turmoil continues between the Populares and the Optimates. Families are divided, taking sides against each other, some fleeing the city, others driving them away, but all are terrified nonetheless. And these internal threats are nothing compared to the dangers Rome is facing from outside. With your recent victories, Rome's conquests of generations are now dropping from its branches like overripe figs and then turning against Rome itself like . . . er . . . like vicious bats that feed on those overripe figs . . ." The courier paused in confusion.

Father sighed at the uncontrolled metaphors and looked im-ploringly at the ceiling while the man regained his composure.

"Most of all, Your Majesty, Rome is in a panic over you—you and your conquests."

Father smiled. "Perfect. Go on, courier."

"The Senate—I myself witnessed the Senate, from the public gallery, on its first day of session to deliberate on Athens' declaration of war. My lord, Rome's greatest leaders, its finest orators, its most prominent citizens, are in utter confusion. The Senate is in complete disarray! Speaker after speaker rose to debate but could scarcely be heard over the jeering. . . ."

"By the people up in the gallery?"

"No, sire, by the other senators themselves! I've never seen the like, not even among the barbarian assembly of Cappadocia! Senator Marcus Albinus rose to speak and proposed placating you by removing the Roman garrisons from Asia. He said the garrisons were a financial burden in any event, too difficult and expensive to administer, and that if they left the territory to you, you would be too occupied to continue being a threat to the Republic."

"Brilliant! Remind me to send Albinus a gift. But wait—you said the Romans fear I am a threat to the Republic?"

"Sire, the Romans speak of you in the same breath as Hannibal himself!"

"And what was the reaction to the good Senator's proposal?"

"My lord, Albinus was almost lynched—by his fellow senators, no less. The wall behind him was covered with rotten fruit and eggs pitched at him by his opponents' hired ruffians. They called him a traitor for neglecting the unavenged souls of the Romans killed last year."

"What next—any other speeches?"

"Yes, sire. Another senator rose to propose funding the Armenians to march against you from the East, but this man was driven from the rostrum for his cowardice, this time by a mob of citizens who burst onto the Senate floor demanding immediate vengeance against you. They screamed for a Roman army to march against you, but the Populares, who control the Senate, have no trustworthy general willing to take on such a task. My lord, the Senate was forced to disband before completing its debates and has been unable to meet in full session ever since, for fear of being overrun by outraged citizens. The leaders are paralyzed by fear and indecision, and none can come to agreement. You, my lord, are the source of Rome's terror; *you* will be remembered by the poets as the very cause of its destruction. The Senate itself will go down in history as your first victim."

Father sat back in his chair, singularly impressed. "This is truly news," he reflected quietly. After a moment of thought, he sat up and gestured for the courier to step forward once again. "Your old wives' tales of rats and ravens I can do without," he continued. "It is facts and events that matter to me. You did well by smuggling yourself into the Senate gallery. Now think, courier; concentrate your feeble mind. What occurred on that one day of the fall of Victory in the theater? No more talk of general panics. What of that one day?"

The man looked at him in puzzlement. If something as astounding as the Senate's collapse was of no import to the King, why had he sent out couriers to investigate events?

"Other than those things, Your Majesty, nothing of importance happened. Except . . ."

"Except what, man?" Father exclaimed impatiently.

"Forgive me, my lord, but I thought it to be insignificant compared to everything else I have told you. In fact, on that day, a Roman general of the disgraced Optimates Party marched north out of Rome with the few legions loyal to him and several talents of borrowed funds. A troop deployment like any other, I assumed. I did not even bother inquiring into his destination."

Father's eyes narrowed. "And what was the Roman's name, courier? Did you inquire into that, at least?"

"Lucius Cornelius Sulla, my lord."

And if Father had been more insightful, he would have known that the high tide for the new King of the Greeks had now turned.

BOOK FOUR

RITES
OF
PASSAGE

In Asia, Roman blades are an object of horror, the Roman name held in loathing, Roman tributes, tithes, and taxes instruments of death.

—Cicero

1

Sulla had achieved his stature late in life, by Roman standards, beginning his career under modest circumstances but marking each of his rises to power with increasing success: as quaestor, he had masterminded the capture of Rome's nemesis, the African king Jugurtha; as propraetor, he had conquered the Armenians and humiliated the Parthians. A few years earlier, he had eclipsed the aging general Marius and attained the rank of consul by the blade of his sword. An aristocrat by birth and a member of the Optimates Party, he was a Roman patriot, but only to the extent of his personal interest. Now the uprising in Greece and the Asiatic territories had attracted his attention, though the Roman Senate had denied him permission to undertake a campaign, forcing him to raise and supply a large army solely out of his own pocket. The Roman troops, normally consummate professionals in both their fighting and their internal administration, would be forced to live not on an extended supply line from Rome but off the fat of the land and on hopes of plunder. Sulla's military situation was tenuous.

The five legions marched directly across Boeotia, on to Attica, and by the time the courier had arrived with his rumors of ravens, had begun besieging Athens and the fortress port of Piraeus, the latter of which was held by Archelaus' forces. Father, however, saw nothing more threatening in this than a stalemate over the winter. After all, the Romans had no navy, so their own forces could not be as easily supplied as the Pontic troops, holed up with their easy access to Father's armada and supply

ships. The barren lands around Athens would be quickly depleted of their crops, and Sulla would either slowly starve or lift
the siege. To hasten matters, Father sent two additional Pontic
armies marching down from the north through Thrace and
Macedonia. We would trap the Romans in a vast pincer movement, cutting them off by land and sea, then destroy them at
leisure.

If any man was equal to the dangers and horrors of siege
warfare, it was the wily Archelaus. For the entire winter he
tenaciously maintained his stronghold in Piraeus, shuttered behind the ancient walls built forty cubits high of closely cut
stone blocks, the work of Pericles in the time of the War between Athens and Sparta. In his weekly dispatches to the court
in Pergamum, which Father read to me aloud, Archelaus fairly
laughed at the Romans' clumsy siege tactics. When their attempt to starve him out proved futile, Sulla built massive artillery pieces, some of which could hurl up to twenty flaming
projectiles in a single throw—for which he even cut down the
ancient trees in the Sacred Grove of the Academy, lacking any
other suitable timber. In response, Archelaus coated his walls
and roofs with fireproof alum, causing the fiery missiles to
bounce harmlessly to the ground and sputter out.

Sulla then dismantled his artillery and built enormous siege
engines. After much effort and loss of Roman life, he finally
succeeded in using explosive mines beneath the foundations to
knock down the Periclean wall—but found, to his stupefaction,
that Archelaus had simply built another one, and another and
another, on the inside perimeters of the previous walls.

Sulla finally resorted to a heroic charge against the battlements, hoping to overwhelm his stubborn adversary by sheer
numbers; but Archelaus, in his fecundity of resources, had
called in the Pontic garrisons from the Aegean islands and Eu-
boea and had even armed and trained his fleet's oarsmen and
was able to drive off the attackers. The longer Archelaus held
on, the more desperate Sulla's position became.

In the meantime, cheerful in his expectations of ultimate
victory, Father settled back into court life in Pergamum. He was
still a young man and utterly confident that he had many more
years ahead of him with which to consummate his plans for a
new Greece. Archelaus was driving Sulla to distraction and de-

feat, and there were precious few other threats to his dominions. The weekly reports from the front seemed so distant as to
be almost unreal—a source of brief commentary between Father and his aides, but little more. Monime could not abide talk
of war in her presence, and though I myself eagerly pressed Father for details on the siege, she always stifled the conversation.
"Really, Pharnaces," Monime would say, with a feigned yawn
or a glare, "warfare is so brutal! Take your swords and go practice with the garrison troops out in the courtyard, if you must.
But I will not have you bringing your bloodthirstiness into the
palace."

At words like this I would look pleadingly at Father, for a
sign that the siege mattered, that he felt there was more to life
than empty court pleasures and Monime's whims; but he would
studiously avoid my gaze and bend over some administrative
document or other. At least he continued to keep his big bow at
his side, despite Monime's protests. Still, it had been months
since I had actually seen him use it, even in practice or the hunt.
I became sullen and uncommunicative to Monime and even to
Father, which he attributed to my age. I retreated into a perpet-
ual slow burn.

All through the next summer the siege continued unabated,
with Pontus' northern forces refraining from the attack, hoping
to simply outwait the Romans. The next autumn, Sulla devised
an outlandish tactic with a lieutenant of his, a wealthy playboy
named Lucius Licinius Lucullus, whose grandfather had been a
Roman consul, his father a felon, and his mother a whore. This
Lucullus slipped past the Pontic armada in a fast smugglers'
cruiser and out into the open sea, with the intent of recruiting a
navy for Sulla, perhaps among the merchant seamen of the
Levant or the seagoing traders of Egypt. His inexperienced
crew sailed directly into a storm and the Pontic pursuers gave
up the chase, laughing at the Romans' stupidity and desperation, as they themselves took safe shelter within the harbor
walls of Piraeus.

The following spring, Athens city, several miles away from
Archelaus' stronghold at Piraeus and defended by only a small
garrison of ill-trained locals and decrepit old men, finally fell to
starvation and a daring Roman assault on an unrepaired portion
of the walls. Sulla himself led the sacking of the city, ordering

his men to carry him, gout-ridden but fierce, in an open litter. Roman soldiers raced through the city's streets and monuments with swords drawn, slaughtering everyone in their path, women and children alike. Even greater than the numbers killed by Romans were those who slew themselves at their own hands, in desperation at finding any mercy from Sulla's troops and in sorrow at their city's ruin. So great was the slaughter of Athens that to this day no one knows how many were killed, how many innocent people fell in the frenzy, though there are places in that city where the blood may still be seen, soaked into the pores of the flagstones. The numbers slain in the agora were so great that the blood was said to be trickling along the gutters under the gates and into the city's suburbs.

Archelaus coldly reported the news of Athens' destruction and then set to work. With the city lost, there was no longer any military advantage to holding the seaport, and he prepared to withdraw and combine his forces with the auxiliary troops in the north. Within a week, he had evacuated all his men in Pontic warships, cleverly holding the Romans at bay with his quickly diminishing garrison until the entire army had departed, along with its war chest and supplies. The Roman victory was hollow.

With thudding oar drums and the golden-horse pennants of Pontus flying jauntily from the masts as if he had gained a great victory, Archelaus sailed the fleet away from Piraeus, around the tip of Attica, and up the Euripus Channel to Thermopylae. There he combined his forces with the northern Pontic army led by the mercenary general Taxiles, which had marched south from Macedonia and was staffed by barbarian auxiliary troops. Archelaus thus had overall command of a hundred thousand foot soldiers and an additional twenty thousand cavalry. Knowing his strengths and knowing the pitfalls of fighting with cavalry and chariots on the broken land of Thermopylae, he marched the army several days' distance to the grassy plains of Boeotia. And there he hunkered down to await Sulla and his thirty thousand starving, unpaid Roman exiles. Archelaus had read his history and knew his terrain. He would not be defeated like Darius or Xerxes. Mithridates was one eastern conqueror who would finally achieve victory on Greek soil.

"Father, I'm leaving."

He set down the game bird he had been eating, wiped his fingers on a cloth, and stretched his huge legs on the couch, contemplating me in puzzlement and irritation. With effort, I held my gaze steady and noticed, as I had for some months, that the skin of his face and arms had lost its bronzed hardness and had become pale and soft-looking from lack of exercise. Ever since the Rhodes debacle he had left the war entirely in the hands of Archelaus and civil administration in the hands of the palace eunuchs. His new empire practically ran itself, with tribute pouring in from all sides and cities tripping over themselves to volunteer their own levies of troops. His time had been utterly his own, yet even with such a luxury as time, a luxury even the wealthiest and most powerful of men can rarely afford, he had squandered much. For three years Father had neglected his riding and hunting, favoring instead his court duties and events and satisfying Monime's whims. The wretched darts of Eros, unlike other arrows, do not kill or wound but rather dissipate, enervate, leave one less a man than before.

I myself had suffered greatly at this, for as always, where Father went, I went, and I chafed at the artificial constraints placed on me by the eunuchs and courtiers, at the female-centered environment of the palace, at Monime's shrewish voice and absurd passions. I sneaked away from the palace whenever I could, to practice my swordplay and archery, my fighting skills and my exercises, but always alone, lacking Father's guidance, lacking even his encouragement. He scarcely noticed my existence or my absences, so wrapped up had he been in the affairs of the palace. Father had become a different man. No longer the fierce warrior and stern leader, no longer even the father I remembered. He was a king still, of course, but a king of eunuchs and harem girls, rather than of soldiers and princes.

And I had had enough. "I'm leaving," I repeated.

Father gazed at me unblinkingly. "Leaving the table or leaving the palace? Our company bores you?" Monime stared, too, her mouth a thin, straight line.

"Leaving the city, maybe the province, I don't know. You were fourteen when you left home. I'm a year older than that."

He started to speak but was interrupted by a servant who stepped forward from the side, handing him a moist linen with which to wash his face, and then Monime interjected with a wordy opinion about a new handmaid she had just acquired. I sighed and clattered my goblet noisily on the table, and Father looked at me in irritation.

"Your studies go well?" he growled distractedly.

I nodded.

"Greek?"

I hesitated. Languages were a favorite subject of study for Father, but it's easy to excel when one has a natural talent. Father was fluent in twenty tongues, but these skills came much harder to me, and for as long as I could remember I had been baffled by the strange dialects spoken around me by ambassadors and heralds, which he seemed to comprehend effortlessly. The only foreign language I had learned to converse in thus far was Gallic, from sitting at Bituitus' feet listening to his stories, but Father derided that as a useless and barbarian tongue. Once, as a small lad, I had invented some foreign-sounding words and recited them casually in his presence, to increase my own importance in his eyes. "*Sulay sulay lulay-o*," I had said, words I must have learned from the garbled call of a shepherd tending his stock. Father's eyes widened in interest at this new exotic tongue, in surprise at my unexpected knowledge. "*Sulay sulay lulay-o*?" he repeated, imitating my enunciation. I laughed, as if I had just played the most brilliant trick in the world on him, and it was only after a few moments of puzzlement that he understood what I had done, and then his booming guffaw joined mine.

But that was years ago. Now was not the time to be overstating my language skills.

"Greek?" he repeated, more insistently.

I took a deep breath and began a halting recitation of Homer's invocation of the Muse at the opening of the *Iliad*:

"Menin aeide, Thea, Peleiadeo Akhilleus oulomenen . . ."

He cut me off impatiently and finished the verse himself. "Latin?" he inquired.

"Latin, Father? Why learn Latin if it's the language of the Romans?"

"*Because* it's the language of the Romans!" he exclaimed. I stared at him in surprise. "If you know a man's language," he continued, "then you know how he thinks, you know whether he analyzes his actions in the passive or active voice, you know whether his vocabulary tends to art and poetry or to war and weaponry. And when you know those things then your enemy is no longer a stranger—he is a known quantity. Speak a man's tongue, and you can think like him and anticipate his moves. And then you need never fear him. '*Qui timens vivet, liber non erit umquam.*' "

"What?"

He glared at me for my ignorance. " 'He who lives in fear will never be free.' Remember that as your first Latin lesson."

I sighed again. I had lost control of the conversation I had started. I stood up brusquely and had begun walking to the door when Father's commanding voice at my back stopped me.

"Pharnaces!"

I turned around slowly, facing his glare.

"What in Hades has gotten into you lately? Monime tells me you are rude to her and the servants."

I exploded. "The servants! I don't need these servants, and yet every step I take I'm dogged by a band of lackeys. If I sweat during my exercises they try to perfume me. If I shoot arrows they cluck about my safety. Pack of hens—I can't do a thing in this house without them pecking at my back. Nor can you!"

Monime gasped at my language and vehemence, but Father's gaze remained sharp and expressionless. "There is nothing you *do* need to do," he said in a low, deliberate tone.

"You're a prince, not an infantry grunt or a scullery boy. Act like a prince."

"As you act like a king?"

He paused in surprise, and his eyes narrowed. "What are you talking about?"

Now that I had started, I resolved not to be deterred. "You are a king," I said, "but you care for nothing."

"I care for defending my empire from Rome."

"Do you? For two years you've left all the fighting to Archelaus—you've hardly set foot out of the city. You hate Rome, you claim, but is that your way of hating? Do you hate anything else? Do you *love* anything?"

He snorted. "*Love* anything! I thought you were talking about the war."

"I *am* talking about the war!" I exclaimed, flustered. "You don't hate; you don't love; you just . . . *exist* here in this palace. You care for nothing. If something displeases you, you snap your fingers and it is removed, and then you go back to smiling and chatting as if it had never existed."

At this, Monime rebelled.

"How dare you speak to your father like this? You mere . . . you . . . you *boy!*"

I sneered at this display of eloquence, and for once, Father backed me. He glared at her and raised his hand to snap his fingers, then stopped himself ruefully. "Monime," he said in a measured tone, "leave us for now."

She stared at him hard, then laboriously sat up on her couch, fixed me with a Gorgon scowl, and walked slowly out of the room in a studied attempt at nonchalance. The softness of court life had not been flattering to her, either. Her youthful figure had broadened, her hips and waist acquiring an unattractive girth, and her face had hardened, from both her attempts at displaying the haughty demeanor of the queen she would never be and her overzealous application of skin-ravaging cosmetics. Father knew I was long past hiding my disdain for her, yet it irritated him when I expressed it openly. As Monime left, he made a visible effort to control his temper and affixed his habitual smile. His eyes, however, remained dark and angry.

"Pharnaces," he said, "Monime complains you practice swordplay in the Great Hall with Bituitus."

I was taken aback. "In the Great Hall? Only once or twice, when it was raining. . . ."

"Glad to hear it. I'm not complaining, mind you—Bituitus is a good man, a good instructor. He knows all my own moves. Let's see what he's taught you."

"What, here?" I exclaimed in surprise.

"No better place or time." Standing up with a grunt, he strode to the sword rack where his guards stored their weapons when off duty and carefully chose a blade, which he weighed briefly in his hand for a moment, testing its balance, before tossing it to me, handle first. He then seized his own massive weapon from the couch on which he had laid it while dining and walked toward me, blade down, chest and face completely exposed. I stood puzzled, not knowing what to do.

"Come on, boy—this is no longer a dining room; it's a battlefield," he said, grinning. "Time for me to work off a bit of this palace fat. Give me your best shot."

"Father, these aren't sparring weapons—the edges aren't blunted; the tips aren't covered. It's too dangerous; these are real blades. . . ."

"Nonsense. If I can't defend myself against a fifteen-year-old I don't deserve to be king and you do. Come on—look, I'm getting too close; I've entered your guard!"

His torso was still exposed, and I swatted at him halfheartedly, not trying to strike but only to ward him off. With a move so fast I scarcely even saw it, he flashed his blade in a powerful counterstroke, setting my sword to ringing and my hand and arm tingling painfully with the impact. The door opened and a startled guard rushed in, but Father waved him off with a grin.

"Bit of sparring, soldier. Stay and watch, if you like."

Nodding uncertainly, the guard retreated to a corner and stood stiffly, observing our maneuvers.

Red-faced, I realized now that Father meant this practice in earnest. Crouching in a fighting stance, I approached him gingerly, aiming to play to my strength, as Bituitus had taught me—to strike low and fast, below the comfort range of a larger opponent.

Father immediately perceived the tactic and nodded with approval. "Good position, boy; keep your balance; rock forward a bit on the balls of your feet, like . . . *so!*" And lunging forward he swiped quickly toward my head, stopping his sword just before it made impact—or just before it *would have made* impact, for I had seen the move coming and lithely stepped under it, popping up just on the other side of the hovering blade.

Father's eyes opened in surprise. "Nice work!" he exclaimed, turning and winking at the guard. "Let's step up the pace a bit here, test the boy's mettle."

Taking a confident step toward me, he lifted his blade and immediately launched into a swift combination of slashes and lunges designed to throw me off balance, to distract me with the immediate threat of the flashing blade so that I would lose control of my footwork and balance. Stroke after stroke he bore down on me, with a strength and speed I could hardly fathom—never had I encountered such pressure in my sparring sessions with Bituitus. Beads of sweat burst out on my forehead as I parried frantically, and I felt myself being backed slowly, inexorably, to the wall behind me. Once I was there, I knew, the game would be over. Stealing a glance at his face between jabs, I saw his expression focused, though utterly relaxed, with a faint smile on his lips. He was enjoying this! And suddenly I felt deep anger, a rage that he could take my concerns so lightly, that he could so casually dismiss the matters I had tried to discuss with him earlier, that he could simply fob me off with what he considered a child's game. Play with the boy for a few minutes to stop him from crying! Burn off some palace fat!

With a strength I did not realize I had, I stood up suddenly from my defensive crouch and unleashed a torrid combination of strokes I had seen Bituitus practicing with one of the army champions, halting my retreat and even taking two or three tentative steps toward Father. His smile disappeared abruptly and he raised an eyebrow in surprise, though he efficiently parried every move. Suddenly this was no longer a mere game, and he paused, stealing a moment to wipe the sweat from his brow.

He nodded once to the watching guard, as if to signal that he would put an end to the match now, before it got out of hand. Turning back toward me, he threw a broad feinting lunge to my right. As I leaned over to block it, he spun to my left almost faster than the eye could see, to pin me against the back wall with the flat of his sword and end the contest.

Except I was no longer there. Having often practiced that

very maneuver with Bituitus, I took the risk that his lunge was indeed merely a feint, and I feinted my counterstroke in return. Dodging quickly under the blade, I spun in the opposite direction behind him, and the flat of his sword rang hollow on the bare stone of the wall. Before he could even regain his bearings, he felt the tip of my own blade pressing lightly at the small of his back.

Father froze. I could not see his face, which was directed to the wall—the only sign I had of his reaction was the red flush that rose up the back of his neck and ears. Behind me I could hear the guard walking toward us gingerly, unsure what to do. I stood panting, grinning in triumph, but only for a moment, for Father suddenly whirled, leaping out of my sword range and simultaneously slashing my own weapon so hard that it flew out of my hand, crashing against the nearby wall with a force that shattered the blade, breaking it cleanly off from the handle. Before I could even react, he slammed the flat of his sword against my stomach, throwing me off my feet to the floor, where I lay on my back, gasping to regain my lost wind. I looked up at him in bewilderment and he, in turn, glared down at me in rage.

"You do *not* threaten the King with a sword in the back," he said menacingly.

"Father, it was only a game; you said so yourself!"

"This was not a game. No man puts a blade to the back of a king save for one who would end his reign."

Now I was truly angry. As if I had started the match! Scrambling up from the floor, I resolved to press my case before he could interrupt. Still panting, I stepped directly before him, chest to chest, so close I could feel his own hot, angry breath on my face.

"So now that you've had a sword prick in the back, you suddenly show some emotion! Do you think I am a threat to you? Is everyone out to assassinate you? Do you care for anything beyond yourself, beyond your never-ending antidotes and omens?"

"You whelp! I'll have you thrashed—"

"You care for nothing, outside your own little circle. Does it trouble you that all Athens is in ruins? That a hundred thousand of your men have been besieged by Sulla for a year? That your own son is treated like a pet dog within his own home? Does it matter to you that—"

"Enough, boy! I will not have you speak to me this way!"

I paused. "Have it your way. You will not have me speak these things. You are the King and you don't *have* to hear my criticism; you don't *have* to care for it. And that's why I'm leaving."

Glaring, he stepped aside with an exaggerated courtly flourish to give me passage. His face was tense with anger, and the line of his jaw whitened in his attempt to control it.

"And so you *shall* leave," he said through clenched teeth. "So you shall. Begone then."

I stalked out without another word, rushing past him so clumsily that I knocked the couch over as I passed.

The next day Monime swept into my room and found me sitting on the floor, gloomily trying to decide what to bring with me and where I was to go. I had not yet thought through the logistics of striking out on my own, and my prospects seemed more daunting every moment that passed. She eased herself down onto a low stool with an ignoble grunt and then started in with her hectoring.

"Foolish boy. You think your father is Hercules—he bats away arrows, shrugs off poison; nothing can stop him or hurt him. He fears no man and no thing, so therefore cares for nothing. Isn't that right?"

I looked at the gear remaining to be packed and muttered that I wished to be left alone.

"But he is flesh and blood," she continued. "Flesh and blood, with a mind always working and sentiments to match. Flesh and blood. And you have hurt him."

I turned to her, trying to mask my surprise by feigning distraction. "Hurt him? And what am I to him, that I could hurt him? You said yourself I'm a mere boy. Machares is the heir."

She looked at me in exasperation. " 'What am I to him?' " she repeated, mocking my tone. "You're everything, you self-pitying idiot! Don't you realize? Prince Machares is the heir by law, but you are all his hope—he teaches you everything he knows. You'll be the commander of his armies, the one to protect and maintain the kingdom, not that sickly scholar

Machares. Last night your father didn't sleep a wink—up pacing all night, alternately cursing you and lamenting for you. I had to go sleep elsewhere, I got so sick of it."

"I'm still leaving."

"Such a determined lad. Where will you go?"

"Why do you care?"

She sighed. "In fact, I don't—not in the slightest. But your father sent me to ask you. You're not supposed to know it's he who's inquiring. I tell you this because I simply can't pretend I care enough to ask you for my own sake. So humor me, and give me an answer to pass on to your father. Where will you go?"

"Where I should have been all along. To Archelaus and the army, to help destroy the Roman legions. There's a transport scow in port, taking on supplies to bring to the troops in Greece. It's leaving tomorrow with the tides, and I'll be on it."

She eyed me curiously and not without a hint of smugness. "It's for the best. The palace is not big enough for you both."

"Thank you for your affection and support."

She smiled faintly. "Oh, my dear Pharnaces, truly I'm not as heartless as you've always made me out to be! I've even arranged with your father to send Bituitus along to accompany you, to ensure your safety. Otherwise, you see, I'd worry about you, poor boy!"

"A fine move," I said sarcastically. "You've never been fond of Bituitus, either."

"Fond?" she asked incredulously. "Fond! It's not for me to be *fond* of your father's bodyguards! I won't have that man come near me!"

At this I bristled. "What do you have against old Bituitus? He's harmless as a lamb."

Monime tossed her head in disdain. "I simply can't abide him. He's too big and too ugly. He's a Gaul, of all things! And he's mutilated."

I looked at her incredulously. "You fill the house with eighty eunuchs, and yet you're squeamish that *Bituitus* is mutilated? The only thing *he's* missing is a finger!"

"Humph! My eunuchs may be mutilated, as you call it, but at least they don't go around flaunting their scar. I can't help but stare at that finger stump every time he's present." She shuddered.

I was boiling. Though Bituitus gave me a different story every time I asked him about his finger, I was certain he had lost it in Father's service, and it infuriated me that Monime should disdain this. I turned back to my packing. "Say good-bye to Father for me," I said, in as manly a voice as I could muster, sounding much more confident than I felt at that moment.

"Oh, I will, little soldier," she said brightly. "I will."

The next evening I stood on the vessel's deck in commoner's togs, watching the workers roll the last urns of wine and oil down the ramps and into the hold. Suddenly a commotion on the street caught my attention and I turned to stare. It was a sight I knew well. Father's royal litter was passing by and had paused just at the foot of my vessel's wharf. *He must be dropping off Bituitus to accompany me on the voyage,* I thought, *or perhaps Father himself is coming to wish me well.*

But it was neither. Instead, as the crowd noticed the familiar litter, men surged around it, cheering, jostling the eight struggling slaves who stood panting slightly with the heavy load on their yokes and calling out to their fellows in the neighboring taverns and food stands to come hail the King. I smiled—this was one of the burdens of duty Father always hated, though Monime reveled in the glamour of being pointed out whenever she and the King ventured forth in public. Yet this was unusual. Father rarely allowed the litter-bearers to stop in the streets before reaching his destination.

The gauzy curtains of the window pulled back, and inside I could see the faint outline of his large shaggy head, reflected off the light of the white plastered wall behind him. Yet in front of him, peering out the window, was Monime—her face pinched and flushed with anxiety as she stared out at the growing crowd of men surrounding the vehicle, some of who were now shouting personal petitions, hoping Father might grant their requests.

Why the long face on the bitch? I wondered. *Certainly not because she's worried on my account. Father must be still in his mood.*

And before the litter bearers had even resumed their dogged trot away from the wharves, I shrugged, turned my back on Monime's searching face, and climbed belowdecks. The captain whistled and the crew cast off lines and began rowing through the tight harbor and out to the open sea. I drew a deep breath and sighed loudly, a mixture of relief and worry.

Bituitus, to my genuine dismay, had missed the boat.

Three days of a favorable wind, and the transport scow crossed the Aegean and put in at a small harbor in Boeotia with its consignment. I stepped onto the wharf and took a deep breath of the air of Greece—redolent of tar, rotting fish, and old wood, the same smells I had left behind in Asia; if I closed my eyes I would not even know I had traveled away from home. Still, I breathed in deeply, for these smells, in all their slight variations and yet their sameness, were somehow holy—for they were Greek.

Glancing up to the street at the foot of the wharf, I was surprised to see a litter, similar to the one I had left behind, though with a different collection of eight sweating bearers—and a hand emerging from the curtain and beckoning me to approach. I sighed. *So Bituitus made it after all,* I thought. He had to have taken a fast pirate cutter and rowed through the nights to beat me here. I strode up to the side of the car, and with barely a glance I drew back the side curtains, climbed in, and sat down, quickly pulling the curtains shut behind me.

Looking at me with a broad grin, massive bow of Odysseus across his lap, was Father.

"What . . . ? Why are you here?" I asked in astonishment.

"Because," he said quietly, as the litter began swaying on the shoulders of the trotting slaves, "you were right."

"Right? What do you mean?"

"Your words the other night were harsh, and they bit deep. You accused me of caring for nothing. But I do care, with a passion. And I decided I could no longer deny that, merely for the sake of a peaceable household. And if that means hating . . . then I hate. I hate Rome and her bullying, corrupt, thieving ways. I hate its conquest of our ancient cultures. And if that means love, then I'll admit to that, too." He paused and glanced distractedly out the window. "Two years," he said. "Two years since I sent the army away to invest Athens. *Three* years since I've last fought. By the demons in Hades—what have I been doing?"

"But I still don't understand," I replied. "You're here now—but I saw you on the wharf before I left Pergamum. How did you arrive so fast? Where is your garrison?"

Father chuckled. "I see the ruse is working," he said, "if I can fool my own son!"

"What do you mean?"

"That wasn't me you saw at the wharf, lad—that was Bituitus, in the litter with Monime."

He paused a moment, letting me make the connection—then I burst out laughing. It was so obvious I could hardly believe it. "You don't mean the Gaul is pretending to be you . . . ?"

Father's eyes twinkled. "And why not? We pulled that trick all the time as boys. Bituitus is the same height and build—"

"But his beard! His accent!"

Father chuckled. "Bituitus is now as smooth-cheeked as you, boy! He's been cleaned up and even fitted for purple. From a distance, as he climbs in and out of the litter, he's the spitting image of me. I've ordered him to ride about the city behind curtains two or three times a day, feigning to be me, while I'm away. Archelaus will defeat Sulla's legions and I'll return in three weeks, and no one will be the wiser."

"And Monime?"

"Monime rides with him. She doesn't mind, do you think?"

I could hardly contain my pleasure at the thought of her confined to a litter with Bituitus twice a day. "No," I laughed, "Bituitus is the perfect gentleman. They'll do just fine."

Father smiled.

"But why the secrecy?" I pressed. "You're king—why sneak around?"

"Loyalties are still uncertain. We've only been in power for three years. There are no Italians, but Rome has ears in Pergamum. It wouldn't do for them to know I had left the city."

"But you've left the city before—on your tours of the territory, to suppress revolts . . ."

"Those occasions were all with the army—or at least with the city garrison, since most of the army is in Greece. I can't leave Pergamum undefended while I travel to Greece—yet I can't afford for Rome to discover I'm traveling alone. Wouldn't Sulla's agents love to catch King Mithridates sailing across the Aegean without his fleet!"

"But why come to Greece at all, especially with no troops?"

Suddenly his face closed up and he peered vacantly outside through the gap in the curtains as the litter swayed on its dusty course down the road.

"You ask too many questions, boy," he said, and I knew I could probe no further. In reality, I hardly needed to ask the question, for he himself had supplied the answer. His hatred ran deep, as did his love—for his people, for his army—and it had been only because of my boyish foolishness that I had failed to see that earlier. I would not doubt him again.

3

We traveled a day and a night until we arrived at the highland plain of Elatea, a beautiful land with good soil and fields, multitudes of prosperous hamlets, and abundant trees and water. Here the main body of the Pontic army was encamped, several miles from a rising hill. On the summit we could see the Roman army entrenched, in a compact formation befitting their small number of troops, but in a near-impregnable position. Father had not sent advance word of our coming, and we marched into the general staff tent unannounced, waving aside the guards at the doorway, who stared at us in astonishment.

Inside, Archelaus and Taxiles were in close conference, heads bent down over a low camp table, peering at a map scrawled into a large wax tablet. They were in heated discussion and did not look up, nor did Father interrupt them. Instead, he merely stood quietly in the doorway observing them. Though it had been several years since I had last seen my "Uncle" Archelaus, he had changed very little. A short, stocky Greek, he was a man of utter practicality, to the point even of shearing his hair close to the skull, contrary to fashion and even to the tradition of his countrymen: "The better to keep the lice tamed," he said. Though he rarely smiled, his narrow gray eyes nevertheless radiated good humor, particularly for me, and as a child I had delighted in accompanying him on his rounds through the camp, almost as much as I did with Father. Archelaus was a lifelong bachelor—his entire existence was dedicated to the army and to serving Father, and though he could command a ransom in gold for his services, his wealth was never in evidence—even here, as a *strategos,* a field general on campaign, he wore the same rough woolen tunic as the common soldiers, his rank distinguished only by the fine leather and the silver embossing on the sword scabbard at his side. After observing the two generals for a moment, Father cleared his throat. Archelaus looked up, an impatient set to his square jaw, and then his eyes opened wide in surprise.

"By the Holy Serpent!" he exclaimed in consternation, scrambling up from the camp bench. "My lord, what brings you here? And the young prince as well?"

Father nodded in greeting. "Gentlemen, please sit. It's been months since I've even left the palace, much less pestered my officers in battle. Young Pharnaces told me I was getting soft"—he winked at me—"and I agreed. Time to earn my keep again, and for Pharnaces to learn the trade."

"But the empire, my lord—Pergamum . . ." The question hung in the air, unspoken yet clear as the ringing of a bell. Roman agents and spies were everywhere, even among our people, and the danger of a coup should they realize the throne was vacant, even temporarily, was very high. Seeing Archelaus' reaction, I now understood Father's wisdom in installing Bituitus as his double and departing Pergamum in secrecy.

"Ah," Father said, glancing at me slyly, "that has been well taken care of. Archelaus, sit down and brief me. How went the evacuation of Piraeus? Your last dispatch had not yet arrived before I left."

"Very well, my lord. We left the Romans not so much as a crumb of bread when they finally broke into the citadel of Munychea, where my headquarters had been. Not a single flagon of wine, not a scrap of papyrus."

"Good, good," Father said eagerly, rubbing his hands together. Already the old spark was back in his eyes, and I could see he was relishing being back on campaign. "Any casualties?"

"Not on our side," Archelaus said with quiet pride, though still refusing to sit down in the presence of his king. "As a final salute to Sulla, I sent a squad of Cilician irregulars to slip back into port from their ships offshore, the first night the Romans had taken possession. They're born arsonists and murderers, those Cilicians. They painted themselves black, infiltrated the Roman lines, and torched all the docks and warehouses Sulla was so happy to save after the siege. Left him with only a ruined shell of a port, to go with the Long Walls he had toppled and the city he had destroyed."

"The evacuation was masterly."

"Thank you, my lord. I am at your orders, as is Taxiles," Archelaus said, bowing low.

Father stepped forward and pulled him back up. "No, Generals, it is I who am at *your* orders. History is full of armies who have been defeated because of arrogant kings who did not leave the fighting to their officers. I am here merely to observe your victory."

Archelaus straightened up. "And the boy?" he asked, glancing at me.

"I'm here to observe you," I said simply.

Archelaus smiled indulgently and relaxed. "And how do you intend to do that?"

"Father said I should leave that to you. Camp messenger, orderly, phalanx commander . . ."

Archelaus chuckled. "Phalanx commander, eh? We'll see about that. In any case, you've done well in arriving now. You'll see us rout Sulla and retake Athens."

"Sulla! He's near?"

"Indeed he is, lad," and Archelaus' tanned and weather-scarred face darkened even further. "Been here all of three weeks. Can't get the bastard to fight, though. He marched his little army up here after we slipped away from him at Piraeus. I believe he's feeling arrogant, thinking he would chase us out of Greece once and for all. But he wasn't counting on our joining with Taxiles' forces. When the Romans saw our combined army, with almost as many horse alone as they have men, they hunkered down behind their palisades, and now they won't move a muscle. I can't attack him behind his stakes and ditches, but I've offered him battle every day. My troops are getting so cocky and restless they're losing discipline. Last week they destroyed two towns and sacked their temples before I was able to regain control. Still the Romans just sit inside their trenches."

"So why don't you just march around them?"

Archelaus winked at Taxiles. "Smart lad. The King knew

what he was doing when he brought you here. We'll make a soldier out of you yet, boy."

As it turns out, going around the Romans was precisely what Archelaus had in mind. The very next day the Pontic forces struck camp, heading southeast on a four-day forced march through the rocky hinterland. They were aiming for a point on the Euboean Channel opposite Chalcis, the nearest port large enough to accommodate the Pontic fleet. From there they would quickly return to Piraeus and Athens, which the Romans had left undefended but for a light garrison, and retake the city, this time with stronger forces, more supplies, and greater determination than ever to starve Sulla and his troops back to Italy.

Father rode with the senior officers, disdaining his normal kingly garb for rougher campaign clothes, to prevent being recognized by the Roman scouts spying on us from the ridge tops. The secret could not be kept from our own troops, however, and news of our arrival sped through the camp like wildfire. As always, whenever Father was present with the army the air fairly crackled with excitement. The men were eager to engage, eager to test the phalanx tactics in which they had trained for so long, to destroy these Romans who had been harassing us. Now, outside the confines of the close walls of Piraeus, our scythe chariots could finally roll, our phalanx move unimpeded into the outnumbered Roman lines. The men were champing at the bit to grant Mithridates a great victory. With Father's arrival the atmosphere was suddenly almost festive, and I could imagine the Romans' wondering what might have inspired the Pontic troops so suddenly.

When Sulla saw our departure he, too, struck camp and followed us at a prudent distance, like a shadow. His forward scouts stayed always just beyond our rear guard's arrow range, and each night the Romans made themselves impervious to attack, digging deep trenches topped with a palisade of spears and sharpened stakes around their closely ordered camp. We wondered at the Roman tenacity—surely, after camping in the barren, rocky land around Athens for the past two years, the Romans had received little food, and even less pay, from Sulla's dwindling war chest, yet each evening, after a hard, twenty-mile march through the rocky high grounds overlooking the channel, they still managed to dig their endless trenches and fortifications. Call it what you will—blind foolishness or stubborn discipline—the Romans had it. And they were not slaves or mercenaries but rather volunteers for a twenty-year hitch. You couldn't help but admire them.

We set up camp near Chaeronea, an ancient Boeotian town that centuries before had been the site of a great victory won by Alexander's father, Philip of Macedon, over the Athenians. The historical significance of this did not pass Archelaus unnoticed, and he thought it a good omen that the victor then had been a great Hellenic king, as he considered Father to be. That night, the early-autumn weather turned unseasonably cold and stormy, with driving rain and cruel gusts of wind that cut through the canvas tent flaps. We suffered the darkness in the cold rain, sleepless and jittery. It was impossible to relax—all we could do was stow our gear and arrange the supply wagons as best we could in the dark and the storm, as scouts fanned out in search of the best ground for the battle we knew would be coming with morning's light. Palisades and entrenchments were impossible under these circumstances, though Pontic armies rarely used such laborious defensive tactics in any event. With twenty thousand horses to feed and pasture, it would be impossible to contain the entire army in a compact array behind a wall, as the Romans did so well. I had developed a new appreciation for their lightness of baggage and cautious defensive style.

We would see how their tactics would serve them in the morning. Impossible to imagine that anyone could stand up to the onslaught of our phalanx, men who had trained for years to fight in tight ranks, flanked by our armored cavalry and scythe chariots. Even Roman legions could not withstand such a charge. They were only men, after all, men of flesh and blood and armed like us, with short swords and spears. True, they were professionals, but so, too, were our own mercenaries. Though our men were largely foreigners, fighting for money rather than for a land many of them had never seen in their lives, the Romans were fighting for neither—Sulla could not offer them the standard legionary pay, nor a country, for as supporters of the Optimates he and his men were exiles from a Popular-ruled city that no longer appreciated or even recognized their very existence. Sulla's Roman troops were men without a home, outnumbered four to one, and lacking even horse or artillery weapons. Their situation was desperate.

Morning dawned cold and gray, with scarcely more light than there had been the night before. The rain increased in intensity, turning into a hard-driving sleet, then a frigid, slushy snow. The terrain before us was a plain, if you could call it that, bounded on the east by a rocky escarpment topped by the citadel of Chaeronea and on the west, a mile or so distant, by the gravelly banks of the River Morion, which ploughed its rough and foaming way from the spiny ridge of mountains before us, to the Euboean Channel some ten miles to our rear. The plain itself was unsuited to our strengths—sloping irregularly both laterally and uphill, peppered with rocks and boulders, and crossed by streamlets meandering from the foothills to the river far to our left. All of these posed serious obstacles to maintaining the formation needed to mount a phalanx charge. Worse, they would reduce the speed and maneuverability of our fearsome scythe chariots. But this field would have to do. We had no choice. There was no time to move our position.

The Romans had arrived.

With a blast of trumpet heard even from this distance of two miles, they marched out from the fortified rock outcropping comprising the town of Chaeronea. Not exactly out from it, for they had not been stationed within the protection of the town's walls, but *around* it, like a column of ants encountering a pebble in its path and splitting the line in two parts, to march without hesitation down either side. As if they had practiced the maneuver on the parade ground for months, the two Roman columns, of three legions on one side and two on the other, appeared simultaneously on either side of the stronghold, marching in tight anapestic rhythm, shields swaying before them and spears locked in the upright, "ready" position. The two halves of the army marched toward each other for a short space, drums throbbing ominously with the beat of the tramping feet, and as they approached, the trumpet shrilled once again and the two columns wheeled toward the front, merging with each other to form one wide, undivided column, marching implacably toward us on a front a quarter-mile across.

No motley collection of pirates and mercenaries these: though battered, their shields gleamed in the dull light with the pride of men who sand-polished them every morning to remove the previous day's rust, tarnish, or blood; though tattered from two years of campaigning, their faded scarlet tunics beneath the armor showed proudly against the dull, sodden landscape. The legions were arranged so precisely that every man could be counted at a glance, in cohorts and centuries as uniform yet distinct one from another as carefully cut flagstones in the street, each identified by its flapping pennants. As the five legions approached, a sudden order was heard, shouted by a herald on Sulla's staff and relayed immediately by trumpet signal, and the troops stopped their forward progress with a single accord. The two flanks whirled to the outside and began trotting away from the center, spreading and thinning the line, as the rearward troops moved forward to fill in the spaces left by their comrades. Not a word was spoken, not an effort wasted.

In the time it takes a man to count slowly to one hundred, the battlefront had been extended from the escarpment on the right to the river on the far left, each Roman standing two sword's lengths apart from his fellows on either side, sufficient for one soldier and his neighbor to protect the space between them. The front rank was supported from behind by the next line of troops spaced an identical distance apart and offset to fill the gaps between the men in front. The array was a mere four-deep, with pockets of cavalry and archers interspersed here and there and one legion remaining in the rear as a reserve, ready to be sent to whichever flank most required its assistance. Though the Romans were outnumbered four to one, the length of their widely spaced line far exceeded the distance covered by our own phalanx, which had hastily formed in a compact, sixteen-rank formation. These men, these Romans, trusted not in the shield of the man on their right, as did the soldiers of the phalanx. Each Roman stood alone, each man responsible for holding the length of line on either side of him.

The frightening implication was that each Roman, alone, truly *was* capable of holding that expanse of line.

My jaw dropped at this display of coolness and precision, but there was no dismay among the men around me. For two years they had watched from the ramparts of Piraeus as the Romans had besieged their defenses and launched assaults on the walls. Precision drill was no novelty to them, and the Pontic phalanx was not without great skill itself in forming rank. I glanced at Archelaus, then at Father, to judge their reactions, but their faces were inscrutable as they calmly chewed on twigs and squinted at the line before them.

"We'll soften 'em a bit," Archelaus muttered to Father and the captains, "before we throw in the heavy troops." Father nodded, and I knew the Romans would soon be staring Death in the face, in the form of the whirling, razor-sharp blades of the Pontic scythe chariots.

These were the vehicles that had torn their way through the Bithynian lines and brought about the destruction of Nicomedes' army. Their killing power was well known throughout the world, and the Pontic armies had the largest scythe-chariot forces ever deployed. No one was under any illusions that a mere sixty of these vehicles would be sufficient to send the Roman army flying, as they had the ill-trained Bithynians. The weapons were designed to work best when launched into the concentrated flesh of an opposing phalanx, for even if the horses were impaled and killed on the upraised javelins of the enemy, the chariots' forward momentum would carve a bloody swath of carnage that could not be easily filled and into which our own troops could quickly charge. Yet even against veteran Roman troops the vehicles were certain to be deadly. Our troops fell silent as these, their most formidable weapons, were brought forward and deployed in three ranks of twenty across the center of our line, spanning the very distance the phalanx covered, about two hundred paces.

The Romans, a quarter-mile across the field, neither flinched nor budged from their positions but stood stolid and imperturbable as ever, waiting in their hyperextended position for us to make the first move. At a nod from Archelaus, the mournful bleat of the *salpinx* rose and carried over the plain; the horses leaped forward with their drivers lashing fiercely from behind; and the sixty chariots dashed bumping and careening over the rock-strewn terrain, sheets of freezing water spraying to the side as wheels caromed through marshy rivulets, to the wild cheers of the Pontic forces behind them.

The implacable Roman legions stood stone-still, flexing

nary a muscle, disdaining even to lower their spears or raise their shields to face the charge thundering toward them. No man flinched, not even in the face of the stinging rain beating into their eyes—Zeus' own fury at their insolence. Our voices rose louder, anticipating the triumph, waiting with bated breath for the crunch and crash of the initial contact, the screams of the enemy as the whirling blades sliced through limbs and rib cages. We tensed in anticipation of the order to commence our own charge, to follow through into the bloody path cut by the chariots' murderous tines, to join in what would surely be a crushing victory over these Romans who had been our bane for two years. . . .

And then nothing.

There was no crunch and clash, no screams or orders to charge. The chariots met nothing, not a single soft-fleshed foe. As soon as the charging horses arrived at the front ranks of the enemy, the Romans, already spaced two arm's lengths apart, simply stepped farther to either side to let the horses pass, and the chariots swept harmlessly through, into the very rear of the deployment. The Romans then closed ranks by quickly stepping back into their initial position.

At this, our cheers fell to silent astonishment, as we saw, behind the thin line of Romans, the reserve legion in the rear quickly surround each wheeling Pontic chariot and shoot down the terrified horses with arrows. The drivers were dragged from their cars and each disappeared under the thrusting swords of a dozen Roman legionaries, and then the bodies and chariots were left where they were, toppled in the field, as the reserve legion quickly reassumed its original formation. In one swift and silent stroke, the Pontic chariot squadron had been destroyed.

Our men were stunned. In the silence that followed, a faint cry was heard drifting toward us across the plain, a hooting chorus of *"Currus! Currus!"* This was soon picked up by more Roman voices until the entire enemy army was shouting the mocking chant. For the first time in my life I regretted not knowing Latin, and I looked quizzically at my father while he shook his head in anger.

"Father!" I called as he turned to give orders to his captains. His earlier resolve not to interfere had been forgotten and he was now taking measures into his own hands. "Father, what are they saying?"

"It is not for the ears of our army to hear," he shot back sharply.

"But the men do hear it, and some will understand it!" I shouted over the clamor. "Our ranks are full of freed slaves who used to serve the Romans. They will understand and tell their fellows. What are the Romans saying?!"

He looked at me with some disgust at my inability to understand Latin. "It is the call used in the Roman Circus by spectators waiting for the next race to begin."

"And what is that?" I cried in exasperation.

"They are calling for more chariots."

The massive charge of Pontic horse that followed was more effective, as it could not help but be against the widely spaced Romans. More than a charge, it was almost an eruption: after the debacle of the chariots, the Pontic cavalry, seeing their king's and their own honor at stake, rushed through our infantry formations and were on the verge of racing into the Roman ranks immediately, orders or no orders. Archelaus and Father were hard put to hold them back until our troops had re-formed their phalanx to follow up on the cavalry. When the call finally sounded for the first wave of the attack, the King's own elite band of two thousand armored horsemen fairly flew along the narrow front, tearing through the blinding rain, directly into the enemy lines.

The overwhelmed Romans in the center of the legions' array collapsed and were destroyed in a moment by the slashing scimitars of the enraged Pontic warriors and the trampling hooves of their mountain ponies. Yet the attackers did not emerge unscathed. To our amazement, every enemy soldier firmly stood his ground; not a man fled, as any other foe would have done when faced with such an onslaught. Our horses were trained to run down and trample fleeing foot soldiers, and the stubbornly immobile stance of the legions confounded them, causing the animals to balk or even pull up short as they approached the Roman lines, thus giving the defenders time to loose their spears or attack animal and rider with their swords.

For every Roman taken down, cut cleanly through the neck by an arcing cavalry scimitar, a Pontic horse was hamstrung or killed. Riders were torn flailing from their mounts and thrown to the ground by Romans working in teams of two or three. Once fallen, the cavalrymen were defenseless in their stiff riding armor, helpless as turtles on their backs. The Romans simply ignored such easy prey to concentrate on the next horse in the attack, and the next, returning to the fallen Pontic horsemen later, after the initial charge had passed. Then with quick sword thrusts they coldly dispatched the fallen riders where they lay struggling on the ground.

From the corner of my eye I saw movement to the right of the hillock on which Father, Archelaus, and I were standing to view the battle. I turned abruptly, just catching sight of a glimmer of bronze through the driving rain as a Roman legionary ducked behind a boulder not fifty paces from where we stood—he must have walked the entire night to circle behind our lines and move into such a position, with an unobstructed view of the entire Pontic command.

Stupidly, with no thoughts but to my own glory, I slipped and scrambled down from the muddy rise and shouldered through the ranks of heralds and couriers waiting impatiently with their horses—and there I saw him, in profile only thirty paces away, his face intent on his view of Father around the far side of the rock. He was no sniper, I saw—few Romans are truly skilled in archery—but on his back I saw the deadly bronze tips of a sheaf of javelins. Few weapons are as fearsome, either close up or distant, as a six-foot spear in the hands of a Roman legionary.

The duck shooting lessons flashed before me, and I slipped my bow from my shoulder, strung it in one easy motion without taking my eyes from the attacker, and nocked an arrow from my quiver onto the string. Yet this wasn't a duck before me, it was a man, and I had never shot at a man in my life. Where does one aim to best penetrate armor? How does one transfer the skill of pinning a live duck with scarcely an injury to that of slaying a full-grown man, before he can put spear to flight and slay you with a bronze warhead, your cranium exploding from the impact like the rag-stuffed sacks we use for target practice?

I aimed carefully, trying to time the gaps between the gusts of biting wind buffeting my face—*look for the thin membrane on the tip of the wing where it would be certain to draw little blood, no, the joint next to the armpit, where shoulder guard meets cuirass; surely there is a crack there, a weak spot . . .*

No! I fairly shouted to myself in my mind. *Don't think! Let the god take possession of your arm, of your aim. Deathless Apollo, send my arrow true. . . .* "Father," I whispered under my breath, "I'm coming! Hold, Father; I'm coming. . . ."

I could hesitate no longer. The man had crouched, and at a sudden surge in the battle, when the attention of all was focused on the mighty clash of the two forces' lines, he leaped to his feet. Racing toward the King, he held the javelin high over his head in an overhand thrusting position, a position that, when loosed, would send the heavy shaft hurtling toward the target, with a momentum and weight that could slam through the thickest armor, even through a solid oaken shield. His eyes were wide open in concentration and his mouth formed a wordless bellow as he raced swiftly toward the King. I knew I could wait no longer—there would be no second chance.

I loosed my arrow, giving no further thought to the direction and speed of the wind, save for aiming just below the height of the chin to account for the downward arc over that distance. The arrow shot invisible and silent, and I blinked as it was loosed, missing its soundless flight and fatal impact. The arrow darted straight and true, through the crack in his armor and directly into the lung—but not stopping him! My heart nearly burst as I saw the Roman falter and stagger, almost dropping to the ground, but recovering and lifting his arm once more to bring back the javelin into the overhand thrusting position. He was only twenty paces away now, then ten, and I drew another shaft from my quiver—*deathless Apollo*—I had no time for a longer prayer than that before I notched the arrow and let it fly, without thinking or even aiming, hoping only for the best but fearing the worst as the Roman now staggered into stabbing range of Father and Archelaus. I tried to shout a warning, to scream for Father to turn around and look, but no words came from my mouth. There was no time to loose a third arrow, and I could not even see the results of the last one—it was all happening too fast. My strength gave way and I sank to my knees.

With a scream, the man tripped, his momentum carrying him directly into the crowd of aides, his shoulder plowing into the small of Father's back as he fell to the ground, javelin dropping from his hand. Father stumbled at the impact, then caught himself and turned, his expression turning to surprise and wonder at seeing a dead Roman lying at his feet, javelin on the ground at his side, its bronze warhead buried in the half-frozen slurry. Only then could my eyes focus on the Roman's body—besides the first arrow I had shot, which had penetrated his carapace through the gap at the armpit, the second shaft also stood erect in the air, like a tiny pole for a battle pennant, its sharp head buried deep in the man's temple, just in front of the helmet line. It had killed the soldier in mid-run, preventing him from loosing his javelin into Father's back. The body twitched, and a thin stream of blood gurgled from the mouth, forming a red pool at Father's feet.

Father and Archelaus stepped forward, swords drawn, as they looked around fiercely for any other enemy who might be near. I rose slowly to my feet, still breathing heavily, bow raised, hand frozen at my shoulder where I had begun reaching for the next arrow. Father looked up, rain sheeting down his face, and caught my eye, then stared at me in wonder. He nodded his head at me, a slow, deep nod of respect, more eloquent in its praise than any words he could have spoken. At that moment, before he returned his attention to the battle, I knew all arguments had been forgotten, all debts repaid.

A sudden cheer rose up from the troops on our side, and Father turned back to the battle. The Pontic cavalry had torn through the Roman lines, bulling an enormous gap in the middle and splitting the legions into two halves. Father saw the opportunity and leaped to a boulder in the midst of the troops.

"Infantry—to victory! For Zeus and for Pontus!" he bellowed, and with a thunderous roar the phalanx, two hundred paces broad and sixteen men deep, stormed across the field, a precision killing machine. Their sprinting steps kept perfect unison with the rapid beating of the drum, shields swinging in lockstep with their precise cadence, a floodtide of hardened fighters, directly into the breach cut a moment before by the deadly cavalry attack. The Romans on either flank of the phalanx saw it coming and immediately grasped our strategy: to divide their forces and then destroy the weaker half with our superior manpower before turning to the stronger half and eliminating it as well. The legions' two flanks scrambled madly to close the gap opened by our horse, constricting the length of their front, compressing and drawing their forces in toward the huge empty space in the center—but it was too late; our phalanx had seized the ground and was now pouring into the gap, trampling the spilled bodies of horses and men littering the sodden muddy plain, fairly leaping in haste to secure the advantage the powerful Pontic cavalry charge had gained.

The horse troops, meanwhile, had passed clear through the Roman lines to the rear and were now wheeling for a second assault from behind, though hundreds of their comrades had fallen on the first charge. Such devastating losses would normally have sent the horsemen reeling back to their own lines for cover. Yet having struggled through to the Roman rear, the Pontic cavalry had few alternatives but to return back the way they had come, to join with the foot soldiers and strengthen the wedge they had driven into the heart of Sulla's army. One more charge through, just like the one they had completed, would wipe out the Roman reinforcements from the flanks, prevent them from linking together, preserve the gap through which the Pontic infantry were now pouring. . . .

As the horsemen wheeled to form up, the torrential rain and steaming animals hindered their view, and in the confusion they were suddenly hit, blindsided by a crushing force, a collision that seemed to come from nowhere, from the sky itself, perhaps. I saw it coming only moments before it occurred, but from our distance we were powerless to warn the riders. For in the scrubby forest just at the edge of the plain where the Pontic horsemen had wheeled after their charge and were now reassembling, a Roman cavalry squadron had been watching and waiting for its opportunity. This band, led by Sulla himself, from the appearance of the long crimson mantle and the high horsehair crest on his helmet, this band of a mere one thousand horse, slammed into our distracted and breathless cavalry with a deadly charge that stunned our riders and left their horses panicked and reeling. I was stupefied—the Roman horse had physically collided with our close-packed cavalry, and now all around the ground was a writhing tangle of kicking horses and bellowing officers, all knees and elbows and wildly flailing hooves, as the animals struggled to rise from the quagmire of mud and blood. The Roman horse had simply run them over. It was foolhardy, even suicidal, for dozens of Roman horse and their riders lay where they had fallen. Those not too stunned to continue leaped up and struggled back to their rear lines or drew swords and fought with those whom they had toppled, making the most of their foray into the midst of our lines before they themselves were cut down.

The Roman cavalry charge was hopeless if the intent had been to rout our own cavalry forces; within moments the survivors of Sulla's brigade had remounted and fled back through the lines and into the woods whence they had just appeared a moment before. The charge was mad, completely uncharacteristic of Roman tactics and methods. But with uncanny precision Sulla had accomplished precisely his goal—delaying the second charge of our cavalry forces until his own flanks could regroup and fill the gap in the center.

With that delay he had forced upon us, our victory, our culminating victory over the Roman legions, faded before my very eyes. Our phalanx had charged into the middle of the breach, but the breach turned to a noose as the Romans, rather than fleeing in terror from the conquerors in their midst as the Bithynians had done, rushed back in. Their own flanks compressed and became denser, like some living thing, like a python digesting a hare, as they surrounded our charging phalanx on all its sides. The battle was no longer a commanded one—now all was madness and chaos as the phalanx disintegrated. The men on the right sought to defend their flank from the Romans methodically attacking them there; the men on the left did the same. The front and the rear were blocked, as the overlapping Roman forces moved to sever our army's contact with its leaders, surrounding the charging Pontic infantry on all sides.

Bewildered, the Pontic phalanx skidded to a stop, and with all hope of re-formation lost, with all hope gone of finding shelter under the shield of one's neighbor, the response Sulla had sought was fulfilled—the phalanx was destroyed, its cohesiveness and unity eliminated. The men were now nothing more than a mob fighting for their lives. Formation no longer existed, only individual soldiers; unity had been eliminated, the phalanx scattered beneath a writhing, battling sea of crimson, the crimson of blood and that of the Roman tunics. It was uncontrolled fury, each man fighting for himself and for his own survival and escape.

Against five intact Roman legions.

Of the hundred twenty thousand Pontic warriors thrown into battle that freezing and fearsome day, a mere ten thousand escaped, including Father and myself. All others perished, their bodies never recovered, their remains stripped of armor and then burned by the legions in a great, crackling holocaust the next day. When it became clear, late that black afternoon, that all was lost to us at the battle of Chaeronea, Father and his generals mounted their horses, and, with the ten thousand infantry that had been held in reserve, marched determinedly down the sodden, rolling slopes to the sea, where the naval armada had anchored just offshore. Ostensibly it had been positioned there to receive from us the Roman prisoners we had expected to capture, and the sailors were astonished to see naught but a bedraggled and heartsick king and the pitiful remnants of the Pontic army floating up to the fleet in rafts, skiffs, and landing craft from the beach. Some of the troops even swam wearily out to the armada on logs, so desperate were they to escape the storm-swept beach and the hellish slaughter of the battle in the hills behind them.

An entire army lost, to a force one-fourth its size. It was a terrible defeat, one that haunted me for years, with visions of Father's pale, silent face as he stood on the flagship watching the receding Boeotian shore while the armada sailed to its base at Chaeris, a short distance across the strait. The driving rain ran down his face, obscuring and mingling with the tears that coursed down his cheeks. His silent weeping added to that of the men who had escaped the terrible carnage with us. The salty tears of ten thousand men flowed into the sea and became one with the sea, and Poseidon in turn yielded his to the men as the salt spray crashed over our bows. All mourned the loss of a great army. It was a short voyage, scarcely long enough to secure our anchor before it was dropped again in the harbor of Chaeris, but the longest day in Father's life.

The Romans were said to have lost thirteen men, but this estimate was not generally believed. I myself saw many more than that killed in the cavalry charges, though in the end, the number of Roman lives lost was of no concern.

Our own losses, however, were incalculable.

4

After a sorrowful return to Pergamum on a pirate cutter, leaving the remainder of the armada and the army's survivors to over-winter in Chaeris, Father did what he had to do to compensate for the enormous loss in men and treasure. He raised taxes throughout the empire, to his subjects' dismay, and the following year levied an additional eighty thousand infantry and ten thousand horse troops, which he sent to Archelaus. But if the first army had been destroyed so effectively by a force barely a quarter its size, the situation facing this new army was infinitely worse, for the new recruits had been only hastily trained and equipped, though they were still the best armed and appointed soldiers in all of Asia. Still, only the cavalry could be relied upon—they consisted entirely of Pontic nobles from the interior mountain clans, the sons of men who had sheltered Father during the years he had spent among their mountain strongholds. They were the best cavalry in the world and utterly loyal to their king.

The outcome of this second phase of the war would have to be decisive: Against all odds, Lucullus, the general whom Sulla had sent by ship to penetrate the Pontic blockade during the siege of Athens, had reappeared recently, with a large fleet of warships he had hired from Syria, using funds he had demanded from the Egyptian royal house. He broke our blockade of Rhodes and wreaked havoc among the Greek islands, forcing their allegiance back to Rome. Precious little of the sea empire Father had acquired two years before still remained.

In response, Archelaus took the initiative by forcing battle on the Romans, this time at Orchomenus, only a few miles from our earlier defeat. This time his position was well prepared—his troops dug in behind barricades and backed by a vast swamp fed by the River Melas, the only river in Greece navigable to its source. The site was carefully chosen facing a broad, treeless plain, ideal for the sweeping movements of the crack Pontic cavalry against the largely unhorsed Roman army.

By the end of the day, the Pontic army had been utterly destroyed.

Archelaus himself came up missing in the head count afterwards, though he was later found floating in the marsh, lost but alive, in a small boat. His son Diogenes, a junior cavalry officer, was dead. Out of the one hundred eighty thousand men Father had sent to Greece, only a few shocked stragglers ever made it back to their homeland alive. There was now no Pontic army, in Asia or Europe.

Sulla could have chased Father to the ends of the world at that point, had he been so inclined. Indeed, on the day news of this second defeat reached Pergamum, half the city fled into the hills, certain that the wrath of Rome would soon be visited upon them. Sulla, however, had been away from Rome for over two years, and the civil war he had left behind was growing bloodier by the day. His wife, Metella, had recently escaped Rome with their children and caught up with her husband in the midst of his campaign, bringing news that his town houses and rural estates had been destroyed and pleading with him to return to protect what was left of their assets. Scores of his followers were killed by rampaging Populares—indeed, that party had even sent out its own army to win its share of loot in the war against Mithridates. Sulla, therefore, resolved to return home quickly and restore an Optimates government at Rome before all he had fought for was lost.

Thus it was an internal struggle between two Roman political parties that saved us in the end, compelling Sulla to seek terms with Father sooner rather than later and to forgo an all-out thrust to destroy Pontus. Marching his troops slowly and deliberately east, Sulla forced the allegiance of the cities through which he passed, crossed the Bosphorus unimpeded, and sent word to all the territories of Asia: the Dream was over, New Greece destroyed—Rome had returned.

That month, Sulla ordered Father to meet him at the ancient ruined city of Dardanus, south of the burning hulk that had once been Troy. There he would negotiate the final terms of the Pontic surrender.

Yet Father refused to bow in defeat. Determined to demonstrate he was still a ruler worthy of respect, he arrived for the council at the head of two hundred sail of ships, his surviving twenty-thousand-man garrison, six thousand cavalry who had joined him from Pontus, and sixty scythe chariots. I joined him, wearing unwieldy ceremonial finery, in company with Bituitus, still shaven-jawed from his stint as the King's double, and a number of Father's advisors and generals. Before being allowed to accompany him, however, I had to prove to Father my usefulness, and this I did by demonstrating my growing knowledge of Latin. Indeed, I had studied the language all that past winter and spring, to the detriment of mathematics and other subjects, for I had taken Father's earlier advice to heart: I knew now who my enemy was, and it was not Euclid or Pythagoras. The language was simple and straightforward, much like the Romans themselves, I was to learn later, with all the strength and logic of the Greeks, whom they so emulated, but lacking in their beauty and poetry.

Sulla arrived in slow and stately procession, with a tiny force of a mere four cohorts and two hundred horsemen, scarcely more than a personal bodyguard. The man was perhaps fifty years old, large and fleshy, his body hinting at the strength and athleticism it had once possessed, which was now submerged beneath the fats and oils of his later life's dissipation. The skin of his face was florid and coppery, with eruptions of peeling blemishes and inflamed pustules on his cheeks and chin and with veiny streaks running across his nose and echoed in his bloodshot eyes, like those of one who starts his day with a flagon of wine for breakfast. His most extraordinary feature, however, was the color of his hair, which, though limp and greasy, still showed a pale pinkish-yellow—something few men from our parts of the world have seen, other than among the occasional Scythian mercenary. We had been informed that the general was uncommonly proud of this almost preternatural hair—he believed it to be a singular gift, a sign of favor from the gods.

Thus, piss-haired, red-faced Sulla arrived at the table virtually unprotected, sweating, grunting, and gout-ridden, but armed with the confidence that accrues only to victors—and shades of Popilius' encounter with Antiochus IV three generations earlier came to mind. I watched Father's weary face and clenched jaw as he observed the insultingly tiny Roman detachment, and I knew he was thinking precisely the same thing.

Sulla stood before us and for a moment his gaze flickered back and forth between Father and Bituitus in irritation. Obviously Sulla had been told Mithridates was a man of imposing stature, with light skin and brown hair, but here he had before him two such giants. Bituitus' ruse in Pergamum had never been discovered, and the Romans were unaware of the similarities between the two men. Quickly grasping the situation, Father stepped forward, and in a gesture of grudging chivalry, he extended his hand to grip Sulla's arm and help the obviously unfit general into his seat. The Roman shook him off with a disdainful shrug and set his large haunches heavily down onto the cushioned chair. The two men stared at each other coldly for a moment as Archelaus, who had undertaken the preliminary negotiations and arranged the details of the meeting, made the formal introduction. Oddly, Archelaus acted almost deferential to Sulla—standing close by his side, referring to him as "my lord," and lowering his voice when speaking to him. In annoyance, Father waved his general off and turned back to his adversary, though remaining silent.

Sulla stared at him a moment longer, eyes as cold and lifeless as a herring's, then coughed impatiently into his red, meaty fist.

"I find it strange you remain wordless before me," he said. "By custom, it is for the suitors to speak first and for conquerors to hold their peace, to hear what they have to say. I take it you accept the terms of the agreement negotiated by your general Archelaus?"

Father, however, was not one to satisfy his adversary with groveling.

"*Ecce vir fortis*," he growled to Sulla in fluent Latin. "It takes a brave man to approach with such a small guard in support. I could, if I wished, order my own troops to attack this very moment, and then there would be little left of the vaunted General Sulla."

Sulla's piercing blue eyes remained cold and expressionless, not flickering for a moment from the lock they held on Father's gaze. The face was soft, the hands thick and stubby-fingered, the eyes piggish and grasping—but behind the layer of pudgy flesh was a will of iron and a calculating mind, and I knew Father had met his equal.

When Sulla spoke, his voice was as equally low and menacing as Father's.

"And if your garrison troops fight as did their compatriots at Chaeronea, King, then my own meager guard has little to fear. Except, perhaps, needlessly dulling their blades on your men's skulls."

"You defeated me in a minor battle. Yet you have no supply lines. Your home city does not even support you—"

"Quit the posturing," Sulla interrupted, clearly impatient to terminate a negotiation he felt he had already settled long before, through Archelaus. "You are in no position to do anything but plead for your life."

Father stiffened and the courtiers behind him recoiled.

"You forget yourself, General," he replied. "I am a king, to the tenth generation and beyond, to a time when Rome was nothing more than a shepherd's village. . . ."

Sulla fixed him silently for a moment and then made an extraordinary gesture. Standing up laboriously, pulling his shoulders back, and lifting his body to its full height, he raised his right fist into the air, above his head. Immediately the two thousand troops behind him spread their feet into a fighting stance, raised their shields in front of their bodies to the "attack" position, and drew their swords. The sound of the steel of two thousand blades sliding simultaneously on scabbard leather was swift and sharp, as menacing as the dead silence that then fell over our entire company as they contemplated the threat implied by the legionaries' action.

"On the contrary," Sulla continued quietly, his pale blue eyes fixed unwavering on Father's face, the irises completely filling the orbits so as to obscure the whites, for all the world like the lapis inserts in a marble bust. "On the contrary, I have not at all forgotten, though I have, indeed, been disappointed. As a king, you should be better versed in the ways of your conquerors, rather than wasting our time with heavy-handed bluffing."

Father exploded, reaching for the dagger at his hip before his arm was seized by Bituitus and Archelaus standing behind him. His face flushed crimson as he struggled against them, and Bituitus' knuckles turned white in his effort to hold back the King, the missing finger of his right hand standing out starkly against Father's purple cloak. Suddenly, with a shudder, Father gained control of his rage, and glaring at Sulla, he snorted in disdain and dropped his guard. Bituitus and Archelaus cautiously released their grip. During the entire outburst Sulla had stood motionless and unperturbed, observing the scene dispassionately, with a kind of clinical interest—the interest of a captor toying with his captive.

"So you think I'm bluffing?" Father spat.

Sulla ignored the question or, worse, dismissed it. "I recognize you are a king, but that is of no consequence. Kings are of use to me only to the extent they maintain peace within the confines of their realms. As you have now discovered, Rome is powerful, though unfortunately not particularly populous. We cannot afford to garrison every little mud brick town on the borders of our empire. That is the duty of the local kinglets and satraps. That is *your* duty."

He spun on his heel, turning his back on Father, who stared at him in rage as Bituitus again poised to seize his arm. Before reaching his own troops, however, Sulla stopped and turned slowly back to Father, as if in thought. Their eyes met again once more, the last time they would do so.

"There are precious few other reasons to keep you alive at all," the Roman said.

The terms Sulla imposed were crushing. Father must give up all his new territories—all the Greek islands and mainland, as well as Paphlagonia, Bithynia, and Cappadocia. He must transfer his entire fleet to Roman possession. And he must pay the enormous sum of two thousand talents from his personal wealth, which Sulla happily added to the treasure of Delphi he had plundered to finance his siege of Athens and Piraeus. Further, Sulla beggared the entire continent of Asia, condemning it to pay an additional twenty thousand talents, equivalent to its entire export production for two decades, an impossible sum to be wrung from the broken and impoverished inhabitants. The Roman army occupied the wealthy and urbane cities of Greek Asia and the troops lived as princes while the defeated populace existed as starving dogs. Sulla not only ordered common soldiers to be quartered in the very homes of Pergamum's inhabitants but also required the householders themselves to pay each Roman wages of sixteen drachmae per day, forty times a soldier's ordinary compensation, plus meals for them and any guests they might invite, regardless of number. A centurion was entitled to *fifty* drachmae per day and two sets of clothing, one for indoors and one for out. The payments were ruinous, and no date was set for them to be lifted.

Only Rhodes was spared the crushing penalty, and the pirates, of course, simply avoided paying anything at all—one intrepid fleet of them actually stole a thousand talents of gold back from under Sulla's very nose in Samothrace, while he was in that province visiting its shrines on his return to Italy. Perhaps the otherwise alert Roman had been distracted, for it is said that when he arrived in Macedonia, intending to voyage from there to the Italian peninsula with his twelve hundred sail, he was accosted by a number of frantic men. There is a park in the region of Dyrrachium consecrated to the nymphs, where in a peaceful green meadow a satyr had supposedly been taken sleeping. The creature was shackled in a cage and brought to Sulla, and when asked by interpreters what he was, he made no answer that any man could understand but only emitted sharp noises like the neighing of a horse or the bleating of a goat. Sulla, it is said, wondered at the satyr, abhorred him, and then ordered him to be destroyed as a monstrous thing—a clear demonstration, if ever one was needed, of the Roman mind's lack of depth and inquisitiveness. Sulla eventually returned to Rome as the recipient of a glorious Triumph—a wealthy man, a victorious general, and perhaps the most wicked ruler that city had ever seen.

To Father's fury, he was never able to avenge himself on Sulla, for the Fates wreaked their own work on the Roman first. His years of decadence ended by corrupting his flesh, raising a purulent abscess on his abdomen, which even the best doctors were unable to diagnose. Upon finally being broken open, the enormous pustule was found to be crawling with maggots of a kind hitherto unknown to medical science. As quickly as the learned physicians attempted to wipe them away, they continued to multiply inside the man's gut. There were no garments, baths, or even food in his vicinity that were not soon filled with swarms of this vermin, such that only his most loyal retainers even dared to remain near him, for fear of themselves becoming infected. Some said it was a vile disease contracted from Mithridates' poisons and thus by stealth did Father obtain the victory over Sulla that his own troops had been unable to achieve. But this was a lie, for no such maggots have ever existed in our domains, nor were Father's poisons ever employed to such purpose.

At Sulla's funeral, Roman ladies bestowed on his pyre such a huge quantity of solid perfumes and other odoriferous resins that a famous sculptor was engaged to mold them into a great image of Sulla himself. When the blaze was finally set, even the suffocating smoke from the melting of this pile was insufficient to mask the stench of the man's worm-eaten body.

Thus ended the struggle the Romans would call the First Mithridatic War. An entire Pontic army had been destroyed, with the death of close to two hundred thousand men. If the massacres at Delos and elsewhere were counted, along with Sulla's butcheries as he passed through the enemy countryside, the tally of lives lost would doubtless total more than half a million. As for the material damage—villages razed, farmland ravaged, temples burned, works of art destroyed—Father's accountants finally gave up even trying to approximate the losses. Equally disastrous was the region's moral collapse: social ties had been severed, satraps overthrown, slaves released, merchants bankrupted, poverty and misery more firmly entrenched than ever. The region was a ruin.

Yet for all the death and destruction Rome had wrought, it had not succeeded in destroying Father's ambitions. For though he had failed in his attempt to unify all the Hellenistic lands under his rule, he had awakened passions—all the latent hatred for Rome, the ancient pride of Greek culture and heritage, memories of times long past, and hopes for a better future, a future free of Rome's hob-nailed military boot. Father returned to our

old home at Sinope, to ponder his mistakes and consider the
strengths of the Roman legions he had faced. He was defeated,
and his kingdom was now the smallest and most fragile it had
been in years. He could almost feel the ghosts of his father and
of his ancestors berating him, for the weakness and decadence
he had exhibited over the past two years, for the marvelous opportunities he had squandered.

His first task at Sinope was to bid a cordial yet tearless
farewell to Monime, whom he sent—for her own protection, of
course—to a secure fortress in Pharnacia, on the eastern edge
of the Black Sea. At this she complained bitterly, deploring her
wasted beauty and ill fortune, bemoaning the Fates who, instead of a loving husband, had given her a heartless master,
who instead of ladies-in-waiting had given her guards and garrisons, a stark stronghold far from her sweet homeland, and
only the dreams and shadows of the possessions she had expected and deserved. . . . I shut my ears to her rantings, as did
Father.

His second task was to prepare—for the next war.

BOOK FIVE

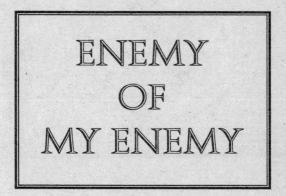

ENEMY
OF
MY ENEMY

Blow lies upon blow, and evil upon evil . . .

—The Pythia of Delphi

1

"The days of the phalanx are gone, my liege. A mass of men fighting in a block can never stand up to the Roman legions."

"By the gods, Neoptolemus—do you never quit?"

"No, my lord. Quit what?"

Father dropped the field reports he had been reading and rubbed his eyes in weariness. Six years had passed since that golden summer when he had conquered Asia and Rome's generals so effortlessly, when for a brief moment he had stood as a colossus, as King of the Greeks and of all their ancient domains. Six years, during which he had aged and smoldered in anger, while I had grown to manhood and been assigned to the cavalry. For me, the future looked bright and exciting. For Father, however, the past years had been the worst of his life.

"Quit calling me 'my liege,' 'my lord,' 'chief ball buster,' and all the other flatulent platitudes my advisors dream up for me," he said to Neoptolemus. "We've known each other almost forty years now, man—we're not exactly young anymore. I don't give a boar's ass what you call me in public; that's for the eunuchs and priests to come up with when I'm in court, and I haven't been in court for months. When we're sitting here alone, trying to make sense of these quartermasters' reports and recruitment figures, call me by my rightful name and get down to business."

Father's demand was trivial, of course, but it reflected a much larger problem he had been searching to overcome. Ever since the disastrous losses to Sulla at Chaeronea, he had recognized that the old ways, the old methods, the old titles, could not hold. Of course Athens was only a vestige of her former self in military terms—no one would have been foolish enough to rely on her manpower. Still, until Chaeronea, he had thought that at least the old knowledge Athens had developed was universal, that it would hold true: that the phalanx was invincible, that control of the sea lanes would lead to victory, that massive cavalry charges could not be withstood, that courting the favor of the ancient Greek deities would tip the balance our way, that pure, unmitigated "Greekness"—with a dash of Persian aristocracy and Asian wiliness thrown in for seasoning—would win the day, over the coldness and brutality of Rome.

Yet the Romans had proven all of these ancient tenets wrong. But how? What advantage did these western barbarians have over the proven strengths of Greece and Pontus?

For six years Father had known he must defend against the Roman attack certain to come in revenge for the Night of the Vespers. To address this, he had installed Machares as king of the Pontic province of Bosporus, on the northern coast of the Black Sea. This afforded us a permanent source of mercenaries, as Machares' primary task was to recruit troops from among the Scythian tribes in that region. It also afforded him ample time to pursue his studies in that quiet little kingdom without pressure to accompany Father on military campaign.

Father mustered the raw soldiers Machares sent at a remote mountain valley he called Camp of Ares, two days' ride south of Sinope, far from the prying eyes of Roman spies and informers. For six years he told his generals to train the incoming Scythians like Romans, as best they knew to do from the knowledge imparted by the occasional Roman deserter who joined our forces. It was the greatest irony—to defeat the Romans, we must become *like* the Romans, at least in warfare, and Father hoped it would be limited to that. Yet for six years the generals had stubbornly continued to train the new recruits in the courageous but witless phalanx formation, backed by useless scythe chariots and heavy cavalry. Tradition and hidebound culture—the *old ways*—had been to blame for our disastrous defeat six years ago. Tradition would have to be thrown out the window.

And now, an additional complication had set in. Six months before, on a cold winter morning when he had called for his morning briefing, he found that Archelaus had bolted. Bolted! Our top general, designer of all the Pontic military strategies, chief negotiator of the Peace of Dardanus, and Father's closest confidant! The man I thought of as a second father, an uncle— Archelaus had slipped away in the night, traveled to Pergamum, and sought asylum from the Romans, before continuing on to the vast estate outside Athens that he had secretly been gifted by Sulla himself!

The defection had devasted Neoptolemus, and shaken Father to the core. Clearly Archelaus, the consummate soldier, felt that there was no more to be gained by fighting for us—that Rome was the future and that remaining with vanquished Pontus was to continue to scourge a dead ox. Such reasoning Father could not understand for the life of him.

"I would fight the Romans if I were the *only* man left in Pontus!" he raged. "Archelaus is wrong! Wrong that our forces cannot stand up to them, wrong that power means right. The traitor! You don't fight for the *strongest* side; you fight for the *right* side! Otherwise you are nothing more than a mercenary!"

"Archelaus *is* a mercenary!" I pointed out. "He always has been. He served you for years, but now we see him for what he truly is—not a Pontic patriot but a mercenary—and he has done what mercenaries do: sold himself to the highest bidder. Could you have expected otherwise?"

"Did he have no honor, no loyalty, no faithfulness to a friend?"

"He did for as long as the money lasted. Sulla offered him more, a fine estate and a wealthy retirement under a victorious government. Leave him, Father; he's not needed."

For weeks Father raged at this loss of his close friend and of all his secrets to the enemy. And the enemy wasted no time using this knowledge. Rome had recently appointed Lucius Licinius Murena as governor of Asia, tasked with keeping a close eye on us and ensuring compliance with the Peace of Dardanus. Murena was a Roman general who had helped defeat the Pontic forces at Chaeronea and whose success in that battle had led to a series of rapid promotions. Now, for the first time in his career, this man had an independent command—he was no longer under a master like Sulla, and therefore credit for any victories he won would accrue to him alone. Only one thing stood in Murena's way; one pesky little detail stopped him from toppling the King of Pontus in a great war: That buggered Peace of Dardanus, which prevented any new war from being started in the first place. Murena seethed at this treaty, which he claimed "did nothing but protect a rogue king and his lawless hordes." With a lawyer's eye to cutting his losses and maximizing his gains, Murena simply chose to ignore it.

Father had fulfilled his end of the bargain—given up his fleet, restored all the territory he had conquered, and paid the devastating tribute. But the faithless Romans did not keep theirs. That summer, Murena led his Cilician legions deep inland, over the Cappadocian mountains, and into the valley of the upper Lycus River—undisputed Pontic territory. There he plundered towns, killed livestock, and murdered and enslaved thousands of men. Worst of all, he pillaged the holy temple at Conama with its six thousand temple servants dedicated to the ancient goddess Ma. The people of Conama led peaceful lives, with fine vineyards and estates funded by income from the sacred temple prostitution. We could not even imagine the sacrilegious plundering of such a holy site.

The blow to Pontus was staggering, and Father was completely taken by surprise. Rome had not marched a huge lumbering army overland from Italy and across the Bosphorus. Nor had it sent a massive fleet laden with legionaries. Either one of these would have allowed him ample time to receive intelligence, evacuate cities, raise defenses, and deploy troops. But this—a mere three Roman legions, striking through the back door at his undefended border with Cappadocia—this he had not anticipated. He had no army or horse available in the area, had made no military preparations, and as he scrambled to send letters of protest, Murena withdrew all his forces back to Cilicia as suddenly as he had led them out. Days later, the ambassadors Father had sent to Murena returned, shaking their heads in disbelief.

"What did he say?" Father demanded, not even bothering to clear the room of courtiers.

"Murena replies," said the herald, "that he can find no proof of the existence of the so-called 'Treaty of Dardanus,' as it had never been ratified by the Roman Senate."

Father's jaw dropped. "Of course it hadn't been ratified!" he bellowed. "When we negotiated it with Sulla the Senate was controlled by the Populares—Sulla was an enemy of the Roman people! But Sulla signed it! By my bloody dagger, that treaty is the grounds for Murena's governorship in the first place!"

The envoy merely shrugged.

Shortly afterwards Murena struck again, this time from the southwest across the lower Halys River. With this attack, Papias saw omens, for it was this same river about which ancient King Croesus had been famously advised by the oracle of Delphi: namely, that if he crossed it to attack the Persians, he would destroy a great kingdom—which turned out to be his own. Unfortunately, it was not clear to us from the signs whether our own fate was to follow that of Croesus or the victorious Persians. The Romans, however, suffered no such doubts. Murena plundered four hundred villages in his lightning rampage—and then withdrew back into Roman territory before Sinope had even received news of it.

Father was in an excruciating position now. He had only just managed to escape his first war against Rome with his hereditary dominions still undiminished and his subjects' loyalty intact. A ruler's primary claim to power is his personal authority; if he is unable to protect his thralls, then a new protector will be found, and word was already filtering in of restlessness among the nobles, who were mortified at the Roman incursions and the King's lack of response. In their eyes, Mithridates was wringing his hands and cowering in terror, or at least so Father imagined they were thinking, because that is how he himself would have thought had he been in their places. Like Archelaus, they began to think Pontus had no future as a kingdom or Father as king.

In response, Father departed suddenly into the hinterland, on such short notice that he alarmed the palace staff in Sinope. The only advance warning we received was the arrival of a mysterious messenger, a Pontic courier who had been sent out from the palace weeks before on what at the time I assumed was a routine delivery of correspondence and who upon his return declared that he bore important tidings from Spain. After Father heard the news from this courier, he called immediately for his horse, shrugged off questioning eunuchs, and thundered into the hills, taking only Bituitus and a corps of veteran cavalry. Neoptolemus and I stayed behind a few days more, to organize the departure of the city garrison and arrange for the shipment of supplies. Fearful of this sudden flurry of activity, the courtiers looked to me for answers.

"Prince Pharnaces!" demanded the palace administrator, Prophilus, a competent Ephesian eunuch. "Where has the King gone? He can't attack Murena with these meager forces! Go at once and talk some sense into him."

I began to berate him for overstepping his authority but stopped when I saw his clear worry.

"The King will be gone for some time," I answered. "Continue your duties in the meantime, and calm the palace staff. Panic here will only sow fear among the city residents."

"The city is already terrified," he replied. "Murena has ravaged the interior, and now the King has departed into the mountains with a token force. What are the people to think? How am I to explain?"

"Tell them," I said, "that he has gone into the mountains to create the only weapon that can stand up to the Roman legions and that it will take much time."

Prophilus looked at me skeptically. "And what is this famous weapon that can stand up to the Roman legions?"

I had no more time or patience to discuss the matter, and I mounted my horse, preparing to lead out the garrison.

"I ask you again," Prophilus persisted. "What weapon can stand up to Roman legions?"

As I trotted away, I turned and shot back the answer over my shoulder.

"His own Roman legions."

The courier's message had come from Spain, a thousand miles to the west, where Apollo's horses dip their hooves each evening into the sea. There a renegade Roman general named Sertorius had several years earlier declared his allegiance to the Populares, thereby making him an enemy of the Senate's new ruling party. Over time, his movement had gained in strength and in numbers of followers, and he now posed a genuine threat to Rome's security. Fully half of Rome's armed forces, led by a young general named Gnaeus Pompeius Magnus, was occupied in flushing him out, with most of Rome's remaining troops engaged in putting down civil revolts on the Italian peninsula. Combined with the tension from Pontus, the danger to Rome was palpable.

It was only a matter of time before Sertorius and Father reached an agreement.

Late one night, two weeks after we had arrived at Camp of Ares, Father was interrupted by a call at the flap of his camp tent, followed by a grunted password in Bituitus' voice. I set down the vials and flasks with which I was mixing Father's nighttime draught of antidote and looked to the door in curiosity. Few men would dare interrupt the King's private time—Bituitus was one of them, of course, but he knew well to do so only in matters of great importance.

The Gaul was standing just outside the door, but before he could murmur a word to the King, a stranger stepped into the room. He was short and stocky, wearing a stained woolen cloak with a frayed hood draped over his head and tattered sandals on his feet, looking for all the world like a peasant farmer. But though dressed in such rough, patched garb, he was clearly no poor man or slave. There was nothing humble about his demeanor, for he strode into the room as if he owned it, shoulders thrown back and head erect, though it was still impossible to see his face under the hood. Bituitus momentarily froze at the stranger's audacity. He made a halfhearted attempt to seize him but then stopped as Father held up his hand. The Gaul's dismayed glance flitted between the King and the strange peasant; then shrugging his shoulders he stepped into the room and stood at attention beside his ruler, glaring down at the man imperiously. The "peasant," far from being intimidated by the bulk and the cold stares of his two hosts, drew himself up to his full height and stared back.

"Greetings from Sertorius," he said in a low, even tone. His Latin was effortless and cultured, and his voice had an almost menacing rasp. He shrugged off his hood, showing the hard, tanned face of a man of perhaps forty, with several days' growth of beard and an unruly shock of flaming red hair. One eyeball was white and shriveled, though he did not hide it behind a patch as the half-blind often do. He faced Father squarely, showing not a trace of humility or fear.

Father stared at him for a moment, expressionless, then calmly walked over and picked up the goblet I had prepared, swilling the contents and grimacing slightly at the taste. In all the years I had poured his draughts for him, I was always amazed to watch him swallow quantities of poisons that would have staggered a warhorse, yet rarely did his face register more than a small wince. Setting the vessel down, he turned to Bituitus.

"I dislike this man already."

The stranger stiffened. "I was not aware my assignment required currying your affection."

Bituitus' eyes widened at this outrageous statement. "Sire," he muttered, "I'll remove him immediately," and he stepped forward to seize the scoundrel.

Father stopped him, however, and eyed the man curiously. "I'll grant he's a prick. That's to be expected—he's Roman. But let's not be too hasty in discarding Sertorius' gifts."

I now realized who the man was, and I protested. "Father, Sertorius agreed to send you a general, his top field marshal, to assist you in building an army. Not a tribune or a *primipilus,* not a centurion, not a mule driver, and certainly not this ape."

Without waiting for a reply, the visitor spoke up.

"Your rudeness is unbounded, young man, though perhaps it is my fault for not properly introducing myself. My name is Marcus Marius. *General* Marcus Marius, second-in-command to Emperor Sertorius, leader of the land forces of Lusitania and Farther Spain, Senator of Rome, and nephew to General Gaius Marius, the scourge of the Gauls. At your service."

With that he unhooked the loop on his rough peasant tunic and cast the frayed garment aside, revealing the scarlet tunic, leather belt, and mailed breastplate of . . . a Roman centurion.

Father nodded grimly and with some distaste, though I was not sure whether this was due to Marius' behavior or to the lingering flavor of the concoction he had just swallowed. "So. Sertorius came through," he said. "Why do you arrive in the dead of night, dressed like a common centurion disguised as a common peasant?"

Marius glared at him haughtily.

"I am a Roman first, a Popular second, and then a senator. I have nothing but disdain for the Optimates and their petty disputes, their finger bowls and their eunuchs. I always dress like a soldier. I eat like a soldier, I march like a soldier, and by the gods I fight like a soldier—a Roman soldier. I would never ask my men to do something I myself am not prepared to do. And I do it better."

"How gallant," Bituitus muttered. "And the farmer's cloak?"

Marius looked at him pityingly. "A Gaul, are you? I can tell from the defective accent. I just came from Gaul. Odd that one of your tribe should complain about shoddy clothing."

Bituitus tensed, but the Roman ignored him and addressed Father. "Your troops have a nasty habit of killing every Roman citizen on sight. I'm not sure how you expected my men and me to ride from Spain, through Roman lines, and into the gates of your camp—wearing scarlet cloaks and helmet crests?"

My blood boiled, but Father shot me a glance that commanded silence.

"You said you are a Popular . . ." Father continued, trying to draw the man into a more fruitful line of discussion.

Marius was just opening his mouth to respond when Bituitus interrupted, something he rarely did. The insult he had suffered a moment before had already passed over, and now the rusty mechanism of his brain was again grinding slowly. "A Popular?" he exclaimed. "Just like the other Roman exiles in our army. And some of Lucullus' legions are Populares, too." He eyed the Roman with wary puzzlement. "Why would his legions fight us if they knew our Romans were of the same party?"

Marius glanced at him disdainfully, as Father answered the question for him. "That is exactly the idea, Bituitus," he said gently. "That's why Sertorius sent us a Popular senator. With luck, Lucullus' legions will still have memories of their old loyalties in Rome."

Bituitus nodded in satisfaction.

"Your men," Father said questioningly. "How many did you bring?"

"Fifty," Marius replied. "Forty centurions and the remainder tribunes of cohort. Sertorius could spare no more."

Father nodded, but I could not contain my impatience. "Fifty Romans! *Fifty?*" I insisted. "What good will fifty Romans do us? All their fighting strength combined is not worth a single one of the insults we have suffered tonight from this lout!"

Father stared hard at the little man, who stood motionless. "Perhaps not. We shall see. But these men are not here to fight, Pharnaces."

Marius snorted. "Oh, we'll fight. But you're right. That's not why we're here."

With a smile, Father finished the idea for him.

"Marius and his men will build the greatest army Rome has ever faced."

In changing the Pontic philosophy of war, Father found it was not enough merely to order his generals to train their armies in the new method. Innovation meets resistance from stubborn veterans who see no reason to change their old ways. Unless the supreme commander himself believes in the new method and forces its implementation, then in times of panic or stress, just when the new techniques are most needed, all will revert to the old. To force the implementation, we needed Romans.

Their job was to complete the Romanization of the Pontic army that Father had begun. What they found was a huge number of ill-trained recruits from a dozen nations, all with their disparate weapons and skills, varying degrees of battle experience, and a diversity of goals, ranging from plunder and wealth, to simple glory, to, in the case of one tribe of northern Iberians, the collection of enemy scalps. Marius informed us from the start that it would be nearly impossible to fashion a cohesive army from this motley collection of thickheaded Scythians and stubborn Pontic Persians. Father did not despair, however, for by a stroke of inspiration he discovered his secret weapon: Roman soldiers themselves.

From his long acquaintance with the pirates, Father knew their fleet was full of Roman deserters, many of them battle-tested veterans and officers, suffering no other defect than of having insulted their commander, or killed a comrade in a drunken quarrel, or had some other petty difficulty that had forced them to flee the legions. In so doing, they had fallen in with the Cilician pirates, who had taught them a new way to make a living. A life of marauding by sea, though a waste of their talents and hard-won skills, was often the only opportunity available to displaced legionaires. Until now.

Soon after Father raised the idea, I took a half-dozen company commanders back to the coastal cities of Sinope and Amisus, where we haunted the waterfront taverns and brothels, listened to accents, and picked out Latin speakers. We cajoled and bribed and begged information from sailors on the whereabouts of any former Roman soldiers, paying them rewards if they assisted us. Our method was successful. Romans are creatures of land, not sea, and Roman legionaries rarely feel at home on a confined ship with a rolling deck beneath their feet. When word of our search spread, we were inundated with recruits, hundreds of them, some of them even pirates from other shores faking execrable Latin accents. Again I was grateful at having learned my enemy's tongue, for I could now speak with my prospects in their own language and choose those most suited to our cause. In the end, our greatest difficulty was limiting ourselves to a manageable number and restraining them on their eager march from the pirate fleet into the dark inland mountains where the Pontic army was sweating and training.

Within days, I showed up back at camp with two hundred of the ugliest, toughest, wiliest, most hard-bitten crew of pidgin-speaking former pirates that had ever set foot on the good gods' blessed earth. Father took one look at them, broke out in roaring laughter, ordered all of them to be scrubbed down, cleaned up, and shaved hairless to rid them of ships' lice, and then, to the astonishment of the aristocratic Pontic nobles who had been the commissioned infantry officers until now, he put his entire infantry into these Romans' hands.

For in accordance with the orders he had given me, every one of those two hundred men, in their days with the legions, had been a Roman centurion. And every one of those centurions, each for his own private reason, bore a death grudge against Rome.

Word of our venture continued to spread, and the stream of exiled Roman legionaries to Pontus continued and grew, to hundreds and then thousands, despite our reputation for being ungracious hosts for Italians. Many of them had even fought against us at Chaeronea and were familiar with Pontic battle tactics. When all was said and done and these Roman exiles consolidated into a single unit under Marius' command, we found to our surprise that we had over six thousand Roman-born, Roman-bred, Roman-trained, and Roman-hardened veterans— a full Roman legion, as perfect a legion as Sulla had ever wielded against us. And it was loyal to no one but Mithridates.

Camp of Ares hummed with excitement. For the first time in years, Father returned to the campaign field, sleeping on the ground, performing morning gymnastics with the men, improvising his antidotes with herbs and other plants Papias scrounged in the forests. As an expert swordsman and bowman, still the best in all of Asia, he himself trained his drill sergeants in the necessary fencing techniques it would take for each man to defend his own plot of ground against an advancing line. Spanish-style short swords like those the Romans used, with sharp tips that could be used to both slash and jab, were issued to every man, to replace the traditional yet clumsy Asiatic scimitars or blunt-ended blades most men were accustomed to using.

Father himself strode through the lines of sweating, grunting recruits, encouraging their successes, whacking shirkers on the shoulders with the heavy flat of his sword, and sparring with the largest and most accomplished of the lot. As if training gladiators for the ring, he instructed the new recruits in how many steps they should retreat before wheeling to the counterattack; how to feint and draw the enemy in to ambush; how to defend themselves in close quarters, with only the hands and a dagger. He organized the army in the style of the Roman legions—centuries of a hundred, cohorts of six centuries, legions of ten cohorts, using the same maniple-based battle formations as the Romans had developed.

He did not slavishly ape the Romans, however—his eye in battle had seen certain weaknesses of his opponents that he did not wish to replicate among his own forces but rather to take advantage of. The Romans were notoriously shy on cavalry, for example—and the Pontic mountain clansmen were the best cavalry troops in the world. They could be put to excellent use in long-distance scouting, intelligence, and harassment of the Romans' forward and rear detachments. Romans were relatively poor archers, preferring to rely on their infantry with the battle-tested cut-and-thrust; yet the Scythians from the northern steppes were excellent bowmen, able to hit a coin on a post from two hundred paces—they would soften up the Roman lines well, before the Pontic infantry actually closed with their opponent. Father trained like a man possessed, urging the men on, fearing the next incursion by Murena's forces, dreading that Rome might again find him unprepared, this time on home territory, with his personal prestige, his very kingdom, at stake, knowing there would be no room for loss.

More difficult even than fighting, however, was training the men in the *disciplines* of soldiers—for actual fighting is perhaps the smallest part of a soldier's task. The true victor in a war is the side that marches the farthest, on the smallest quantity of biscuit; that digs the deepest entrenchments and builds the highest ramparts; that posts guards that remain alert the entire night through; that anticipates every strength and weakness the enemy might have and counters them with a trump of its own. This was Marius' task, for in these areas Roman armies excel beyond any army in the world.

On his first day, touring the army's encampment, Marius noticed a *conturbernium,* an eight-man squad, diligently digging at fortifications without wearing their sword belts. Marius was appalled, particularly since these Pontic soldiers formed part of a century commanded by one of the exiled Roman centurions, who should have known better. Marius ordered the hapless centurion lashed until half-dead and the squad assigned to two months' ditch duty as punishment for their sorry example. The next day he issued orders to be read by every centurion to his troops, requiring every soldier to be armed at all times.

"The more you sweat now," he wrote menacingly, "the less you'll bleed in battle."

The Pontic troops were outraged—never before had they been required to dig trenches while wearing heavy sword belts, particularly when there was not the remotest threat of an enemy attack. In protest, after the reading of the regulation, the squad that was being punished launched enthusiastically into its next ditch-digging assignment, this time duly wearing their sword belts—and nothing else. Marius, covered with mud from his own entrenching efforts, came striding past the fortification works that afternoon, wondering at the snickering and the sidelong glances being cast his way. Upon encountering the protesting soldiers diligently shoveling in the nude, he stopped, frozen in rage. All chuckles around him fell to silence. The men found, to their great discomfort, that their new commander had no sense of humor. This time, the eight legionaries were executed for insubordination.

Father gritted his teeth in anger when told the tale but refused to take action.

After this, camp discipline improved remarkably, and to the extent Marius was hated and feared by all but the Roman exiles Father was loved all the more, for his smiles and words of praise and his occasional mitigating of Marius' harsh punishments. As Father strode through the camp, men cheered, flocking around him to touch his garments, to hear his greetings in their native tongue. Company champions challenged him to wrestling and fencing matches and considered it an honor when he trounced them and then helped them back up from the ground. He was a god again, a hero among Pontics, Scythians, and Persians alike, every man of whom would readily give his life and stake his honor for Mithridates, for this was history in the making; this was an army such as had not existed since ancient times, one that could challenge even the might of Rome. Marius walked through the camp anonymously, respected by his Roman troops but despised by the rest; nevertheless, he was effective in all he put his hand to, and Father relied on him as he did no man, except perhaps Bituitus and myself. The rogue Roman general and the Pontic king developed a wary symbiotic relationship that benefited from their respective strengths and served them both well.

And in the end, they created the most formidable army in all of Asia.

Zeus Stratios, who marshals the thunder! If in the past I have served thee well among the deathless gods, hear me now. Thou, Olympian Zeus, lord of lightning, enthroned in the clouds: If ever I roofed a shrine to please thy heart, ever burnt the long, rich marrow bones of oxen and goats on thy holy altar, heed now my prayer."

The great canyon below us rang to the echo of Father's fierce cry, and a hundred thousand men stood silent, in wonder and awe at the words he invoked, commanding the great Zeus his attention, Zeus himself, in a form and with a title they had not heard before, *Stratios*, "Leader of Armies." Father stood alone on the edge of the cliff, a mere arm's length from a thousand-foot fall to the foaming, crashing torrent in the gorge far below. The river's distant roar could hardly be heard but only felt, its damp coolness sensed through the skin as the air rose out of the gorge to the hot plain above.

As his terrible invocation to the King of Gods died to an echo, thunder, the thunder of Zeus himself, rolled out of the clear sky from over the gorge, faintly at first, then building in volume and intensity to an explosive roar before culminating with a deafening crash and ceasing as suddenly as it had begun. The men, Mithridates' army, the greatest land force in Asia, recoiled in fear. Father had summoned the god, and the god was listening. The priests with their enormous kettle-shaped drums in the cave below the lip of the cliff were doing their work well.

Father turned to the enormous altar that had been constructed at the cliff's edge. Dry wood had been piled high around it, and the flat stone in the middle had been carefully laid with the quartered body of a huge white bull, which he himself had slaughtered with a curved flint knife a few moments before. He drew his sword, the one he carried at his side at all times, in battle and in ceremony, even in sleep. Many of those present had felt the heavy weight of its flat on their backs if they had shirked their drills, and many others had feared precisely that and had worked all the harder to avoid it. He drew the sword and pointed it first at the altar and then up to the heavens, as this was a sacrifice to the Olympian gods, not to any mere hero or Underworld deity. Again he raised his mighty voice in invocation.

"Hear me, fleet-footed Apollo, god of the silver bow, far-striking archer, thou who strides the walls of Olympus sacrosanct. O distant, deadly bowman, whose arrows pierce the ungodly with their burning flame, attend my prayer; reward my deeds!"

With a cracking explosion that made the front ranks of men fall back in terror upon their comrades behind, the stacked wood at the altar burst into a ball of flame, engulfing carcass and wood and stone all as one, raising a black acrid column of smoke high into the air. The men's eyes opened wide, and they murmured to one another in awe and fear of this ruler, this king whom even the gods obeyed. Sulfur and saltpeter on a pitch fuse were Papias' tools for creating the display, though this did not detract from the gods' might, for sulfur and saltpeter, too, were creations of the gods, as was Papias himself.

Father stood motionless, staring into the heat and brightness of the flames, until the roar of the burning fuel and sizzling flesh had subsided and he was able to step again before the men. At a signal, a hundred officers began shouting to the troops, dividing them quickly and efficiently into two halves, with a broad path separating them, running from the lip of the canyon in the front to the rear of the gathered army. When space had been opened to Father's satisfaction, he nodded and again raised his sword straight into the air. The men froze and fell silent as his voice rang out once more.

"Terrible Ares, fiery God of War, destroyer of men, stormer

of ramparts, reeking of blood: Smite thine enemies with thy death-dealing sword. Let glorious victory be mine!"

A low rumble suddenly arose from the back, at the end of the path. Men on each side of the space instinctively drew back, widening it farther, as the sound resolved into the distinct thunder of hooves. Four Pontic scythe chariots, driverless yet maintaining perfect alignment and formation, careened madly down the path dividing the troops, each drawn by four flawless white chargers, eyes rolling and tongues lolling at their effort. The flashing blades on the rims spun in a transparent blur, humming dangerously close to the men, who shrank away as the carts, two by two, roared up to where Father stood on the cliff edge. The thunder, the explosion, the galloping horses—it was all in the dream I had had since a boy, that terrible vision of Father's face through the haze of smoke and the clash of battle, of crowds of men preventing me from coming to his aid. I shook my head to clear my mind of the image and peered at him again through the smoke of the fire.

Standing fearlessly and motionlessly, he faced down the chariots as they drove toward him, two on his left, two on his right. At the last moment he would raise his arms in a signal and the horses would skid to a halt, demonstrating that even beasts and implements of war were in thrall to this hero. The lunging horses drew closer and every man held his breath, but still Father stood motionless, his face without expression, staring down the crazily racing beasts with their lethal cargo.

The thunder commenced again with a crash, but the horses did not stop. Rather, they surged forward, roaring past him on either side, the whirling blades on the wheels missing him by a mere few hands' breadth. Without the slightest hesitation, the two lead chariots with their horses plunged over the edge of the cliff, followed immediately afterwards by the two trailing cars. The thunder exploded in a terrible climax and then fell silent. Not a sound was heard—not a whinny or a scream—and any noise produced by the landing at the bottom was too distant for us to perceive, or perhaps they never landed at all but simply flew away to be possessed by Ares, the war god, whose sacrifice they had become. The silence was ghastly, and a hundred thousand men stood frozen, staring at the man who had become like a god before their eyes. This man over whom poison held no sway, whom the Roman Sulla feared to kill, whom even the gods hastened to obey. Their king, my father.

He stood silent, staring at the men, at his hundred thousand chosen, who for the past months he had personally trained and armed. He drank in their silence, with a hint of a smile, widening into a mocking grin on a face that was now beginning to grizzle with age but which had lost none of its perfection and handsomeness. As he raised his sword in a salute, his voice rang like a bell over the heads of his men and echoed across the canyon behind him, with the only sound the low rumble of the thunder.

"Listen to me, you two-legged oxen, you beasts of burden laboring under the Roman lash!" he shouted to the troops, goading and taunting. "Hearken to me, you slaves and jackals! Were you not born of the loins of women, in the same manner as Romans, in the same fashion as kings?"

A low growl, an undercurrent of excitement, rose from the troops. His voice carried, loud and commanding, over the echoing canyon as the men crowded forward.

"And do your enemies not eat as you do, bleed as you do—*die* as you do?" he roared, and the men began to rhythmically beat their shields in approval.

"The ancient gods have spoken!" he cried. "You men, who have come here from a hundred nations, have been forged into a single army, just as your hundred nations themselves will soon be forged into a single nation, a single empire. We will create a Hellenic empire, rivaling and surpassing the glory of Alexander's great conquests of old. Within you runs the blood of ancient heroes and warriors; within you pulses the blood of kings! That bloodline, that glorious destiny, must not be denied!

"Join me in this holy campaign, and earn glory, glory that not only will accrue to you throughout your life but after death will honor all your posterity! It is glory and honor, men, not gold or cattle, that will make you heroes—and heroes you will become, with offerings heaped and libations poured to your ghosts, that you may never wander hungry and desolate through the dark caverns of the Underworld, as do lesser mortals and impious Romans. You, heroes, shall drink from the largest cups, ride the greatest of ghost steeds, germinate the fields, and caprify the fig trees that your descendants have planted. The gods are with us! We shall show the Romans that it is we who are destined to rule, we who may no longer be driven like sheep—we shall battle and defend, kill or be killed. We shall all become as kings!"

As the thunder rose in volume the men's murmuring rose, too, and they realized that in this, in the thunder and fire, the horses and the whirling scythes, they had witnessed a great thing. Once more Father's voice rose, this time barely audible among the chorus of baying men.

"Death to Murena!"

"Death to Murena!" the cry returned, though I realized it was not the canyon echoing back this time but the men themselves.

"Death to Rome!"

"Death to Rome!" a hundred thousand voices roared, and the oath was repeated over and over in a hellish crescendo, and seeing the men's fervent expressions, the utter loyalty and breathless excitement etched in their faces, their love—yes, love!—and adoration for their leader, I knew that they believed, that any doubts his armies may have harbored since the great defeats at Sulla's hands had now been wiped away. A new army had been born, a new king, a new Pontus—a new Greece!—and only Murena's three Roman legions stood between Father and immortality. I looked again at the men's expressions, and I knew them to be victors.

Rome had started its second war with Mithridates, but Mithridates himself would finish it or finish his kingdom in the process. And Murena—either way, Murena, that jackal, was as good as dead.

3

As expected, Murena was unsatisfied with his first two invasions of the Pontic interior and so decided on a third incursion—this time to Sinope, the Pontic capital itself, which would cement his place among heroes and afford him the Triumph in Rome he craved. Scarcely bothering to hide his intent, he marched his three legions by full light of day along the most heavily traveled byways of the Asian interior, openly plundering cities and slaughtering civilians as soon as he crossed into Pontic territory. The infuriated highland chieftains nearly mutinied when Father withdrew his entire army southward and deployed it inside the walls of Sinope. The chieftains considered this an act of cowardice, of the King protecting his own assets at the expense of his people, but Father had a completely different strategy in mind.

When word arrived of Murena's third attack, Father ordered a veteran cavalry commander, Gordios, to lead five thousand heavy cavalry from Sinope around behind the Roman legions, a long ride through several distant mountain passes. "Watch Gordios carefully," Father ordered before I left with the squadron. "He's a good soldier, a good leader. His men are rough, but he controls them well. You will learn much from him."

Indeed, I learned more than I ever expected. Scarcely three days after our departure, Gordios was thrown from his horse on rocky terrain and landed heavily on his shoulder. His collarbone snapped like a reed, jutting out through the skin, and as he writhed in pain, the jagged end pierced the jugular vein in his neck, causing him to bleed to death in moments. Our force now had no leader. Returning back to Sinope for new orders would take too much valuable time. I could not hesitate, though whether Father would have approved of my actions I could not say.

"Men!" I called as Gordios' captains gathered around in silent shock. "The King appointed me as second to General Gordios. With his death, I will assume command. We have no time to linger here. Bury the body, to avoid the smoke of a holocaust, and let's be on our way."

The men did not move, and in response to my order I heard murmurs of dissent. My claim to leadership was not exactly true—in the haste of our departure from Sinope, no provision had actually been made for the general's death, and the men suspected this. "He's only twenty-three years old," a grizzled Roman exile stated matter-of-factly. "Never even seen a battle before."

I stared at the man, whom I recognized as a Roman cavalry tribune named Marcellus—a quiet sort but one who, by his complete competence and self-assuredness, caused men to look to him unquestioningly. He was an effective leader of his cohort of Pontic horsemen and no doubt had been among his Roman forces as well, before his defection to us. Yet his words of dissent were a direct challenge to me. My stomach knotted, though I dared not show my fear. Every eye was upon me, every man gauging my reaction. It was a critical moment that I could not afford to let slip. I drew myself up to my full height, which, as I was a son of Mithridates, was not inconsiderable.

"I've seen every battle my father has waged for the past fifteen years, Tribune," I retorted loudly, fixing a steady gaze on the man. "I killed my first enemy at Chaeronea. Is there a man here who can claim that? Is there a man here who even *survived* Chaeronea?"

Silence followed.

"Is there a man here who was raised from a boy in army camps, whose toys were the markers of battlefield maps, whose very mother's milk was sour wine from an infantry flask?"

Silence still, as the men avoided my hard gaze.

"I will not force you to follow me," I continued quietly, still staring directly at Marcellus. The men leaned forward to listen more closely. "There may be men among you who are more experienced, more capable, than me. If so, ride away now, return to Sinope, and obtain your commission from the King. Whether he will reward you or execute you for abandoning my command I cannot say—that is your risk to take. As for myself, I will continue on to complete our task, and that is *my* risk. We leave now, for those who are with me."

One of the men spoke up. "He's young, but he's a full prince, son of the King himself!"

"I do not claim authority from my parentage," I responded dryly, cutting his enthusiasm short. "I will not command your lives and your families, as a prince could do. Follow me freely, as you followed Gordios; or return to Sinope to explain to the King why you did not."

At this, even the tribune Marcellus, who had originally objected, nodded curtly and remounted his horse. There was no further dissent.

After a week of difficult riding, mostly by night on the faint mountain trails that only the hardy riders of the Pontic interior could discern in the moonlight, we had completed our circular route and caught up with the Roman rear guard just as they emerged from the forbidding Trocmes mountains and were preparing a tricky crossing of the rain-swollen Halys. Once the legions had accomplished this, we knew, they would have a clear path down the gentle valley road on the left bank, across the rolling Paphlagonian plains, and up to the gates of Sinope itself. Our mission was to distract and delay them in this task for as long as possible.

My Pontic horsemen were masters of the game. Orders to them were superfluous, and as their ponies raced forward it was they who led me, not the other way around. Born and bred for cavalry warfare, the fierce riders thundered down the steep, gravelly cliffs of the river canyon in the glimmering moonlight, splitting spontaneously into smaller squadrons of thirty horse each, which surrounded the encampment, itself separate from the main body of Murena's forces several miles away. Galloping into the midst of the sleeping legionaries, we slaughtered every man we could find, running down individuals as they raced into the woods, leaping off our own ponies to drag away those scrambling into the rocky defiles or attempting to scale the crumbling shale cliffs. Within moments, half a thousand Roman soldiers lay dead, without ever knowing the identity of the phantom cavalry that had appeared at their rear in the dead of night.

Nor was our work accomplished yet. In the morning, our cavalry scouts slipped in close to Murena's main forces and set fire to the woods upwind of them, confining the enemy to the gravelly riverbank as the inferno raged behind them. This prevented the Roman construction gangs from obtaining timber for their bridge building, forcing them to send heavily armed squadrons of tree cutters far upriver to procure materials, which they then had to float downstream as cumbersome rafts. Days of delay resulted, requiring the efforts of hundreds of additional men. And as the Romans doggedly persevered in their bridge building, I sent groups of raiders out to harass the Roman supply columns that poured daily over the ridge on their long trek overland from Cilicia. The trick to successful small-scale warfare with a meager body of troops, I found, was to fight only at night, when the Roman troops were most vulnerable on the unfamiliar terrain, and to promise my men they could keep all the plunder they captured. During those weeks we spent haunting the ridges and mountains above Murena's army and supply routes, we lived well, on the food and supplies meant for three legions of well-fed Romans.

Though exasperated at first with these setbacks, Murena strengthened his rear defenses and ultimately paid us little heed, as his scouts had informed him that our entire force was scarcely one-third the size of his. He shrugged us off. "You're nothing but a fly on his ass," a captured Roman soldier told me disdainfully as I interrogated him. "You've cost him nothing but a few days' time before we destroy your pathetic kingdom."

I laughed and ordered the prisoner released for his bravery. *A few days' time.* That's all we needed.

When Father received word by smoke signal and courier that we had met our target, he himself swung into action. He set out from Sinope with fifty thousand troops eagerly awaiting their chance. A forced march of a hundred miles takes a well-trained Roman army five days. Father's troops took only three—and when they arrived at the Halys late the third night, the men were rabid to engage.

Father stationed his forces in a thick wood behind a low range of foothills just out of sight of the Romans across the river. My men and I had been informed of his imminent arrival two days before by cautious smoke signal and had stopped our cavalry harassment, allowing the Romans to proceed with their bridge building, which they finished the morning after Father's forces arrived. The Pontics on both sides—my cavalry on the rocky ridge above the river and Father's infantry in the foothills beyond the other bank—were awakened before dawn by the Roman bugles, and within an hour the first column of legionaries had traversed the wide stream unopposed and established a beachhead on the other side to support the crossing of the remaining troops and supplies.

Crouched behind a foothill no farther than it takes for a horse to become winded in a sprint, Father's fifty thousand men watched impatiently as cohort after cohort of Romans cautiously crossed the makeshift bridge. The cavalry and I stood motionless on the heights above them, armor and shields glinting brightly in the sun, watching the crossing from our own side. But it wasn't until a full half of the legions had passed over and Murena himself began the crossing that Father finally gave the signal to attack. From our vantage point above, we had a view of the battle usually afforded only to circling vultures.

The legions' collapse was instantaneous. The Romans had deployed their main defenses and archers in the wrong direction, facing backward against *us*. They were caught completely unawares by the thundering charge at their front from the King's heavy infantry. With a roar and a flurry of drums that sent throbbing waves of sound crashing and echoing off the rocky escarpments, fifty thousand men leaped up and raced in a disciplined rolling mass toward the surprised legions where a mere half of Murena's army held the beachhead. Meanwhile, the remainder of the legions struggled to evacuate their rear-facing position and cross over the river to assist the troops in the front.

After hastily reversing their positions, the leading Romans were astonished to discover that they had been surrounded by a Pontic army of Roman-style columns arranged in centuries and cohorts, deftly deployed in a half-circle formation facing the river. There was no escape, but for the rushing waters behind them.

The Romans fought valiantly, though they could do nothing against Father's overwhelming forces. What most hampered them, however, was their lack of leadership—for Murena, the legions' general, was stranded in the very middle of the bridge, his forward progress blocked by the troops before him who hesitated to advance into the chaos they witnessed on the far side of the river. His backward progress was prevented as well—for it was just at this moment that I called out my own signal to attack, sending my forces screeching and bellowing their tribal war cries, skidding down the slippery gravel cliff and into the remaining supply columns and rear guard who had yet to cross the torrent.

The carnage was indescribable. The Romans bravely stood their ground, even in the very teeth of our attack; yet their position was hopeless. Nothing could withstand the murderous charge of our horse troops from the rear, nor the disciplined yet furious march of Father's fifty thousand infantry in the front. They systematically rolled over the despairing Romans of the vanguard, butchering them to the last man or driving them, armor and all, into the torrent. By the time Father's forces and mine had met in the middle of the bridge and clapped shoulders in salute, not a single living Roman of the original fifteen thousand who had awakened that morning to the bugles' call remained alive in the field.

After the slaughter, as the captured enemy weapons and armor were being collected into a vast heap for distribution, the tribune Marcellus sidled up to me on his horse. For a moment he was silent, and I pretended not to see him as I continued to direct the cleanup work on the battlefield. Finally he spoke up.

"Sir," he said in his abrupt camp Latin, "I'm man enough to admit I'm wrong when I'm wrong. You showed your command today in battle. My apologies for doubting you earlier."

I looked for a moment longer at the gravel riverbank, strewn with thousands of Roman corpses. Wild pigs and dogs were already beginning to emerge from the scrub behind us, rooting into the bodies, seeking their own share of the plunder. I shouted an order to heap the dead into a communal ditch to be burned. It was a matter of honor—not even Romans deserve to be gnawed by pigs. Then I turned back to Marcellus.

"Your doubts were understandable, Tribune, and your caution commendable. I would have asked the same questions, in your place. But I trust there will be no doubts of me in the future. They might be construed as disloyalty. Which I will not tolerate."

"No, sir," he replied. "There will be no more doubts." He wheeled his horse and trotted off to take command of the cleanup operation himself.

"So you've come of age," said a deep voice. I turned to find Father sitting on his horse just behind me. He had been listening to my conversation with Marcellus.

"You now command a full squadron of Pontic cavalry, with veteran Roman tribunes," he continued. His words were light-hearted, but his face was not. Rather, his eyes flashed fire.

"Alexander was younger than I when he commanded a whole army," I replied.

Father did not smile. "And just as a wise commander should do," he said, "you have demanded utter loyalty from your subordinates. You have received their obedience, and from the looks of their plunder bags, you have amply rewarded them."

"I have."

"And what is to be *your* reward for assuming authority without my approval?"

I bristled at his sarcastic tone. "Gordios' death was tragic, but someone needed to take command of the squadron. We didn't have time to seek out your orders—"

He slammed his meaty fist down onto his thigh, startling his horse. "Some would call what you did mutiny," he said, his face tense.

"Mutiny!" I exploded. "I saved your plan of attack, and your attack saved Pontus! And you accuse me of mutiny?"

"I accuse you of nothing," he replied, his tone controlled. "In fact, I applaud you, for you did precisely what I would have done in your place."

I nodded and began to turn my horse away, but Father reached over and seized my reins, drawing my horse up tight against the side of his own. By turning away before he had dismissed me, I had treated him as an equal—a grave mistake.

"Pharnaces," he continued in a low voice, looking at me hard. "I trust that you took your king's best interest to heart when you assumed command of the cavalry. I, too, demand utter loyalty and obedience from my subordinates. And know this now: I make no exceptions." He peered at me with expressionless gray eyes for a moment, then wheeled his horse and cantered off. I stared after him, angry and shaken.

History, as they say, is written by the victors, which is why Roman historians have little to say of the destruction of Murena's army at the battle of Halys. For of the fifteen thousand Roman soldiers who had set out from Cilicia on this third incursion into the interior, only Murena straggled dazed and half-dead into Roman Phrygia several weeks later. He had survived by tearing off his armor, leaping into the water from the bridge, and swimming to safety miles downstream; indeed, through the manipulation of certain facts, he was eventually even able to arrange for himself a Triumph in Rome, based on the success of his earlier raids.

Which only proves that a great defeat can be just as effective as a victory in gaining praise for one's record, provided that no witnesses survive to recount the truth.

BOOK SIX

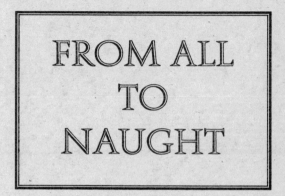

FROM ALL TO NAUGHT

Honor is gone, loyalty feeble and pale.
Sin prevails over virtue, lawlessness over law,
and lost is the common cause of mortals to dissuade the gods
from reaching them in their jealousy.

—Euripides

1

In the fifty-eighth year of life, most men of privilege are, if not dead, at least long passed into retirement, spending their time tending their estates and raising bountiful harvests of grapes and grandchildren. Father did neither. Indeed, except for the fact that records showed he had now been governing Pontus for a full thirty-seven years, one would almost have thought he was two decades younger than he was, that he had somehow discovered a spring of youth. Far from having settled from his enormous height, becoming stooped and stiff with years, Father still held his back as straight as a soldier's. His muscles had lost nothing of their hardness, nor his shoulders and back their tautness and strength. His hair was still the long, flowing chestnut mane as before, and his speed and agility were unsurpassed even by the professional wrestlers who traveled from city to city. His skill at horsemanship and archery remained legendary, and as an orator he was second to none, capable of both debating fine points of philosophy and haranguing troops in the field, not to mention telling raunchy jokes in every language of Asia, the true test of one's fluency in a tongue. Only his hands gave sign that he was human rather than god, for they were not the hands of a divinity, nor even of a king, but rather those of a common soldier—the knuckles scarred with cuts and scrapes, palms rough and hard as cured oak from handling weapons and tools. Calluses covered the thick, meaty slabs of his palms, with dirt worked deep into the cracks, impossible to wash out. His hands were a road map of the travels, victories, and losses in his life.

The man was ageless, rendered immortal from the effect of Papias' daily antidotes. And the old herbalist himself also remained hale and spry, perpetually a hundred and five years of age, or so it seemed to me, though hearty as a man many decades younger. He took his responsibilities as seriously as the life-and-death power he held in his hands, as seriously as I took my own position, which had expanded suddenly and enormously—for Father had promoted me, even at my young age, to the rank of full field general, in recognition of my performance at the battle of the River Halys five years before. I now commanded all the Pontic cavalry, the most powerful force in the army.

In that fifty-eighth year of his life the kingdom, too, was prosperous, after emerging from its second war with Rome; the plunder that had been stolen by Murena had been recovered, and the original terms of the Treaty of Dardanus had been ratified anew, and this time formalized by the Roman Senate. My half brother, Prince Machares, was proving to be an effective, though unwarlike, ruler over the distant kingdom of Bosporus. And the pirate fleets, though semi-independent, still followed Father's orders closely enough as to be considered by all as his private navy. They controlled not only the Hellespont and Bosphorus but indeed the entire Mediterranean, from Spain to Syria. Not a ship could pass, not a Roman senator could travel, without word's being passed to a local squadron commander by signal flag or watchtower and orders given to sink and plunder or to let pass unmolested. Rome's domains may have been enormous; yet if one counted Father's control of the high seas, his empire was larger yet.

Rome's fortunes remained unclear, as the outcome of the Social Wars was still in doubt; and since it had never avenged itself for the Night of the Vespers years before, the memory of that event remained a constant source of anger and calls for reprisal in the Senate. Indeed, every trouble and fear that beset Rome anywhere in its dominions was blamed on Mithridates. The Thracians had revolted on the upper Danube? Surely they were in the pay of Mithridates, the senators screamed, calling for Father's blood. A grain shortage in Egypt? Romans were certain that supplies had been secretly diverted by Mithridates' pirates, and Rome's streets filled with rioters chanting Father's name. Behind every setback they saw Pontic maneuvering. To Rome, Father was a scourge, a bogeyman to children and grown men alike, a mysterious, invisible threat whose assassins and poisons were everywhere at once, yet nowhere they could be seized. He was a threat to Rome's authority, indeed its very existence. Mere mention of his name could throw the entire city into an uproar. Most of the accusations were blatantly untrue, though a few of them had enough basis in fact as to lend credence to the rest. Father relished the role.

Still, there were clouds on the horizon, for that fifty-eighth year was not a quiet one. In that year a singular event occurred, which was to set the stage for the rest of his life, indeed for the remaining existence of Pontus itself.

That winter saw the death of the man who had long been a thorn in Father's side, King Nicomedes of Bithynia. Normally the death of one's rival and enemy should be cause for celebration. Indeed, Father did rejoice, for one night only. His satisfaction, however, was short-lived. For Nicomedes, despairing of his weak country's continued independence, had determined on his deathbed not to bequeath his kingdom to any of his dissipated sons. His last act as king before giving up the ghost was to transfer his entire kingdom to Rome.

The implications were enormous. A Roman fleet based at Heraclea, the main Bithynian port on the Black Sea, would be able to open up the valuable sea lanes through the Hellespont that Pontus currently controlled. This would allow Rome unfettered passage between the Black Sea and the Mediterranean, for commercial as well as military purposes, opening our entire northern territory to Roman expansion. Roman legions garrisoned in Bithynia would have easy access to Pontus via the flat coastal lane, laying open the wealthy core of our kingdom that had not been plundered for decades. By invitation of Nicomedes, the Romans would soon be on our very doorstep.

We needed to reconquer Bithynia before the arrival of the Roman fleet, or all hopes of future empire would be lost.

It was a desperate measure. If we won, we would merely win Bithynia—a kingdom Father had already conquered in the past and where he knew there remained little of value as plun-

der. Yet if we lost, there could be no hope of returning to the
Peace of Dardanus or any other similar treaty. Nothing less
would do for the Roman Senate than the complete destruction
of Pontus and the removal of Father's head. The risk was
great, the potential gain low—but anything was better than
waiting for the Romans to take possession of their new domain and then conquer Pontus at their leisure.

Father spent that winter preparing his army. He collected an
additional sixteen thousand cavalrymen from the Persian clans
in the interior, any one of whom could have held his own
against ten of the clumsy mounted mercenaries the Romans
used in battle. A hundred forty thousand infantry were gathered and trained by our Roman exiles to fight in the maneuver-
able formations that made the legions so formidable. Besides
these forces, Father had dozens of tribes for allies, who supplied crowds of road builders, baggage carriers, sutlers,
smiths, wrights, and all other manner of men an army re-
quires. To soften the blow to the tribes' homelands caused by
the temporary loss of all these able-bodied men, Father distributed two million *medimni* of wheat—a truly staggering
volume—which he shipped directly from the royal storehouses
in Sinope, to the cities along the coast.

Marius and his Roman legion still formed the hard core of
the enormous army; and even a hundred scythe chariots were
brought to Camp of Ares for drills and to raise the men's
morale with the frightful whizzing hum of their blades, though
Father refused to put them into actual battle again. That spring,
the army traveled into the inland mountains for additional training and another sacrifice to Zeus Stratios, Leader of Armies.

2

The army marched south and west along the coast and crossed the borders into Bithynia without meeting so much as a band of vagabond boys throwing rocks, much less a Roman army. Offshore, the pirate fleet shadowed our progress, with a convoy of fast cutters flitting in and out of the armada, maintaining communications with Sinope, Prince Machares to the north, and the various coastal garrisons. The day before our arrival at Heraclea, the garrison and leading citizens abandoned the city, and the Roman warships that had been sent there recently to take over the Bithynian naval arsenal also fled, far down the Asiatic coast to the fortress city of Chalcedon, on the Bosphorus. Although Chalcedon's harbor facilities were not nearly as expansive as the fine port of Heraclea, they still allowed the Romans to bottle up the passage between the Black Sea and the Mediterranean. After allowing the troops to plunder Heraclea, we soldiered on.

The next objective was the Bithynian capital, Nicomedia, which, though also garrisoned by Romans, offered only token resistance and was quickly overrun. Our troops experienced a near-miss, as the Roman proconsul, Caius Aurelius Cotta, remained until the very last moment trying to organize a disciplined retreat. He slipped past our lines just before we closed around the city. As at Heraclea, all citizens of importance fled to Chalcedon, abandoning the capital's wealth, including the late king's treasury. To our great surprise, the wealth was enormous—old Nicomedes must have been secretly hoarding it for decades, while all along claiming the most abject poverty when questioned by his Roman masters. With the plunder, Father's war chest had multiplied in just a matter of weeks, though we had yet to enter into battle.

The target now was obvious—all roads led to Chalcedon.

When we arrived on the outskirts of that city several days later, we set up headquarters on a high hill to the east, overlooking the city walls, as well as the entire Strait of Bosphorus to the European side, with the Propontis to the south and the Black Sea to the north. The Roman fleet, led by the Roman naval commander Nudus, was tightly bottled up within the city's harbor, though it would not be an easy task to capture the vessels from seaward. A heavy bronze chain had been placed across the narrow opening to prevent the Pontic fleet from entering, and rock-hurling engines had been installed on the steep hills rising up on the three sides, with a range that could cover the entire harbor, should our marines somehow cut through the chain. Our three hundred decked warships, massed at anchor just out of range of the engines, closely watched the fire signals communicating our actions from atop the hill. Their marines and ship-based catapults stood at the ready.

We deployed the entire Pontic army in a stunning array of wealth and might. The aristocrats of the mighty inland horse troops pranced their stallions and displayed their finely wrought cavalry armor, while the foot troops watched in admiration, cheering loudly at the battalion of scythe chariots that had accompanied the army thus far.

"We'll give them a show, first," Father told his generals as we stood on the hilltop, carefully observing the city two miles below. "Cotta has few Roman soldiers—the garrisons of Heraclea and Chalcedon only. The rest of his men are citizen levies from Cyzicus, to the south—artisans and cobblers. Strike some fear into their hearts. Chalcedon will fall like a stricken duck."

We nodded. The plan was working already. We had scarcely finished our discussion when the massive gates opened, and Cotta himself marched out, side by side with a Roman officer in rich ceremonial gear. They were accompanied by a small armed guard.

"Who is the officer marching with Cotta?" I asked.

"That would be Admiral Nudus," Father replied.

I chuckled. "You're joking—are the Romans so short of family names they have to resort to 'Nudus'? We'll make him live up to his name—see how he marches *exposed* to our archers?"

Father guffawed at the pun. "Ha—so you still remember your Latin! He's coming to surrender the city, I'll wager."

But rarely in history has a Roman army surrendered as easily as that. Tactical retreat, perhaps, but never an immediate surrender in the face of a siege. Indeed, just behind Nudus and Cotta marched the entire armed forces of Chalcedon, including the Cyzicene levies that had recently joined them—scarcely twenty thousand men, less than a fifth of our forces, but like us arrayed in all the finery they could muster. The army wended its way deliberately along the flagged road toward our forces, dipping in and out of sight between the myriad buildings and garden walls of the prosperous outer suburbs, to the edge of the inhabited area. Our troops stopped all their activity, even their talking, to observe this extraordinary sight. It was not as if the Romans were unaware of the size of our army—we had been parading our men before their eyes for half a day, and the foothills were black with the dense mass of our attacking forces. But even Father's eyes bugged as he watched the enemy calmly deploy into battle formation on the broad, flat plain between the suburbs and our own hillside position.

"Fools," he muttered. "Cotta hopes to repeat Chaeronea here, defeating an army that outnumbers them. Idiots! I have more Romans in my own forces than he has on the entire Asian coast!"

"Don't be hasty," I cautioned. "They may be preparing a ruse. We have no idea how many troops might be hiding in reserve inside the city walls."

He glanced at me. "Well spoken," he said simply. "But we'll give them no time to deploy reinforcements."

At his signal, a shout rose from the Roman exile legion he had placed in the vanguard of his massive forces. At the pounding beat of the huge drums, the troops of the Pontic army set off in their swaggering Roman step, implacable and relentless, shields swinging hypnotically and rhythmically to the Pyrrhic cadence that every Roman soldier, from conscript to tribune, learns from his first day in the legions. The message Father was sending to Cotta and Nudus was unmistakable: They were not facing a mere ragtag lot of conscripts brought over at sword point from starving tribes in the interior. This was a Roman army before them, a Roman army as Roman-born and as Roman-trained as their own; and their own mere twenty thousand conscripts would be trampled into the cobblestones before the day was through.

As if to put his own personal seal on the attack, Father nodded his head toward Craterus, who grinned, pulled the visor down over his face, and then bellowed to his scythe-car drivers to move out. Thundering around the left flank of Father's advancing legion of Roman exiles, they deployed in the very center of the front lines, weaving in and out between each other in a dazzlingly choreographed display of horsemanship and precision, scythes flashing and humming evilly as they approached Nudus' waiting troops. Even from this distance, we could see the enemy lines wavering—the formation was fragmenting as the local militia in the rear lines turned hesitantly and began retreating to the city walls, one eye still on their Roman comrades in the front lines to observe their reaction.

But Father had not yet finished with his demonstration. At a piercing whistle, five thousand horse troops on either side of the lines leaped forward, galloping toward the flanks of marching infantry, which was now a half-mile before them. As they thundered across the plain, they extended their own lines, creating a vast front extending far beyond the defenders' outer wings, preventing any hope of stragglers' escaping, and threatening to envelop the defenders' entire army from the sides. Now even Nudus' front lines, Romans themselves, halted and began to retreat, falling back into their original marching column and preparing to withdraw down the road by which they had come moments before, in their habitual dignity and precision.

As the horses raced forward, Father completed his well-choreographed display. Seizing a torch from an attendant, he strode to the signal tower, clambered the dozen rungs to the top as nimbly as a boy, and set fire to the pile that had been massed on the platform. Instantly a ball of flame rose from the naphtha-impregnated straw and branches, and a thick column of black smoke rose into the sky.

A moment later, faint cheers floated over to us from the distant pirate fleet anchored just outside the harbor. Fire erupted from various points of the inner harbor, from Roman ships anchored within, and from the warehouses and arsenals lining the shores as Neoptolemus' catapults surged into action with their flaming warheads. Columns of black smoke, echoing the single one behind us, erupted around the harbor, springing up like poisonous mushrooms in a dung heap. As Nudus' troops turned away from us and retreated toward the city walls, they, too, could see the fire and destruction raining down onto the harbor, and discipline could not be maintained. Scythe chariots, warhorses, and a wall of Roman shields were roaring down at them from their rear, while their city was bursting into flames behind the protective walls to their front. With a grunt of satisfaction Father leaped down from the tower and resumed his position nearby, arms crossed before him, huge muscles swelling against each other before his chest, Persian trousers flapping gently as the wind-whipped smoke swirled around us.

The rout had begun.

The scythe chariots hurtled down on the fleeing Romans. Though the charioteers were under strict orders to veer away at the last moment, Nudus' troops did not know this, and their discipline could not hold. Troops in the rear crowded in panic against their comrades in front and were in turn pummeled by those arriving from behind. Shouts and crashes erupted from their ranks as the trailing troops, stalwart Romans who had been stationed in the front ranks of the formation on the plain, were hit hard from the rear by the missiles of our Pontic army.

The narrow stone road onto which the twenty thousand defenders were now funneling in their retreat became impossibly clogged. Unable to make headway along the jammed road through the suburbs, thousands broke rank, scrambling and tumbling over the garden walls on either side. Hampered by their battle gear, they hastily threw aside cuirasses and helmets, shields and even swords, anything that would slow their flight toward the city walls looming just before them, but with so many obstacles still to cross. The defenders clambered over the fences and stumbled into the small terraces and plots of the householders. They then hastily rose to their feet and crashed through the adjoining houses and sheds, fleeing desperately to the next low fence, over which they again flopped in terror, kicking and shoving at their comrades fleeing before them in the same mad panic.

They were blank targets for our crack archers, two thousand of whom I hastily moved up to fire upon the defenders in their crazy lurching through the arbors and kitchen gardens. The Armenians, the best bowmen in the army, stood just at the edge of the plain, taking shelter behind the first of the stone walls. The scrambling defenders were so closely packed in their terror that the archers did not even need to aim—merely setting arrow to string and pointing in the direction of the walls could not help but strike home. Other archers, a corps of Colchians, stood farther back and aimed into the densely packed mob still surging down the narrow road, shooting their arrows in high arcs that fell upon the fleeing Romans from straight above their heads, acquiring greater speed in their fall and increasing their lethal power.

Within moments Nudus' forces had been reduced to bloody chaos, the bodies of those killed and wounded impeding the flight of those behind, causing even more of their fellows to fall victim to the lethal cloud of arrows. Our own Roman legion had by now been called to a halt, as had the scythe chariots and the cavalry—there was little point in squandering precious Pontic blood when the defenders themselves were so effectively wreaking their own destruction.

Nudus bravely remained in the rear of his retreating forces, doing his best to organize them, despite the arrow protruding from his shoulder. Cotta, however, panicked at the very beginning of our attack. Somehow he made his way to the front of the fleeing army and was one of the first to reach the city gates. Rushing inside, still in full view of our command post on the top of the hill, he was practically carried through by the flow of terrified men behind him. Yet inside he met with equal terror among the townspeople, who were being pummeled from seaward by our artillery. The fiery missiles of the Pontic fleet's catapults and ballistae rained down in such volumes that the defenders on the walls scurried for cover, abandoning their own engines. As Nudus' army poured into the city through the half-opened gates, Cotta decided he could take no more, and as senior Roman authority in the city he gave his orders.

The massive gates swung ponderously shut.

A roar rose up as the remaining defenders outside, fully half of Chalcedon's army, realized they were trapped between the closed city walls before them and the steadily advancing Pontic forces behind. They shouted and pleaded for the garrison to open the gates to let them pass inside, but Cotta remained firm. When Nudus and his officers arrived, they waved their helmets with the officer crests to the defenders on top of the walls, bellowing and ordering them to open the gates, but were unable to elicit any more of a response than a few ropes hesitantly let down from the watchtowers. Dozens of panic-stricken men leaped for these tenuous lifelines, but Nudus' guard drove them away with their swords, clearing room for the general to be hauled up to the battlements to safety.

There he could do nothing but watch the terrible fate of his men below, and we needed to do nothing to encourage our troops to bring the battle to its conclusion. After waiting patiently for the single clogged road to clear of living defenders, our own Roman exile legion funneled onto it in perfect marching order, picking its way over the mounds of dead and wounded left by the panic-stricken defenders ahead of them. The squadrons of Pontic archers maintained their lethal barrage. Arriving at the walls, our troops found Chalcedon's defenders milling like terrified sheep. Most of them, dropping their weapons and armor, simply fell forward on their faces in surrender. They were roughly pulled up by the hair or shoulders and passed back through the Pontic ranks as prisoners of Mithridates. Some others, particularly the Romans from the garrisons, kept their weapons and actually tried to defend themselves or escape but were cut down in plain view of Nudus and Cotta on top of the walls. Three thousand Roman garrison soldiers were killed under the proconsul's eyes. The rest were taken prisoner.

That was not the end of the battle, however, for the pirate fleet outside the harbor continued its withering volley on the city. At the same time, a team of smiths was carefully ferried up to the harbor chain under the shelter of our warships and, after much feverish work, cut through the barrier. As the sawed ends of the bronze chain sank beneath the waves, swift cutters and triremes loaded with marines poured into the anchorage, setting up their own barrage of arrows at the Chalcedon naval defenders, who scurried to take cover beneath their decks or, if moored by a wharf, dropped over the wales and fled the city. The Roman fleet that had been so carefully brought here from Heraclea for protection was left virtually unguarded.

Our pirate vessels stormed triumphantly into their midst— but motley as the sailors were, they were veteran warriors still and knew value when they saw it. Rather than the rampant destruction and pillaging in which the land army was engaged at that very moment, the pirate captains each chose a Roman vessel against which to pull alongside and unloaded their marines onto its decks. The Pontics scrambled below to kill any defenders still in hiding and then unshipped the oars, dipped blade to water, and calmly rowed back out of the harbor. It was a magnificent feat, one that set all of us on the hill, even the generals themselves, to cheering like boys in the cheap seats at the Hippodrome. The armada captured sixty fine Roman warships intact, each one better than the best of our own, and destroyed six others whose defenders had resisted too stoutly. In this entire process we lost fewer than two dozen men.

Although it was not full revenge for our defeat at Chaeronea, still, the victory was a great one for the Pontics, one that showed Father's true genius as a commander. All Bithynia was once again added to his dominions, and he regained full and clear access through the Propontis between the Black Sea and the Mediterranean. Volunteers now flocked to his army from every corner of Asia and the Greek world, much as they had years earlier, before the siege of Athens. Our path was again laid for us, our destiny clear. The move would be south, toward the Greek cities of Ionia, Pergamum, and Ephesus and into the critical sea lanes of the Aegean. After conquering Bithynia and routing the Roman garrisons, there was little now that could stop us.

3

Within days of the great victory of Chalcedon, word came of the arrival of another Roman army, under the command of Lucullus, Sulla's old lieutenant. He had recently been elected consul, which normally would have been ample reason for him to stay in Rome. However, he was on rather tense terms with Pompey, the commander responsible for putting down Sertorius' rebellion in Spain, and this, combined with certain unsavory bedroom scandals in which Lucullus' name had been mentioned, had given him the notion that a campaign in Asia might be the path to cleaning up his reputation.

Lucullus arrived in Cilicia shortly after our own march into Bithynia, heading a total of five full Roman legions, thirty thousand men in all. If our dream of restoring the empire was to survive, indeed if we were even to retain newly reconquered Bithynia at all, this new Roman army would have to be dealt with.

For a time Father was indecisive. No experienced commander would lightly provoke a pitched battle against Roman legions, even if he outnumbered them five to one. I pointed out that Lucullus was commanding precisely the same number of men as had Sulla when he had defeated our forces at Chaeronea. Father retorted that in those days he had been fighting with undertrained mercenaries, under the command of the traitor Archelaus, using scythe chariots and a Greek phalanx. We now had a full Roman legion on our side, and the native Pontic forces had been trained by Sertorius' officers in Roman battle tactics. We also had a secure supply line to our base at Sinope, and raw materials across the Black Sea. And like Sulla in the past, Lucullus was weak in cavalry. All these points I conceded, yet still I was reluctant to admit that we had a clear victory ahead of us.

But Lucullus hesitated as well, for he knew that Mithridates was no longer the same man, nor his army the same army, as the one Sulla had defeated. With his five legions he advanced slowly and cautiously through Phrygia to the border of Bithynia, where at a little river-crossing named Otryae they met our forces.

We had the fortune of arriving first and so chose the field of battle and fortified our position strongly, Roman-style, behind a series of spike-filled ditches, palisades, and other barriers. Lucullus tried for several days to join battle, sending heralds out with provocative challenges, ordering skirmishers to attack our firewood parties, even feigning a night retreat, hoping to tempt our watching army into plundering his camp, while he waited in ambush. Father, however, was not to be fooled. He had learned his past lessons from the Romans well and preferred to hunker behind his barriers for a time, carefully observing his foe from a distance, spying out its strengths and weaknesses, hoping to draw Lucullus into an impatient or arrogant move on which he could pounce.

Finally Marius decided there was nothing further to be gained by waiting and volunteered to lead our Roman legion, supported by half the Pontic auxiliaries, against Lucullus' wing held by the two veteran legions. By doing this, Marius calculated not only that his was the stronger military force but also that Lucullus' veteran Populares would balk against battling Roman exiles of their own political party, and might even give up the field without a full-scale battle. Father enthusiastically agreed, and the following day the gates of our fortifications were opened and Marius' legion, supported by sixty thousand Pontic auxiliaries led by Father, marched out against the left flank of the Roman forces awaiting us.

Lucullus' troops were at first surprised at this sign of Pontic willingness to battle, but the plain separating the two armies was broad, and there was plenty of time for them to deploy to receive us. Lucullus was a consummate professional and would not have been caught unprepared, nor did Marius expect him to be. This was to be a pitched battle, on a broad, flat plain ideal for both our cavalry and the wide-open fighting tactics of the Roman legions. The stronger side would win, and I had no doubt which that would be—for we still held another eighty thousand troops within the fortifications in reserve.

Just as our trumpets sounded the attack, however, a deafening boom tore through the air, out of a clear blue sky, thunderlike in pitch though ten times as loud. The roar rattled the brains of our men and terrified the horses. Both armies threw themselves to the ground in terror, certain it must be the arrival of the gods themselves, and the terrible roar grew louder, combining with an eerie high-pitched whine that grew in intensity, seeming to come from above us yet from all around, surrounding us, leaving us no way of escape. Both armies lay prostrate, waiting for the gods' deathblow to strike, and even Father, who was beside me at the time, leaped from his horse and crouched on one knee, leaning forward on his fingertips like a sprinter before a race, preparing either to be knocked flat to the ground or to stand to meet the deities.

The very air split before us, and a blinding flash, like the sun itself, exploded out of the empty sky. A fiery object seared through the ether with a deafening roar and slammed into the ground between the two armies' lines, throwing a shower of dirt high into the air that for long moments afterwards pelted us with burning clods and particles of molten metal, covering both armies with a thick layer of dust and residue. For a long moment, men shouted and animals screamed in terror; and then there was silence—an unearthly, unnatural silence, but for the faint echo of the now spent explosion off the distant hills on the edge of the Phrygian plain. All lay motionless, as if dead, each man wondering whether he was with the shades. Turf and hot metal fell around us, pelting us like a foul, deadly snow.

When the showers of dirt had slowed and we were able to look around, we saw nothing but an enormous crater, twenty arm's lengths in diameter, ploughed into the earth before us directly between the two armies. Wisps of smoke still wafted from its center. Father rose cautiously to his feet, stiff in his cavalry armor, and picked his way through the prostrate forms of his men. Many of them still had not even peered up and lay covered under a layer of fallen dirt and rubble. I walked beside him, and we were soon joined by Marius and several other officers, making our way in dead silence toward the crater, the only sound that of our sandals on the newly turned soil.

From the Roman side, I saw officers doing the same, including one whom I immediately recognized as Lucullus. Within moments, all were standing at the edge of the crater, peering into the hole, Romans on one side, Pontics on the other. No man said a word; no arrow was shot, no spears flung. Mithridates and Lucullus, deadly enemies, stood no more than a horse leap's distance from each other, looking in, where all we could see was a lump of molten metal, iron perhaps, still red-hot and sizzling at its edges from the moisture of the soil but rapidly cooling as the dust and dirt settled upon it. The two men looked at each other, holding a long, cool, appraising gaze, each seeking to determine whether the other had identified some divine meaning from the event. Finally, Father slowly shook his head to the side, a soft and subtle negation, and Lucullus reciprocated with an identical gesture.

The gods had spoken, and the commanders had understood. There would be no battle today, here at this spot, at Otryae. Zeus had sent a sign, a terrible warning, to both sides, and it would be heeded. The two armies would retire. Neither would be dishonored. Both would respect the will of the gods.

We broke camp and removed our fortifications, secure in our trust that the Romans would hold off from any attack even while we were in a vulnerable and exposed position. The Romans watched the proceedings from a distance and did nothing to hamper us. We then returned to the coast to undertake the siege of Cyzicus, seizing supplies on our way and burning the countryside behind us.

Lucullus followed slowly, at a safe distance, bedeviled by the ravaged land through which he was left to travel, cautious to extend his supply lines behind him back to Cilicia. Two hundred thousand men had met on the battlefield. Yet not a single arrow had been fired, not a single sword thrust. All scores still remained to be settled.

4

Cyzicus lay at the end of a long peninsula, protected on three sides by the sea, with a harbor on its tip safely sheltered behind a narrow entrance. As long as the harbor remained secure, the city could be supplied by sea indefinitely. The landward entrance to the city was a thin strip of land that could be easily defended by a small force. The base of the peninsula lay just in the shadows of the Adrasteia Mountains, a short range of cliffs and rocky outcroppings that with little effort could be made impregnable against an invading army. The city thus benefited from a series of barriers daunting to even the most powerful invaders: the mountain range, the funnel-like neck of the peninsula, and finally the powerful walls of Cyzicus itself, defended by well-fed and well-armed citizens supported by their sea allies.

The city had to be taken, for along the entire length of the Propontis—the narrow strait separating the Mediterranean from the Black Sea—this was the only remaining Roman outpost. With Rome controlling this harbor, it could launch retaliatory raids against Pontic trading vessels, even serve as a base from which to attack the kingdom. With Cyzicus taken, however, Pontus and our allies would once again have undisputed control of the critical sea lane.

Yet siege warfare was not our only weapon against Cyzicus' defenses. For some weeks, Pontic agents had been hard at work distributing bribes in the Adrasteia Mountains at the base of the peninsula. The Cyzicene defenders there had built fortifications, cleared trenches, and established supply lines back to the city—but when we approached with our one hundred sixty thousand fresh troops, unbloodied from the encounter with Lucullus, the agents' work bore fruit. Fully half the advance defenders, ten thousand men, surrendered immediately to my cavalry. They were allowed to disperse peacefully through the Pontic lines into the countryside, with a stipend to assist them on their way.

The remaining defenders, disheartened at their colleagues' desertion and at the vast size of our forces, immediately abandoned the site. They did not even have time to fall back to the middle position they had envisioned, the trenches across the narrow peninsula—the Pontic cavalry's swift advance saw to that, capturing the position almost as soon as the fleeing Cyzicene defenders arrived and driving them in a hasty retreat back to the city at the tip of the spit of land.

Our army marched slowly and deliberately down the length of the peninsula and set up siege beneath the city walls, just out of missile range of the defenders. Meanwhile, the supporting armada anchored itself securely outside the heavily defended harbor, and the fleet of transport vessels began deploying to supply our army by sea. The situation was virtually identical to the one we had faced and won at Chalcedon only weeks before.

I was bothered by our deployment, however. The army was safely ensconced on the peninsula, with only one side to attack and one side to defend. Yet in the rear, the Adrasteia Mountains were as much a curse as a boon. If they were not carefully secured from the Romans, our army could be bottled up in this small space with no chance of escape, other than an awkward retreat by sea.

Father laughed off my concerns. "Marius and the exile legion are in the Adrasteia," he pointed out, "along with two legions of auxiliaries. They can hold off Lucullus."

I scoffed. "Marius has only half the troop strength of Lucullus, and his auxiliaries are green. How long can he defend our rear, even dug into fortifications?"

Father shrugged. "Long enough. Not all an army's strength relies on troop counts. Marius and his exiles are Populares. So, too, are half of Lucullus' legions. Those troops won't fight against a leader of their own party—Marius is a senator! The

Populares are rising again in the Senate, and any man who opposes Marius on the battlefield will be throwing away his future. Half Lucullus' forces will defect to our side within the week."

I remained skeptical. "Who told you this—Marius? Every exile believes his standing among his former citizens remains as high as it once was. Things have changed. Marius has been away from Rome for years. Exiles are forgotten the moment they leave their country."

"If that's true," he countered, "then I would have been forgotten many times in the past."

I conceded his point but still doubted. "The legions don't give a fig about home politics. They may once have supported the Populares, but that was years ago—they're old; some of Lucullus' veterans haven't seen Rome in two decades. And most of their commissions expire within a year—their only concern is to get through the fighting safely so they can retire."

Father smiled. "There you have it—another reason they won't fight. They'll take the easy road the first chance they get. Turn against Lucullus outright when Marius gives them the word, or at the very least just lay down arms and let Marius walk through their lines. Meanwhile, our job is to take Cyzicus. The faster the better. It'll silence the doubters, shake their loyalty to Rome. Rome's power will fall."

Within days he had restored and strengthened the trench across the neck of the peninsula, constructed artificial heights around the city on which to mount siege engines, and built a double mole out to sea, which completely blocked harbor access, preventing the city from being supplied by water. Father worked methodically and steadily, for his troops were not the only ones that had become Roman by training—he, too, had taken on the mentality of a Roman military engineer, gauging chances of victory as much by the relative slope of the land and catapult trajectories as by troop counts and cavalry tactics. Siege towers were built, ten or a dozen, including one enormous ugly affair that stood a hundred cubits high and could hold two hundred men huddled within its depths, ready to rush the walls when it was pushed within boarding range. The terrible vehicle was painted black, with glowing green eyes on its upper tower and protruding teeth fashioned on the side of the drawbridge that would be let down onto the tops of the ramparts. By daylight, the figure looked ludicrous, but at night, with its enameled eyes glimmering eerily in the torchlight, the camp artists' mastery of the element was evident. The huge dragon struck fear into all who saw it, and during our preparations the defenders took special aim at this particular vehicle with the flaming tar pots they periodically hurled at us with their engines from within the walls.

While the land engineers were busily constructing their siege devices, the fleet outside the harbor was not idle. After they had completed construction of the mole, all resources were dedicated to building that most difficult of weapons: a waterborne siege engine, a *sambuca*. This consisted of an enormous tower, built of strong wooden beams and draped with wet hides, ropes of seaweed, mud, and other noncombustible materials. It stood six stories tall, carefully calculated to exceed the tops of the city walls. A squadron of archers, armed with flaming arrows and soot pots, manned the top level, while just below them a ramp hung by chains, designed to be lowered onto the top of the battlements as soon as it had been brought within range.

This device was floated on two massive *quinqueremes,* the largest warships in the fleet, each with two hundred seventy rowers arranged in three banks of oars. Each ship in turn was stabilized by sturdy pontoons fastened to the side to prevent rocking, like a training canoe used by boys. The quinqueremes had enough stability to float even this enormous structure, which was so tall it could look into the windows of the city magistrate's palace towers. The original city planners had clearly not anticipated the Pontic sambuca.

For the entire summer the city was pounded. The defenders inside survived the onslaught as best they could, patching holes in the walls and repairing toppled battlements. Deserters brought us word of increasing hardship as food supplies dwindled and the city's wells turned brackish. Still, the siege was taking far longer than planned, and the Pontic troops were growing restless, for there was precious little for them to do besides remain battle-ready. This was a war of attrition, of engineers and quartermasters, and thus far those specialists had performed adequately; but the men had been trained as Romans, to fight as Romans and to entrench as Romans—and Romans were not accustomed to waiting on a beach.

Nor did Lucullus' Romans wait, either. In early August Father and I looked to the army's rear in the Adrasteia and saw an astonishing sight—Marius and his men complacently surrendering their stronghold on the cliffs, with Lucullus' forces filing into the positions they had previously held, all in full view of our troops on the peninsula below. Father stared in stupefaction for a moment, then set his face impassively. Seizing our horses, we rode out to meet Marius' exile legion on the road.

We encountered their vanguard as they marched onto the Cyzicus peninsula, and here Father called a halt, ordering a pavilion to be set up for a conference. Marius arrived an hour later and was escorted to the tent as his men were ordered to halt and rest for the remainder of the day.

Upon arriving at the tent where Father, Bituitus, and I waited, Marius bowed to the King, nodded affably to us, and sat down uninvited. He clearly knew the question on our minds.

"The ruse goes well," he opened, without preliminaries. "As we expected, Lucullus' commanders are completely supportive of our intent, and have no desire to challenge our legion of Populares. The situation is in good hands, my lord."

Father stared at him in silence a long moment before standing and walking slowly across the carpet of the tent to where Marius sat facing him on the camp chair. He towered over the Roman, whose face betrayed no hint of concern, though his eyes darted swiftly to each side as if he suddenly realized he had made a mistake by entering the King's tent with no supporters or guards of his own—he was the only Roman present.

Father bent down, placed his huge hand over the Roman's head, and lifted him bodily to a standing position, as easily as if he were a rag doll. As Marius grimaced in pain, Father released his grip and then placed his own face directly into the Roman's.

"You were not invited to sit down," he growled in quiet fury, "and the situation is *not* in good hands. It is in Lucullus' hands. Your tactics are as bad as your manners."

"By the gods!" Marius sputtered, his face registering outrage and humiliation. "The tactics are sound! I would have consulted with you had there been time—"

Father whirled toward the tent opening, gesturing furiously at the view of the cliffside stronghold, which was now crawling with Roman troops. "I would call you a traitor if I didn't know how utterly stupid you are. You have surrendered our defenses to the Romans!"

"I'll be damned . . ." Marius protested, and then glancing at the angry faces surrounding him, he adopted a more conciliatory tone. "Your Highness, negotiations require concessions by both sides." He paused for a moment, struggling to put into a few quick words the complex deals he had been brokering with Lucullus' commanders. "Let me explain. Lucullus already suspects the loyalty of the Populares among his legions, afraid they might give up the game to us. He knows how influential I am. He's positioned veteran Optimates legions just behind them, keeping the Populares on a short leash. They wouldn't have been able to turn on Lucullus in battle, as we had planned."

"So why are they now controlling *your* position on the Adrasteian heights?" Father hissed.

Marius flushed but carefully maintained control. "I had to throw the Populares a bone," he said slowly, "make it look like we surrendered to them, dispel Lucullus' suspicions, so he would trust them to oppose us. Otherwise, they wouldn't get the opportunity to abandon Lucullus in a later battle and give us victory. It was the only way I could . . ." Even Marius now realized how paltry the reasoning sounded, and his voice trailed off plaintively.

Father stared at him in disbelief, then disgust, as he strode to the entrance of the pavilion and peered out at his troops, at the Roman exiles setting up camp beyond, and at the slopes of the Adrasteia, now black with Lucullus' five legions—Populares *and* Optimates, indistinguishable one from the other.

"If only there were a mark," he said quietly, as if musing to himself, "a clear mark, to recognize a man's worth. Wit and stupidity are everywhere, and are passed randomly from one generation to the next. I have seen virtuous offspring of worthless parents. By Zeus, *I* am the offspring of a worthless parent. And now I have seen the reverse: this son of a noble father, with the blood of Rome's greatest general and senator, proves himself to be a traitor! No, I take that back—it takes deliberateness and intelligence to be a traitor. This one is merely . . . an *idiot*."

Bituitus broke the silence that followed.

"Sire," he said in his guttural Gallic accent, fingering his sword and dispassionately eyeing Marius. "Shall I be rid of him?"

Marius' eyes flickered in consternation, and I noticed one of his kneecaps began to twitch. The man's terror was but barely concealed. Yet Father remained motionless and silent, staring out the tent door. I stepped forward.

"Wait, Bituitus. Marius' officers will soon be seeking orders, and asking after him. What would we tell them?"

"Nothing," Bituitus growled, "or if you have to, tell them Marius took sick and will not be leading them."

"Let him go. Send him back to his men." Father's words were hard-edged and bitter.

We stared at Father and then at Marius, who had not dared to breathe during the entire discussion. For perhaps the first time, Marius' life had hung in the balance. He had been subjected to a trial, found guilty by the jury, but released by the judge—something one does not readily forget. On this Father was counting.

As Marius hurried out of the tent, I looked at Father questioningly.

"His men saw him enter this tent," he said, in response to my unasked question. "They would never believe he was suddenly taken ill. Marius' Romans are more loyal to him than to me, and they would rebel. Besides—for better or worse, Marius is the best Roman officer I have."

"He will never again test your patience with such stupidity," I said, understanding now the need to spare him.

Father stared hard at me. "True," he said in barely controlled fury. "Yet we must still live with what he has cost us."

With that, he strode out of the tent. As Father had foreseen, even after the Popular legions had taken over the stronghold on the Adrasteia, Lucullus still mistrusted them, and a few days later he rotated his younger, more reliable troops into their position, completely blocking our land route off the peninsula. The besiegers were now the besieged. Marius returned to his troops and Father did not mention the incident again.

But it only got worse from there.

5

Though the Romans occupied the Adrasteia Mountains, they were too outnumbered to assault our forces—just as we lacked the strength to storm Cyzicus. The situation bogged to a stalemate for all three sides. The city's supply lines were cut off by the Pontic army, the Pontic army's own land communications were cut by the Romans on the cliffs, and the Romans suffered from their long supply line to Cilicia, which was under constant attack by guerrilla warriors supporting Pontus. It was turning into an endurance match.

To force the situation, Father attempted moral pressure, the pressure of family and tribal ties. He bound three thousand Cyzicene prisoners who had been captured weeks before at the battle of Chalcedon and mounted them on ten pirate vessels, which he had rowed into the harbor. The day was miserable—though still only early autumn, it was unseasonably cold, with a biting wind and chopping waves slapping loudly against the vessels' hulls. As the squadron laden with Cyzicene captives approached the seawalls, the leaden, glowering skies opened as if on cue, and a torrential downpour swept over harbor and city. Sheets of rain poured upon the wretched prisoners huddled on the open decks. Heavily armed Pontic guards stood stoically in sodden blankets, holding chains binding the prisoners to keep them from leaping overboard. Archers lined the yardarms and rigging above their heads, bows drawn and dripping arrows aimed, to prevent any mishap during the dangerous maneuver. The Cyzicene defenders on the wall, watching numbly as their countrymen were paraded before them in the harbor, held off from firing their own weapons, waiting to see what Mithridates might do. Scattered cries and wails rose from the walls as women recognized their husbands and sons among the men lining the decks of the ships.

Father waited on the Pontic flagship for the downpour to slow, though as the clouds thickened overhead and the wind cut through our soaked woolen cloaks he finally gave orders to commence. His ship was brought to the fore of the squadron, within hearing distance of the populace lining the seawalls, and a bullhorn was produced. A man was then brought forward, a Pontic herald actually, who had been mussed and dirtied like one of the captured Cyzicene troops and taught a carefully crafted script in his role as a "prisoner" representing his comrades.

"Allies and friends!" he shouted through the bullhorn in passable Ionian Greek. The crowds on the walls fell silent. "You see our wretched condition, a fate we deserve because of our treachery in supporting Rome. We have killed fellow Greeks and fellow Asians and supported the barbarian Romans. Noble King Mithridates has wreaked his revenge, ravishing Heraclea and Chalcedon, besieging Cyzicus, and seizing us as his prisoners!"

The man fell silent for a moment as guards on the deck pretended to lash out with their whips at prisoners, raising cries of anguish from the watching townspeople. The "prisoner" again raised his bullhorn.

"Citizens of Cyzicus—you are our last hope, our last chance for mercy. The King has agreed to release us and spare our homes and families if Cyzicus surrenders to his forces. He will make us part of his great empire, his New Greece, and forgive all our aggressions. Three thousand of us are here on the ships, and more in the camp! All can return if you only give the word. If you refuse, however—"

Again shouts rose from the guards, with the cracking of whips. The populace on the wall gave a collective moan of despair.

"If you refuse," the herald shouted, "you will have betrayed not only us but our great Greek tradition. Even the Spartans, known to prefer death to surrender, made covenant with the Athenians to spare the prisoners captured at Sphacteria during their great war. Would you raise yourself up even above the honor of the Spartans? Surrender now, friends; spare our lives!"

More cries and wails rose from the wall, but this time in response not to the "prisoner's" words but rather to the strikes and blows from Cyzicene guards in the city, who leaped to the walls and hastily drove the civilians away from sight of the fleet, swearing at them and swinging the flats of their swords against the backs of the fleeing women and old men. The gusts rose and the ships struggled to maintain alignment in the harbor, finally scattering back to their anchorages. Only our flagship remained behind to hear the Cyzicene response.

Peering up through the driving rain, we could see the detachment of fierce guards lining the top of the wall, shields at the ready, eyes glaring sharply out from beneath the visors of their helmets. Their armor and exposed skin glistened wetly with the cold soaking from the sky and the stinging waves crashing against the wall beneath them. Their ranks parted, and an old man emerged from among them, his armor dented and worn, his shield unpolished. Even from this distance, white scars were visible on the brown skin of his upper arms. He was clearly an ancient, seasoned warrior.

"Pisistratus," Father snapped, looking at him. "He fought for me once. He's a fine old veteran. But he knows me better than anyone. And I know him." He sighed and began to turn away. "This day's over."

"Mithridates, you pig!"

The man's voice boomed over the crashing waves and the wind. Father froze and peered up at the man through the pelting rain.

"You threaten us by pleading to our women and children!" the old man bellowed, in a strong voice that belied his years. "You appeal to our cowardice to seize our city. But it is you who are cowards. You who parade helpless prisoners on your decks as if they were trinkets to be bartered."

"They are your own men, Pisistratus!" Father boomed out, annoyed. "I appeal to no emotions but those you elicit yourselves. I offer mercy for your people. Take it or leave it, as you see fit. I care not, for I will have your wretched city either way. The only difference is whether you prefer to live or die when I take it."

"Jackal!" the man screamed, enraged at Father's indifference. "Greek honor is not yours to call upon but mine to bestow. You bring prisoners before me, those who surrendered beneath the walls of Chalcedon. Soldiers who surrender forfeit the right to influence those who still fight. Slay them or sell them, it's of no concern—to the brave warriors of Cyzicus, your wretched prisoners are already dead!"

Father stared up at the glowering old warrior, then turned away, wiping the sodden hair from his eyes. The pants clung to him, cold and wet, like a second skin, and he was shirtless and armorless, with no protection from the driving rain. He seemed impervious to the elements, a man of wood, of iron, of an iron that did not rust or age. Yet even for a king on whom the rain and the cold have no effect the taunts of a brave soldier rankle, pierce the skin, and disquiet the heart. Father shook his head, and Neoptolemus shouted to the pilot to return to anchorage. The prisoners were herded belowdecks, half-dead from their exposure to the elements, despairing at the Cyzicene general's words.

Even as we rowed back through the harbor, we were replaced by the warships and the sambuca, the mighty sàmbuca, engineered to withstand even the harsh conditions it was now facing. We transferred to one of the warships crowding into the harbor, flame-hurling machines at the ready. Over the wind we could hear the women inside the city walls, weeping at their leaders' rejection of our offer.

The coordinated assault began on the land, and from our position on the ship we could see the arcs of flaming missiles—naphtha-impregnated bales, fire arrows, red-hot stones, tar-filled barrels—launched from batteries of siege engines just outside the landward walls. A horrific pounding drifted to our ears as the rams came into play against the gates. On the hills above, the Pontic legions massed in full battle array, standing stoically in the driving rain. They watched the massive assault and tensely awaited the orders to attack, the moment the gates lurched open or a position on the weakening walls crumbled. Cyzicene officers on the battlements rushed from crisis to crisis, plugging breaches, commandeering men to stack stones into gaps, directing archers to position, even forcing terrified women onto the walls to stamp out fires, carry water, and drag down the wounded.

The huge sambuca approached, rocking and swaying, the top of its tower crowded with armored assault troops sheltered behind a wall of shields. The body of the structure, open at the back, teemed with two hundred additional troops, poised to dash up the five flights of stairs the moment contact with the walls was made and the boarding planks dropped onto the battlements. The terrifying machine, perhaps the largest wooden structure ever seen by man, cut slowly through the sheets of rain and splashing waves, and at sight of it the troops manning the ramparts wavered, retreating from the walls where the landing was to be made. Officers shouted at them to repel the monster, but the ramparts were narrow, capable of accommodating only two or three men abreast. It was a terrifying thing for such few men to charge into the teeth of the approaching engine, with black-faced Pontics peering menacingly over the tops of their shields.

The sambuca came within range and the boarding planks slammed down onto the tops of the ramparts just at the corner of a looming watchtower. The Pontic troops loosed a roar that carried even above the wind, and dark-helmeted assault troops raced across, leaping onto the walls and careening two abreast into the narrow file of Cyzicene troops awaiting them there. Cutting down the first two defenders, the Pontic attackers stepped over their bodies and slashed into the next two. Our troops were superior in training and in strength, but the Cyzicenes were not fleeing—rather, they continued to block the narrow ramparts, even with their dead bodies, as the Pontics jammed up on the planks, unable to funnel onto the narrow catwalk. The rowers below struggled mightily to hold the ships steady against the mounting waves battering them from both fore and aft, as the huge swells rebounded off the seawall and crashed back into the bows of the vessels. Steadily they held; it would only be a few moments before our assault troops overran the defenders lined up to die on the wall before them. . . .

Yet as we watched in horror, a firepot, a bucket-sized wooden barrel filled with pitch and lit with a short wick, flew over the top of the watchtower and onto the deck of the nearest quinquereme. As the firepot cracked open upon impact, the oily flames spread in a broad puddle across the deck, pouring through the loosely spaced planks onto the top tier of rowers below. Bellows of pain emerged from the rowers' benches, and several sets of the long oars in the bow ceased their pulling as the occupants released the handles, entangling them in those of their neighbors. It was not a fatal attack, nor even one that was unexpected; but it was enough. The Cyzicene troops in the watchtower rallied at this minor success, and dozens of firepots and additional hand missiles were quickly launched at the now hesitating quinqueremes.

By now the wind had risen to gale force, and though the sambuca remained stable, its enormous weight was proving impossible for the rowers to manage. Try as they might, they were unable to hold the ships steady at the seawall against the driving wind and smashing waves, and the soldiers on the wall rained down fire and arrows at the ships at almost point-blank range. With the roaring wind, the oily fires quickly spread, engulfing planking and rails and dripping through the slats onto the hapless rowers below. From our vantage point, we saw that the entire top bank of rowers had now abandoned their positions, fleeing the flaming droplets pouring onto them from above; even the second bank of rowers was hesitating, as several oars from that level, too, were suddenly dropped and now dangled uselessly from the side of the craft.

A horrible realization struck us. "Withdraw the sambuca!" Father roared into the wind, but with the lashing storm he might as well have been shouting into a hole in the ground.

With its loss of rowers, the port-side vessel was no longer able to hold steady against the wall and began drifting back, spinning against its twin and rotating the entire mass—sambuca, bridge, and vessels—away from the ramparts. Men standing on the boarding plank and waiting to leap onto the walls were suddenly left hanging and dropped into the crashing sea below. Several poised just on the edge of the tower teetered dangerously before being hauled back to safety by their comrades inside. Most tragically, the heroes who had already managed to leap across to the walls were now isolated—separated from their comrades, even from the covering fire of the archers mounted on the top of the sambuca, who were clutching the walls of the spinning, rocking craft for balance.

The captains below gave orders to retreat, and the rowers back-paddled furiously out of range of the tar pots, calling in vain for sand buckets to extinguish the spreading fires. As they did, the stress of the rocking waves proved too much for the towering engine. With a groan of splintering wood, followed by a loud crack, the load-bearing timbers shattered, sending the entire contraption collapsing into the water. The starboard quinquereme was upended, the other crippled, and two hundred men toppled into the frothing waves. The harbor assault had to be abandoned.

After repelling the sambuca, the Cyzicene defenders rushed their forces to the opposite side of the city to fend off the fierce assault from landward. The fighting was desperate. Our battering ram had actually opened a breach through the gates, until the Cyzicenes brought up a load of copingstones—sharp-pointed triangular pieces used in construction for building corners and archworks—and dropped them onto the makeshift shelter protecting our ram, shattering the wooden roof and forcing our men to retreat. Other rams they caught in nooses or with "wolves," huge iron tongs let down the walls with cranes. Citizens cushioned the surviving sections of wall with baskets of wool or linen screens from their own homes, softening the impact of the iron bolts fired from the catapults and the stones hurled by our ballistae.

At one critical part of the wall, the flaming barrels of tar launched by our assault troops struck home, spattering sticky flames over a broad surface, which were fed by the roaring winds. Mortar turned to powder in the terrible heat, and the battlements collapsed. As the Pontic troops rushed in to scale the breach, however, they were quickly repelled—the stones were red-hot, even glowing, and the troops' hesitancy as they picked their way through the smoldering rubble allowed the defenders to drive them back with a company of archers. When the stones finally cooled, we found the gap had already been plugged with another hastily erected wall of debris.

We beached our vessel outside the harbor and we rushed on horseback to the landward side for Father to direct the assault from there. Yet as darkness fell, the wind increased even further, making it difficult for a man to even stand steadily, encumbered by a five-foot shield that acted as a sail. Under a steady rain of fire missiles now pouring down from the walls, our exhausted Pontic troops were forced to abandon their siege engines and retreat from the front line. The results could not have been otherwise. Despite the pelting sheets of rain, flames spread in all directions from the burning tar and naphtha and quickly engulfed the valuable machines. Towers of fire burned brightly, illuminating the battered walls of the city on the one side and the discouraged, sodden Pontics huddling without shelter or the consolation of victory on the other.

It is said that at that very moment the goddess Athena appeared in the ancient city of Troy, farther up the coast. Her gaze was wild, her breath panting, and her gown torn and drenched with water, as if she had just undergone a terrible ordeal—and the wide-eyed priests recalled that the defiant city of Cyzicus was dedicated to that very goddess. Troy's inhabitants were so moved by this spectacle that they erected a monument to the event, which stands to this day.

Indeed, the fickle favors of the gods were much on our mind that night, as Father gazed in rage at his flaming engines, now destroyed. He swore under his breath at the fruitless months of labor and waiting, all wasted. Yet his eyes did not linger long on the walls, for the city was now far down on his hierarchy of concerns; nor on his troops, who would recover to resume the siege tomorrow.

Rather, his gaze was directed up, to the cliffs of Adrasteia, where the ten thousand Roman campfires of Lucullus' army, in perfectly aligned grid and symmetry, burned brightly through the raging storm.

6

With the onset of winter, it became hard to tell who was more desperate—the city of Cyzicus, our besieging and besieged Pontic army, or Lucullus' restless and hungry Romans. We were feeding over three hundred thousand mouths on our barren peninsula, only a third of which belonged to fit fighting men—all the remainder were camp followers, slaves, and women we had foolishly acquired on our march to Cyzicus the previous summer. Added to this was the huge number of cavalry horses, an enormous burden on our supplies; and then the winter storms that shut down the fleet's ability to land provisions for us on the open beach inland of the city harbor. The massive army, which had never been able to store up food, passed immediately from a state of plenty to one of starvation. Sickness and disease ran rampant through the camp. Three hundred thousand people, poorly fed and worse sheltered, were crammed into a confined area, where even the most rudimentary sanitation had been neglected, since we had thought the conditions would be only temporary. Something had to give.

The pack animals were the first to go, the vast herds of Bactrian camels and mules, slaughtered as meat for the troops. This alone infuriated Father, who could foresee what would be next. When told that a hundred Pontic cavalry horses had been sacrificed to feed the starving men, he exploded.

"Not the horses!" he roared, knowing that the crack Pontic cavalry was the one clear trump he held over the Romans. "Better to eat the camp followers than our cavalry!"

And he did not smile when he said it.

Inside the city, things fared no better. The citizens were desperate, and cases of cannibalism had been reported by deserters and captured prisoners. Plague, too, had erupted and was threatening to spread outside the confines of the walls, and to prevent this I instructed our Pontic troops to shoot on sight any Cyzicenes who attempted to escape the city. Several weeks earlier there had been signs of rebellion within the walls against Pisistratus' harsh rule, and Father was confident the city would capitulate before our own situation deteriorated too far. But the inevitable had happened: Lucullus was finally able to get word to the starving citizens, by means of homing pigeons, that the army encamped in the Adrasteia Mountains was actually a Roman relief force, rather than Mithridates' troops. In one stroke, this new knowledge lent spine and determination to the besieged citizens, and they resolved to wait us out, knowing that we too were hemmed in on all sides and starving.

Yet Lucullus, too, was in a dire position. Pontic allies in the surrounding countryside had stepped up their harassment and increased their attacks on the tenuous supply line Lucullus maintained with his base in Cilicia. The harvests had long since been collected or destroyed, so there was little to be had by foraging. And the troops, who like well-trained fighting men everywhere had little patience for inaction or siege, were growing impatient with Lucullus' hesitancy.

It was only a matter of time, to see which side would break first.

Well into the winter, a heavy snowfall buried the troops in their huts, muffling the interminable wailing that wafted from the city, even stifling the smoke of the Romans' campfires, at which our own soldiers, having long ago run out of wood, stared almost as longingly as they did at the skinny shanks of the unused cavalry horses. With the snow, our hopes froze and shattered. Fearing the loss of our forces to starvation and disease, Father decided to abandon the siege of Cyzicus.

At Neoptolemus' orders, six warships of the armada, with full complements of crew, were collected at short notice from their various safe harbors in the nearby islands. Fearfully hugging the coastline as meager shelter from the howling winds and towering waves, they wended their way to the beach where the army was huddled. Father stood in the gravel, freezing water lapping at his sandals, and looked unhappily at the tiny fleet, compared with the hundreds of thousands of men, followers, and beasts for which he was responsible. He made his decision.

"Pharnaces," he ordered, "take the war chest and hostages by ship. Row to the ports along the Propontis where the fleet is dispersed and order the sailors to muster at Lampascus. Take Bituitus with you; display him as my double. When the Romans see him on board, they'll think I've fled. Marius and I will take the legions and cavalry around the Adrasteia and meet you in Lampascus." He made no mention of how he would manage to fight his way past the Roman lines, nor what would happen to the camp followers.

At these words, all around him broke out in protest. When he observed this, his cheeks flushed, despite the biting wind that cut through the thin woolen cloak he wore over his armor.

"We have no choice!" he shouted to the growing knot of soldiers who were beginning to gather on the beach, intrigued at the arrival of the six ships and peering through the stormy seas for more. "If the whole fleet were here, it couldn't carry even a fourth of our people! Convoys would be needed, repeated trips back and forth. Impossible in this weather."

"That's not what they're shouting about," I said, raising my voice above the gale and the growing protests of the soldiers around us. "They're angry that you also do not take the safety of the ship. Marius can lead the troops overland to Lampascus, if that's what we must do. Many men will be lost, though some will make it. But if *you* are killed, all is lost. The men will have no more will to fight, and the Romans will slaughter them. No, better for them to know that you have escaped and are waiting for them. You must take the ships."

He stared at me. "Abandon my men? You're asking me to abandon my men? To go on alone, with the war chest, carried by a squadron of pirates? Are you mad?"

I laughed bitterly. "You've trusted the pirates with your life before—why not with the treasure as well! Better it fall into their hands, better *you* fall into their hands, than into the hands of the Romans."

"Ha! So now I'm an old man, who needs to be coddled and can't slip past the Romans myself?"

I became deadly serious. "Father, you can't hide. The Romans know your every move; there are spies and traitors everywhere in a camp of starving men. A part of the army may slip past Lucullus to safety if you are not with them. But if you lead the men, every Roman will know that. They'll see you in your purple, and if you wear a plain cloak they'll know you for your height. Lucullus has offered twenty years' wages as a bonus to the man who brings you down—you'll be dead the moment you set foot out of our camp. The army stands no chance if you take them—but some may survive if you lead the way, by sea."

He bit his lip as he stared at the ships, rocking and swaying in the water just offshore, the sailors on board impatiently gesturing and waving to us every time we looked their way, nervous about remaining any longer than necessary away from the shelter of their ports.

"Very well," he said quietly, and the men around us immediately dropped their voices to an excited murmur. "But I will not yet go to Lampascus. The pirates will ferry me only as far as Parius. That island is a half-day's row from here. There I can remain in contact with the army, and return at short notice. Ha! From there I could swim if I had to!"

"I've been thinking," Bituitus interjected. Everyone fell silent and turned to him in surprise, for it was rare that he contributed to discussions of strategy. His face was stony and his eyes fixed straight ahead—the big Gaul was in the laborious grip of an idea. "You can still use me as a double. Send me with Marius and the troops. Give me your purple. That will draw the Romans' attention away from the ships and the camp followers here. Maybe it will buy them an extra day or two to escape."

Father reddened in anger and began to protest, but one look at Bituitus' determined expression silenced him. Grudgingly he agreed and boarded the vessel. Behind him, almost hidden among the squadron of guards who would be accompanying him, walked immortal Papias, bearing a sack of roots and plants. The old herbalist, I noticed, looked singularly frail and wispy, and it occurred to me how astonishing it was that he had even survived the harsh conditions we had lived through in recent months. Yet when he glanced up to where I was already standing on the deck, I saw that he bore a fire in his eye that matched Father's own.

That evening, Marius and the army, absent the camp followers, slipped off the peninsula under cover of darkness and skirted the Roman legions. Morning quickly revealed the ruse, and word spread of the sighting of "Mithridates." Lucullus gave chase with his legions, leaving only a body of auxiliaries behind to guard the camp followers on the peninsula until his return. The Romans caught up with Marius and the troops as they were crossing the Granicus River, and in their frozen and exhausted state the Pontics fought poorly, with over twenty thousand killed or captured, including many of the cavalry. Half the survivors died of exposure in the mountains before Marius was finally able to rally them and lead them to Lampascus, where they were taken inside the walls of the frightened city.

Meanwhile, Lucullus' army hurriedly returned to the peninsula to plunder the Pontic encampment, and there they massacred the entire body of camp followers, down to the last women and children, two hundred thousand or more. More than retribution for the Night of the Vespers years earlier, it was an act of frustration and fury at seeing Mithridates once again slip through their grasp.

Lucullus entered Cyzicus in triumph, while the legions set off to besiege the loyal city of Lampascus.

And Father? Separated from his beleaguered army, he stood raging on the docks of Parius, stranded in the tiny port by the furious winter winds.

BOOK SEVEN

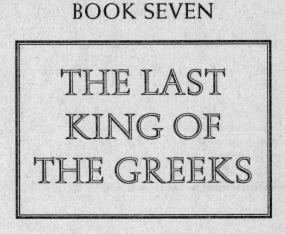

THE LAST KING OF THE GREEKS

It is impossible even for a god to escape the decree of fate.

—The Pythia of Delphi

1

"Otus, you old bear-flogger, is that you?"

It was the first time in weeks I had seen a smile on Father's face. No betting man viewing the situation, and all rational men are bettors, would find cause to put money on Mithridates. Our Greek allies had deserted us. The Scythians refused to send more mercenaries. Ancient King Tigranes of Armenia, Father's own son-in-law, ignored his letters. Agents we sent to recruit soldiers from among the fierce northern tribes went over to the Romans or deserted to the tribes themselves. And Father's domains were reduced again to his original tiny kingdom of Pontus, which he had inherited over forty years ago—forty years of planning, fighting, bleeding, and dying, to bring him naught but destruction and a Roman army pounding on his door.

Certainly the pirates had shown great courage in evacuating the Pontic army's survivors, including Bituitus and the Roman exile Marcellus, the cavalry tribune who had once challenged my leadership, from their besieged position at Lampascus. Yet Lucullus had not missed a beat; he sensed momentum, the favor of the gods. He captured the ship transporting Marius and executed him, though not quickly or honorably—for in a mock triumphal ceremony, in full view of all the sailors of his fleet and the captured Roman exiles, he had Marius mounted on a crosstree in that barbaric exercise the Romans call crucifixion and then lopped off his hands, feet, nose, and ears, pruning him like a fig tree in winter. It was a deliberately brutal message, and its effect was not lost, for it caused most of the other exiled Romans fighting for Pontus to scatter in discouragement.

Still this was not enough—Rome's goal was to destroy Pontus once and for all, and like a bloodhound it could smell its quarry nearby. Lucullus' fleet systematically wended its way along the kingdom's northern coast, matching pace with his legions onshore, and our coastal cities had fallen one by one. Now even Sinope itself was besieged, and thousands of panicked inhabitants had packed their belongings and were rushing to the safety of the mountains. For hours, Father, Marcellus, and I, leading a squadron of cavalry and heavy infantry, had been forcing our way along the refugee-clogged roads from Sinope south into the interior mountains. If it wasn't Lucullus' legions barring our cavalry's path, it was a column of farm carts five leagues long, snaking along the narrow dirt tracks.

Father on his war charger pulled up alongside a large, gaily painted wagon, its canvas tarpaulin depicting scenes of gladiators and wild beasts. The tiny driver on the awning-shaded platform in the front at first looked with puzzlement and alarm at the gigantic rider who had pulled alongside him, filthy from the road but armed with curved saber, daggers strapped to each thigh, and the huge horn-and-ash bow strapped to his back. There was no longer anything royal about the King, apart from his fierce and commanding demeanor. He slept on the ground, ate hardtack and meat roasted without salt, and bathed and slept only rarely. At sixty-two he had the strength and stamina of a man half his age. But the cares of the past year had taken their toll, and his face reflected the strain. The midget driver, his expression partially obscured in the shade of the awning, peered up at us.

"Your Majesty, it is indeed I!" an excited voice called huskily. "Only recently returned from my performances to triumphal acclaim in the palaces of the pharaohs of Egypt, to whom I had been sent with honor and tribute by the astonished court of the Persian King of Kings, after having been—"

"Enough!" Father interrupted, laughing but staring at the driver with a puzzled expression. "But who is it that speaks, Otus, and why do you remain silent? By the gods, you gypsy dwarves confound me; you live decades but age not a year; you—"

He in turn was interrupted by hoarse laughter as the flap of the tarpaulin behind the driver opened and a tiny wizened man crawled out, toothless smile creasing his weathered face like the ripened cracking of a piece of fruit, the very image of the brown-faced driver, though thirty years older. If ever I could have seen the future, it was now, for looking at the old man I could see exactly what the younger would be in his own dotage. The secret of immortality had been discovered by this tiny pair of Armenian travelers, and if the older one's soul was not passed on to his offspring, his body most certainly had been, and perhaps his memory and wit as well. In the end, is this not immortality to the same degree as any other?

"A pleasure to see you, my good king," Old Otus rasped, "and to find you in such astonishingly good health! Allow me to present my son, Otus"—the younger man smiled as broadly and toothlessly as his father, stood up on his short legs while keeping a cautious hand on the reins of the mules, and bowed with a flourish—"and my grandson. . . ." A tiny, bony brown head popped out of the tent flap beside the old man, peered at me wide-eyed, grinned not toothlessly but black-toothed—it was only a matter of time before he would be as much a gum-scoffer as his sires—and popped back into the tent. Odd-sounding growls and snorts emerged from within.

"Let me guess," I said, looking curiously at the old man. "And the boy's name is Otus?"

"By the glib tongue of Apollo," the man cackled. "You have a future as a fortune-teller! . . . Prince Pharnaces, I presume? I remember you well from an earlier visit to your extraordinary kingdom. A mere princeling you were then, clutching fearfully at your father's knee. The ape's penmanship surpassed yours—do you remember?"

Father roared at the recollection, but Marcellus leaned over to murmur in his ear. This was not the time to be trading jokes with old acquaintances. The garrison at the stronghold of Themiscyra was awaiting the troops we were bringing, to defend the pass to the strategic city of Cabira, only three days' march away. The leading cohorts of the Roman legions would be arriving within hours, and if the fort was not strengthened they would seize it, turning our own mountain defenses against us. Yet Father shrugged off Marcellus' urgency with irritation.

"By the gods, you Romans have raised even nagging to a military art! How often do I have the chance to speak with new men, who are free of fear and responsibility? Otus, you dog-thumper—you travel when you will, say what you like, crap where you please, and the rest of the world be damned. Truly kings covet your lot."

Old Otus looked down at his scaly bare feet and then back up wistfully at Father.

"Perhaps so, my lord—but I would say it is we who envy the likes of you, we who must worry what to put in our mouths day to day, how to fill our bellies. Glory falls to kings, not to humble old men—"

Father interrupted him with a snort. "Ah—but in that very glory lies my grief. I, too, must worry what is put in my mouth, by others, in the form of both words and food, and how to fill the bellies of fifty thousand men besides myself. I bear fifty thousand times the grief you do."

Otus looked bewildered. "But are those the words of a king? You jest, my lord. You were not born for a life of ease, nor one of poverty, like my own. The gods have given you a gift, command over men, and by disparaging the gift you mock the gods. Please, sire, the topic is ill-chosen. Let us speak of other things."

"Very well. What word, Otus—where do you truly come from recently?"

The old midget's face fell in disappointment that the King did not believe his previous boasting about the pharaohs, but he perked up immediately.

"Most recently, my lord, from Italy, whence I'm sorry to report, we were forced to . . . let us say, withdraw. On your account."

"Withdraw!" countered Otus the Younger scornfully. "We had to flee for our lives when you misspoke your patter, Old Windbag!"

"Aye, so I did," Otus Senior nodded ruefully.

"What! On my account?" Father exclaimed in puzzlement.

"In his introduction to our show," Otus the Second explained, "the dotty old codger mistakenly claimed we had been the toast of the Court of the Great King Mithridates, rather than the pharaohs of Egypt. You never heard such howls of rage. If rotten fruit were edible we could have eaten for a month, from just what we scraped off the sides of our wagon. He might as well have said we were the minions of Hades, the way mothers hide their children and grown men take cover at the very mention of your name, Your Majesty, pardon the frankness. Word spread ahead of us and we couldn't enter a town the whole length and breadth of the Italian peninsula. We figured it best to not risk crucifixion by staying in Europe; the only safe place for us is Pontus itself. We've spent the past year trundling up through Greece and Macedonia, just arrived in Pontus this past spring—and the Romans are still pursuing us. Apologies for dragging the legions along behind."

Old Otus simply nodded in agreement at this assessment of their predicament.

Father stared at the motley wagon and midgets wide-eyed, not knowing how to respond, until Marcellus again touched his shoulder, and I, too, urged Father to move on. Nodding curtly at the trio of Otuses, he prodded his horse to catch up with the troops ahead, still cursing and forcing their way through the shouting, disorganized throng.

Themiscyra was not a city but rather a fortress, a castle, a stronghold on the black-watered River Thermidon said to have been inhabited by the ancient Amazons. It stood on a promontory overlooking the single viable pass into the mountainous Pontic interior for miles in either direction. The road through the pass was broad and well traveled. In fact, there was no doubt the Romans could bull their way past if necessary, in hardheaded Roman fashion, by simply rushing through in a mass and emerging victorious on the other side by dint of sheer numbers. But the loss of life they would suffer by doing so, from the formidable artillery engines mounted on the walls of the fortress above them, would be atrocious. Moreover, leaving the castle untaken behind them as they made their way into the Pontic interior was not an option: Our army would be able to surround them, cut off their supply lines, and force a retreat or starvation. No, the Romans would have to take Themiscyra by force, and we knew that Lucullus could do it. No fortress in the world could stand up to Roman guile and determination.

But we would make Lucullus pay dearly for its capture.

Every day the fortress held out would be more time for Father's newly gathered army to consolidate. The Romans were far from home, with a badly stretched supply line. Time was our ally.

A day after we arrived with the extra troops to reinforce the garrison, Lucullus' advance forces were sighted, followed soon after by the main body of legionaries. They wasted no time gawking or wondering but set to work with an alacrity that makes Romans and other soldiers mere mortals.

Marius had long ago showed us that the legionary has a weapon that is the bane of the civilized world, one more formidable than the dual-edged Roman short sword, more effective than the bronze-headed javelin, of greater defensive strength than the concave bronze-sheathed shields. It is a weapon in which the legionary is trained from his first day of induction and which he uses daily, in peacetime or in war, on the march or hunkered in camp under siege from flaming missiles. And upon their arrival at Themiscyra, every able-bodied Roman immediately whipped out this most fearsome of all weapons:

The legionary's shovel.

Before even breaking to rest or scouting for supplies, the Roman troops had unpacked their shovels and commenced digging, and the dirt flew, and the dust rose. In the space of an afternoon, a Roman camp for thirty thousand men had been constructed just beyond range of our catapults. Before dark it had been ringed on all sides with a trench twelve feet deep and three feet across, the dirt thrown up into an embankment ten feet high inside the ring, topped with a thick palisade of sharpened stakes. Inside, four sturdy walls were constructed of felled trees, guarded by squat log towers twenty feet high, stationed every fifty feet and surmounted by bolt-hurling field catapults. Inside, a space of a full two hundred feet was left between the walls and the tent line, a distance calculated to prevent our missiles and burning arrows from reaching the tents. This space was occupied by prisoners, cattle, plunder, and supplies. Within a mere few hours, the Romans had constructed a stronghold that would be the envy of a lifetime's work of many civilizations poorer than theirs, a fortress impregnable.

Yet this was not a permanent stronghold they had built. This was the Romans' usual daily campsite. Every day of a legionary's working life he would dig such a trench, construct such an embankment, hew trees, and build such a palisade. All to be torched at sunrise, when the legions marched off to their next encampment. Javelins, when thrown, may miss their mark entirely. Shields may cave upon impact with a Scythian battle-ax; and a sword, though reliable at close quarters, still dulled, broke upon ribs, or shivered if struck upon armor. But the shovel—the shovel was the legionary's best friend, his most faithful protector, the one weapon that allowed him to sleep soundly at night, behind his magnificent trenches and embankments. The shovel could stop a cavalry charge cold, stymie hordes of barbarians. Rome conquered not with its brutal leaders, not with the strength of its soldiers, not with the ingeniousness of its weapons, but with the most rustic, pigheaded, inglorious, gods-bedamned tool of them all—the shovel.

And in this was Themiscyra's fall. The fortress was well stocked with food and the cisterns full, for the garrison had long anticipated the coming siege. Refugees from the countryside were well lodged against the inner walls all around, and even Otus' animals received provisions and were exercised, much to the consternation of the garrison troops upon first seeing the lion, wolf, and bear. These creatures had initially been prevented by the Pontic sentries from entering, though Otus had assured them that the beasts were properly sedated and defanged. It was only by Father's intervention that they were allowed passage behind the safety of the walls, on his personal guarantee that they would cause no harm. The stronghold was secure. Food and water were not a problem; the walls were unscalable, the steep approaches unsuitable for Roman battering rams or siege engines.

Yet the Romans doggedly set upon the attack with their fearsome shovels. Within a week, a thirty-foot section of Themiscyra's main wall had collapsed, undermined by a tunnel burrowed beneath it from the legionaries' camp. The sandy soil had been carefully shored with stout timbers, then the tunnel stuffed with straw, tinder, and pitch-coated firewood. Our sentries on the wall first sounded the alarm at sunset, when they saw black smoke rising from a line of airholes that had been surreptitiously punched from the tunnel ceiling up to the ground. Moments later, with a low rumble, one of the fortress's closely fitted stone walls collapsed into a pile of rubble, burying several of the guards who had been standing upon it, as all of us inside stared in stupefaction.

At the same time, we heard the Roman trumpet call to charge, and an entire legion, commanded by Lucullus himself, rushed out of the twilight under a hail of covering arrows and small-shot fired by portable ballistae they had dragged outside the Roman palisade.

Fortunately, we had not been caught completely unawares, for at that very moment Father had been conducting drills on the fortress's small parade grounds, just adjacent to the breach in the wall, and a good number of armed troops were in the vicinity. After the initial surprise, the Pontic garrison scrambled to the top of the demolished wall, taking cover behind tottering battlements and tower debris. They began heaving building stones down onto the legionaries, who themselves were having a difficult time scaling the structure in the semi-darkness, hampered by their helmets and shields. At length the Romans were repelled with heavy losses, while we lost not a single life, except for the unfortunate guards crushed by the initial collapse of the wall. Nonetheless, a gap had been created, which the garrison spent the entire night filling, doing two weeks' worth of stone humping in a mere three watches. The wall of rubble was finally raised to the same height as the undamaged sections on either side and we managed to lodge several hundred sharpened stakes into the cracks between the collapsed stones on the outside, to hamper any new attempts by the Romans to scale the weakened section.

But the Romans still had their shovels.

Peering over the walls the day after the attack, Father could see the path the next such assault would follow, for the rock outcroppings between the fortress and the Roman camp limited the routes any tunnelers could take, unless they were willing to bore through solid rock. Even this would not be unthinkable for Romans. Identifying the most likely direction from which the next tunnel would come, he gathered his own makeshift team of miners at that point of the walls and called for a bowl.

"A bowl?" I repeated, uncomprehending, after our troops had gathered with their own shovels and shoring equipment. A bronze bowl, a *krater,* used for mixing wine with water before serving, was brought by a priest from the nearby temple of Artemis and given to the King.

"Behold our new ears!" he said, and then motioning all to silence, he set the bowl upside down on the ground by the wall, knelt, and put his own ear to the upended dome. With a grim smile, he motioned me over to listen.

Amid the shuffle of the men around me I could clearly hear, through the bronze of the bowl, the clanging and chopping of metal, the scraping and pounding of tools against soil—digging. The Romans were below us and not far distant. Thirty men took their turns listening, and their eyes grew round at the mysterious sounds from beneath the earth. They needed no further urging to set to their task.

That night, contact was made with the Roman gallery at a tangent to our own wall, five arm's lengths beneath the surface, and the first Pontic miner to punch through was surprised to find it abandoned—in fact, he had entered just as the Roman shift was changing and had sufficient time to quickly reconnoiter the enemy tunnel, which was comparatively large: well shored with stout timbers, tall enough for a man to stand stoop-shouldered, and broad enough for three to stand abreast—or two with armor and weapons. Hastily backing out and plugging the hole he had just made, the Pontic digger crawled back behind Themiscyra's walls to report his find.

Father rubbed his hands. Identifying twenty eager volunteers, he armed them with daggers and swords, all that would be necessary for a confrontation in the tight confines of the tunnel with unarmed Roman diggers. Armor and shields would only impede them. At dawn, the men descended naked one **by one,** white teeth grinning out of black-painted faces.

On the parade ground above, a hundred men lay sprawled on the earth, as if dead or injured. In fact, each had pressed his ear to a bowl or concave shield and was listening eagerly for the sounds of the underground battle. They were not disappointed. Muffled shouts came filtering through the layers of sand, the clang of metal on metal as the hapless miners defended themselves against the underground Pontic attack. More shouts, groans even, and then silence.

Father strode over to the tunnel entrance to greet his returning warriors. None came.

Suddenly the sentry on top of the wall above us shouted out, "Romans emerging!"

I leaped up the stone stairs of the inner wall three at a time to the sentry position. "Show me, soldier!" I demanded.

But there was no need for the soldier's directions. Before us, just out of bow shot, a squadron of armored legionaries, caked head to foot in sandy red clay, emerged from the main gates of the Roman encampment, dragging behind them a long rope. Trussed to it at evenly spaced intervals were the twenty Pontic volunteers we had sent down the hole scarcely an hour before. All were bloodied, their naked torsos and unprotected heads torn by the stout weapons the Romans had inflicted upon them in the ambush. The bodies, one or two still twitching with life, were laid in a row, face up, sufficiently far from the Roman trench as to not offend Lucullus by their stench but too close for us to retrieve. There they were placed to bake in the hot sun in full view of our sentries, a foul testament to the Romans' cunning. That night, the sounds of cutting and digging continued, from what seemed at least three different places. We were helpless to stop it, unable to determine precisely where they might be or what to do if we did know.

In the garrison headquarters that evening Father shook his head in resignation at reports that the Romans were massing behind their gates for another attack.

"We're losing the fortress," I said.

He eyed me. "That was never in doubt. You have to pick your battles. Some you know you can win, though it may be that you only *think* you know. Some you know you'll lose. But sometimes the ones you know you'll lose can be the most costly to the enemy. That is what I had hoped to make of Themiscyra. We don't need this fortress—we need time, at least one more night! The army is still collecting in the mountains."

Suddenly distant shouts were heard from the Roman encampment.

"The attack has started," Father said, rising swiftly.

I was surprised, because I had not felt the collapse of any walls, nor heard reports of smoke plumes from airholes. Rushing outside, we found the entire Pontic garrison standing along the wall facing the Roman side, watching agog as the legionaries' camp fell into chaos. The ranks of infantry preparing to storm our walls had been broken, and Roman cavalry squads thundered pell-mell through their own camp, brandishing torches and firing arrows at dark shadows racing through. Roars and shouts were heard, and a squad of naked, dirt-encrusted diggers burst through the Roman gates to the outside. They pushed past the astonished sentries and leaped into the trench outside the palisade, where they lay rolling in the mud. Father watched the spectacle in amazement, as even Lucullus had difficulty restoring order to the legions who had lost their normal relentless discipline. Order was eventually restored, but by that time darkness was about to fall and it would be impossible for the Romans to launch an effective attack against the walls.

From the Roman gates soldiers appeared, each leading a balking mule by the halter, dragging heavy burdens behind them. In the waning light it was difficult to identify the five black mounds trailing in the dust—three enormous figures, two much smaller. It was only when they were brought alongside the row of festering bodies from our previous attack that we were able to make out the corpses of a bear, a lion, a wolf, and an ape—along with a midget.

Father turned back into the fortress in horror.

"Otus!" he bellowed. "By the balls of Neptune, where is that old relic? Otus!"

After a moment, Otus the Younger, the middle-aged midget, was fetched and came running forward, stopping before us. He was barely higher than Father's knee.

"Your Majesty," he said quietly, peering into the King's face, tears streaming down his cheeks.

"Otus, Otus!" Father raged. "Imbecile! What have you done? What has your *father* done?"

"He was a sick old man, my lord, but this was his wish. He has bought you one more night."

"One more night?" Father said. "But . . . those animals . . . they were toothless! They were meek as lambs! How . . . ?"

"They have always been sedated, my lord. They take their poison daily—like you." The midget allowed himself a wan smile. "But we ran out of their herbs two days ago, and here in the fortress we had no chance of finding more. The beasts were awakening, for the first time since they were cubs. They would be a danger to the refugees. So Father Otus decided upon this measure. He himself rode the wolf into the tunnel. And we gave the beasts additional encouragement to be brave in the face of the Romans."

"Additional encouragement?" I repeated. "What additional encouragement do you give wild beasts?"

Again Otus smiled. "We rolled hornets' nests down the tunnel behind them. There was only one direction the animals could run."

I recalled the view of the screaming Roman diggers racing out of the camp and leaping into the mud of the entrenchment and now understood.

That night, with the entire garrison and old Papias, we slipped out a secret postern to the rear of the castle and filed along a narrow trail cutting through the terraced gashes of an ancient quarry. Blocks of limestone stood derelict where they had been lifted and propped from their graves a century before, glowering sentinels whose clean, hard faces were stained and shadowed by creeping growths of lichen, their surfaces skinlike and menacing in the silver starlight. We silently knifed the Roman sentries posted at the abandoned mortar kiln below the quarry, swam the horses across the Thermidon, and raced into the mountains along goat tracks Father had known since he was a young boy hiding in these mountains with his friends. Themiscyra and all the civilian refugees surrendered to the Romans the next day.

2

After two days of hard riding through the steep, gravelly canyons of interior Pontus, we arrived at the hidden valley of Cabira, where we were met by our army of forty thousand. Marius was long dead, of course, and most of the Roman officers under him had scattered with the winter storms in the Propontis. One important exception was Marcellus, whom Father had appointed commander of the few remaining Roman exiles. But apart from these few Roman loyalists, this was a now purely native army, levied solely among the powerful chieftains of the interior, horsemen to the last, loyal to the royal family for the past six generations, familiar with Father and his companions since their days roaming these mountains half a century before. Their ways were known, their fighting styles tested. Father greeted hundreds of them by name, inquiring after their families and homes, remembering their distant relatives, joking with them in their local dialects. These were men he could trust, men who, because of their isolation or wealth, had held off from the Pontic wars until now—but now that the kingdom itself was under siege, they called together their vassals and thralls at this secret valley. Lucullus would meet his match here at Cabira, at Mithridates' last stand.

The Roman general did not even hesitate. After capturing Themiscyra with nary a struggle, he seized several shepherds, tortured them for information, and marched straight upon us. Rather than hunkering down in our stronghold, however, Father and I led ten thousand horsemen straight out to meet the Roman vanguard, encountering them in a narrow ravine a half-day's fast march from where they expected to find us. After a fierce clash, the Roman advance cohorts broke and fled, scattering into the brush and escarpments. Our Pontic horsemen ran them down, splitting their heads like melons with scimitars or simply trampling them with their swift ponies, while Father, Bituitus, and I sat our horses on a rise in their midst, watching. The Roman vanguard was slaughtered to the last man, some five hundred of them, with the exception of a tribune named Pomponius, who, it turned out, was Lucullus' cavalry commander. He was dragged before us bleeding from a terrible injury from a scimitar stroke, his helmet split asunder and the skull of his brow nearly hacked away. Nevertheless, though barely able to stand, he took one look at Father, hawked, and spit a great gob of phlegm on his feet.

The Pontic captains were outraged and immediately began roughing the soldier up even worse, but Father stopped them, forcefully shouldering his way through his own men until he stood face-to-face with the panting tribune and placed his gigantic hand under the Roman's throat.

"*Salve, Tribune Pomponii,*" he addressed him, in a studied and menacing Latin. "Your entire cohort has been destroyed, and I hold your life in my five fingers. I will not mince words. I need a message brought to Lucullus. Tell him to withdraw from Pontus, and I will let his army go in peace. If not, his legions will be destroyed, just as your miserable crew was here today. Do this, Tribune, and you shall be my friend. I treat my friends well. Refuse, and . . ." He tightened his fingers around the Roman's neck for an instant as the man's eyes bulged.

The Roman dropped to his knees, clutching his bruised throat, while the Pontic captains crowded around him, muttering at his defiance.

"Step back!" Father roared. "Give the man some air—he has a mission!"

Pomponius struggled to his feet, recovering his breath only with difficulty, and straightened his shoulders. Blood had crusted on his head and face, covering one eye completely and making it difficult for him to see. Yet none of the fierceness had left his countenance as he glared at the King.

"Your friend!" he rasped hoarsely. "Your friend! By the

gods, if you yield to Lucullus I will be your friend, not before. Otherwise, kill me if you will, but I will always be your enemy!" And again he began hawking and eyeing the King's feet.

Bituitus stepped forward and slammed his massive fist into the man's stomach, doubling him over and dropping him to his knees.

"Piss-ant Roman," the big Gaul growled. "You are too faithful to your master by far."

Pomponius looked up, eyes watering from retching.

"Your taunt is my boast, Gaul."

Bituitus drew his sword and took careful aim at the man's swaying head as the Pontic chieftains erupted in shouts of encouragement and backed cautiously out of blade range.

"Dog," Bituitus hissed. "You'll bleed for that. Your head will decorate my tent pole."

The Roman smiled through his split and bleeding lips.

"Pedicabo te." Fuck you.

Bituitus flushed in fury and drew back his sword for the stroke, but Father stopped him, stepping between the two men.

"Hold, Bituitus. By Zeus, if only your wit were as sharp as your blade. The man is strong—he will not be broken. I would expect nothing less if you were captured by Lucullus."

Bituitus lowered his sword slowly, but the long-haired and bearded Pontic captains, who understood nothing but the fact that this man had insulted their king, erupted in outrage at Father's words.

"Think!" Father shouted. "We are asking this man to betray his country and his general, to become a traitor—and for this we are to reward him? Would you expect leniency from Lucullus if you were to betray me? The ultimate betrayal, your own life for your country's! This man is loyal—he, of all Romans, deserves to return to his homeland. Give him a horse and send him back to Lucullus. Whether we make him our friend or not, he will convey the message."

With angry mutterings, a horse was procured and bloodied Pomponius strapped to it, to prevent his falling off in his weakness. He was then led away by a Pontic scout, to be taken back down the road whence the Romans would soon be arriving.

The Romans were now in a desperate position—far from their base, in the heart of enemy country. Lucullus would be de-

stroyed if he marched through the valleys or across the few
plains in the region, where our Pontic horsemen could cut him
down at will; yet the mountains were too rugged, the risk of ambush too high, to confine himself there. When he learned the
fate of his vanguard, well before arriving at Cabira, Lucullus
marched to the top of a small hill, one somewhat isolated from
the surrounding heights, and there entrenched a solid camp, a
Roman camp, one impossible to attack, and hunkered down to
decide what to do next.

For three days, we paraded our forces before the Roman
camp, sending horsemen galloping within catapult distance of
the stolid legionaries, hoping to lure them out to battle on the
plain below their hilltop. And for three days Lucullus refused
even to launch any missiles from his guard towers at the Pontic
cavalry, taking all our humiliating taunts and jeers silently, as
patiently as a hermit, his guards lining the palisades and watching our ever more daring maneuvers. Time was on our side—
we would starve the Romans out of their stronghold, if
necessary.

On the fourth day, our spies reported that a large supply train
was making its way north from Cappadocia to provision the
Roman camp. Father leaped at the opportunity to deal a deathblow to his foe. He sent a full complement of cavalry, near
twenty thousand riders, thundering south to intercept the convoy, while he remained behind with the infantry to maintain the
siege on the Roman camp. I stayed behind as well, hobbled by
a wound.

Lucullus saw what was at risk, and even before our own cavalry could be dispatched, he sent ten infantry cohorts, a full Roman legion, marching out to escort the convoy to safety. We had
no word of the outcome until two nights later, when four hundred Pontic horse straggled back into camp.

"My lord," said the squad's senior officer, a loyal cavalry
captain from Pharnacia named Myron who had served with us
for many years. He tumbled off his quivering horse at Father's
feet. "All is lost."

Father stood in stupefied silence, unable even to muster the
words to demand an explanation.

"The Romans ambushed us," Myron groaned. "Drew us into

a ravine where we couldn't maneuver the horses, and cut us down."

"All twenty thousand of you?" the King whispered, stunned. "The Romans were only one legion. . . ."

"No, not all of us, my lord," Myron mumbled as if ashamed, though he, in fact, had fought bravely. "Many, but not all. Four thousand, perhaps five thousand."

"And the rest? Only four hundred have returned. Where are the rest?"

"Scattered, my lord, scattered to their homes. When they saw the battle had been lost, they despaired of returning to you, and feared for their families with the Romans now in control of the southlands. Your cavalry is gone."

Myron was wrong, though not by much. An additional one or two thousand survivors trickled in during the night, but no more. Father could scarcely comprehend it. His infantry alone was incapable of standing up to Roman legionaries, and without horse, our one advantage over the enemy was gone. So, too, were our eyes and ears, for the wide-ranging cavalry scouts kept us supplied with information on the Romans' movements and the surrounding conditions. Without horse, we must retreat from the open valley in which we had been besieging the Roman camp. We must flee back into the mountains.

For the first time in my life, I saw Father near despair. His one bit of fortune was that the cavalry survivors had made their way back faster than the Roman infantry could pursue. The main body of the Roman forces was still several hours down the road; it would be some time before Lucullus himself would receive confirmation of his victory. If the gods were with us, if we acted quickly, we might still be able to disengage and melt into the hills before the Roman army had consolidated its forces for an attack.

Normally, the slowest part of any army is the baggage train. In an emergency, most of the baggage can be left behind if necessary—but not all. Chief among the baggage that must be retained at all costs is the war chest, along with the accompanying army records, maps and related documents, the royal regalia, the personal savings of the senior officers, and other such items, which are bulky and difficult to carry. Mules and carts are the preferred mode. Cabira had been the *de facto* capital of

Pontus for over a year, since the siege of Sinope had begun, and therefore all official records for the entire country, as well as much of the royal treasure, were here. This baggage was not merely spare armory and tools. It was critical that it be saved, that it not be left behind to the Romans.

Father made a rash decision. So as not to panic the troops, he quietly ordered a convoy of mules to be prepared for immediate evacuation, before news of the general retreat was released to the army as a whole.

But there are no secrets in an army as inbred as that of Pontus. Scarcely before the orders had even been issued to load the valuables, the false rumor flew among the ranks that the King and his senior command were sneaking away by dark with their assets, abandoning the troops to fend for themselves. This was preposterous, of course—Father had been in many tight scrapes during his life and had never abandoned his men—but it was a rumor that the common soldiers, nervous already at the news of the cavalry disaster, were ready to believe without a second thought. Each man concluded that if the officers were fleeing, he himself could do no better than to run as well. And when the rear gates of the Pontic camp were opened to let the baggage mules slip through on their head start, they were rushed by a mob of frantic men. The gods of Chaos and Rout set to work.

The tumult and confusion that engulfed the camp were indescribable. Officers were sought out and slaughtered. Captains who had always held the awe of their troops were cut down like thieves, their bodies hoisted into the air, gleaming a bloody red in the torchlight. Even the chief priest Hermaeus was trodden underfoot and smothered at the camp gate, an indication of the utter terror that had gripped the camp—for no men in their right minds would dare to so mistreat a priest, for money or for fear. By the avenging gods above, it was the worst night of my life.

And Lucullus, up on the hill, saw it all.

Without waiting for dawn or even for the arrival of his ten cohorts still in the field, Lucullus organized his soldiers and bet everything on one massive attack. Our guard outposts had deserted us with the outbreak of the riots, and the Romans descended without warning upon our panic-stricken camp. Before we knew what was happening, shrill Roman trumpets were blaring their signals in our very ears, and the echoes had not even subsided before all hell was loosed upon us.

They took no care for tactics or precautions—they simply burst through our gates like a hurricane, storming over everything in their path, tents, latrines, men already dead and dying from the mob action that had taken its toll. Fires were trampled, torches sputtered out, and all was darkness but for the ghostly gleam of the starlight above, reflecting ironlike and malevolent on the Romans' whirling swords. Pontic officers shouted to bring their troops to order, to face the onslaught, to organize a coherent line of defense, but to no avail—scarcely had the words left their mouths than they were cut down, by Romans in their midst or by their own men. It was every man against the Pontic officers and every Roman against the Pontic soldiers and no man against the Romans. Each Pontic soldier fled where best he was able, stumbling blindly in the dark, trailing blood from wounds inflicted by comrades and enemies alike, falling over writhing bodies impeding his path. Men raced in all directions, seeking only the path of least resistance, a place of shelter, a ditch or mound or small copse of trees. The disaster was overwhelming.

At first Father and I tried to rally the troops, though we wasted precious time before we even realized the reason for the panic, the misunderstanding that had led to the mutiny in the first place. During this time we were very nearly killed by our own men. A dozen rioters recognized Father and surrounded his horse, attacking him with their daggers. Caught utterly by surprise, he kicked with his feet and spurred his horse forward, but they leaped upon the animal's neck and by sheer weight of numbers pulled it down and tumbled Father off. Leaping clear of the fallen animal, he scrambled up, drew his sword, and began slashing his way in the darkness to where he could see the outlines of Bituitus and me against the starry sky, ourselves under attack as well. He hacked his way through the tumult, bellowing his rage at his own men. Yet before he could arrive, our horses, too, were tumbled, and we toppled into the melee. Only the darkness and confusion and the rioters' own greed for the horses and for whatever riches they might have been bearing saved us from instant death.

Bituitus and I scrambled up from beneath the mutineers and the flailing hooves of the terrified animals. I leaned heavily on the Gaul's shoulder, my leg in excruciating pain from the fall. Somehow we made our way over to Father, who by now had taken understanding of the situation, discarded his purple tunic, and ceased the bellowing of his instantly recognizable voice. He was furious at seeing all destroyed by his very own men, but there was nothing for us to do. Wearing neither helmets nor armor, we seized shields from bodies lying on the ground, drew our swords, and joined the chaotic flight out the rear of the camp.

Jostled on all sides by panic-stricken men, we rushed blindly along the dark, crowded road, like rafts careening down a roaring river. Men shouted and screamed on all sides of us; bodies jostled against us as men tripped over stones or their own comrades. Fighting was out of the question—it took all our senses and strength merely to remain on our feet, for to stumble and fall beneath that fear-maddened crowd would have meant certain death. Yet even our best efforts were not enough, as suddenly we heard the battle trumpet, again almost in our very ears, accompanied by the thundering of mounted cavalry. The Romans, who had ridden through to the far side of our encampment, were now chasing down Pontic survivors, slaughtering them in the dark—and searching for Mithridates, the greatest prize of all.

There was no chance of escape—the hooves sounded on both sides of us, and on the road ahead forward progress had stopped as well, as men bunched up, blocked by the cavalry that had cut through from that side. Terrified men scattered to the four winds, trusting in the darkness of the night to lead them between the legs of the Roman horses. Now all men avoided one another, knowing instinctively that to cluster in a group, to form a dark spot of a target in the graying light, would be to invite a rush from the marauding Roman cavalry. Each man fled like a rabbit, diving to the ground when overtaken by racing hooves, hoping to be trampled rather than lethally hacked, and suddenly we found ourselves alone on the road, as chaos and terror reigned all around.

We kept our heads, and better yet, the gods finally had pity upon us and sent us a meager portion of fortune. Peering through the penumbra and the dust churned by the stamping cavalry, we saw, unbelievably, one of the baggage mules that had been packed with treasure and sent ahead—the very cause of the mutiny. It was plodding along the road through the midst of the chaos, without rider or driver, as stolid and unthinking as if treading a solitary mill path, its comrade mules having long since been killed or taken fright. Thinking to use the animal to escape, we raced forward, but our sudden movement was detected by a roving squad of Roman cavalry. We could not have been recognized as officers in the half-light, yet it was of no consequence. Wheeling their horses, they thundered toward us, drawing their swords.

There was no time to flee, nor place to flee to, for enemy cavalry stalked the entire field. Arriving at the mule ahead of us, Father drew his blade and with a great slashing motion brought it down full-strength—into one of the swollen bags of gold that had been bundled onto its side.

With a solid clash of metal on metal, the sack burst open and gold coins flew in all directions, pouring in a heap at the mule's feet and leaving a glittering trail of gold staters on the ground as the blow spurred the lethargic animal into a braying trot. Raising his sword again, Father slashed it down onto the other side, splitting open that bag as well, showering silver tetradrachmae in all directions, and this time causing the mule to sit down on the spot, in protest at this undignified treatment. Father had time to raise his sword once more, to give the stupid beast a mighty whack across the back with the flat of his weapon, attempting to make it get up and run, but to no avail, and he tried no further. The gods had been good thus far and it would be unseemly to complain—best not to push our luck.

At the sight of the gold spilling into glittering mounds on the ground, the cavalry riders pulled up short. Like Atalanta spying the golden apples Melanion tossed on the ground before her in the footrace, they lost all sight of their original goal. Leaping off their horses, they dove at the bewildered mule, ripping off its half-empty baggage sacks, scooping up handfuls of plunder, and shoveling it into the helmets they had torn off their heads. We wasted no time. Leaping onto three of the horses the Romans had abandoned, we thundered off down the road, threading our way between the bands of Roman cavalry racing to the fallen gold like flies to dung. They gave us not a second glance. Nor were we pursued farther, for despite their overwhelming victory, the Romans preferred not to extend themselves but rather to stay and plunder our camp by daylight.

No man in history, I am certain, has raised as many armies as did Father during his three wars against the Romans. Yet, I would venture to say, none has ever lost an army as quickly as he did that night. The men who scattered did not regroup, but for a skeleton force of perhaps two thousand, of varying degrees of armor and health, who eventually tracked and joined us in the dry canyons of the upper Lycus over the next several days. The remainder simply disappeared, killed by the Romans or having slunk off to their homes in shame. Between the space of a sunset and a sunrise, the last Pontic army, forty thousand strong, had disappeared from the face of the earth.

3

For six months we ran like thieves, dodging from castle to castle in the remote Pontic hinterland, clashing in small skirmishes with Lucullus' scouting parties. For the first few weeks after the debacle at Cabira the Roman cavalry rode hot on our trail, eager to capture the ultimate prize that had eluded it for decades. We avoided even the hospitality of Father's old vassals, as Lucullus pulled his political strings as deftly as his military ones—he tortured and killed anyone found to have given us aid as we passed through their territory and rewarded with gold or political office those who had ignored our demands for provisions or, worse, who gathered their own militias and chased us away like starving dogs. Our beautiful capital of Sinope finally fell to the Romans—demoralized, starving, and deserted by its last seagoing line of defense, the pirates, who had departed for more profitable waters. The city was burned to the waterline, its inhabitants scattered. Amisus met a similar fate shortly afterwards, and Pharnacia could only be next as the Romans methodically pushed farther east, tightening the noose.

To the south, Cappadocia was occupied; to the north, sea access was cut off; and the Roman army was advancing, pace by measured pace, from the west. We still had mountain strongholds to give us temporary shelter, but they were falling rapidly, and with each defeat another crack appeared in the loyalty of those that remained, making our safety and secrecy all the more tenuous. A king can rarely travel in secret, even among staunch allies. In every town we entered, Father was openly hailed by the populace for his stand against Rome and secretly vilified by those who feared we brought destruction in our wake, like a deadly plague. It became too risky even to spend the night within the walls of a castle—there had been too many ambushes, too many raids by wide-ranging Roman assassination squads.

Our band dipped into villages on market days to provision ourselves and then thundered out again as fast as we had arrived, spurning any ceremony or escort, making camp in hidden locations where we could escape quickly, avoiding campfires by day, which might attract the enemy by their smoke, seizing and silently garroting any Romans careless enough to stumble within our grasp. All this we did in hopes that news of our whereabouts would be muddled or lost, but to no avail. For every scout we killed, three more were visible watching us on the horizon. For every chieftain who proclaimed his undying fealty to the King, ten shepherds and farmers could be found willing to betray our location, for the price of a silver tetradrachma or two.

It was impossible to regroup under these circumstances. New forces could not be raised; recruits could not be trained. We could barely feed ourselves, and soon of the original two thousand that had reunited after the fall of Cabira barely half remained. Father no longer even bothered hunting down deserters—in the past, such traitors had been treated even more harshly than captured enemy, for in his eyes, the enemy was at least loyal, even if to the wrong cause, and therefore held some redeeming qualities. Now, however, desertions elicited nothing but a weary shrug from the King.

The sparkle of energy had gone from his eye, replaced by a weary squint. His flowing hair, always worn long and loose behind his back in emulation of Alexander, turned from chestnut brown to steel gray in a matter of weeks. His frame, though still massive and strong as it had ever been, was now leaner and rangier from hours in the saddle and irregular rations; he had even lost the confident spring in his step I had always tried to emulate, and now strode with a preoccupied gait, a slight stoop to the shoulder, a worried cast to his expression. Since the fall of Cabira, Father had become old, like a man who had for years drunk daily from the elixir of life but who had suddenly lost the formula and whose true age of sixty-two was now catching up with him in a rush. Only one ruler in the entire region was older, his own son-in-law Tigranes of Armenia, who was perhaps another twenty years his senior and was said to be decrepit and bordering on dementia. Armenia was to the east, the only route still open to us ahead of the advancing Roman legions, and it was from old King Tigranes that we would seek refuge.

As we threaded our way through the narrow gorges and defiles of the rough interior, Father's thoughts were not on how he could save his possessions and kingdoms—the time for that was long past. Rather, they were on how best to deny the Romans the use of these possessions. The castles we passed now were torched by our own hands as we departed, their treasure and royal records packed to be taken with us or buried in secret locations. Many of the local chieftains loyally acceded to this terrible step and combined their garrison forces with us in the withdrawal east. Even castles and strongholds not on our route were destroyed, as Father sent trusted officers fanning out in all directions, bearing dispatches ordering his vassals to remove everything of value and join him across the border in Armenia. Most obeyed, and the Romans, as they picked their own way east, found fortresses in smoldering ruins, the vital records of Father's rule and campaigns destroyed, and Roman informants put to the knife.

Yet the most sensitive embassy of all was one I myself led to the coastal city of Pharnacia, where dwelt the women of the royal harems, sent there for safekeeping years before. My orders were to pack up and remove any women whom Lucullus might consider worthy of a place in his Triumph in Rome. I thundered into Pharnacia with a small squadron of Pontic soldiers and an old eunuch named Bacchides, whom I could trust to recognize the great ladies, some of whom had been sent to the cloister before I was even born. We arrived only a day before the Roman fleet secured the seaport and two legions of Lucullus' army closed the roads out of the city behind us. A safe rescue of the delicate women, some of them elderly, would be impossible. The Romans would capture them, probably rape them, and carry them to Rome, the worst disgrace they could suffer, not to mention Father himself. There was only one solution.

The King's two elderly sisters, my aunts Roxana and Statira, whom I had not seen since my childhood and whom I did not recognize, were the first. Roxana, the old harpy, went down fighting, cursing Father to Hades for the fate that had left her a lifelong, bitter virgin, unable to marry him after his disastrous union with Laodice yet prevented from marrying any other man of lesser rank. She bitterly drank down the goblet I handed her of warm mare's milk laced with arsenic and lay down on her cot. Between her final convulsions the old woman mustered just enough energy to grasp my sleeve, pull me down close, and spit in my face. She smiled in satisfaction as she died.

Statira, though several years younger than Roxana, had lived as her virtual twin, also forbidden a normal life. Unlike her embittered sister, however, Statira was almost cheerful at her fate. She took the cup and calmly held it aloft to inspect it, striking a noble pose like some tragic queen of the Greek dramas. As she drank she winced involuntarily at the burning in her throat, but unlike her sister she composed her expression, lay down, and gave thanks to her brother for affording her the opportunity to die a death noble and free, rather than enslaved by the Romans.

Though I had scarcely known these two women, the experience unnerved me greatly. I have fought in battles, killed men, dressed my own wounds. Yet the deaths of these women shattered me. There were still dozens yet to die, an entire palace full of them, the distant female relatives of these great ladies, obscure members of the royal family whom I scarcely knew had existed, crowds of maidservants, concubines of the King whom he had received in years past as gifts of state but whom he had barely known or known only briefly before shelving them with the others. Worst of all, there was Monime. As much as I wished, I could not recuse myself from the task, could not simply assign it to Bacchides. Father would require a firsthand account. I steeled myself for the task with a cup of uncut wine and then strode to her quarters. Though I arrived unannounced, she was waiting for me.

Monime was the most pitiable of all creatures, the most unwilling to accept her fate, perhaps because, unlike the King's sisters, hers was a fate of her own creation, rather than handed to her by the gods, by the accidents of birth. When Father had first chosen her from out of the crowd two decades before, she had been offered a fortune in gold for the hire of her charms.

This she could have accepted, serving as a smiling courtesan for as long as her favors pleased the King and then departing free and wealthy after that. But by holding out for the diadem of a royal concubine, she accepted not only the status but the fate that went with it—namely, that a concubine is the slave of the royal bed for life. When her favors decline, she is retired, like a worn-out track horse, to the stable of other faded concubines. As a seventeen-year-old beauty, such thoughts of perishable glory had not crossed her mind. With her banishment to Pharnacia only a few years later, however, the notion of her fate began to sink in. Now, with my arrival, it took on the form of mortal reality.

When the imperturbable Bacchides and I appeared at her apartments, Monime was furious. I had not seen her in years, but the angry expression on her face, the disdainful words on her lips, brought rushing back all the painful emotions I had experienced living in her household in Pergamum as a boy. As she fixed her haughty glare on me, I momentarily froze.

"Have you no words of greeting for your stepmother?" she snapped. "Have you no kiss for my cheek? Or perhaps murderers like you are unable to show proper respect and affection for their betters?"

"You are not my stepmother," I responded stiffly. "Father never married you, and for good reason."

Whipping off the diadem that she had continued to wear every day like a queen, she dashed it to the ground, scattering pearls and tiny jewels to all corners of the room. Ranting, she stormed through the halls bemoaning her fate and crying upon all the gods in heaven to strike Mithridates down, to infest me with a loathsome disease, to avenge her fury. Bacchides observed her patiently.

"My lady," he interjected after a moment, "you no longer share the King's bed, but you are not past the beauty of your prime." For a moment she hesitated in her tantrum as she considered the eunuch's unexpected compliment. "Indeed, your loveliness has, if anything, only increased and softened with the passage of time." Cautiously she composed her face and straightened her robes, almost as if preparing for a suitor. My heart filled with disgust at the ease with which she was able to shift her emotions, like an actress in a bawdy play.

"Naturally," Bacchides continued coolly, "any man would feel most fortunate to be in the presence of such a lovely specimen." I couldn't believe it. The woman actually began preening, plumping her hair, glancing coquettishly into a wall mirror. What could the eunuch be thinking, talking like this? I stood tongue-tied, silent as a stump, as she responded.

"Thank you, Bacchides—it is a rare man who even *notices* how hard a woman tries to keep up her standards, especially under the abominable conditions here. Naturally I'm certain that all this is simply a mistake. . . ."

"Indeed," the eunuch continued, a faint smile on his lips, "your rare beauty has not been forgotten by the King." Monime blushed like a virgin. "He is terribly worried. Consider your fate if the Romans were to capture you—do you imagine you would be leaving the palace with your honor intact? The first grubby-handed legionary who scaled the walls would head first to the Harem Palace. . . ."

Monime flushed white and recoiled. "How dare you speak to me of such horrors!" she hissed. "Even if the Romans were to seize me, I am a full royal concubine. None of them are worthy of me; none are at my level, barring perhaps Lucullus himself. . . ." She stopped and her gaze flitted back and forth between Bacchides and me, and with growing horror she realized she had spoken the words that would seal her fate.

"Precisely," the eunuch said evenly, pouring from the ewer of milk and mixing the fatal syrup. "It is precisely that— Lucullus' seizing of the King's most valued possessions—that must be prevented. For the King's sake—and for your own." He held out the cup.

Monime staggered back in despair, and then with a flash of inspiration she looked at me, her eyes pooling with tears. "Pharnaces . . . have you nothing to say to all this? Is there nothing that moves your heart? Are there any memories of our years in Pergamum that are not hateful, any that are not poisoned by bitterness? You were only a boy then, you know; all boys suffer anxiety; you needn't blame me for your anger. . . ."

I looked past her, willing myself to keep a stony, neutral expression, refusing to be moved by her pleas. My mind flew back many years, to when Bituitus had first approached her in the crowd to demand she be brought to the King's bed and had

been repelled by the Greek meaning of the name Monime—
"all alone." I now realized how insightful he had been in his
interpretation.

"Pharnaces?" she continued, tentatively approaching and
placing a hand on my shoulder while keeping a wary eye on
Bacchides and the cup. "Did your father truly send you to do
this to me? It doesn't have to be like this. He is an old man,
Pharnaces, but I am still young, as are you! You are his heir—
you needn't follow orders you will regret after he is dead."

"I am not his heir. Machares is. I am only a soldier."

Her face hardened for an instant, then returned to its soft,
pleading expression. "No, your father thinks nothing of
Machares. He's only a lapdog. You are his true favorite. Anything you do will be forgiven; it always has been. He needn't
even know! I could simply slip out the back and you could tell
him later that you did your duty. . . ."

My mind reeled. *Loyalty—the highest value Father placed in
a man. He would forgive even a Roman if he was loyal to his
master. Yet did Monime truly deserve this fate? The woman was
resourceful—perhaps she would survive the Roman invasion.
But no, how could I even think that? How could I disobey? If a
man betrays his father, he betrays his very self.* I looked at
Monime, at the makeup streaking her face, the mouth composed in a pathetic plea as her words continued to flow, sooth-
ing and honeylike from her lips. But then I saw her eyes, which
despite all her skills could not hide the feelings in her soul—
they glared at me with a hatred and malevolence I had never
seen before, even from enemies with whom I had grappled in
battle. Her eyes pierced me, but I had long ago become immune
to her poison, and my own stony glare mocked the tears and
blandishments with which she tried to soften me. All I could
feel was disgust. I turned away and motioned for Bacchides to
administer the cup.

Monime screamed. Tearing off the linen scarf she used to tie
her hair back, she raced to a torch sconce on the wall, pierced
the fabric through a protruding nail, stuffed her head through
the knotted loop that still remained from its use as a headdress,
and threw herself to the floor, bearing the full weight of her
body against her neck.

The linen did not hold. It tore immediately, but the strain of

Monime's lunge carried her forward with the momentum, and she hurtled against the wall with a sickening crack. As Bacchides leaped to her side, she crumpled slowly to the floor, her head at a terrible angle to her body.

Monime was still alive, but her neck had snapped like a twig. She was unable to move the rest of her body or even to swallow the draught Bacchides offered her. Filled with loathing at Monime's final words, I could not stay in the room a moment longer and strode out. Bacchides fulfilled her last wish quickly and painlessly, bringing me the still-bloody knife as a testament to his deed.

The following week Father and his entourage crossed the Euphrates on hired boats and passed into Armenia, beyond Roman control. We were met on the riverbank by a high embassy from Tigranes. To our astonishment, we were immediately surrounded by a squadron of Tigranes' burly personal guards, the Immortals. Our troops were disarmed, and Father, Bituitus, and I were politely escorted, not to the Great King's palace at Tigranocerta, but rather to a dreary hunting lodge he owned, in the mountains hard by the border.

We were under arrest, forbidden from leaving this rustic castle under pain of death. Father's protests were disregarded, his letters and demands to his son-in-law ignored. Even my requests to foray into the surrounding forests to seek the herbs and duck's blood necessary for Father's daily dosages were refused, until our own supplies became depleted and Father began suffering seizures and convulsions from the lack of the drug. Only then was a local apothecary made available to us, who provided us with the necessary ingredients for Papias' *pharmacon,* at criminally exorbitant prices.

That winter, the last fortresses of interior Pontus surrendered to Lucullus and the Romans retreated back to their strongholds on the coast. Father sent numerous embassies to old King Tigranes, demanding his release from captivity and insisting that he be treated in a manner befitting the King of Pontus and sworn enemy of the Romans. These messengers often passed other heralds, bearing Roman standards and messages from Lucullus, ordering of Tigranes precisely the same thing, that Father be released from captivity—and turned over to Rome. What Rome had been unable to obtain by force it now demanded by diplomatic pressure.

And Tigranes had yet to answer either side.

BOOK EIGHT

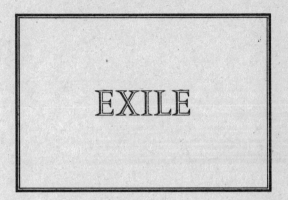

EXILE

Whether to pronounce thee man or god, I know not,
Yet I think rather that thou art a god. . . .

—The Pythia of Delphi

1

Tigranes was a king of meager brain, though endowed with a goodly supply of malicious wiliness. Any king capable of surviving as many years as he had, despite the treachery and plotting that go part and parcel with being a member of a dynastic royal family in the East, must have a certain well-honed instinct for political intrigue. Yet Tigranes' distinct fortune was this: In the sixty years of his reign and the eighty years of his life he had never faced any significant threat. Not that Armenia was a particularly powerful kingdom—certainly it had its share of gold and manpower, which in a good year could rival any in all of Asia. Yet Parthia, its neighbor to the east, was far wealthier, its territory extending from Syria to India and across the great desert of Arabia. The Ptolemies in Egypt ruled over a much more cohesive population, with rapid communications along their great river that would allow them to draw up an enormous army and navy in the time it would take Tigranes' messengers simply to find the best mountain passes to cross his kingdom. Rome, of course, was the most aggressive power in the Mediterranean, with the best trained forces and the most professional leadership; and Pontus, to the west, was powerful, ambitious, and wealthy.

All these threats Tigranes had for many decades resisted, and because of his success, he now thought very highly of himself—so highly, indeed, that he had recently taken on the self-bestowed title of Great King, King of Kings, and built himself a royal capital in the Armenian mountains, Tigranocerta, that was the equal, for sheer opulence, of any city his fellow kings might have matched. Tigranes' treasury was laden with gold and silver, precious metals, statues, furniture, and valuable artworks; the massive walls of his capital, a full fifty cubits high, were surrounded by stables at their base, housing the King's immense herds of camels, elephants, and thoroughbred horses; and in the forested outskirts he had built a magnificent palace, laid out with large parks, hunting grounds, and artificial lakes.

Personal credit for his success, however, was undeserved. Neighboring Parthia had been wracked for years by internal struggles that had sapped the strength of its rulers; Egypt was crippled by the inbred and spiteful reign of its Macedonian "pharaohs," the last of a dying breed as Rome consolidated its control over the region. Rome had never been interested in Armenia, deeming it too distant to efficiently conquer and administer. And Pontus—well, Tigranes was a friend to Pontus, or so Father believed; it was to Tigranes whom many years ago he had betrothed his daughter.

Now Father sought to call in the favor, to enlist Tigranes' support in regaining his kingdom, in advancing his dream—or at the very least, in protecting him from Lucullus' legions. Instead he found himself under arrest an hour's march from the border. The scoundrel Tigranes hesitated as to where his sympathies actually lay in this struggle and wanted to keep Father in a convenient position to be handed over to the Romans if the occasion merited.

Indeed, Tigranes even refused to allow Father to plead his case in person, as Lucullus' troops marched ever closer in their implacable conquest of Pontic territory. Finally, however, Tigranes deigned to grant an audience to an ambassador whom Father might choose, at a hearing to be attended by Lucullus' representative as well. It would be a trial, with the ambassadors serving as counsels to the plaintiff and defendant and with ancient Tigranes as the dotty judge. Lucullus' brother-in-law Claudius Pulcher would plead the Roman case, seeking Father's handover. I would be his defending attorney. I traveled in all haste to the palace at Antioch, where Tigranes was holding court at the time.

In the Great King's view, as advocate for a prisoner I had

few rights and little status. Indeed, I was not even allowed to present a cogent case. Arriving at the palace at the appointed hour, I was shown into the audience chamber, the air so thick with swirling incense and the perfumes of courtiers and pages that I could scarcely breathe. Though I was wearing the purple tunic and finely worked armor of my rank, a prince and a general of cavalry, I was forced by the guards to drop to my knees, then to my belly, at the gnarled, wrinkled feet of the monarch. Only after making humiliating obeisance to him was I allowed to stand to plead our case, before this man whom I had never met but who in fact was my own brother-in-law.

Such a man I had never before beheld, nor do I hope to do so again. As sturdy and robust as he may once have been, for I had heard stories of his handsomeness and strength as a youth, he was now as shriveled and withered a creature as I had ever seen, nor would I expect any differently from someone in his ninth decade of life. Bald as a babe, with nary a fringe or tuft, his tiny head appeared shrunken and withdrawn inside the neck hole of the ornate breastplate he wore over his trunk, one that perhaps may have fit him well six decades earlier, but which now dwarfed and dominated him like the shell of a tortoise. Spindly brown arms jutted from either side, fingers drumming impatiently upon the carved lion-paw armrest of the throne, and chickenlike shanks emerged from beneath the long ceremonial robe he wore under the armor, one foot positioned out slightly before the other, toes pointing in my direction. It occurred to me that perhaps the custom was for me to have kissed them when I had been lying on the floor. Certainly the irritated grimace on his face indicated that I was not in his favor.

"My wife's half brother Pharnaces, you say?" he rasped to the elderly eunuch who was standing at his side with a scroll in his hands, announcing each arrival to the half-deaf king.

The eunuch had said no such thing, at least not yet, and had cleared his throat to begin formally announcing me when the king interrupted him.

Peering straight at me with rheumy eyes, Tigranes leaned forward as much as he was able. The knobby head bobbed toward me, no doubt with the shoulders and chest attached to it, though the heavy chest armor remained immobile.

"You need no introduction," he said, coughing. "You're the

very image of your father, whom I last saw when he was perhaps your age . . ."—I consciously stood up straighter at this compliment, thrusting out my chin in an authoritative military stance, as he continued—". . . though I must say you appear much smaller." He dismissed me with a curt wave of his fingers. "Your father's current circumstances have already been made known to me."

Without allowing me to utter a word, a guard seized my elbow and forced me to step aside, to a line of several vassal kings and chieftains who were attending the hearing in hopes of having their own disputes settled. The eunuch's clear, childlike voice rang out above the soft murmur of the court.

"The Tribune Appius Claudius Pulcher, Ambassador of the Roman general Lucius Licinius Lucullus."

A man of perhaps thirty strode forward in full Roman ceremonial regalia, jeweled short sword strapped to his left hip, polished helmet propped under his right arm with the crimson horse hair of the crest plainly visible. His handsome, tanned face displayed all the disdain for these eastern ceremonies that he could muster, and arrogance was written in the cast of his jaw, in his very posture. My eyes bored into him, so intense was the hatred I felt at that moment, yet he ignored my presence completely, a gesture more disturbing than if he had glanced at me with an expression of loathing in return. In the end, disregard is the greatest of all insults.

"King Tigranes," he pronounced in a loud voice when he had approached the throne, his tone like that of a father to a distracted toddler. He seemed to have purposely disregarded Tigranes' title of *King of Kings,* a subtle though grave violation of protocol. Though I saw that his guard escort put the same pressure on his elbow as he had on mine to force him to the floor in obeisance, Pulcher shook him off in visible irritation and remained standing. The court gasped at this overt display of rudeness to their king, then fell silent.

"King Tigranes," he repeated, when he noted that all eyes were upon him. "I thank you for the magnificent gifts you presented to me yesterday upon my arrival in Antioch. I regret to say that I cannot accept them, for I have come not to negotiate or to parley, but to deliver an ultimatum from my general."

Tigranes' eyes bulged from his skull-like head and a blue

vein throbbed visibly at his temple. Had any of his own people spoken to him thus, so peremptorily, so disrespectfully, those would have been their last words, and indeed I noted the guards' hands moving to the hilts of their scimitars. Yet though coughing and working his mouth, the King said nothing, and the tribune continued.

"General Lucullus sends you cordial greetings. He also demands that you turn over to him King Mithridates Eupator VI of Pontus forthwith, bound in chains, to be placed on trial for his crimes before a Roman tribunal."

Tigranes rustled some more inside his armor, though his fingers had by now stopped their tense drumming. Squinting at the young tribune, he visibly struggled to control the rage he felt at the Roman's arrogance and presumption. Within the Armenian court it was considered disgraceful, a lack of good breeding and control, to allow anger to show in public. Breathing deeply for a moment, he forced a wry smile at the corner of his mouth, which I could just see over the gold filigree collar of his breastplate.

"You mentioned an ultimatum, Tribune," he wheezed. "What does your general propose if I do not do his bidding?"

"Then, King Tigranes," Pulcher announced in a voice as sonorous and confident as his initial greeting, "Rome will make war upon you until the criminal king is handed over to us to be brought to justice. Armenia will be destroyed."

He paused for effect, though it was hardly needed. The entire court had frozen in astonishment at his audacity.

"I will be departing in the morning," Pulcher continued. "Your answer before then, if you please." He then nodded to the King, spun curtly on his heel, and marched out the way he had come, roughly shouldering through the silent mob of eunuchs and courtiers who had crowded up behind him to hear the extraordinary exchange.

The answer was foreordained, and whether or not Lucullus truly did desire war against Armenia, Pulcher's flagrant challenge left Tigranes no choice if he wished to retain his own authority. Calls were issued to muster the Grand Army of Armenia, scouts were sent to monitor the Roman legions' movements—and Father was at last summoned to the Great King's presence, not to receive punishment but rather to advise old Tigranes on the strength and tactics of this new invader. With his thousand Pontic exiles cooling their heels behind him, Father set out to meet with the sovereign, at the place of the army's mustering, a secret stronghold in the mountains of Taurus.

"Tigranes doesn't believe the Romans will invade?" Father asked incredulously.

"He relies on his courtiers," I answered. "They claim Lucullus wouldn't even defend Ephesus if Tigranes chose to march against him."

"Then how does he explain the two legions that have just entered Armenian territory from Pontus?"

"Just that—a mere two legions. Tigranes says it's a diversion, for the Senate's benefit. Pontus has been subdued, but Lucullus still wishes to retain his command. He can't do this, however, unless he can show he's engaged in a campaign. His other three legions are still mopping up in Pontus, so two legions is all he can spare. That's ten thousand men, with a couple of thousand mercenary horse. Tigranes believes he'll raid a few border towns, beat the bushes looking for you, and then withdraw when the Armenians put their foot down."

Father considered this for a moment in silence.

"Then why Tigranes' own buildup? He's mustering the Grand Army."

To this I had no ready answer, though I myself had spent the past several weeks in Tigranes' entourage, observing the troops' arrival. The Armenian cavalry, in particular, were a formidable lot, professional warriors known as *kataphractoi,* garbed toe to knob in armor, with their massive horses sheathed in bronze as well. Such heavy cavalry were unassailable. One attack was all it took, one charge by these horse-mounted hoplites, who like their foot-bound brethren fought in close phalanx formation. If the enemy were not destroyed immediately, they were sufficiently softened that it would take only a quick cleanup by the trailing infantry to achieve complete victory.

I shrugged. "It may be the Grand Army, but it's not completely his doing. Tigranes himself would rather ignore Lucullus until he goes away. Calls him a pimple on his ass. But his young chieftains are baying for Roman blood. They haven't fought in years and are hot for battle. It's they who've done the mustering. Tigranes is just watching in amusement."

Father shook his head in disgust. "For years I've asked Tigranes to join with me against the Romans, and he's put me off every time. I gave up a perfectly marriageable daughter to that lout. I see I should have been talking to the chieftains."

"You'll have your chance to do both this afternoon. Tigranes is summoning you to a meeting of his general staff."

Father threw back his great shaggy mane of steel-gray hair and adjusted the curved dagger fastened to his belt.

"Oh, he'll get an earful, that old horse thief. Believe me, he'll get an earful."

In Tigranes' capacious field tent, Father and I, accompanied by the Pontic general Taxiles, who had joined us recently, explained the situation to the old king, emphasized our experience against the Romans, and made our proposal. Taxiles was our representative—as he was the lowest ranking among the three of us, it was more diplomatic that he speak first, to allow King Tigranes to respond more freely without fear of offense should he feel it necessary to be critical of our plan.

Not that Tigranes was fearful of offending us.

"My lord," Taxiles confidently stated, "Lucullus has now advanced to your capital, Tigranocerta, so far without opposition from your forces—"

"It is merely a feint, General," Tigranes interrupted, in a scolding tone. "His legions will scatter as soon as the Grand Army appears. The further we let him advance into our territory, the more completely we will be able to crush him. Let him come."

Taxiles paused and eyed the king closely. "Our experience, my lord, is that even in defeat, the Romans can inflict painful losses on their foe. Certainly your forces are overwhelming. But why risk losing even a few of your magnificent warriors?"

Tigranes glared at him balefully. "I dislike your tone, soldier," he declared. "You seem to imply that my forces are somehow inferior to these parade-ground Italians. They may be able to inflict pain on *inferior* warriors"—and he glanced at Father, who sat listening impassively, tenting his thick fingers, eyes half-closed—"but not on the Grand Army, on its own territory. These are Lucullus' veteran legions, are they not? They must be near the age of discharge by now, old men all of them. And only two legions at that. My very knees tremble. Are you quite finished, General?"

"Not quite, Your Majesty. I absolutely acknowledge your forces' overwhelming skill and numbers. Nevertheless, I believe we must seek to destroy the enemy with minimal loss to your troops. Allow Lucullus to approach your city, even to besiege it, to dig his infernal entrenchments. Your true strength, my lord, is your cavalry, both the kataphractoi and the light-armed riders. Control the open country around the Roman lines. Prevent the enemy from foraging. Tigranocerta is strongly garrisoned. The walls can hold for months. Lucullus can be starved into submission without risk of pitched battle. Victory can be yours without loosing an arrow."

Tigranes eyed Taxiles malevolently, then addressed Father. "It goes without saying, of course, that this is precisely the tactic Lucullus used against you at Cyzicus three years ago, is it not? There would not, perhaps, be a touch of vengeance in your plan that distorts your good judgment?"

Taxiles opened his mouth to speak, but Father himself stood up, gesturing to his general to be silent.

"Indeed there is not, Brother King," he rumbled patiently. "It is a sound strategy that uses your strengths to best advantage and capitalizes on the Romans' weaknesses."

Tigranes tottered to his feet, wheezing and defiant as a child, his eyes reddening with rage, looking from Taxiles to Father and then finally settling on Taxiles as being closer to his line of rheumy vision. "Are you suggesting, General, that my army might be unable to defeat the Romans in pitched battle? That we must skulk on their flanks and deny them biscuit to achieve victory? Are these the manly tactics the Pontics have employed—to such *overwhelming* success, I might point out—in their own wars with the Romans?"

Taxiles glanced sidelong at Father for support and then back to the enraged old king, maintaining his straight military bearing.

"No, Your Highness, it is a carefully considered—"

"An *insult* is what it is!" the King screamed. "You insult me and are a traitor to suggest such a strategy! I shall have your head for your impertinence. Guards!"

Taxiles looked about wildly as two guards stepped to either side of him, but Father moved even more quickly. Stepping directly in front of Taxiles, he faced down the old king in a calm but commanding voice.

"With reverence, Brother King. I, too, am a sovereign, and Taxiles is my subject. I shall deal with him as he deserves. His fate is not your concern."

Tigranes stared at Father, peering at him as if through a haze, struggling to focus on his face through the cloudiness of his cataracts and rage. Finally he took a deep breath and dropped heavily back into his seat, supported under the arms by a courtier on each side. The guards at Taxiles' sides relaxed.

"Very well. Mithridates, you and your men are to return to your quarters on the Pontic border, to await my further instructions. Your counsel has been useless, and I shall pursue it no longer. Your incompetent advisor Taxiles and your son, General Pharnaces, shall remain with me, as surety for your obedience. Begone with you all; you make me ill."

Father turned, his jaw set in fury, and strode out of the tent beside me, with Taxiles close behind. With scarcely a word Father packed his meager kit, mustered his company of Pontic exiles and Armenian guards, and set out on his return to the hunting lodge before the sun had even set. His gray head was set as defiantly as ever, and his massive shoulders, burdened with the long ash bow and quiver of arrows he was never without, betrayed not a hint of the discouragement and despair he surely must have felt at this repudiation. He had sworn never to be conquered, by gods, Romans, or allies, no matter how hard fate might treat him.

Yet as he cantered off into the mountains, I reflected on the odds facing us. Never to be conquered. Gods, Romans, and allies seemed to be in league against us to do just that.

It took four months for Tigranes to complete the mustering of his troops. The enormous force was three hundred thousand strong, and it took another two months for it to wend its ponderous way to Tigranocerta, which had been encircled by Lucullus' two legions since mid-summer.

The siege of the city was as porous as a sieve, however—with only ten thousand troops at their disposal and a mere handful of horse, the Romans could do little to choke the lifelines of a city with a population thirty times as large, guarded by a sizable garrison. They blocked the main routes into the city, of course, but dozens of paths, trails, and tunnels outside and around the walls allowed trade to be carried on almost as usual—even between the inhabitants and the Roman troops themselves. Tigranes knew there was no need for him to hurry. The city could not be starved into submission; to take it, the Romans would have to actually attack, which was unthinkable, given the size of their forces. The only thing that puzzled the King was why the Romans dared to remain in their entrenchments outside the walls, risking being hemmed in by the city garrison on one side and the Grand Army of Armenia on the other. As Tigranes never tired of chortling within my earshot, Lucullus must be even stupider than Mithridates.

By the first of October, Tigranes' forces were in position among a low range of foothills overlooking a small river above the city. The Roman entrenchments were just across from us, and the city walls beyond that. Lucullus' strategy was truly baffling. It was impossible to believe he hoped to join battle against such overwhelming odds, yet he rebuffed every herald we sent him with offers of negotiation or a peaceable withdrawal of his forces. He remained entrenched, hot, dusty, and hungry, for our scouts even witnessed the Roman forces slaughtering several of their precious horses to feed their troops. Yet still he made no move.

Tigranes' patience was wearing thin, and his chieftains were calling for blood, some even begging the Great King for the honor of attacking and destroying the legions immediately with their own commands. Tigranes put them off, waiting to see what Lucullus might do. In one of the rare discussions I had with Tigranes, I urged him to entrench his own army, to not risk sending out individual units, even kataphractoi, against the Romans—the Great King should hold every man at the ready for a combined action. He raged at me, calling me a coward and a traitor, threatening to crucify me alongside the Roman generals if I dared insult him again with such treacherous advice. From that point on, I kept my mouth shut and observed.

On October sixth, the enemy suddenly burst into activity. At the sound of trumpets, the Roman troops clambered out of their trenches and began forming up in a flat area on the bank, across the river from our own huge array. The Armenians, at last seeing movement from their foe, set up a deafening cacophony of jeers and catcalls, braying like asses at the Romans, crowing like roosters at their cowardliness. Individual squads of horsemen broke away from the Armenian lines, sprinting down to the near bank of the river and then dashing back after chucking a spear or loosing an arrow in puerile bluster, which the Romans ignored. Three Armenian staff generals, observing the meagerness of the Romans' troop strength, fell to laughing and casting dice for shares of the plunder to be taken that day. Even I was beginning to believe that Lucullus had finally made a fatal mistake.

At the sound of the trumpets the Romans began marching west, downstream along the banks of the river, at a fast trot. It was a full retreat, and Tigranes hastily called his own generals, ordering them to deploy the Armenian army, to sweep down upon the Romans and destroy them once and for all. With shouts and cries the men hastened to obey, and dust roiled up from the plain around us. The eager horses of the kataphractoi stamped and pawed, nipping at the necks and haunches of their brethren, restless at the long wait in the foothills and the palpable excitement of the men.

Smiling, Tigranes approached us, swaying on his overly large charger.

"So you see, General Taxiles: The great conqueror Lucullus now runs with his tail between his legs. What is your advice now?"

Taxiles remained tight-lipped, staring at the departing Roman column. "I note, my lord, that when Romans set out for a long march, they carry their breastplates and shields in bundles on their backs with the rest of their kit. These men, however, are wearing full armor. They have even removed the leather dust covers from their shields. I urge caution."

The King's face reddened in anger and he wheeled his horse away from us awkwardly. The troops behind us laughed and jostled into formation, but the couriers rushing to and from the general staff suddenly fell silent and pointed, drawing our attention to the Romans' path. A mile downriver the Romans had come to a ford, and rather than continuing on their way, they were now crossing, wading through the hip-deep water to the side on which we stood. The vanguard of the procession, the men the Romans call the *aquiliferi,* who bore the two legions' eagle standards, emerged from the stream and again took up the patient, trotting progress I had seen so many times, following the banks of the river—but this time directly back toward us. At the head of one of the columns was a tall soldier in a swirling purple cloak, marching on foot and surrounded by his glittering escort. As he approached, his demeanor and his very expression were unmistakable—it was Lucullus himself. His sword was drawn and carried before him. This was a gesture a Roman general would make for only one reason—as the signal for attack.

A hush fell when the troops behind us saw this maneuver, broken only by the querulous voice of old Tigranes standing a few feet away from me, his tone half-question, half-complaint: "Taxiles! If these men are coming to negotiate, they are too many; but if they are coming as an army, they are too few." The general and men within earshot around us let loose nervous laughter. Taxiles, however, continued to stare at the Romans, his face utterly straight.

"My lord," he said in a loud voice, "the Romans are *not* coming to negotiate!"

Tigranes turned toward us, for the first time looking flustered and confused. All eyes were upon him, and the men behind us continued to jostle and trip over themselves in an effort to find their units and fall into formation, their visibility and breathing hampered by the choking dust rising up all around.

"What!" Tigranes wheezed. "Do they dare attack?"

Without waiting for the King's command, his division generals and chieftains wheeled their mounts and plowed into the men behind us, shouting orders to fall in, slapping wayward horses and foot soldiers out of the way with the flats of their swords, calling through the dust and the chaos for their units. It was utter madness. Men at the rear of the army, who had not yet seen the Romans' approach, nevertheless heard the confusion and shouts from the front. Thinking that the rout of the legions was beginning without them and that they would miss the opportunity for plunder, tens of thousands of men surged forward, colliding with the milling troops and horses already scrambling for position in the center and further adding to the confusion. The noise from the ranks behind us was deafening, the confusion indescribable. The Armenians struggled to organize, but they were packed too closely; they could not maneuver, only jostle. I saw Tigranes' mouth open in shouted command, but his faint, rasping words were carried away like the dust in the cloud.

The Romans continued their trot in easy procession, in perfect step with the throbbing beat of the cadence drums, ten thousand men rising and falling in unison as they steadily closed the distance between us. The individual ensigns on the banners could now be made out through the Romans' own miniature dust cloud, and then the legion insignia on their shields.

Suddenly shouts arose from our flank, nearest the Romans' former camp. A squad of Galatian mercenary horse in the service of the Romans, perhaps five hundred or a thousand, had been left behind the palisades when the Roman foot troops had marched out earlier. While all eyes had been focused on Lucullus' audacious maneuver downstream, these plains horsemen had calmly swum their mounts across the river below us, fallen into a tight formation, and unleashed a charge—directly into the flank of Tigranes' force of kataphractoi.

The ululating war cries of the Galatian tribesmen assaulted our ears. Not knowing the source of the attack or even the numbers of their assailants, the Armenian horsemen scattered like a flock of birds into which a boy has thrown a stone, bereft of formation and tactics, spreading across the plain and full into the ranks of the milling cavalry behind. The bearded, half-naked Galatian tribesmen thundered into the midst of the Armenian lines, hacking and slashing and screaming their foolish heads off, striking terror into the hearts of a body of horsemen thirty times their number. Yet as quickly as they had appeared within our ranks the Galatians withdrew, forcing their way back out again and racing down the hill to the water's edge, where they drew themselves up in a cheering, milling band. They had killed few men on our side and lost even fewer themselves in their mad foray—but their timing was perfect, the effect fatal.

Just as the Galatians pulled back, just as the Armenian ranks were at the peak of their disorder, Lucullus himself, leading a point guard of perhaps two cohorts, a thousand men, slammed into the front ranks of our army, bulling his way on a broad path straight through the now terror-stricken Armenian foot soldiers who had scarcely had time to draw their swords. Within moments he had cut through the very heart of the army to a hillock in our rear, where his men turned and began launching their javelins at the astounded Armenians, who a few moments before had thought themselves so distant from the front lines.

Tigranes' terrified troops rushed forward to avoid Lucullus' murderous assault in their rear, colliding full with the eight remaining Roman cohorts who had, meanwhile, calmly arrayed themselves across the front. The panic and chaos were absolute. By now the kataphractoi had come to their senses and were racing back into the dust cloud, striving to recover their formations and organize a resistance against the enemy, but it was too late. They ran headlong into their own fleeing foot troops, crushing and trampling them beneath the horses' hooves or driving them back into the swords and javelins of the Roman legionaries, who stood their ground in the growing muck of blood and piss like avenging gods. The infantry turned to flee but were blocked by the densely packed ranks of reserve troops behind them, themselves fleeing both Lucullus' cohorts in the rear and the madly racing Armenian cavalry. It was a complete rout. The Romans calmly waded into the fray to finish the slaughter.

Such was the discipline of the Romans that they stopped not even to take plunder or to strip valuable armor from the bodies. Rather, as the Armenians broke through the thin Roman lines by sheer force of numbers, the cohorts remained completely controlled. They split into smaller, orderly units to press the pursuit against the largest mobs of terrified Armenian soldiers as they scattered, racing into the hills. For seven miles the Romans continued their infernal trotting, mowing down Armenian stragglers and deserters as they went, killing those they captured, ignoring those already fallen, pressing the attack until finally turned back by darkness.

The Armenian army was decimated. We had no way of knowing even how many men had fallen or how many had simply fled and then drifted shamefully back to their homes. But in the dispatches that Lucullus published and triumphantly addressed by courier to rulers, commanders, and encampments in every corner of the world, the general claimed that one hundred thousand Armenians had died—and only five Romans. Future historians may scoff at these numbers. Personally, I marvel at their restraint. Never before had Rome achieved such an overwhelming victory, against any enemy.

Tigranes himself, the scoundrel, was among the first to turn tail, along with most of his general staff, and because he had a fine horse and was unencumbered by the heavy armor of the kataphractoi, he was able to easily slip through the lines and put good distance between himself and the foot-bound Roman column. I have no shame in confessing that Taxiles and I accompanied his small group, since we had been disarmed from the beginning and would have had no opportunity to defend ourselves in battle. Nevertheless, the King's behavior was abominable. As he raced from the destruction of his army, his head and his hands shook in terror and he was unable even to speak coherently. When he noticed one of his sons accompanying him, a young prince serving as page to the general staff,

Tigranes ripped the golden diadem off his own head, a gesture a king never makes except to lie down, and pressed it on the young man. Perhaps Tigranes hoped by this means to transfer responsibility for the debacle or to divert the attention of the Romans away from himself, should they succeed in capturing him. To his credit, the young prince would have none of it, though he dared not refuse the crown or hand it back to his father. Fleeing at full gallop across the plain, Tigranes' son accepted the crown from his father's hand, dropped back to the rear of the group, and passed it on to one of his slaves, who in terror at possessing such a hot coal simply threw it away. The pursuing Romans later found it, I am told, and presented it to Lucullus, who displayed the relic to great acclaim in his later Triumph in Rome.

According to survivors who later caught up with us, the city of Tigranocerta, seeing the rout of the Grand Army, immediately capitulated. The population within, many of them Greeks and other foreigners imported as slaves from other parts of Tigranes' empire, overthrew the Armenian garrison. The Romans took immense plunder, so much that for once the hungry legionaries were persuaded to spare the lives of the townsfolk.

Being immensely wealthy already, Lucullus accepted none of the plunder yet indulged himself in his own decadent fashion: The city's magnificent theater had just been completed before the siege, and a company of well-known Greek actors had been trapped inside the town. After the initial rounds of looting and rapine, the legionaries settled down for a complete cycle of Greek dramas, sponsored by Lucullus himself. For many of the Roman soldiers, country boys by birth and upbringing, it was their first exposure to the arts, and they were so appreciative of the performance that they donated a huge portion of their plunder to the surprised actors. After that, at Lucullus' orders, the entire city of Tigranocerta—palace, theater, agora, everything—was dismantled stone by stone, the inhabitants chased away across the desert, and the site left desolate—which is as it remains to this day.

3

Roman prisoners told us an amazing story.

After the conquest of Tigranocerta, talk had turned to Lucullus' becoming the new Alexander. Indeed, it would have been impossible for a Roman general fresh from an overwhelming victory in the East not to harbor such aspirations. His distance from Rome, the continuing chaos in that city, and his own success bolstered his ambitions. To Lucullus, the vast wealth of Parthia was there for the taking, just beyond the Syrian desert, like a piece of ripe fruit hanging on a tree. It would be a small thing for him to seize it—indeed, a Roman army had invaded such territories in the recent past, though with poor preparation and against robust foes. Crassus the Triumvir had been killed in that attempt. Now, however, the Parthians were emasculated, and Rome had built a reputation that made the world tremble. Lucullus sent word to the Roman legions garrisoning Pontus, ordering them to march to Armenia to join him in his magnificent campaign.

Yet his veterans saw things differently. In fact, the soldiers of two entire legions, all of whom had been mustered at the same time twenty years before, had now completed their service and were up for discharge. They were comfortable in Asia and Cilicia, where they had been stationed on garrison duty, and they set out on the road for rugged Armenia only reluctantly. They absolutely rebelled against risking their lives in a march across the desert to unknown lands, against a powerful and numerous enemy, when even now each veteran was due his discharge bonus and forty acres of bottomland for his retirement. Well before those legions even arrived in Armenia, they sent word to Lucullus of their response to his summons—they would not advance with him to Parthia.

Lucullus was no fool. A general who suffered a mutiny of his own men was more disgraced even than one who had lost to the enemy. He could not risk an invasion of the East with his troops' loyalty in question. Accordingly, he gave in with as much grace as he could muster, absorbing the sullen new legions and marching the entire army south, to the lowlands of Syria, where the weather was warmer and the plundering easier.

And Father claimed his rewards from Tigranes for sheltering him at the hunting lodge during his winter of defeat and for reforming the bewildered officers of the Grand Army of Armenia.

No, it was not treasure he demanded, for of that there still remained copious amounts hidden in forests and mountain caves in Pontus. Nor was it land and a satrapy, though Tigranes certainly offered this to him, seeking no doubt to keep him close at hand should Lucullus resolve to return to Armenia later.

The reward Father demanded was twofold: The first part involved a slave girl Tigranes had recently purchased from traveling Greek traders. Hypsicratia was her name, a terrifyingly stern and beautiful Scythian girl almost as tall as Father, with a thick mane of hair the color of golden cassidony, and shoulders and thighs of a musculature that would strike envy into a Roman gladiator. She was so ferocious and her strength so great that for the short time Tigranes owned her he had kept her in slave shackles, for fear she might endanger his entourage if set free. The men looked upon her in awe as a descendant of the mythical Amazons. When Father first saw her, there was no question but that she was to become his prize.

Tigranes did not sell cheaply, though there was little use he could possibly have made of the strange, pale wench, who spit and snarled at him whenever he dared approach. Ten magnificent Pontic war chargers was his price, and Father was glad to pay it. Immediately upon completing the transaction, he strode up to the magnificent creature and ordered her unshackled. Hypsicratia stood rubbing her wrists for a moment where the irons had chafed her; and then with catlike speed she pounced at the Armenian guard beside her, seized the dagger from his belt, and leaped away. She then dropped into a crouch, cursing furiously in her barbaric tongue, ready to take on all comers.

The men erupted in a shout and Bituitus and the guards immediately stepped forward, yet none were eager to rush in and disarm the tigress. Father, however, stood unperturbed, calmly observing. Shouldering through the excited mob of men, he approached the furious girl while speaking to her softly in her Scythian tongue, for all the world like a trainer calming a wild young filly. The men around fell silent, admiring the girl's magnificent beauty and wondering at the King's calm confidence. Stopping in front of her, well within reach of her dagger, he, too, fell silent, staring hard at her face, her flashing eyes and flaring nostrils. Seemingly satisfied with what he saw, he spoke a few more quiet words to the girl, then turned his back on her—and walked away.

Bituitus and I tensed, hands on our swords, ready to leap forward in an instant to kill the warrior maiden if she attacked. To our astonishment, however, the set of her jaw softened slightly, and her shoulders relaxed. Cautiously she stood erect, towering over the men around her, glaring fiercely at their faces. And then with a practiced gesture, she thrust the knife into the belt of her ragged slave tunic and strode resolutely after Father, matching him step for step. He never looked back as she followed him straight to his tent and went in behind him, to the amazement and envy of us all.

The other reward Father demanded from Tigranes was men. Four thousand of them he received, well-trained infantry mustered at the mountain camps the previous spring. These he combined with an additional four thousand Pontic and Roman exiles who had survived Pontus' previous defeats and joined him in Armenia over the past year. And at the age of sixty-four, fierce, stubborn, unbroken King Mithridates walked with eight thousand fighters and a yellow-haired warrioress, over the storm-whipped passes of Pontus and into the Lycus valley. On a freezing winter day he appeared in Conama like a phantom from the Underworld, to the amazement and acclaim of its citizens. If Lucullus was unaware of Father's maneuver at the time, he would not be for long: We captured the town's Roman garrison, set them on asses, and ran them off south, to the seaports of Cilicia. It would be only a matter of weeks before Rome was informed and would again erupt in panic and outrage.

Mithridates the Great had returned.

BOOK NINE

LAST
MAN
STANDING

Nor are those gods, that have the name of wise,
Less false than fleeting dreams. In things divine,
And in things human, great confusion reigns.

—**Euripides**

1

How great the irony. As desperately as Father despised Rome, all his fortunes hung on the balance of domestic Roman politics. Thus far, he had been unlucky. He had mustered thousands of men in armies over the years and had won and lost great and decisive battles but had never fatally cracked Rome's great, resilient armor, for he had had the misfortune to face two of the greatest generals Rome had ever produced— Sulla and Lucullus. His fate was bound to Rome, as much as was Sulla's fate; yet Father's bonds were the bonds of defiance and hate, while Sulla's were bonds of . . . perhaps hate as well? Had Sulla, too, not been driven from his homeland, at least for a time, by events beyond his control, by rivals more powerful than he? Was Lucullus not delaying his inevitable return to Rome after all these years for fear of what awaited him there? One does not hesitate to return to a woman one adores, nor to a city one loves. Perhaps Father had much in common with the men he fought, though he refused to speculate on such things. It was simpler merely to fight those men, to draw the sharp distinctions between *them* and *us,* to oppose them and wreak vengeance on them, to fill one's life and mind with such anger as to eliminate the need for anything deeper, anything more troubling. Despise them with your soul and your gut and every fiber of your body; despise their treatment of conquered peoples and their rape of your ancestral lands; despise them with a ferocity borne of defeat and injustices suffered.

But do not look too closely at the similarities between you and them. That would only weaken your will.

Lucullus had now been deprived of his commission. His term as consul had long expired; his plans for conquering the East had faded; his legions were clamoring for their discharge. And news of Father's return to Pontus and his raising of yet another army had capped his disgrace. Lucullus was being recalled, by the very politicians whom he himself despised. The Senate would award him a Triumph, of course, for his military conquests over the years, but it would be a hollow one, with the bare minimum of military escorts and awards. Small comfort for an illustrious career.

Father, on the other hand, had much cause to rejoice. He had outlived and outmaneuvered his two old nemeses. Admittedly he had lost battles; but now he had returned, unharmed, to his ancestral kingdom, finding it largely intact but for some token Roman garrisons in the major towns, which he could eliminate without great trouble. Despite his defeats, it was Father who was the last man standing and who therefore had won the war. Father's resurrection, his return to power, stupefied the Roman world. The Senate was exasperated by the legions' failure to destroy us, and the Roman people—the Roman people, furious that the earlier reports of Mithridates' defeat had borne false, thwarted in their demands for vengeance, were threatening to take out their rage on their own leaders. It was not merely Rome's reputation and prestige that was at stake but its very survival.

But the Senate had one last solution to offer:

Gnaeus Pompeius Magnus, known to all as Pompey the Great.

He was the ordained favorite of Sulla. A mere thirty-four years old, Pompey was fresh from a great victory over Sertorius' rebels in Spain, commander of Rome's largest body of troops, and the terror of the Senate, now that he had cleverly switched his party affiliation and put himself at the head of the revived Populares. Pompey was now looking for a task deserving of his ambitions and power. Mithridates was the only challenge worthy of such a man.

With the Senate undecided as to how best to handle the renewed threat from Pontus, it appointed Pompey as a general-at-large. This meant he was given almost unlimited power to accomplish his task—in fact, his terms of command were so broad that he would be allowed to levy any soldier or ship in all of Rome's domains, whenever he chose. Pompey would rank at the same level as every constitutionally appointed Roman governor or proconsul—yet all Roman allies and clients were ordered to place first priority on supporting him and fulfilling his requisitions. Five hundred ships were armed for his use, with six score thousand footmen and five thousand horsemen. Twenty-four senators, all of whom had previously been full generals, were assigned as his lieutenants. Most important, he was appointed for an unprecedented three-year term of office, rather than the customary one-year term. If it came down to a competition for resources between Pompey and a shorter-termed governor, it was clear whom the local petty officials and populace would obey.

Thus in that year, Father's sixty-fifth, the Roman Senate threw against us our most fearsome adversary yet. If Pompey's plans bore out, he would be marching on us with an army even more powerful than that which had besieged Athens two decades before. Yet at the same time, Lucullus' activities were shut down, and so Roman operations in the East were effectively frozen. The Roman bureaucracy had given us a window—a year at most—during which we could consolidate our reconquest of Pontus. If, after Pompey had completed his preparations, he found Father once again firmly seated on his throne, in possession of his strategic seaports and mountain strongholds, he might think twice before seeking to retake them from us. We had one year in which to firmly establish our control. There was no time to lose.

The first city we had retaken after our return from Armenia, Conama, became our new royal capital. Unlike Sinope and Amisus, it was largely intact, its public buildings undamaged by Roman looting, its population unharmed, though starved and demoralized. To the people's amazement, Father threw every resource he had into making Conama a new seat of empire. Enormous infusions of cash—treasure he had stored for years in secret caves and troves scattered about the Pontic interior, ancient offerings to forgotten gods that Father now claimed as his own, confiscations from wealthy landowners who had collaborated with the Romans—all these resources were applied to rebuilding the lost glories of ancient Pontus.

And wonderful things began to happen. Offers of double wages yielded at first a trickle of hungry workers, followed by a few hundred more, and within weeks thousands of skilled laborers began pouring into the city from all over the eastern Mediterranean. Engineers were imported from Greece and Syria, bearing plans for great structural and mechanical marvels. Architects and sculptors arrived in such quantities they had to be lodged and fed in a tent city on the outskirts, which the inhabitants dubbed the City of Dreamers. Musicians, actors, and poets filled the theaters and performance halls, overflowing into streets and taverns, keeping the City of Dreamers wide awake until far into the night. Academies sprang up like mushrooms after a rainstorm, representing every field of study and philosophy, from the sublime to the ridiculous, attracting instructors and curious followers from all over the known world. An enormous aqueduct began rising, spidery scaffolding clinging precariously to the limestone archways looming elegant and airy over the newly paved agora and the freshly plastered facades of the public buildings. Baths and gymnasiums were built; bids were tendered on a new coliseum.

And throughout the entire Pontic interior, across all the smaller cities the Roman legions had not bothered to occupy during their march to Armenia, it was the same. More funds were invested in these towns in one year than had been seen during their entire previous existence. Taxes were canceled, new temples established; slaves were manumitted and their owners compensated at twice the going rate. Father was feted as a conquering hero whenever he entered one of these dry, dusty outposts, and word of his coming would cause the entire countryside to empty as men and women rushed from their farms and trades to throw themselves at his feet. Never had I seen such adulation for any man, never such worship for any god, as Father received in that golden year after his return from exile.

Only his closest advisors were concerned at the frantic pace of his rebuilding, at the ruinous expenses he was incurring. All of us knew, of course, that he had squirreled away thousands

of talents in earlier years, when Pontus had been flush with pirate tribute and Roman plunder. Yet Father's current efforts
left us agog.

"It's madness!" I exclaimed as I examined the ledgers. "You
can't maintain this rate of building—you'll be bankrupt in
months!"

He smiled serenely.

"One year is all I ask," he said. "Keep the funds flowing for
one year. One year to create a new Golden Age, to cement the
people's loyalty to us, to make the Romans see that Pontus
will never be destroyed. One year—and Rome will understand
that our New Greece cannot die, that it is we, not Rome, who
are immortal! In one year Pompey will be knocking at our
door. And regardless of the outcome, after that encounter we
will no longer need our old savings. Either Pompey's own
treasure will be ours . . . or the opposite. Spend it, Pharnaces;
spend it! Let the world see the beauty and glory that Rome
hopes to destroy!"

Yet though Rome had suspended its aggressions, the threat
of its garrisons on Pontic territory still rankled. After confirming the solid start to his vast construction program, he handed
responsibility over to his civil advisors and returned . . . to matters of war.

With his core force of eight thousand troops, Father set his
sights first on the Roman occupying legion led by a general
named Fabius, based in the Cabira valley, the site of the panic
two years earlier that had resulted in our terrible defeat. Fabius,
in his great Roman arrogance, believed that no force would
dare attack him without overwhelmingly superior numbers and
that Pontus' troops, in particular, were too busy building spas
and gymnasiums in the cities to pose a threat to his position.
Father cannily exploited this belief. Leaving decoys in
Conama, in the form of tradesmen and laborers disguised as
Pontic soldiers, he filtered his troops through the mountains in
small bands by night, resting and planning by day, garroting
Roman scouts in the darkness before they could sound the
alarm. Without a single betrayal, in complete secrecy, our entire
force mustered in the darkness within three bow shots of
Fabius' camp. We had descended upon the unwitting enemy

seemingly from nowhere, like hornets gathering to the site of their threatened nest, like restless shades risen from the Underworld to torment the living.

Like Mithridates returned from the dead.

2

Silhouetted against the dawn sky that crisp morning at the head of his silent troops, Father looked not so much a mortal man but a Titan, emerged from his dark lair beneath the iron mountain. His vast mane of hair, flowing loose over his shoulders, glowed the color of polished steel, and the months of traveling had burnt his skin a deep umber, like the age patina of polished heartwood or the glowing coals of Hephaestus' forge. His eyes were shadowed beneath his heavy brow, yet the determined set of his mouth betrayed a slight smile, the supreme confidence he felt as he gazed at his men. His great warhorse was not armored as that of a Greek hero's but simply painted in bright swirls in the fashion of the Persian horsemen of Pontus, bold barbarian designs calculated to strike fear into the heart of the enemy by their very strangeness. Strength emanated from deep within him, through the taut muscles of his back and shoulders, through the very veins of his hands grasping the ash-wood javelin shaft. In the pre-battle stillness and silence the men themselves seemed to take courage from his strength, straightening their shoulders and growing before my very eyes, while he slowly paced their foreranks, waiting for the optimal moment to launch the attack.

Just as the top edge of the sun sent its piercing rays bolting from the horizon behind us, illuminating the Roman sentries on the palisade below in the blinding light, he gave a silent nod. The men exploded in a fierce roar and leaped from the copse in which they had been hiding, Father astride his war charger at the very front of his troops.

The Romans scrambled from their blankets in astonishment and confusion and struggled into battle positions, leaving armor and half their weapons lying uselessly in their tents. Despite Fabius' complete surprise, he did not order his men to hunker like cowards behind their infernal trenches and palisades but rather led them out to the front of their camp in true Roman fashion, encouraged, no doubt, at his realization that our forces were scarcely larger than his own. Yet the gods, this day, supported the righteous.

The battle lasted a full day. Father had two horses shot out from under him, and finally he resorted to stalking the front lines on foot, bellowing in a demon's voice and challenging every Roman to hand-to-hand combat. Battle raged around him, the Pontics and Armenians inspired by his vast silhouette striding among them through the clouds of dust. The Romans were slowly but surely being driven back. As darkness fell, Fabius realized he had been bested. Meanwhile, news of Mithridates' campaign spread like wildfire through the region, and volunteers and auxiliaries poured through the mountains to our assistance by the thousands, from every direction. Fabius ordered his men to fall back behind their fortifications.

As Armenian scouts cantered through the groves and fields, cutting down Roman stragglers who had become separated from the main force, Fabius' situation became desperate. His camp was strong, but it was surrounded, and prisoners informed us he had insufficient supplies to survive a siege. Fabius would have to attack, try to break through our lines before our own forces grew even stronger. And he would have to do so, with his exhausted, injured troops, the next day.

Yet the next day, to our astonishment, the Roman lines were twice as numerous as before! Fabius, in his desperation, had resorted to a step unprecedented in Roman history—he had freed the slaves in his camp, armed them, and distributed them in the battle lines among his trained legionaries. When Father first saw Romans clumsily swatting with their swords and using their javelins as canes and clubs, he thought the legionaries had drowned their sorrows with too much wine the night before. But when he realized they were untrained kitchen slaves and stable hands he roared with laughter and disdain.

"So, Fabius!" he shouted derisively as the Roman lines encountered our superior Armenian and Pontic forces. "What soldiers are these? Is it the Saturnalia so soon?" Even in the clamor of the fighting a chorus of hooting laughter could be heard from the Pontic ranks, at this mocking reference to the Roman festival when slaves don their masters' clothes and reverse their roles. Fabius, on the far side of the field, visibly stiffened at the taunt, though he refused to look our way.

Again the Romans were driven back. Their formation broke and the battle turned to a rout. Scullery workers and pantry boys scrambled up the embankment in terror to take refuge behind the pointed stakes of the palisades, and even the regular legionaries were not far behind, stumbling and tripping over one another in their mad dash. During our charge, Bituitus' horse, shot through the eye by an enemy arrow, rolled to his back, tipping his rider heavily to the ground. As the big Gaul staggered to his feet, an enormous Roman legionary leaped at him, striking a massive blow with his sword that split Bituitus' shield in two and sent him rolling to the side from the impact. Surely that man was a champion within his cohort. Yet springing like a cat before the Roman was able to recover his stance, Bituitus lunged, driving his own blade to the hilt into the Roman's groin, just below the edge of his mailed corselet. The man stiffened in shock and then doubled over with the pain of his disemboweling, grasping Bituitus' blade as if seeking to pull it from his body with his own hands. Bituitus placed his foot on the man's thigh and jerked the sword out, dismissively pushing the Roman into the mud and then cursing as he saw that the blade had broken off in the Roman's body.

I cantered over to his side, cutting down another attacker who leaped up against my horse. "Well done, Bituitus!" I shouted over the clamor and fighting, tossing him my cavalry scimitar as he bent to pick up the fallen Roman's shield. "How'd you lose your finger, old man?"

He grinned through the dirt and blood encrusting his face and saluted with the mutilated right hand that had fascinated me since boyhood. "Knife slipped scalping a Roman!" he shouted back.

Father led the final Pontic charge on foot, bearing a Roman shield that he, too, had picked up from the ground, waving a bloody sword, and surrounded by his own squadron of Roman exiles as bodyguards. I remained on my mount and was returning to the flanks to lead a charge of Armenian horse when I saw a heart-stopping sight.

Just as Father and his troops reached the walls of the palisades, where the gates were still open to let pass the fleeing legionaries, the defenders loosed a withering hail of missiles from the watchtowers. The attacking Pontic forces raised their shields and continued to forge ahead, cutting down the fleeing Romans before they escaped into the heavily fortified gate. Father raised his shield to protect his face from the shower of stones and arrows, but large as he was, the Roman shield he carried did little to shelter his broad shoulders or the lower half of his body. As I watched, a pointed sling bullet, like those used by the Cretans, as long as a thumb and just as thick, slammed into his shield, denting it deeply, and another riveted his shoulder guard, though he shrugged off the impact as if it were an insect. Still he advanced, sword raised and bellowing encouragement to his men, while a furious volley of sling stones flew around him, whizzing past his face as if he were favored by the gods. With the gold plating on his armor reflecting blindingly in the evening sun, he was the very image of a god, of Apollo himself—the Sun God! His charge was mesmerizing, into the very teeth of that hail of deadly bullets, yet it could not hold— the slingers on the wall had found their range, had recognized the enemy king, and now every defender on the ramparts was loosing his missiles at one man, at his shattered and destroyed shield, which he struggled to hold before his face for protection.

Suddenly a whistling lead bullet from a well-wielded sling slammed into his knee, shattering it in a burst of blood. Father's face contorted in pain as the leg buckled and he fell heavily to the ground, rolling onto his back to grasp his injured knee with one hand while raising the remnants of his shield for protection against the fierce hail of missiles.

I jerked my horse's head around and raced over to assist him. The men following behind their fallen king were still leaping over him in their momentum, unaware, until they were virtually on top of his prone form, that he was lying on the ground.

Yet the Roman defenders in the watchtower above had seen him fall, had seen the vast bulk of the man they had toppled, and there could be no mistake in their minds as to whom the sling stone had struck. They now concentrated all their fire on his writhing body. Dozens of stones, arrows, and lances slammed into his shield, cracking and shattering it as he rolled and struggled to stand. The King's own Roman bodyguard had by this time seen his fall and raced to his assistance, three of them sheltering his body with their own shields as the others set up a murderous counterfire of spears against the defenders above. The Romans raining their missiles down on us hesitated at this fierce attack as they squatted beneath their shields, and the pace of the shooting suddenly dropped. Lying in the mud in excruciating pain, Father lowered the pieces of the shattered oaken plates that had once been his Roman shield—and then the javelin struck.

I did not see who loosed it, though undoubtedly it was one of the determined watchtower defenders. Bituitus told me later it was a burly veteran, whom he himself then impaled by the throat against the back wall of the watchtower with a mighty heave of his own spear. But that hardly matters now. The Roman javelin flew through the air, whistling at its sudden release from the thrower's finger loop, seeming to snake around and between Father's bodyguards, whirring like a hornet directly through the tiny gaps that had been left between their interlocked shields. It slammed into Father's mouth, a four-foot, iron-tipped missile thrown at close range from the top of a watchtower. Father's head snapped back sickeningly with the impact as he thrust backward against the hard ground, and blood and tissue spattered over the feet of the horrified guards surrounding him.

A cry rose up, a simultaneous cheer from the defenders in the watchtower above and a bellow of rage and dismay from the guards below. The Pontic assault troops, most of whom had not seen what had transpired, nevertheless heard the uproar and, sensing trouble, an ambush perhaps or a localized defeat, suddenly slackened in their attack. Men ceased to run, drawing up aimlessly just outside the Roman gates, looking to their sides and over their shoulders at what their comrades might be doing, waiting for orders. The battle cries of the attackers suddenly diminished, and it was this sudden silence that seemed to bring back awareness to the fallen king.

Half-senseless, Father threw aside the guards bending down to assist him, lurched to one knee, and roared at the top of his lungs.

"Continue the assault! Charge the Roman dogs! Charge!" His voice strangled in the blood that filled his throat, and he sank back down behind the shields of his mercenary Romans— but not before the entire attacking force, and most of the enemy as well, had caught sight of him.

His appearance was horrific—half the right side of his face, it seemed, had been torn away where the warhead had exited his mouth. Blood sheeted down his neck and covered the shoulder plates and carapace of his armor. His face was twisted in fury and pain and his eyes rolled white in his head as he collapsed backward and was then hidden by the backs and shoulders of his guards. The dream, the dream I had—Father passing in and out of my sight as men moved in front of him, face pale as death, seeming to look for me, searching for me—I was living the terrible dream. Yet this was no dream. I was surrounded by grim-faced cavalry officers, armor and limbs sticky with the residue of battle, the taste of dirt and blood in my mouth, javelins and arrows whizzing by my face.

I whipped my horse furiously, trampling over the fallen and shouting for the men in front of me, Pontics and Romans, to yield as I bulled my way through them. My heart leaped into my throat at the sight of Father lunging up with his destroyed face, still calling for the attack, yet dying even as he did. I shouted to him to hold, to hold on, yet the words would not pass my lips— as in my dream, I was struck mute at the terrible scene. The entire Pontic force dropped its pursuit of the Romans and stood silent, defending themselves with their shields from flying missiles, but with one eye on the spot where the King had fallen. Nothing, after such a sight, nothing could compel the men to continue with the attack.

Fabius' troops struggled to scurry inside the shelter of the palisade and close the gates. Meanwhile, six of our men, led by grizzled Bituitus, struggled to carry Father's weight as he writhed and thrashed in pain, bellowing to be released to continue the charge.

"Cowards!" he roared, spewing blood. "Laggards! Release me!"

"Get *down*, sire!" Bituitus implored as Father struggled to escape their grip.

"I will not! The bastard Romans are on the run! Bituitus, you *stupid* . . . you lame-assed Gaul, you . . . Release me!"

Bituitus had had enough. Drawing back his arm, he dealt the pain-maddened king a mighty blow in the temple with the flat of his hand, stunning him into silence. Surely the Gaul was the only man in Asia strong enough to accomplish such a thing and brave enough to even consider it. No one protested. Father fell back into the men's arms and they staggered away, half-dragging, half-carrying the King, to a low swale in the terrain out of arrow range of the Romans.

For four days Father wavered between battlefield and Boatman, between life and death. His handsome face was destroyed—the heavy warhead had slammed into his mouth at an angle, shearing off all his front teeth at the gum line and emerging from his right cheek just in front of his ear, opening a gaping hole through which the shattered remnants of his right jawbone protruded. The weapon's wooden shaft had broken off upon impact, as it was designed to do by the clever Roman armorers, to prevent the enemy from picking up an intact weapon and hurling it back—so the iron had passed clean through. The army surgeons looked in dismay at the terrible injury and shook their heads. They did not even bother contemplating his shattered kneecap.

All felt there was no hope. All, that is, but the ancient Scythian Papias. When the army surgeons threw up their hands in despair, the cunning old sorcerer booted them out and set to work with a determination matched only by the strangeness of his muttered chants and groans. He was watched only by Bituitus and myself, and by the fiercely loyal Hypsicratia, who remained by Father's side day and night, pale as death, snarling like a tiger if anyone attempted to remove her.

Papias sedated Father from his pain, using a distillation of Caucasian crocus, red as newly carved flesh. Torn gums were packed with wool lint and flax; the gaping hole in the cheek was sewn with gut filament, but since so much of the skin had been ripped away, the remainder had to be pulled excessively tight, stretching down the corner of his eye. This prevented Father from shutting it completely, causing the eyeball to dry out and wither. Salves and vulneraries were applied to the stitches to promote healing and his chest poulticed with a febrifuge to draw from his body the fiery heat and congestion that were sure to set in. A hollow reed was carefully inserted through his mouth and into the lungs, which Papias employed to suck out the blood Father had inhaled, which had given him an ominous, raspy breath. Papias spit the lung debris into a silver bowl I held by the side of the bed. Father's head and jaw then were bound tight with strips of clean linen.

Most important, the antidote was administered, through another reed threaded into his esophagus, to prevent the convulsions and seizures that would otherwise occur. In fact, old Papias administered a double dosage each day as the patient tossed and moaned on his cot in a painful fog of misery and drugs.

On the fifth day Father sat up, his remaining eye bloodshot but clear of the haze in which his mind had been wandering, and he signaled for water, which he drank messily with a ladle through his broken teeth. He swallowed a quantity of strong wine and a medicinal broth made of the livers of field mice, delicate yet nutritious, flavored with squill. He then looked up at my worried face.

"Well," he croaked, "I suppose now you truly *are* Alexander."

"Alexander?" I asked in puzzlement.

"Do you remember Phrygia?" he replied.

I hearkened back to our conversation long ago, after I had slept in the room of the great conqueror, and smiled. "How could I be Alexander?"

"Because with only one eye, and a face like a Gorgon's, I now look like his father, Philip!" He laughed painfully, without daring to smile, then fell serious again. "Help me outside to see the troops."

Never, I believe, has a commander's arrival been so welcome as was Father's, from the land of the dead. The cheers resounded among the mountain cliffs surrounding us as far as the camp of the Romans, who were still nursing their own wounds behind their palisades, cornered and besieged by the roving bodies of horse troops I had stationed on all sides. Since the last battle, fighters had continued to pour into our camp, and the army now numbered over twenty thousand—and the sight of old Mithridates, without voice and with only half his face, but sitting up before them, with a body like Hercules', moved them to a riot of celebration.

The men surged about him, showering him with the locks of hair they had cut in their grief at what they thought was his death and praising the gods for his survival. To the men, Mithridates was no less than a god: No mere mortal could have survived such an injury; no man could have continued to urge the attack after suffering such terrible pain. No human so grossly wounded could possibly lead these men in final victory against the Romans but him.

And while Father encouraged the men by his mere presence, he in turn was strengthened by their cheers, which did more even than Papias' ministrations to heal his broken body.

3

Though father recovered quickly, the Romans took advantage of the reprieve given them, and within two weeks General Triarius, commander of Rome's forces in Asia, had received word of Fabius' predicament and marched to his relief with two full legions. Forcing his way past our encirclement while Father was still weak and unable to rally his troops, Triarius combined his forces with those of Fabius and took charge of the entire army. The Romans were now strong enough to break through our lines and march through open country to the seacoast and safety, which they commenced to do, in a southwesterly direction.

As the Romans withdrew, Father followed cautiously with our own continually growing forces. He was not sufficiently confident in their abilities to attempt a full assault but nevertheless sought an opportunity. He insisted on riding his own horse unaided, which he preferred to walking, as his injured knee gave him much pain. He rode among his soldiers, aligning their positions, engaging them in drills and exercises even while on the march, and trading jokes and banter.

He grew stronger by the day and more horrid to look at. Leering down at the men with his one good eye from his tremendous warhorse, he was a terrifying sight to those who had not known him before—his hair by now white as snow, with a thick, grizzled beard covering most of his face, save the long scar running ear to chin down his right jawline where the javelin had punched through. This jagged line, raw though healing quickly from the effect of Papias' salves, gleamed pink and wormlike through the adjoining whiskers. Indeed, though he still resembled a god, he was now more like old Zeus or Poseidon than Apollo. There were no Roman jowls or fatty Latin chin for him but rather the same strong jaw and aquiline nose, the same piercing, intelligent stare. From the left side, he was as kingly and stately a monarch as had ever sat on a throne. From the right, however, men shuddered in repulsion at the twisted grimace into which his face had healed, a horrifying caricature of what it had once been, all the more disturbing for belonging to the same person as the beautiful visage on the other side. His face had become a disturbing theater mask, comedy and tragedy, one side grinning, the other leering. Yet on Father, both comedy and tragedy were now equally and simultaneously visible, his whole life writ large on his face for the world to see.

Triarius withdrew and Mithridates advanced—cat and mouse, neither side making any decisive maneuver, until Roman politics once again played into our hands.

A Roman cavalry captain, fatally injured with an arrow through the spine in a skirmish with a small company of our scouts, was brought into camp for interrogation before he died. When asked Triarius' intent, the wounded soldier laughed in our faces.

"General Triarius will destroy you all before Lucius Lucullus does it himself, which he should have done five years ago!"

At these startling words, the interrogators quickly summoned me to the dying soldier's side to hear this extraordinary claim.

"Lucullus?" I said. "What of Lucullus?"

The Roman, only semi-lucid at best, apparently saw no need to disguise his general's strategy.

"Lucullus is marching through, on his return to Rome. His troops will be here in a fortnight. Triarius will present him with your pathetic king's head, before Lucullus can take it himself!"

There was no further information we could glean from the man, so I ordered him put out of his misery and brought the strange tidings to the King.

Strange, I say, because with our network of spies among the chieftains, traders, and shepherds throughout the land surely we would have known weeks in advance of any incursion by a force the size of Lucullus'. Tigranes in Armenia would not have allowed the Romans to pass through without sending word to us, if only to request our assistance. Any landing of a Roman fleet in Cilicia would have been immediately noted and communicated to us by pirate signal. And even if Lucullus did attempt such a landing, with his legions of mutinous old men awaiting their retirement bonus, he was in no condition to undertake a risky march into the Pontic interior. After Father and his advisors discussed the matter half the night we came to the logical conclusion: Lucullus and his force were nowhere near the vicinity.

Father allowed himself a smile with his twisted lips. "The only news better," he concluded, "would have been if Lucullus were indeed close by."

He chuckled but did so alone. None of the rest of us understood what he was talking about.

"Think like a Roman!" he hissed at me, his voice still hoarse from Papias' throat-reeds. "I taught you Latin so you could understand their speech; I showed you battles so you could understand their weaponry and tactics. But you miss the most important lesson—if you cannot put yourself into their minds, you cannot defeat them!"

"Into their minds?" I questioned. "What is there to guess at? Triarius believes he will be reinforced soon, so all he needs to do is hunker down and wait. We cut off his communication and supply lines and starve him out—"

"No!" he roared, and I could see that though he had regained his health, he had lost his patience, as if his injury had been the first sign to him of his own mortality and he was rushing to accomplish what he could while he still had time. Clearly, my thickheadedness was an impediment to his plans.

"Think like a Roman commander. *Think,* Pharnaces! If Triarius wants any chance at glory, any chance at advancement or a Triumph in Rome, he must defeat me here, now, *before* Lucullus arrives. Once Lucullus is here, Triarius will be only a subordinate. He can't hunker down and wait—he must attack me now!"

"But Lucullus is *not* coming . . ." I rejoined.

"True, but Triarius doesn't know that. He's laboring under false information. Or perhaps he *does* know that Lucullus is nowhere near but wishes me to think he is, and so he planted that false information among his men, knowing that word would reach me. Which it did."

My head spun. "But why would he want you to think that Lucullus is coming—or if he truly *is* coming, why would Triarius want you to know that?"

Father sighed heavily. "Now you must take your mind out of the Roman's head, if it was ever there in the first place, and put it into mine, as commander of the Pontic forces. If I thought Lucullus were approaching—which I don't—what would I do?"

"Split up your army, of course. Send a force of heavy cavalry to harass Lucullus in his approach, and leave the remainder here to besiege Triarius."

"Precisely. You're not as dense as you sometimes seem."

"And then"—light was beginning to dawn—"and then Triarius would see that our forces were down to half-strength, and would take that opportunity to attack us. Whether or not Lucullus is truly coming, whether or not Triarius *believes* he is coming, he wants *you* to believe it so you will split up the army and he can defeat us!"

"You understand, General," and he turned the left side of his face toward me, laughing with the good side of his mouth, his healthy eye twinkling, as the rest of his face was obscured in the shadows. "And we shall give him the satisfaction of knowing that his rumor of Lucullus was well received."

The next morning Father split off five thousand cavalry, which I myself led thundering off to the southeast, ostensibly to intercept Lucullus on his approach. Triarius waited a full day, to ensure that good distance had been placed between the King and his crack Pontic horsemen. And then, on a plain overlooked by a craggy fortress known as Zela, a site I was to know well a few years hence, Triarius turned like a cornered dog and attacked.

This was precisely what Father had hoped for, and he proved equal to the task. Having known in advance that Triarius would pull precisely this, Father had his men march in full panoply with weapons at the ready, advancing from position to position rather than their normal helter-skelter, uncaring, dusty slog along the road. When he and the infantry emerged from the deep valley through which they had been marching, onto the dry, desolate plain of Zela, the advance scouts had already warned him of the Roman entrenchments that had been hastily dug an hour or so before, awaiting our arrival. As Marcellus commanded the half-legion of Roman exiles and the remaining cavalry, Father took personal command of a cohort of Armenian veterans, maneuvering them into the front ranks of the army. Without even pausing to muster troops or to parley position with the enemy's heralds, he bellowed out the war cry and met Triarius' legions head-on.

Father fought the entire day in the front rank, on his war charger, as the cohort under his command led the effort to push Triarius back toward the fortified camp the Romans had constructed at the far end of the plain. The enemy fought valiantly, unwilling to cede—until from the canyon beneath the rocky fortress, on their right flank, the trumpet sounded, and I led the five thousand horsemen who had split off the day before, streaming across the undefended grounds and straight into the Romans' astonished right wing. The legionaries were too stunned even to flee, and countless hundreds were simply trampled under the sharpened forehooves of the tribal horsemen or split down the cranium by the flashing cavalry scimitars. The survivors finally gathered their wits, regained a semblance of order, and beat a retreat back toward their camp, tripping and stumbling through the muddy entrenchments they themselves had dug, which were now their own most formidable obstacles in gaining safety from the rampaging Pontic army pursuing them.

Joining up with Father during the rout, I noted the grim satisfaction on his face at facing regular Roman legionaries, not Bithynian auxiliaries or Chalcedonian mercenaries, but true Roman soldiers in full regalia, on foot, broken in line, dropping their shields and fleeing before him. It was a sight he savored as he trotted along in the midst of his foot troops, fast approaching the undefended walls of the Roman encampment.

My work done and my cavalry now running down straggling Roman legionaries, I broke off the chase and cantered toward Father through the chaos and shouting, aiming to congratulate him. He sat tall in the saddle, hardly a sign of his near-fatal injuries, but for the odd shape of his helmet where he had removed the right cheek plate to accommodate the swelling he still suffered from his injuries to that side. Trotting on foot beside him was the usual squad of Roman exiles he maintained as a personal guard, arrayed in the complete Roman regalia and panoply they still retained even after years of service to the King.

Suddenly I noticed an enemy centurion struggling up from the ground where he had been lying facedown and over whom Father and his guards had stepped unheeded, thinking him dead. The man was severely wounded, for he could barely make it to his feet, but stand up he did, in armor and clothing almost identical to those of the exiles surrounding Father. Tottering and swaying for a moment before gaining his bearings, he suddenly realized he had just been passed over by the Pontic king and was now actually behind enemy lines, isolated from his own unit, which had already fled behind the palisade walls or been killed in the rout.

I was about to ignore him, to consign him to capture and handling by the auxiliaries and camp followers behind us, when I saw the man fix his gaze on Father's back, hunch up his shoulders, and begin trotting toward the group of Roman exiles surrounding the King.

A flash went off in my mind as I suddenly realized the danger. With a shout I dug my heels into the flanks of my mount and sprinted forward, fighting my way through the chaos and masses of men running before me, who dove away from my lashing whip and my animal's hooves while I struggled to make way through to the King.

I was too late. Never taking my eyes off the wounded centurion, I watched in horror as he caught up with the Roman guards, falling into step with them and maneuvering his way close until he was trotting alongside Father's mount, struggling to disguise his limp and trailing a thin stream of blood behind him.

"Seize the centurion!" I bellowed, finally making my way through the swarms of men to within earshot of Father and his guards. "Seize the Roman!"

Father looked up at me, a mixture of pride and confusion in his eyes, and his men, too, looked around, startled at my sudden appearance in their midst, shouting for one of them to be seized. Only one man knew my meaning; only one knew his own evil intent. Seeing me about to run him down, the rogue centurion suddenly whipped out the short sword from the scab-

bard at his hip and, raising it above his head, brought it down
with all his remaining strength into the closest part of Father he
could reach from his position—his huge, unprotected thigh.

Father roared in pain and rage as his horse, startled and confused, reared onto its hind legs and pawed frantically in the air
with its forehooves before slamming back down to earth. I
thundered up, shouldering through the bodyguards who were
still ignorant of what had happened, and with a single swoop of
my scimitar sliced through the centurion's neck beneath his
cheek plates, sending a fountain of hot blood streaming over
the haunches of Father's flailing horse. The momentum of my
stroke sent the head spinning beneath the feet of the running infantry, and the body itself crumpled slowly into the dust, iron
Roman fist still clutching the sword handle.

Father's wound was terrible, a deep gash through the fiber and
muscle of the thigh to the very bone itself. For a moment it lay
open, the femur white and exposed between the two crimson
walls of meat wrapping it from either side, so much like the
haunch of an ox being slaughtered that I shuddered. For a moment the wound failed even to bleed, and Father looked down at
it in pain and dismay, and then blood began gushing from the
severed artery like a fountain, and he turned pale. I leaped off my
mount, slapping the animal away, and strode quickly through the
mire and muck of battle that covered the field. Father, too, dismounted, half-tumbling onto his uninjured leg or, rather, onto
the leg injured less recently, and his face twisted in pain as his
weight fell heavily onto the shattered and still-splinted knee he
had been so careful to favor. A dozen shouting men reached out
to seize him, rushing to stanch the gushing flow of blood from
his huge limb, and Father threw off his helmet, rolled his eyes
into the back of his head, and lost consciousness.

Just as had occurred before, once the King fell, word spread
quickly through the army and the attack broke off, allowing the
surviving Romans to limp and struggle behind the spiked walls
of their palisades unimpeded.

One of Father's guards hastily improvised a tourniquet to
stanch the bleeding, and within moments Father woke from his
swoon. He was groggy at first, but as his wits returned to him
and he recognized the concerned faces hovering over him he
became suddenly angry.

"Lift me up," he groaned. "Lift me up so the men can see I am alive."

Bituitus protested strenuously, but I saw immediately what Father intended—just as Alexander, when wounded in India, showed himself to his troops to allay their fears, Father hoped to prevent his own men from scuttling certain victory out of fear for him.

"Lift him up!" I ordered, seizing Father by one shoulder myself, and Bituitus, with a moment's hesitation, began to help me. Father's head lolled backward in another swoon, and I supported its heavy weight with my own shoulder until he revived.

"Resume the attack!" Father rasped throatily, weak from the loss of so much blood as would have killed a normal man, if not a horse or a bear. "We had them running—destroy the Romans!"

Marcellus came thundering up on his horse, face still aflame with the fury of the charge he had just led and anger at the fall of the King.

"Prince! Prince Pharnaces!" he bellowed.

I glanced his way angrily. "Not now, Tribune! Can't you see the King is wounded?"

He leaped off his horse, strode to where I stood supporting Father, and seized me by the shoulder. I almost struck him with my free arm in my fury, but the earnest look on his face stopped me.

"Prince Pharnaces—are you mad? The army can't stop now—we'll lose all we've gained! Leave the King to the physicians—you must take command, *immediately,* or the King's fall will have been in vain!"

I stared at him, without moving, as if in a trance. Take command of the army? With Father still alive? How could I betray him . . . ?

"Prince Pharnaces—*now*! The men await!"

Snapping out of my thoughts, I nodded and handed Father to the guards. Leaping onto a nearby horse, I raised my sword high above my head, waving it in a broad circle, like a pennant, calling the attention of the centurions and cohort commanders who had drifted to the site of the assassination attempt.

"The King lives and rules!" I bellowed, and as word spread through the gathering forces of worried men, a cheer arose.

"The King lives and rules!" I roared again, but this time the wave of cheers that met my words almost knocked me over, so great was the effect such news had on the men. Astonished at the fervor I had awakened, I continued the simple harangue.

"He lives, and his will is that the jackal Romans be destroyed this day!" I shouted. "We shall drive the Romans from the face of Asia! *Resume the attack!*"

With a thunderous roar the men raced back to their units, forming into the ranks they had abandoned moments before, and leaped toward the palisades rising scarcely two hundred paces before us. Turning to seek out Marcellus and send him back into action with the Roman exiles, I was astonished to find Father looming over me, mounted again, his face pale and drawn. He stared at me hard, penetrating deep into my eyes. A memory flashed to me of my confrontation with him after the battle of Halys, when I had first assumed command of Gordios' cavalry squadron.

"I ordered the troops back into battle," I told him matter-of-factly, uncertain how much of my harangue he had heard and whether his wits were about him.

He nodded curtly. "So you did," he rasped, swaying on his saddle. "And again you assumed command without my authority."

Still he doubted! This was the final straw. I exploded at him, though the old man could barely see straight for pain and loss of blood. "*Without your authority!* You yourself ordered the troops to press the attack, even after you were wounded!" I bellowed. "What do you *want* of me? Am I a general or just your mouthpiece? Do you accuse me of mutiny every time I apply a tactic? Are you an immortal god, knowing all and seeing all?"

He stared at me, his face exhausted, and I fell silent. An army surgeon, Timotheus, ran up, appalled that Father had somehow managed to climb onto his horse, and the physician seized the beast's reins. Father brushed him off for a moment longer.

"You did right, Pharnaces," he said, his voice at almost a whisper from fatigue but his eyes still glaring fiercely. "But remember your position; remember it! I am not dead yet."

I sighed and shook my head, exasperated that after so many years of faithful service to him he could still doubt my intentions. "And I rejoice in your survival," I said solemnly.

He looked at me closely. "You say that as if you truly mean it."

"I do mean it. But the Roman Triarius is not dead yet, either, and that must be addressed."

"Triarius will not survive the night," he replied, "nor Rome the year."

But Rome did survive the year, and Triarius the night, though only his own conscience, if he has one, may tell if he was able to live with himself for his conduct. For seeing his forces routed, Triarius took all the able-bodied men from among the survivors and fled to safety in Roman-controlled Cappadocia. In so doing, he committed the unthinkable, the unpardonable—he left behind seven thousand Roman corpses, their ghosts hovering unhappily between the jawbones of their unburied skulls. Triarius' act was one that disgusted us for its perfidy, tainting even our joy at capturing the Roman baggage, treasure, and supplies left behind in their panicked retreat. Our only regret was that we had failed in the complete destruction of the Roman force, which would have been possible had we not hesitated in fear at the King's injuries. Among the dead were twenty-four tribunes and a hundred fifty centurions, an enormous proportion of the Roman force's leadership, evidence that the demoralization of the legions was complete, as the soldiers had fled the field while leaving their officers to fight and die behind.

Shortly after the battle, we received word from Greek merchants that Lucullus had finally returned to Rome and been awarded his Triumph. His ceremonial escort was meager—a mere fifteen hundred sick or wounded legionaries, the only ones who had not scattered to their newly assigned land parcels upon being discharged or who had not re-upped under Pompey's commission. Yet what Lucullus lacked in manpower he more than made up for in sheer, opulent, eye-popping wealth, all of it plundered from Pontus and Armenia.

Besides thousands upon thousands of empty suits of armor from dead Armenian kataphractoi, which Lucullus set up in ghostly ranks in the middle of the Circus Flaminius, his trove included the beaks of a hundred captured Pontic warships; ten gilded scythe chariots; a life-sized statue of King Mithridates crafted of solid gold; twenty litters overflowing with silver plate, each carried by eight staggering slaves, and another thirty-two bearing gold plate; fifty-six mules laden with silver ingot; and another hundred and seven bearing silver coin. All of this was deposited before the steps of the Capitol, a massive donation to the Roman people and the guardian deities Jupiter, Juno, and Minerva. Every soldier in the eastern campaigns was awarded nine hundred fifty silver drachmae, a mind-boggling sum. After the triumphal procession, Lucullus sponsored a general celebration, in which he lavishly feasted the entire city and all the surrounding towns and villages from his own personal wealth.

Thus he concluded his career, like one of those ancient and cheap comedies that begin tediously yet end with a guffaw, for his early life had been marked by dogged campaigning and governance and his later years by feasts and banquets, mummeries and torch dances, and other such frivolities. Lucullus was resurrected, from his status as goat of the legions, to the wealthiest and most popular man in Rome.

During the triumphal celebration, one senator apparently had the temerity to point out publicly that scarcely a year before, Lucullus had sent Rome an official dispatch boasting of his final conquest of Pontus and neutralization of Mithridates. Upon being confronted with this accusation, it is said, Lucullus simply shrugged and said that, at the time, it was true.

But now Rome must take Pontus all over again.

4

Pompey was true to his boasts of invincibility. Within three months, he had eliminated the pirate threat in the entire Mediterranean basin. He sent Roman squadrons to North Africa, Sicily, and Corsica, flushed the rogues from their lairs, and herded them to the huge, permanent pirate base on the Cilician coast. Here there was a semblance of a battle, but the pirates' enthusiasm was dampened when Pompey captured some four score and ten of their galleys, dozens of transport vessels, and twenty thousand men. Yet rather than incurring the pirates' enmity, he instead caused massive confusion and dissent among their ranks, by releasing to them an offer, unauthorized by the Senate but respected nonetheless, of a free land grant in Greece or Asia to any pirate who agreed to surrender his ill-gotten wealth and submit to Rome. The pirate force dissolved like Caspian pack ice on a summer day.

My greatest surprise at this was that Father was not in the least surprised.

"I learned my lesson from Archelaus," he scoffed. "Pirates are mercenaries, no more, no less. They see no profit in fighting against a Roman war fleet, unless they aspire to govern Rome. I have nothing to offer them at the moment, so even an acre of Boeotian gravel bottom to grow lentils beats the prospect of life as a Roman galley slave if they refuse." He spit out of the open right corner of his mouth, a habit he had developed since his injury, to prevent the inevitable, unkingly drooling that would occur if he did not. Whether spitting or drooling, he was cursed by a continual unsightly runoff down the side of his whiskers, a distracting sight to one not accustomed to it.

"It doesn't matter," I pointed out. "You hold the Pontic interior. Thirty thousand foot and three thousand horse, a standing army. Sinope and Amisus—you can do without the coastal cities. Even to keep them would leave you beholden to the pirates."

He sniffed, shrugged his great shoulders, and stood up. Things could be worse, I thought. But not by much. Rome's greatest general was now camped on the coast of Cilicia. He had a mighty host, a combination of loyal legions transferred from Spain and Italy and Lucullus' remaining forces, who were familiar with the region. Father, on the other hand, was in his sixty-sixth year and still suffering the pain of three recent wounds, none of which showed any promise of healing completely. His vast program of civil construction and financial reforms would soon exhaust all available funds. He led a large but untrained army of tribesmen in the forested hills and canyons of the interior, but food and supplies were increasingly difficult to come by—Roman armies had occupied and pillaged the region so brutally that the few farmers who remained hardly bothered to plant crops, fearing they would be burnt or stolen before they could be brought to market.

Our advisors counseled parley with the Roman general. Go-betweens from Pompey had implied there might be room for peaceful settlement. Pompey was eager to return to Rome, to take up the governance functions he felt were due him. Father simply wished to be left unmolested by the legions, confirmed as ruler in his hereditary domains, allowed to continue with his rebuilding of Pontus. Pompey would require that the King declare himself a friend and ally of the Roman people. Father could not stomach this but hinted that he still retained a last hoard of gold in a distant fortress, which could be made available to the general were he to make peace. The Romans counteroffered, and Father gave slight ground. Slow progress was made.

Things seemed to be lurching and limping toward a middle ground when Pompey, always through back-door channels, floated a demand that Father flatly rejected. Not only did he reject it, but he slammed the door on all possible future negotiations, for the insult it implied. For Pompey required, before any face-to-face meeting could be arranged between the two men, that as a sign of good faith Mithridates surrender all Roman exiles he retained in his camp—three thousand of them.

Father refused, remaining loyal to the men who had stood by him over the years, even in the face of certain defeat should Pompey initiate all-out war. A vassal's loyalty to his lord, he said, was the virtue most to be admired above all others. He would not torture captured enemy soldiers who remained loyal to their commanders, nor would he punish slaves who followed their masters into treason, even treason against himself. How then could he remain a man if he were to surrender the very soldiers who had stayed loyal to him for two decades, who had followed him into battle, who had saved his life when he had fallen? He would rather, he said, have lost both legs to injuries at Zela. He would prefer, he said, to have had his entire head taken off by the javelin rather than merely his right jawbone. Actually, to the Roman heralds who brought him the fatal proposal from Pompey he was far less articulate, or perhaps more so, depending upon your perspective. He said only two words, of unsurpassed eloquence:

"Fuck Pompey."

The scandalized heralds scuttled back to Cilicia. Within the month, Pompey attacked.

The Roman general moved in with his legions, advancing ponderously across the Cappadocian plains and into Pontus. The man was a proper soldier and a sound strategist, even by the high standards of Rome. But where he truly excelled was in administration. While our army lived hand-to-mouth, spending half its days foraging for food, haggling with peasants over a few moldy grains of wheat, or painstakingly hunting down deer and antelope in the mountains, Pompey's men marched on full bellies. They crossed into Pontus trailed by an enormous supply line extending all the way to their Cilician base, bearing not only the obligatory biscuit and wine on which the legionaries could survive for weeks on end, but water—carts loaded with hundreds of barrels and skins of fresh water drawn from secure sources, making them impervious to all our attempts to hinder them by poisoning wells or diverting streams from their path. It was impossible for us to break the supply train, for we could not concentrate sufficient force behind the Roman lines to effect any permanent disruption. Worse, Pompey had a knack for simply absorbing our allies into his own forces by bribery, or promises of safety, as he did the pirates. Slowly and systematically, with infinite patience, it seemed, he drove us back through the interior mountains, drove us toward a corner, toward the Roman fleet massed on the Black Sea coast, or toward Armenia, where Father was loath to throw himself on Tigranes' mercy a second time. Our options were dwindling daily, and Pompey knew it. Our own soldiers knew it as well.

O Lord Aion, elusive God of Ever-Extending Time: *Slow* is not the word to describe Pompey's advance. His progress was *excruciating,* toying with us as we retreated, unwilling to take even the slightest risk, to engage our infantry in full battle. Try as we might, we could not draw him into the ambushes we planned—his legions refused to emerge from their fortified camps until we retreated behind the next set of foothills. He guarded his river crossings with squads of heavy infantry, deploying mercenary horse and bowmen in the hills above the fords to protect the all-important baggage train. We seized an impregnable mountain fortress from which we could destroy them with boulders and missiles fired from the walls. The Romans refused even to attack but rather besieged us with trenches, remaining far beyond arrow range, seeking not so much to starve us but to *bore* us into surrender with their grim, complete silence, their absolute lack of aggression.

Twice in two weeks Pompey sent heralds under a flag of truce, issuing his former offer, for Father to surrender his Roman exile troops and declare himself a friend of Rome, in return for which he would be left to rule his ravaged kingdom in peace. Twice Father sent the emissaries back with an angry refusal. On their third attempt, Father ordered the heralds fired upon. When I protested his actions, he responded that it was better to violate diplomatic law by firing upon emissaries than natural law by betraying men loyal to him.

For forty-five days we withstood, holed up in that pestilent fortress. We were reduced to eating our baggage animals, even wild dogs and cats we found inhabiting burrows under the walls, though Father forbade us from slaughtering the cavalry mounts. From the heights of the wall we could spy the relentless arrival of Pompey's laden baggage train, herds of goats and cattle driven in for the slaughter, cartloads of wine. Looking around at my troops one day, I saw gaunt faces and dry, cracked lips from the tiny rations of fetid water each of our men were allotted, the rancid mule meat and wormy wheat tack. Even Bituitus, huge, muscular, immortal Bituitus, had begun to look thin and aged, a frail imitation of what he had been in his prime. I knew we could hold out no longer.

On the next moonless night we made our fatal decision. I looked up at the heavens as Papias and Father stood beside me.

"What star is that, traveling in the sky?" I asked.

The old Maeotian spoke without hesitation.

"Sirius," he said. "Close to the sevenfold voyaging Pleiades, still high overhead."

"The omens are right for the deed, old man?" Father asked in a somber tone.

Papias squinted at the sky for a long time, then spoke carefully. "They are, sire."

Father strode across the sward flanking the fortress keep, in the shelter of which our sick and injured soldiers, twelve hundred in all, lay shoulder to shoulder in military formation—two full cohorts, a writhing, moaning, horizontal army. Stepping to the first injured man, he stopped, looked down at the prone shape, then slowly knelt beside him on one knee and pulled back the blanket covering him. A sickly, sweetish smell wafted up to our faces, the smell of death. The man's leg was gone from the knee down, the result of a Roman arrow taken in the shin two weeks before, followed by the camp surgeon's hacksaw of healing. The tissue around the wound was visibly rotting, taking on the scaling and the purplish luster of gangrene.

"He will be dead within two days," Papias muttered, stepping closer to peer at the soldier's leg in the torchlight. The wounded man stared at the sky, expressionless, seemingly oblivious to our presence. Taking a deep breath, Father nodded shortly, pulled his dagger from the sheath, and without further hesitation drew it swiftly and efficiently across the man's throat. The head dropped silently to one side, eyes still staring at the heavens. Father stepped over him and to the next man, a Pontic I recognized as a veteran scout. No blanket covered him, for the weight of it was too painful to the charred flesh of his torso and thighs—the result of an encounter with an enemy firebomb hurled by ballistae that had killed several other of our men. This soldier had carefully watched our action with the man beside him. Now, as Father approached, he closed his eyes and thrust his chin up, toward the stars, exposing his throat to the blade in acceptance of his fate. Father placed his hand gently on the man's shoulder, murmured a word of thanks, and then sent him, too, to the gods.

Having set the example, and accompanied by twenty Roman exiles selected by lot, Father swiftly and silently slit the throats of the other prostrate soldiers, each in turn. Those who were conscious and understood what was happening awaited their fate in stoic silence. The healthy troops stood by somberly, watching in bleak resignation. No protest was issued, nor was any even considered. No comparisons were made to Triarius' hasty abandonment of his own dead and wounded at Zela. The swift, silent death of our twelve hundred injured men was preferable to the fate they would have met had they been captured alive by the Romans.

After Father dispatched the last remaining soldier he strode stiffly back to the massive gates guarding the entrance to the fortress, joining the small knot of Pontic and Roman exile officers observing the grim proceedings. His face was stern and expressionless, but in the dim light of the torches flickering from the sconces set in the stone behind us streams of tears ran down his dirty cheeks and coursed into the matted beard. Pausing for a moment, he turned to the silent mob of men crowded behind him, accepting of his actions, but wondering nonetheless.

" '*Better it is to die as a soldier,*' " he said softly, translating Euripides' elegant Greek into his men's Pontic, " " '*since die we must. And though the man who dies hath pain—to all his house accrues praise and pride.*' "

Without further pause for sentiment or misgiving, he nodded to the soldiers atop the wall above us. The men set to with the winches, and the massive gates swung ponderously open, silent and smooth on their carefully oiled hinges.

The two thousand remaining horse of the Pontic cavalry thundered through the gates, followed in close formation by the ragtag but fiercely determined foot soldiers, with the Roman exiles in the van. All baggage, all treasure, all remaining supplies, shelter, and spare weaponry were left behind. We would have but one chance to break through, which we could do only if every man was in fighting form. Even old Papias gamely took up sword and dagger. No man could be spared to transport equipment. If we were defeated, such burdens would be of no use anyway.

But for once, Pompey, meticulous, ever-watchful Pompey, was caught with his loincloth at his ankles. Our cavalry stormed through the dozing line of Roman sentries at a weak point we had reconnoitered in advance; our infantry scrambled across the ditches and over the staked palisades the Romans had constructed to prevent just such an event, and before the alarm had even reached the Roman staff headquarters a half-mile distant, Mithridates and thirty thousand emaciated troops had disappeared into the darkness, leaving the Roman legions confused and then triumphant as they swarmed, not after us but into the fortress we had just left, to plunder the baggage and treasure we had left behind. As we galloped away through the darkness the cheers and shouts of the legions followed us for miles, and I saw Father shaking his head at his enemies' stupidity and avarice and perhaps at his own prospects.

We had reached the end. Before us lay the massive Euphrates River, separating the kingdom of Pontus from Armenia, the very terminus of Father's reign. Here the river flowed through a deep gorge, bounded by cliffs, and around a sharp bend in which a long rocky outcropping, like a peninsula, diverts its flow. There is no ford for dozens of miles, and indeed even boats would have difficulty crossing the rapid current. It was no accident but rather an explicit message to the men that we marched the army over the narrow neck of land protruding several miles into the bend of the river and then out to its end. From here the army could no longer run. It was bounded by the river gorge on three sides, and the fourth side consisted only of the steep, narrow road we had just climbed. Within hours, this last pathway to safety was itself blocked by Pompey's determined Roman legions, who camped directly across it. Only one army could emerge victorious from this position.

That night Father stationed four cohorts across the narrowest part of the peninsula, commanded by his Roman centurions, to block Pompey's advance on our camp. The next morning, Roman assault troops launched a fierce attack. Initially, they were repelled, but as the day wore on and the heat and strain began to tell on our hungry and weakened troops, they were hard pressed, though not yet driven from their trenches. Late in the afternoon, increasingly urgent messages began arriving from our beleaguered defenders, requesting reinforcement. Initially, Father was at a loss; because of the terrain, the battle line was short and compressed—there was literally no room to deploy a large body of troops in support of the two thousand already there.

"What we lack in space for more troops we must make up in quality," I said.

He waved dismissively. "Our best troops are our cavalry. But the ground is too broken, the defile too narrow, for horses. They can't maneuver."

I concurred. "You're right—our best troops are the horse troops. I'll take them in as reinforcement—without horses."

He looked up at me sharply, and for the first time in days I saw the brightness of hope in his eyes. Our cavalry were the best archers and swordsmen in the army. Clearly they were the men who could make the most difference with the most compact force.

"Take the cavalry," he growled. "Dismounted."

With the arrival of our horsemen, on foot, the reinforced Pontic line stood and even advanced slightly beyond its original position, as the Romans struggled, too, with the same difficulty, their inability to overwhelm us with numbers because of the broken field. Even their crack Galatian horse were sharply repelled by our foot-bound Pontic archers. As the day closed, the two armies fought to a draw, and with sunset Father wearily turned to his cot and to the capacious comforts of his fierce concubine, Hypsicratia. With the tension of the recent siege and flight, combined with his lingering wounds, Father had been spending more time alone with his pale and beautiful prize. This night he was exhausted and fell asleep with her almost immediately.

The disaster came about shortly after nightfall, when Father's guiding hand was absent from the scene. From what I was able to reconstruct long after the sequence of events, this is what occurred:

At our line of defense, the Romans' mercenary horse finally ceased their relentless charges and used the remaining light to pick their way carefully back over the broken terrain to their camp for the night. Our unmounted Pontic cavalry, who had fiercely defended the position all afternoon, saw this retreat as a golden opportunity to unleash a fatal blow on the Galatians. Naturally, however, our horsemen could not attack without their mounts. So, eager to deliver the attack before the unsuspecting Galatians had completely withdrawn to safety behind Roman lines, I ordered the Pontics to leap from their trenches and race back to our own encampment to retrieve their horses.

In the gathering dusk, however, our guards at the Pontic gates misinterpreted this action. They saw a mob of their own dismounted cavalry racing back to camp in no order or formation, and in the tension of the moment they could only assume the worst: that the Romans must be hard on our heels. The guards threw down their weapons and abandoned the perimeter, running into the camp as if their lives depended upon it.

At this point, the retreating Galatian horsemen looked back and realized that something was amiss—the trenches and ramparts they had been charging all day were now deserted. They immediately turned back to investigate and then, hearing the turmoil in our camp, sent an urgent message back to Pompey. Even absent the message, the signs of disturbance must have already reached his ears: the shouting and uproar from the panicked Pontic camp could no doubt have been heard as far as Armenia. The cautious, slow-moving Roman general this time did not hesitate, and the legions formed up for an extraordinary night attack.

We were hindered not only by our stupidity but by the gods themselves. As the Roman legions reached our palisade, a full moon rose directly behind them, low on the horizon. It gave sufficient light to identify the outline of a man, but because it was so low, the shadows of the attacking Roman legions reached long, almost as far as our own walls. This handicapped the few Pontic archers who still remained at their guard posts, who were unable to accurately measure the space of ground between them and the enemy. Misgauging the distance of the attackers while staring into the moonlight, the archers shot their arrows too soon and missed their marks. The Romans scrambled through our trenchworks and into the Pontic camp, still moving with their customary deliberation. By the time Father was roused, all Pontic resistance had collapsed. As had happened at Cabira, the Romans were fighting not defenders but the chaos of fleeing men.

In the slaughter and devastation, in the sheer confusion and surprise, we were unable to rally the troops for a defense. Leaping to his horse, Father called to all those around to follow him. In the shadows and moonlight I saw other figures, too, seizing horses, including one intrepid Pontic guardsman who vaulted in full armor onto the back of a gleaming white Roman cavalry horse, heaved the surprised tribune off the saddle, and then seized the reins to sprint after the King.

Forming a ragged column of eight hundred horsemen, we raced through the crowd of milling men, Romans and Pontics slashing at each other in a frenzy. We surged out the main gate of the camp whence Pompey's troops had just arrived and toward the base of the peninsula, the only path off the narrow neck of land to the open ground beyond. It was an impossible task, and I can only believe that it was the confusion and terror of the moment that even led us to consider it. We were met full on by the main body of the Roman infantry just arriving from its own camp, and a hail of arrows decimated our meager force, killing dozens of men and horses on the spot and dispersing us in every direction. In the chaos and slaughter, Father and I, along with the Pontic guardsman, Bituitus, and several others, were forced to the side, off the path, away from the approaching legions, in the only direction we could run—on the cliffs to the gorge. Without time to utter a prayer or even a shout, we drove the horses over the edge and off into the emptiness of space.

How far did we fall—twenty arm's lengths? Fifty? A hundred? It may have been less, but it felt an eternity, and it killed several of our group upon impact, for we found their bruised and lifeless bodies later, washed onto the same gravel beach a half-mile down the bend where we dragged ourselves gasping and sputtering from the water. Those who had managed to keep a grasp on their horses in the water were saved. Those who had become separated from their mounts sank under the weight of their armor; it was as simple as that. In the end, a mere four of us in our immediate party survived the fall: Father, Bituitus, myself, and the fierce Pontic soldier who had stolen the Roman war charger. It was only a few moments later, when the soldier decided that the ill-fitting bronze corselet was too uncomfortable and so discarded it to ride bare-chested, that I realized the soldier's identity: the ice maiden Hypsicratia herself, of the flowing hair and Amazonian shoulders. So Father had not lost everything.

Of the thirty thousand men in the Pontic army, the Romans killed one-third during the sack of the encampment. The remainder were captured to be sold into slavery or dispersed into the night, to be hunted down later by the grim Galatian horsemen. Some few survivors made their way to the fortress of Sinora, a three days' march or stagger to the north. Our small band also took refuge there, to the astonishment of the elderly chieftain and tiny Pontic garrison manning the stronghold. The Romans, probably believing we had perished in the fall off the cliff, did not pursue us, and so we were able to recover and take stock, for a time. Over the course of a week or two, other survivors straggled in, even a few squadron of horse, as well as a cohort and a half of battered Roman exiles led by the resourceful tribune Marcellus. This yielded us a remnant of some three thousand men from the original army, most of them injured and starving.

Father, exhausted and in pain, ordered me across the border to Armenia, to assess King Tigranes' disposition and determine whether he would be willing to afford us refuge again against the Romans, as he had done five years before. I did not have to travel far before finding my answer. The moment I set foot off the ferry over the Euphrates I was met by a delegation of Armenian elders. Apparently, Pompey's agents had been to see the Great King first, on the off-chance that Mithridates might somehow have survived and been tempted to seek exile in Armenia. Unfortunately, the elders said, the Armenians could not offer us hospitality. In fact, it would be best if I myself were to leave the territory at once.

Tigranes had put a price of a thousand talents on Mithridates' head. There would be no refuge in Armenia.

BOOK TEN

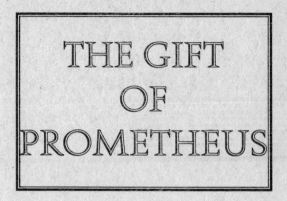

THE GIFT OF PROMETHEUS

Through me, mortals ceased to foresee their doom. Blind hopes I made to dwell within their breasts.

—Aeschylus

1

Our situation was not promising: three thousand half-starved foot soldiers; several hundred cavalry; a small stronghold deep in the Pontic interior on the border with Armenia, at which an angry and ambitious Roman general with five legions would be arriving within days; and an enormous price on Father's head.

Yet as he led me down into the cellar of the fortress of Sinora he simply smiled mysteriously.

"All things are possible," he said, "with enough gold."

And gold he had in plenty. Heaps of gold, chests of coin, piles of bullion, high stacks of intricately wrought plate, mounds of jewelry, rings, bracelets, necklaces, crowns—I had accompanied the man my entire life, but even I was dumbfounded when I walked into the storeroom of that remote outpost and found gold heaped to the ceiling and spilling into the corridor, enough to pay his entire army for a year or more: which was precisely what he intended.

"Where . . . ? How . . . ?" I stammered.

Father shrugged. "The Romans have been seizing my fortresses for five years now. When I can, which is not often, I order each fortress's treasury evacuated before the legions arrive and carted to a safe house. This"—he gestured around him at the dank crumbling walls, the bare earthen floor, and the leaking, moss-encrusted ceiling—"is the last safe house."

The last treasure of Pontus, and he the last king. The army was gone, the fleet dispersed, the population enslaved to Rome.

Castles destroyed, concubines and sisters killed, so many thousands of men sent to the land of the dead, all for the preservation of this, this . . . Suddenly the enormous wealth heaped before me seemed paltry and shabby and I turned away at the thought that the wealth and might and glory of generations of my ancestors had been reduced to these coins and trinkets.

Father stared at me, knowing what I was thinking.

"And yet you doubt," he said. He looked at me disbelievingly, almost angrily.

I was beyond fearing his wrath, and I turned to walk away.

"You doubt!" he continued. "Yet with gold, one can regain what has been lost, win back one's freedom, buy back the glory of one's ancestors. . . ."

Listening to him, to his determination to begin again, to scramble back up the impregnable wall the Fates had placed before him, I felt a weariness so deep it penetrated my very bones. I could foresee nothing good from the gold, nothing in its favor, I could see it only dragging us down further into the depths to which we had sunk. I looked at the gold, and I could see only that it was an enormous weight, a burden that I thought I could bear no longer.

"This gold . . ." I said.

He would never understand. Ever the dreamer and planner, he would never see that it was time to accept the inevitable. What could I say to dissuade him?

Then it occurred to me. How were we to even carry it? It would be a crushing load, weighing tons. This, then, was the answer.

"We don't even have carts to carry our food and weapons," I said. "We must flee north, now. Pompey will be here within days, if not hours. We can't carry this gold."

He stared at me, disappointed at my lassitude, at my discouragement, at the exhaustion I felt so intensely that I was not even able to think problems through. He placed his great heavy paw on my shoulder, as he had not done in months, perhaps years. Without thinking I glanced to the side to see if anyone was nearby. It would be shameful to be seen as such a cripple, a weakling needing to be bolstered by his father. I was a full general of the Pontic army, a prince of the kingdom of Pontus. I threw back my shoulders and lifted my head and Father dropped his hand back down to his side, beginning his slow, rolling, stiff-legged gait back to the stairs that rose up from the cellar entrance.

"The gold will not be a burden for the army to carry," he said. "It will be divided up among all the men, according to their rank and deeds. Each man will carry a year's wages in gold on his back. No man will refuse such a burden, and many hands will therefore make it light."

"You'll distribute a year's wages to the army, half of whom are mercenaries and exiles? And after they receive this windfall, you believe they will stay with you and fight at your side?"

"You speak as if I have a choice," he said quietly. "If they choose to desert with the money, then I am no worse off than if the Romans had seized it. And as you say—we have no carts in which to carry the treasure. But I know my men, Pharnaces."

"You must, if you are willing to entrust them with such wealth."

"They will not desert me. I know my men."

For decades Pontus had been preoccupied with Rome alone and with the territories to its south and west; consequently, contact with the peoples of the eastern Black Sea, the Iberians and their neighbors the Albanians, had not been maintained. Nor would those fierce and unfriendly tribes have welcomed our civilizing influence. They were nomads, short and broad-shouldered, ruddy from their clime, but altogether lacking in moderating qualities. They lived solely from hunting, fishing, and raising vast flocks of sheep, and few were capable of scratching any sort of living from the soil, though their lands, where tended, were the most fertile I had ever seen: Vines planted only two years before bore abundant harvests of grape, and wheat fields yielded two and sometimes three crops a year. These men engaged in little trade, were ignorant of the use of money and even of weights and measures, and could barely count past one hundred. Their language was broken into a multitude of dialects, their tribes into dozens of warring clans, and their religion was a bizarre mixture of superstitious rituals, dominated by orgiastic cults and human sacrifice. They venerated mystics and madmen. Yet despite their lack of civilization, they could assemble massive armies. The Albanians alone could put up to sixty thousand infantry and twelve thousand cavalry in the field, the Iberians even more.

With only three thousand troops we could not hope to conquer these peoples. Yet with Rome breathing down our necks, we could not spare the time to negotiate with and placate them. We had only one option—to bull our way through before they even knew we were there.

Not a man deserted us, even under the wretched conditions through which we forced them. Leaving Sinora, Father, Marcellus, and I drove the troops like madmen, marching day and night, catching the small parties of Iberians we encountered unawares, overcoming their outposts and snuffing their signal fires. A week after marching out of Sinora, we stormed into their rude, mud-hut capital, having lost scarcely a dozen scouts to javelin attacks by the defenders. The Iberians had been so ignorant of our lightning approach they had failed even to close the city gates. In their astonishment at our arrival, seemingly out of nowhere or from out of the sky itself, the city's inhabitants fell prostrate before us, surrendering to us without lifting a blade.

Father marched straight to the agora, the central meeting place, gathering his troops behind him and summoning the fiercest expression that he could, which was not difficult given the fearsome condition of his face. As the citizens assembled, trembling, Father sternly announced his identity and mission.

"Behold the Great King Mithridates of Pontus, Conqueror of the Romans, King of the Greeks, and Sovereign of All These Lands!" he bellowed in Greek, and a temple priest translated his words into the local tongue in his quavering voice. The crowd's frightened murmurs dropped to a hush.

"I come not to enslave or plunder you," he continued, "though I will not hesitate to do so should you fail to obey my commands. Bring me your wretched king!"

The people looked around at one another with wild gazes, unsure how to react. A conquering army had stormed into their fortress, was claiming peaceful intent, and yet was demanding delivery of their king? Confused voices filled the air.

"You do not obey my order?" Father roared, his eyes flashing as all fell silent again. At my signal, the troops behind him fell suddenly into attack position, shields high before their eyes, swords raised. "At the risk of destroying your pitiful town with all its inhabitants, bring forth the Iberian king!"

This time there was no hesitation. The decrepit old headman, even more emaciated than our soldiers and lacking most of his teeth and hair, was led trembling through the crowd and up to Father's feet, where he threw himself down, prepared to die for his hesitance to obey the King of Pontus, whose ancestors his own forebears had battled for countless generations.

Father, however, after gazing fiercely at the old man, suddenly bent and raised him up by the forearm, speaking to him a few words in the Iberian tongue, which none from among our ranks but the strange girl-soldier Hypsicratia understood. At Father's signal, she stepped forward to stand by his side, bare-breasted and wearing a battered hoplite helmet, her face half-hidden behind the cheek plates and nasal, golden hair flowing wildly out from beneath the rim. She towered over the Iberians, and her glowering presence seemed to strike more fear and awe into their hearts than even us and our motley collection of Romans and Pontics. Her hair and torso had been dusted with gleaming flecks of gold filed from one of the ingots Father carried, and fluttering from the shaft of a long Roman centurion's spear that she brandished in her right hand was a banner bearing the winged horse of Pontus. After a few moments of parley, Father dismissed the old king and again stepped forward to address the crowd.

"Through my benevolence, and your wisely cooperative king, your city has been granted a reprieve from my wrath!" Father intoned. "Go back to your homes, Iberians, and see that in all that you do, you show reverence to the gods, and to Mithridates the Great!"

Thereafter, for the five days remaining of the march to Colchis, we were accompanied on our flanks by a large squad of sullen Iberian warriors, who cantered ahead whenever we approached a village, to head off any spontaneous attacks by their tribesmen and to arrange a market for our troops. Peace had been made between the two kings, and the old Iberian monarch was assured that we would merely be passing through and needed only safe-conduct and provisions. It also did not hurt that the simple tribesmen believed we were under the protection of the goddess Athena herself. The golden giantess

Hypsicratia, whose grandmother, in fact, was from those parts and had taught her the Iberians' strange and ancient language, had played her role well.

Upon arriving at the Colchian seaport capital of Phasis, we were received hospitably but nervously by the city fathers. In generations past the Colchians had been a fierce, warlike people, supposedly descended from Greeks who lost their way when returning from the Trojan War. In recent years, however, the Colchians had become soft and fearful, swaying like reeds in any political wind, supporting first Mithridates, then Rome. For a day we were feted, our kits replenished and our horses tended. Then we were firmly urged to be on our way, before the Roman fleet received word of our presence and sailed on the city. Father had expected this reaction. He pursed his lips stoically, as best as he was able with a distorted grimace, and we moved on.

Our goal, twenty days' hard march north of Colchis, was the forbidding "Scythian Gates," the narrow pass between the rocky shore of the Black Sea on our left and the bare, icy Caucasus Mountains on our right. In those mountains dwelt the fierce tribes of Achaeans, a brutal barbarian tribe of Scythians who had never been conquered by any ruler and who occupied territory that, as far as was known, had never been traversed by land. These men were half-beast—inhabiting rude stone huts, wearing the skins of animals, and living off the treasure and bodies of hapless sailors who foundered in the treacherous coastal rocks and shallows. The Achaeans were said to wear rawhide shoes set with spikes to allow them to climb icy peaks more deftly than goats, and to slide down snowy slopes faster than diving swallows by riding tiny boats made of dried skins.

The deeper we trudged into their territory, the more horrific the stories of them grew. Some said they were creatures who had not yet mastered the use of iron, who used weaponry made of flint and stone. Others claimed they were master smiths, whose deadly missiles were marvels of ingenuity and cleverness. They were men who ate men, who drank their victims' blood from cups fashioned of the scooped-out hollows of their brainpans, who tore their enemies' hearts still beating from their chests. It was even said that they delighted in inflicting the foulest tortures on women, in the very sight of their own husbands and children.

Of these fearsome tales, it was this last one we were least concerned about, for the only woman in our party was Hypsicratia, and she, of all of us, required the least protection. While the soldiers wrapped themselves in furs and hides if they could or in simple cloth if nothing else was available, Hypsicratia remained true to her blood and rode without covering; in the worst conditions, she might resort to a cold bronze corselet under a light wolfskin cape draped over her shoulders. Thus she traveled through the sharpest gales, pale skin smooth and unpricked by the biting wind, matched in size and fortitude only by the sixty-seven-year-old king, who also disdained outer garments. The formidable ice maiden could hold her own against ten of the enemy. Nevertheless, we marched every day with increasing trepidation.

Not a living being did we see. The coastal villages through which we passed were deserted, burnt to ashes in anticipation of our arrival. The freezing wind scoured the barren ground, and the gray hills above us, treeless and swept bare by the harsh winter storms, showed no sign of life, not even a flock of goats or a brace of partridges. The very earth seemed bereft of movement. All was so silent, but for the moaning of the sharp wind, that the creaking of the hard-frozen earth under our sandals seemed to reverberate and swirl around us like the dust devils on the eroded, scabrous hilltops. The troops could not discern the source of the sounds made by their comrades ahead of them or to their flanks. They jumped at the unexpected shouts of a cavalry officer or a lame soldier, sounds that seemed to be signaling an attack from the hills above us but in reality were merely the routine trampling and rustling of the army at march, echoing off the steep cliffs rising up to our right.

Once, as I marched in the van of the army, my men rounded a bend and came upon an ancient Scythian shepherd and his wife huddled miserably over a tiny dung fire, a dozen or so scrawny sheep milling nearby. They were the first living creatures we had seen since departing Colchis, somehow neglected during their tribesmen's flight into the mountains. The old pair looked so worn and their sheep so starved and stringy that though we were hungry, we had not the heart to seize their animals. Our soldiers merely marched along in silence as the couple stared wide-eyed at our procession.

When I passed them by, I nodded and looked into their eyes, at the deep creases etched into their faces, and wondered if I would ever live so long as to have such a careworn face. Is a long life a reward from the gods or a punishment? It depends upon whether you live comfortably in a palace or huddled starving on a frigid Scythian steppe. Old memories flooded back to me, of pleasant days I had spent in the company of shepherds in Pontus as a child, days when such hardship as this would have been inconceivable. *"Sulay sulay lulay-o,"* I murmured without thinking—my garbled old childhood shepherd's call, my first foreign tongue. The old man stared back at me solemnly and touched his forehead and lips with the tips of his fingers in the Scythian gesture of respect.

"Sulay sulay lulay-o," he replied.

After three weeks of cautious, steady progress we approached the northwestern terminus of the Caucasus range and the narrowest point of our path, the fearsome Gates. Before us, even the flat beach on which we had been walking narrowed, developing a steep upward slope into the foothills above, which became increasingly treacherous to cross on the icy terrain. At one point a glacier from the mountains above us stretched out a long, muscular arm, a veritable river of ice two miles wide, extended in a frozen, silent, deeply cracked mass down to the ice-rimmed crust of the sea.

Our way was blocked by the dangerous field of ice before us. There was no way to determine where the water began or the land ended, no well-defined border between the two elements. Ice caves, tunnels, and pits riddled the vast expanse. Where the pack seemed solid beneath our feet, careful listening could discern the ebbing and flowing of the tides in the undercut below. Solid glacier suddenly gave way to heaving ice pools where the seawater beneath had broken through. Here and there horses, with their weight concentrated on small, sharp hooves, broke through the thin crust without warning, rider and baggage disappearing into the freezing blue depths below. Even those able to be fished out perished of exposure within heartbeats if not immediately stripped of their wet gear and set before a fire.

After a day of picking through such obstacles while progressing scarcely a mile, Father made a decision. This "beach," if one could call it that, would have to be abandoned. The glacier's confrontation with the sea was simply too dangerous. We would have to move inland, over the range of foothills, to the long, shallow valley beneath the towering Caucasus Mountains. There the glacier would still have to be traversed, but we would at least not be fighting the sea along with it. We would be venturing away from the security and guidance of the coastline, for what this was worth, and into the silent, frozen interior of the land of the Achaeans.

Traversing the barren white landscape was treacherous. Weeks of howling wind had transformed the surface beneath our feet to a sheet of smooth ice. A slip and a spill meant landing with a bone-crunching thud on your tailbone or shoulder, and then sliding down the slope until you could dig into the ice sufficiently with fingernails or tools. If the slide was not arrested, it was fatal. Crevasses spread across the surface of the ice like broken veins on skin, like the shattering of brittle pottery. They had no visible bottom and could swallow a man or a horse into their gray silent maw without a trace. As one looked down the slope from the top, toward the foothills that ran to the sea, the jawlike cracks were utterly invisible—their overhanging lips on the upper sides completely obscured the frozen, silent death within. There was no way to avoid a crevasse in front of you while sliding down the hill. The only defense was to not fall in the first place.

Javelins and spears were fashioned into walking sticks; hatchets were kept in hand, to be hacked into the ice to break slides. The men strapped their shields onto their chests—for falling onto the smooth bowl of a shield on your back would send you skittering down the hill like a skipping rock on the water. They tore their fur capes into strips and wrapped them around their feet, not for warmth but for the additional traction the hide afforded on the bottoms of their sandals. At Father's orders, they roped themselves together in groups of five or six, in the hope that if one man slipped, the others left standing would have the strength to stop him. The technique worked for the most part—unless the first man falling brought down his neighbor as well, in which case the weight and momentum of two sliding men would be too much for the three remaining

standing. Within the first half-mile I saw two full strings of
men slide screaming and clawing over the lip of a crevasse.
Both times, the surviving army stared in horror at the place
where their comrades had disappeared, and then silently continued its march, one plodding step at a time.

Throughout the day we trudged, roped together like prisoners or madmen, all equal now in rank and burden, for whether
you were a king, a general, or a captured baggage slave, your
progress depended upon your strength and balance on your own
two feet. The officers and small cavalry squad walked beside
their nervous mounts, careful to position themselves uphill of
each animal to prevent being swept down if the horse should
slip and, conversely, using the beast itself as restraining barrier
to save them should they lose their own balance.

A mile or so in the distance before us loomed the Scythian
Gates. The steep Caspian Mountains on the right side formed a
sheer ice cliff, as if the glacier, like a gray, solid river, here
dropped from the heights in a frozen waterfall; on the left, the
coastal foothills rose up before us in an equally steep and stark
cliff face, this time of bare, frozen granite. It was a portal, truly
a Gate, a mere thirty arm's lengths wide, through which the
army would have to pass. Thus far we had seen no sign of the
terrible Achaeans, and the men had held their breath for so
long, for so many weeks awaiting the feared attack, that they
would be almost relieved if it came—*when* it came. Depending
upon our deployment, a battle at the Gates might even be to our
advantage—in the solid, narrow pass there were unlikely to be
any deadly crevasses to threaten, and the sheer walls on either
side would prevent our inadvertent sliding. Yet the danger was
real: If there was to be any ambush at all, it would be here. The
men tensed visibly and became even more silent than usual,
though it would still be another hour before we could pick our
way through to the pass. I steeled myself for the attack to come.

The Achaean commander was brilliant. Knowing we would
be on full alert once we arrived at the Gates, with veteran
troops and seasoned leaders in the front ranks, he played to his
own strength and to our weakness. The ambush came not within
the narrow confines of the Gates but before—on that frozen
slope a mile distant, as our troops were still struggling merely
to stand, to place one foot in front of the other.

With a shrill, terrifying battle cry resounding from the cliffs around us, an army of strange fur-clad creatures scrambled over the lower lip of a long crevasse on the slope above, where they had built a hidden inner ledge on which to await our arrival. Hairy, rounded beings they were, more simian in appearance than human, with bushy brown beards and piercing eyes, peering from beneath close-fitting woolen cawls. Their padded fur jerkins looked soft and ungainly yet afforded them protection from arrows almost as effectively as bronze armor. On their feet they had strapped hobbed soles, nails that emerged from their sandal bottoms, affording them as sure a grip on the ice as if they were walking on soft sand. They were barbarians in the truest sense of the word, half-animals, screaming for our blood like a troop of apes, lacking in all formation and discipline— yet numbering a full ten thousand, thrice our own number, and strong and well fed to boot.

We scrambled to close ourselves in formation, for we had not expected the ambush so soon. For the first time in nearly two decades Father reverted back to his old lessons of ancient Greek warfare, and even the Roman exile commander Marcellus supported the tactic.

We formed a traditional Greek phalanx.

The army was already in a compact unit, with individual groups roped together for safety. With the attack of the howling Achaeans, the men consolidated their positions, those on the uphill side raising their shields before them, linking the rims and turtling up to protect themselves and the men still struggling to fall into position behind them. Arrows rained down upon us from the barbarians above, heavy obsidian-tipped things that shattered like glass upon impact with a shield or armor but cut huge, penetrating holes into soft tissue they struck. Father rushed to the front of the battle line I was hurriedly creating, shielded tenuously by Bituitus and Hypsicratia, one on either side of him. He roared out orders and hastily fitted an arrow to his own bow, heedless of his safety as the barbarians caught sight of him and the heavy tipped missiles thudded into his comrades' shields.

Though half-lamed by his earlier wounds, the King was still the strongest soldier, the best bowman, in the army, and brushing aside Bituitus' heavy shield, he stood up in full view of the enemy, took careful aim with his enormous bow, and loosed a mighty shot. Unerring and true, the arrow slammed into the throat of a huge warrior in the enemy's front line, a leader of sorts, lifting him bodily off his feet. The man fell onto his back, writhing with the arrow emerging three feet in front of his eyes, and began a slow slide down the slope toward the front line of our own troops, leaving a long crimson trail on the ice in his wake.

The barbarians roared in fury at the killing of their chieftain, and our troops reciprocated with a bellow of triumph. Our formation had now been deployed. We formed a compact mass, two hundred soldiers broad with shields linked tightly, a bronze wall fifteen ranks deep, each rank supporting the men in front, shield boss against back, pressing and digging in, calves and feet straining to maintain a grip on the sheer, icy surface beneath. At a call from Father that carried even over the shouting of the troops, the Pontic army began its slow, step-by-step advance, carefully but inexorably moving forward over the ice, each man focusing on the shield in front of him, concentrating all his will on sliding his feet to the next toehold scuffed into the hardpack, clearing his mind of all but the killing to come.

When the barbarians saw that their initial volley of arrows had had no impact but to speed our deployment, their fury increased. Heaving javelins at our lines, they began rushing down the slope toward us, their own tread certain and secure with their hob-nailed sandals and a lifetime of practice on the ice. Our archers in the rear ranks let fly a flurry of deadly missiles that stopped the enemy's advance, but for a moment only; the dead and injured Achaeans merely toppled onto their backs and resumed their forward progress, sliding at pace with their attacking comrades. As the Pontic archers continued their furious volleys into the enemy, the line before us thinned and wavered: We were being charged by a sliding wave of enemy dead, tumbling and skidding toward us down the slippery slope, followed close behind by the living barbarian army who continued to tread surefootedly down the blood-reddened ice traversed by their comrades.

In a moment the first wave of enemy corpses hit our ranks. Our lead men saw them coming and anticipated them, jumping and stepping over them like obstacles in a training course, bracing themselves for the more dangerous impact of the living fighters following close behind. Our middle and rear ranks were not so fortunate. Unable to see beyond their own shields, they were upended by the sliding cadavers as surely as if the enemy had rolled logs down upon them from the heights. With curses and shouts the middle-rankers were bowled over, tumbling backward onto the shields of the men behind them, and those in turn onto their own fellows, until the ranks in the rear realized what was happening and braced themselves to absorb the impact. Entire columns of our troops were brought down by the grisly obstacles as Pontic soldiers tripped and fell into the fur-clad arms of their dead enemies and continued the sliding roll down the slope. For those still roped to their comrades, a tenuous salvation was possible as the survivors dug in their spear points or shield rims and held fast to the ice. Others, however, dozens, who had cut their ropes to maneuver better within the phalanx, slid despairingly as they gained relentless momentum, skidding off down the hill to the crevasses below.

The main body of enemy hit our front ranks like a battering ram, with a crash that all but knocked our phalanx backward. The two armies paused for that fleet moment of impact, and then, again like a battering ram, the enemy bounced off, unable to penetrate the interlocking bronze of our shields. Its momentum stopped, the enemy roared in brave defiance and began slashing and hacking at us with great bronze battle-axes, engaging furiously, pouring their rage into their sword arms and seeking, by pure, dumb determination, to drive us to our knees.

Though phalanx fails against a trained Roman army, it scores its bloodiest success against a mob. Railing against our lines was like beating their heads against a bronze-clad door. After the initial clash of the two armies, I bellowed, "Forward, Pontus!" and a resounding cheer rose from our lines. Step after grunting step the solid block of shields resumed its implacable march, men neatly stepping into the gaps created by their injured and fallen comrades, disdaining even to wield their swords or their javelins—all effort was placed into holding the heavy shields before their eyes, maintaining the alignment with their fellows on the right and the left, stepping slowly and steadily forward, an oxlike advance of utter discipline, of death-dealing precision, into the very teeth of the barbarians' desperate slashing.

The barbarians paused in dismay and astonishment, for despite outnumbering us three to one they had made as much impact on our lines as if they had attacked the sheer rock face of the cliffs themselves. Still swinging furiously with their weapons, they assumed a steady retreat, not orderly by any stretch of the imagination, for they had no visible discipline or formation, but with no signs of panic, either.

Until Hypsicratia stepped forward.

With a shrill, piercing war cry in a language alien to my ears, she leaped away from Father, whom she had been protecting with her own shield as he bellowed orders to his officers, and raced forward, ahead of the front line of our phalanx, into the very thick of the enemy. Towering over barbarian and Pontic alike, she swung her shield and broadsword, using both as weapons, crushing helmets and skulls and shearing through necks and ribs with the blade. As if by one accord, both barbarian and Pontic stepped away from the maddened warrioress, clearing a space around her through which she stalked, eyes glaring bloodshot anger, nostrils snorting steam like a war charger, mane of yellow hair flowing wild from beneath her battle helmet, magnificent breasts bare and taut beneath the open wolfskin cape, heaving from her exertion.

Shrieking her otherworldly battle cry, she struck out at the barbarians, who cowered back at this wholly unexpected weapon. As word spread among their lines that a goddess had appeared, panic ensued. None would dare face the wrath of this tigress, this Fury whom even the cold wind did not affect, whom arrows could not strike. At first singly, then in groups of six and ten, the Achaeans turned their backs and fled. A cheer rose up from the Pontic forces as we picked up our pace and drove after them, though we were quickly outstripped by the fleeing enemy with their nailed sandals. They scrambled up the slope, leaping across the ice, across the narrow crevasses and around the ends of the wider ones, the locations of which only they knew. Seeing we would never be able to catch them, I called our own exhausted forces to a halt, which they did of good will, all but one—Hypsicratia.

As if in a mad trance, she continued her dash up the side of the mountain, slipping and scrambling, single-handedly pursuing the entire fleeing Achaean mob. We watched in wonderment as she shrieked and thrilled at every straggler who crossed her path, cutting them down like swine being slaughtered. Father bellowed after her, "Hypsicratia! Stop!" but because of the shouts of the enemy or her own blood rage she would neither hear nor obey. Slathered in frosty gore, she raced forward, to the roars of encouragement from the Pontic troops and the bellows of outrage from Father—until suddenly she crouched and sprang in an enormous leap, blade whirling, to kill a faltering enemy tribesman. As she landed, she overshot her mark, lost her footing—and dropped out of sight into a chasm, her fierce battle cry fading into a distant, echoing wail and then silence.

I stared, aghast, at the space where Hypsicratia had been. From ice she had come to us, that strange Hyperborean goddess, and to ice she had returned.

The Pontic army fell silent, eyes flitting back and forth from the blue-gray gash of the crevasse, across the bloodstained glacier, to the horrified expression of the King. He gaped at the point where she had disappeared. Turning slowly back to his men, he stood a long moment, his lips working as if he was trying to say something. Then he set his jaw, adjusted the bow slung across his back, and resumed his trudge across the bloodied and empty ice. Though the men followed him willingly toward the Gates and safety beyond, by the discouraged slump of his shoulders I saw that for him, the battle had been no victory.

I had once asked Father if there was anything he loved. I knew now that he had truly loved the slave girl Hypsicratia.

For the past twenty-five years the northern Black Sea kingdom of Bosporus had been ruled by Machares, Father's son from his ill-fated marriage to his sister Laodice, and heir to the kingdom of Pontus. I had not seen my half brother that entire time, ever since Father had appointed him king of that cold, windswept northern territory. Six years ago, however, when Lucullus first conquered Pontus, Father sent me to Bosporus with orders to Machares to raise an army of Scythians to assist in our reconquest. At the time, I looked forward to reviving our old friendship.

Yet Machares had received me more like a leper than a long-absent half brother. When I entered the modest reception hall of the palace in his capital city of Panticapaeum shortly after my arrival, I strode joyfully across the room to give him an embrace, believing he would be as delighted to see me as I was him. He remained seated on his high-backed throne, eyeing me coldly, while the two Scythian guards who fronted him stood stolidly in my path, refusing to let me approach closer. Undeterred, I stopped short and saluted him, calling out my greetings.

"Machares, you old dog, twenty-five years a king now, while I'm still carrying Father's water flask in the army! But you've ruled this godsforsaken outpost so long you've forgotten me! Come, give your brother an embrace; let us toast our reunion, and Father's reconquest of Pontus."

Still Machares remained seated, and I looked more closely at him to see if I could discern any physical impediment. He was older, of course, as was I, but still strong and fit, still in the prime of his life. Yet his face looked far sadder and more care-worn than a king's should, especially one who had governed a kingdom in complete peace for the past quarter-century, without a single threat to his rule.

"I have no good news for you, Brother," he said, "nor may I toast Father's new venture."

My jaw dropped. "You refuse his request? Do you even know what it is?"

"Knowing Father, he is requesting troops. He has conscripted men from me many times in the past—indeed, that was part of his purpose in placing me here on the throne, to ensure a supply of Scythians for his armies."

"And . . . ? Have you no men for him? Has a plague killed them all off?"

He laughed hollowly. "A plague—in a way, yes, but it has not killed them off."

"What are you talking about?"

"You're not the first to arrive to discuss this matter of Father's needs. A Roman delegation was here just last week."

"What does that matter? Roman delegations are everywhere. I trust you gave the scoundrels vinegary wine to drink, bedded them down for the night with syphilitic whores, and sent them packing on the next trading scow to Italy."

Machares trained his gaze on me without a hint of a smile.

"Not quite, Brother. As a matter of fact, it is you, I'm afraid, whom I must send away on the next ship out of Panticapaeum. I have signed an alliance with Rome."

My mind raced, a tumble of thoughts and accusations, questions and demands, but in the end, no words came. No explanations he could give could possibly satisfy me. There was no reason to even keep up pretenses. I turned to leave in furious silence, but he called me back.

"Pharnaces, wait!"

I paused.

"You cannot sweeten this news to Father," he said, "nor should you."

"Of course not," I replied coldly.

"But why return at all? Can't you see the old man's fighting a losing battle? He has been for years. No man can stand up to

Rome! No man can rail against the tide forever—it may flow away from him for a time, but he can't take credit for that, because it is far bigger than anything he can ever do—eventually the tide just returns, higher than it was before, and anyone who tries to defy it is a fool. So it is with Rome, Pharnaces. Father is old; he can't see the big view; he's so embittered he can't admit defeat even when it's hopeless. Why should I risk my rule, send my men away, for a hopeless cause? A 'New Greece'—it's impossible, a preposterous dream. But you and I—we can step back, examine both sides like rational men; we can back the right horse. Right, Pharnaces? Can you deny what I've said?"

He was almost pleading with me, looking to me for assurance. Always the scholar, always the rational thinker, the one who disdained tall tales by the campfire, preferring instead the skepticism of his philosophers. Now, however, he looked not to Plato but to me, for confirmation that what he had done was right and proper and in the best interest of all.

Perhaps it was. Perhaps there are reasons that trump even loyalty and faith.

But this was not one of them. I turned to go and this time did not look back.

Thus my last contact with Machares some six years before, at a time when our position was critical, but not nearly as critical as it was now. Believing that Father's reign in Pontus, and indeed his very life, had come to an end, Machares had at that time declared his allegiance to Rome. Indeed, the fool had even sent Lucullus a crown of gold, weighing a thousand staters, as a pledge for his alliance. Lucullus, in turn, had responded in a haughty manner, declaring that so long as Machares paid the customary annual tribute to Rome, he would be allowed to rule peacefully and without interference in his remote kingdom on the steppe.

It was a cheap conquest for Lucullus, who probably never harbored any intention of leading troops so far afield in any case, for such meager hope of gain; and it was cheap insurance for Machares, who now could be assured of undisputed control over his distant domain, in his muddy little capital on the northern coast. All was well for the petty prince—until that spring, when the Old Man appeared out of the blue at the gates of his city. We were stinking and hairy from weeks without bathing, bloodied but alive after three months' march through unexplored territory thought to have been impassable—and Father was prepared now to settle with the son who had betrayed him by declaring his loyalty to Rome.

We were still several days out from Panticapaeum when a party of envoys arrived from Machares, sent to explain away the Prince's earlier conduct. They were met with glowering silence and dismissal from Father, and a second embassy was then sent, begging forgiveness for Machares' misplaced loyalties. They were driven from the Pontic camp, and the army merely picked up its pace toward Panticapaeum, like sharks smelling blood. The last set of heralds galloped into camp the very day we arrived at Phanagoria, on the narrow strait separating the Asian mainland from the peninsula. These men threw themselves at Father's feet, scooping handfuls of dust from the ground and pouring it onto their heads, wailing and crying like eunuchs on Machares' behalf, for mercy from the King's wrath.

Father looked down in disdain at the three men, one of whom he recognized as a former servant of his, Euthradorus, whom he had lent to Machares years ago as an advisor. The other two were counselors Machares himself had acquired in the interim, whom the King did not know.

Ordering the men to stand, he paced wordlessly before them for a moment, staring at their faces almost with a sense of satisfaction as they recoiled at his massive frame and wild mane of snow-white hair, but most especially at his hideously deformed visage, so different from the handsome, kinglike features they had expected. Suddenly, and without warning, he drew the scimitar from his belt and with a catlike pounce, astonishing for a man of his age and size, he leaped forward, swiping the blade through the air with a hiss, and neatly sliced through Euthradorus' neck. The head, eyes still opened wide in shock and bewilderment, dropped to the feet of the two other terrified ambassadors, followed a moment later by the body, which crumpled softly from the knees and then rolled to the shoulder, almost as if there were still life within to guide it in its slow, gentle fall.

Without pausing even to wipe the sheen of blood from his blade, Father slid it back into the sheath at his hip. He then removed the medallion he wore about his neck as a sign of office, a golden minting of a Pontic stater depicting a flying horse on one side and his own likeness on the other. This he placed over the head of the first recoiling ambassador. Then quickly loosening a large golden ring he wore in the lobe of his left ear, he presented this into the hands of the second.

"Tell your master this," he growled, looming over the two quavering men threateningly. "Thus I deal," kicking the head of the fallen Euthradorus to one side, like a boy's ball, "with those who betray their loyalty to me, who call my ambition a 'preposterous dream.' And thus"—here he gestured to the magnificent gifts he had bestowed upon the two terrified survivors—"I deal with those willing to suffer even great humiliation for their own master. Euthradorus I had known and loved, and he was mine; yet he betrayed me. You two I ignore and despise, yet your loyalties are correct. Now get out of my sight."

It did not take a Maeotian diviner to tell Machares what his fate would be were he to fall into Father's hands. In terror, he burnt every ship in his little navy, every fishing vessel on the docks, every merchant craft that had had the bad luck to berth in his port, to prevent the Pontic army from crossing the strait over to Panticapaeum. But for an army that had just undertaken a march more brutal even than Xenophon's three centuries before, such an obstacle was easily overcome. Other shipping was obtained, makeshift rafts were built, vessels requisitioned from tribes to the east and the south, and an attack on the capital was made ready. On the very eve of our invasion, Machares, seeing himself cornered, resolved his dilemma in typically Pontic fashion, swallowing a fatal dose of poison. A war between father and son had been averted.

Father rode into the relieved city in triumph, to acclaim as great as that with which he had been greeted upon his arrival in Sinope nearly five decades before.

His first act upon taking office as newly crowned King of Bosporus was to send envoys to Pompey, announcing his accession to a new kingdom and offering peace to Rome if the general would in turn recognize him as legitimate ruler of the northern domain. His second act was to send out a virtual battalion of eunuch ministers the length and breadth of his new land. Their orders were to announce the conscription of the largest army ever seen on these shores. He seemed to have no doubt that the masts of Roman warships would soon appear on the southern horizon of the Black Sea.

Perhaps it was the strain of the difficult winter marching through the Achaean wastelands or perhaps a delayed effect of the injuries he had received the year before at the hands of the Romans. In any event, for the first time in his long life, the old fighter was disabled by ill health. He made his best effort to disguise it—energetically participating in the welcoming celebrations the city of Panticapaeum held for him and performing in the chariot races and archery events, to demonstrate that he was a worthy king of these backward, superstitious people. Yet after the initial flush of excitement at gaining a new kingdom had worn off, it was evident to all that Father was no longer the same man he had once been.

Grieving over the loss of Hypsicratia, his kingdom, and perhaps tardily for other deaths over the years, he fell into a kind of death himself. He ate only red food, like that reserved for occasions of mourning and which by ancient tradition may not otherwise be consumed: blood pudding, lobster and crayfish, boiled ham, oat cakes steeped in the fermented juice of red berries. For days, even weeks on end, he shut himself up within the *gynaeceum,* the women's quarters of the palace, remaining asleep for many hours past sunrise. Apart from the two most elderly females in the harem who had medical skills, he consorted with no women, preferring instead to keep to himself in a darkened apartment filled with Machares' collection of ancient scrolls and treatises in a dozen languages. Abandoned were the witty feasts and the arranged debates between Greek men of letters he had so enjoyed during the peaceful years of his past reign. Dramatic events and sacrifices to the gods on feast days were held without him, and foreign dignitaries were received by his eunuchs. Father preferred his unpadded couch in the cool, gloomy apartments, immersed in studies and receiving visitors only for the most dire emergencies.

The day-to-day administration of his kingdom he assigned to me, a straightforward task and one that I rather enjoyed. I had inherited all of Machares' eunuchs and advisors, who were a capable lot, honest and knowledgeable for the most part. The kingdom's needs were so simple that I found my responsibilities actually amounted to little more than handing down rulings on foregone conclusions and settling disputes between various tribal chieftains. All quite lacking in challenge, given the four decades I had spent at Father's side watching him perform precisely these same tasks, as well as my own experience as a general. Yet there was one labor that Father refused to delegate to any person—the raising of his new great army.

The core of his force, as always, would be the veteran Roman exiles who still accompanied us, led by Marcellus the tribune. Many of these men were now well past the age of retirement, but in emulation of their master they remained unwilling to admit defeat by mere Chronos, the lackluster and insipid God of Time, who saps strength by long and uninspired siege rather than by manly assaults. These stouthearted centurions were ably supported by the rest of the Pontic and Armenian veterans who had accompanied us on our journey through hell the previous winter. This force, however, was scarcely three thousand men, the equivalent of a mere half a Roman legion. More were needed.

Hence Father's urgent dispatch of the most capable eunuchs and heralds who had formerly been in Machares' service and who were now sent out across the kingdom to conscript warriors. By mid-spring recruits began pouring into Panticapaeum by the thousands—pale-skinned, painted bastards, savages to the core, as undisciplined as street mongrels but fierce as wolves. These were horsemen and spearmen of the steppe, tribesmen who had scarcely ever seen more than a hundred people gathered in one place at a time, who had never fought in bands of more than thirty, for whom the very notion of battle discipline and tactics was something unmanly, unworthy of their keenly developed shooting and riding skills.

Marcellus cursed when he saw the grinning, gap-toothed, long-haired mob descending from the hills behind the sea and pouring into the makeshift training camp he had constructed outside the capital city. He groaned when he heard the newcomers' barbaric language, unable to be understood by any of the Romans and even barely by Father himself; and he tore his hair in frustration when he saw the barbarians' skills at sword fighting and hand-to-hand combat, the most important techniques of all to master, for a Roman army to fight like a Roman army. But he watched in amazement after drill was completed each day as the new recruits retreated to their ponies for impromptu horse races, games, and shooting demonstrations.

"Sire," Marcellus concluded after one of his initial progress reports to Father, "a cavalry force will be more fruitful than converting these men to infantry. By the gods above, dressing them like soldiers and making them march is like putting a fine toga on an ape."

At this Father hardly even cracked a smile.

"Nonsense, Tribune," he retorted. "To fight Roman legions, you need Roman legions. That means infantry—does it not?"

"Not with this lot," Marcellus grunted. "It's a waste of my time and theirs. They're already the finest horsemen I've seen, without the benefit of training. But they're dumb as posts. Why make them what they are not, when they already excel at what they are?"

"Infantry, Tribune. Infantry."

Marcellus grumbled but ultimately gave in. The new recruits continued to pour in. By summer's end thirty-six thousand men had been conscripted and passed through basic training, sixty cohorts of six hundred men each. The equivalent of six Roman legions, precisely the number Pompey was marching with, and organized in exactly the same way.

Yet while the men trained, Father, brooding and nursing his ulcered face, caught up in his cycle of despair and hatred, refused to leave the darkness of his study.

3

The Romans, rather than immediately pursuing us north-
ward to Bosporus, first struck eastward across the barren
interior mountains to the Caspian Sea, easily subjugating the
barbarian tribes that opposed them. Having set foot in those
frigid waters and declaring them subject to Rome, Pompey then
turned and marched his legions back to Colchis, fighting his
way through the same tribes, who by this time had organized in
a loose-knit confederation to oppose him but were no more successful the second time than they had been the first. Arriving
back at Colchis near the end of the campaigning season, Pompey missed the opportunity to attack us in Bosporus that year.
Perhaps hesitant to lead his legions through the uncharted territories along the east coast of the Black Sea, Pompey held out
for easier gains. An opportunity presented itself when Tigranes'
son in Armenia, tired of waiting to inherit the crown, issued an
invitation to Pompey to assist him in taking his throne by force.

Without a doubt, the prospects for plunder in Armenia were
greater than in Bosporus. And Tigranes would be a much easier
conquest than would Father, whom Rome had tried to crush for
decades yet had failed. But Pompey was loath to admit of such
reasonings aloud. Instead, at a banquet he gave in Colchis for a
group of merchants provisioning his army, he declared mockingly, in response to their queries, that it would be more profitable to invade Armenia than to march across dirty glaciers to
pursue a decrepit old king living in a capital of mud huts.

The merchants' news traveled quickly, and within days I

was summoned into Father's rooms in the women's quarters. Expecting to find him delighted that Pompey was abandoning his northern campaign, instead I found him pacing the room in a fury.

"Decrepit old man!" he fumed. "Capital of mud—this from a *Roman,* giving *me* lessons in aesthetics?!"

"It's not important," I rejoined. "He said such things to mock you, knowing the merchants would report his words. What is certain is the Romans are departing. We can halt the preparations for war and return to peacetime. Farming and fishing— that's what these people do best. They are unsuited for fighting."

Sitting down heavily, he glowered at me. "We'll do no such thing," he countered. His tone was even, but the deep anger was clear.

I looked at him in surprise. "The Romans have left. Even now they are marching to Armenia. Reports are that they will continue on to Syria after that. There is no need for additional siege engines or training in field tactics. We should disperse the recruits."

He stood up and raised his voice. "We will do no such thing!" he thundered. "My destiny—and *your* destiny, Pharnaces!—is not to be king of a mud-hut realm. That is not the fate of a descendant of Darius, of a King of Pontus. That will not be our fate!"

I looked at him closely and curiously, unsure whether to take his words at face value. So many things had passed, so many deaths, so many defeats. Could he seriously be thinking again of taking his old throne? Did he still harbor his faded and tattered dreams of a New Greece?

Outside, the sun had dipped below the horizon, and the small room in which we sat fell into shadows. Nevertheless, neither of us lit an oil lamp or opened the shutters to the torchlight from the sconces outside. He turned to me in the gathering gloom.

"Do you know what I fear most?"

Rarely had he spoken in such a way to me before. "A man like yourself?" I asked. "I suppose you fear the possibility of death at any moment, from poison or in battle."

He sat silent for a moment, thinking.

"Do you recall the story of Prometheus?" he asked. Seeing my puzzled expression, he continued. "The great Titan saw that men lived like animals, like little ants dwelling underground in sunless caverns, laboring at random, ignorant even of the weather. But Prometheus taught them to observe the seasons by the rising and setting of the stars. He invented numbers for them, taught them the groupings of letters to be a record of the past. He brought oxen and horses under their control, showed them how to mingle bland herbs to make powerful medicines, to interpret dreams, to work copper and iron, to make sacrifice to the gods. Every human art was given by Prometheus. But greatest of all, he gave men the gift of the gods—fire—making men like gods, giving them comfort and protection and allowing them to look past the desperation of the moment. And like the Roman invaders, who seek only to destroy superior civilizations who precede them, the upstart god Zeus punished Prometheus for his defiance, for his love of culture and civilization, for his devotion to mankind. And what was this punishment?"

I searched my childhood memory of the tale. "He arranged for the creation of woman."

I saw a hint of Father's grin flashing in the dim light. "Yes, well, actually that was the punishment of mankind. But *Prometheus* was punished by being bound forever to a high rock in the Scythian mountains, where the hot sun burned him and the frost froze him. His liver was gnawed out each day by an eagle, and then renewed at night for further torture the next day."

"I would prefer the punishment visited on mankind."

"Ah, but nothing is as it seems. The old myths are not just stories but the accumulated wisdom of the Ancients. Prometheus' gift of fire was not merely that; it symbolized an even greater gift to man—the gift not to foresee coming doom. Pharnaces, no man of action—no *thinking* man of action—fears the possibility of dying at any moment. That is something that hangs over any man's head, not just a king's. A farmer may be killed by a tipped cart or the kick of a mule. A shepherd may be brought down by snakebite, a sailor by drowning in a storm. What is most to be feared, though, is not the *possibility* of dying at the next moment but rather the greatest horror of all: the *certainty* of dying after fifty or sixty years. How does a man come to grips with that? Think about it—you are *certain* to die!"

"But I *don't* think about it, at least not often. Hardly anyone does."

"That's it; *that's* the gift Prometheus gave to mankind! Blind hope for the future, the ability to look past the presence of impending death. Without such ignorance of his fate, mankind would be eternally crushed by terror. It is death that defines the existence of life, as grief defines joy and sickness health. Yet more important, it is our ability to ignore certain terror that gives us awareness of possible joy. That ability to forget is blind hope."

I looked at him in puzzlement. "Why do you tell me this?"

"Because I seem to have missed Prometheus' gift."

My voice must have reflected my skepticism. "How can you say that? You're not crushed by terror. Mortality is a terrible thing, so terrible that men choose not to think on it, and wisely so. Prometheus' gift is a boon, and you've not been spared your portion of it—how else could you continue to risk so much, to drive headlong into battle, to continue struggling, after suffering so much?"

"My solution is not to ignore death but to fight it. To strive for immortality."

"What? In your potions and antidotes? Father, those don't ensure immortality; they merely prolong the reckoning—"

"No, no. I've found a more effective way. The way to ensure immortality is to seize it outright from those who possess it."

"What are you talking about?"

"Listen, and don't interrupt, to the fate of Rome, the city men call Eternal."

While I sat in the darkness on a couch across from him, he related to me the stupendous vision his fertile mind had devised during the months he had spent alone in his rooms, nursing his wounds.

He had plotted the destruction of Rome itself.

In Father's solitude, he had conceived a magnificent fantasy—strength based on weakness, his own and that of the Romans.

In the East, he had been defeated. Rome ruled supreme from Greece to Parthia, from Armenia to Egypt. The Black Sea itself, with the exception of the small area around our own little territory in the north, was nothing but a Roman lake. Even if Father were able to revive his old pirate allies from the comfortable stupor into which they had fallen, he would be unable to build a navy of his own—there was the question of money, of course. And even beyond that, he had no materials with which to actually build warships, in a kingdom consisting largely of a treeless plain. The East was Rome's strength and Mithridates' weakness.

The West, however, was another story. The barbarians of the West had repeatedly revolted and attacked over the past few decades, and in the process entire Roman armies had been wiped out. Was there any reason to believe that such a disaster could not happen to Rome again? The West was Rome's weakness— and if it was not yet our strength, Father would make it one.

His plan was fully formed, and he had been contemplating it for some time, back when he had first begun gathering the army of recruits to counter the Roman attack on Bosporus—which he always knew would never come.

Just to the west of our kingdom lay the mouth of the Danube, the undefended gateway to Rome's western territories. Following the length of the mighty river upstream five or six hundred miles—an unremarkable task for a leader who had led a half-legion of starving refugees a similar distance around the eastern shore of the Black Sea—one came to the Alps, within easy marching distance of the low mountain passes into Italy. These lands were populated by warlike, wealthy but demoralized tribes who themselves had been only recently defeated by Rome. Could there be any doubt what their reaction would be were Mithridates suddenly to march up through their broad river valley at the head of a mighty army of Scythians, bellowing for reprisal against Rome and accompanied by a column of siege engines, catapults, and other mechanical marvels?

The scenario was breathtaking: a march from Panticapaeum to the Alps, gathering mighty hordes of barbarian allies as he progressed, from all his former clients and trading partners. With a nucleus of trained soldiers—the wild men his eunuchs had spent the past year recruiting and his core of hardened Roman and Pontic veterans—he could gather hundreds of thousands of Thracians, Germans, and Gauls and sweep into undefended Italy from the north, while unsuspecting Pompey dallied in the East. It would be the greatest coup the world had ever seen. Father would be renowned as the savior not only of Greek civilization but of the whole world, wrenching barbarian and cultured nations alike from the life-sucking grasp of Rome.

All these years, he had not realized what was before his very eyes: The New Greece was not to be constructed in the East, where generations of Roman dominance blocked his progress, but rather in the *West*—where Rome's hold over the barbarian tribes was tenuous. Like Alexander before him, Father had finally found that rare combination of place and timing, that fortunate confluence of unlikely circumstance and sheer opportunity, that would finally bring his vast plans to fruition.

It was the most audacious plan he had ever devised, perhaps the most daring in history, and I was completely taken in, overwhelmed by the grandeur of its scope, by the feverish light in his eyes and the rising enthusiasm in his voice. In that darkening room I could see his very features harden in intensity, regaining the expression of confidence and command he had had years before, and the angry wound in his cheek seemed almost to recede before my eyes. He stood and began pacing the room in excitement as he explained the strategy, stopping and starting, increasing and slowing his pace as his mind raced and he improvised tactics, experimented with harangues, and drove his men to conquest and victory, all in his mind's eye. With a start I noticed that his limp had disappeared and the slump he had acquired since the battle on the glacier had gone. His gait and posture were now those of the conquering warrior he once had been. He was rejuvenated, strengthened, he had become as an immortal, and I suddenly realized the source of his immortality: his utter belief in himself and his life, his utter disdain for death. He had become a Greek hero, an Achilles or an Ajax, fighting with an inner light, an invisible force that supplemented his physical vigor and made him so much more powerful, more deadly, more *enduring* than a man relying on bodily strength alone.

A guard walked past in the corridor, shining a fleeting flicker of torchlight through the door's viewing slit, which skittered like a lizard across the opposite wall of our room. And just as suddenly as I thought I had understood Father a moment before, with that brief gleam of light, I realized now that I was dead wrong.

The passage of the torch had lit up Father's face, reflecting an expression he had allowed himself only because he thought it was too dark in the room for me to see. It was an expression of exhaustion, drained of energy, yet at the same time almost *desperate,* as if too little time remained for him to do what he had to do. And just as assuredly I knew again that the secret of his immortality was not hatred for death but rather hatred alone: unfulfilled, unsatisfied hatred that could give him no rest, that would not even let him die before it could be consummated, before he could be released of its grip. Even though the same blood of Darius coursed through my veins as through his, I knew that I could never *hate* as deeply as did he, for that hate was to him his very lifeblood, his food and his antivenom, so powerful as to make him indestructible.

Yet this was a man who could not be resisted. With my misgivings overcome by the sheer force of his belief, I agreed to his campaign to conquer the world.

When the plan was announced first to the Pontic officers and then to the soldiers themselves, the King was hailed as a conquering hero, a brilliant strategist now embarking on the culmination of his life's work. Preparations were accelerated and training redoubled. There was no fear of Pompey's being informed of the plans and invading Bosporus by land or by sea to intercept us—as I had predicted, the vain general had now completed his invasion of Armenia and set off for the debauchery of Syria, where he would quarter his troops and consolidate the wealth of his conquests. Harsh winter set in, and final preparations were made for us to commence marching at first thaw.

Yet as spring drew near, second thoughts arose, and the formidable march up the frozen Danube began to seem hazardous. Plans that could cheerfully be toasted over the wine horns of winter banquets, vast wealth that could be imagined over the glowing coals of cozy campfires, suddenly seemed less achievable when the frost began melting and the baggage animals began to be packed. Men whispered the worst—that Mithridates did not intend to actually achieve victory, merely renown; that he had been so stung by Pompey's contemptuous remark that he vowed a violent death in glory, rather than a peaceful end in oblivion; that in his terrible desire for self-destruction he would drag his entire kingdom with him, to the very Gates of Hades, merely to tweak the beak of the Roman eagle. Hannibal, it was said, even Hannibal with his elephants, with his great victory at Cannae, with his ten years of invasion and plunder in Italy, had been unable to break the Roman spirit. How then—and here voices would drop to a whisper—how then could an old man, even one as vigorous as the King, succeed where the mighty Hannibal had failed? Every soldier in the army began to have misgivings, and officers began hearing rumblings from the troops and from one another.

But the most reluctant of all were those who stood both the most to gain and the most to lose from the venture: Marcellus and the Roman exiles.

4

Life as son of a concubine had inured me to any ambition to rule a kingdom as Father had done. My skills and my goals lay in leading armies, and in this I was accomplished, though the administration of civil affairs was not beyond my ken, either, and I performed my tasks well in Panticapaeum. Naturally, opportunities to seize power from Father had not been lacking over the years—yet my own loyalty to him and fear of the consequences were I to fail, were I to commit the unforgivable crime of betrayal, prevented me from ever giving more than fleeting attention to such thoughts.

Such was not the case among certain Roman exiles, however, particularly restless Marcellus. Several times over the years he had engaged me in subtle conversation, attempting to create in me the desire to take power for myself, and on every occasion I had rapidly rejected such nonsense. My one mistake was not to have had him executed on the spot; but like Father, I have a weakness for the loyalty of subordinates, and Marcellus had always been loyal to me, and a good soldier besides. Had I only realized that his betrayal of the King was, in reality, a betrayal of me as well, I would have acted differently. Rather, I flattered myself at the Roman officer's ambitions for my personal cause, convinced that both his military skills and his fealty to me were indispensable. I laughed off his entreaties to overthrow Father and ignored the poison bubbling beneath the surface of his obedience.

Marcellus and his comrades would not be easily dismissed,

however. If I were not willing to openly take control of my destiny, they would be only too happy to force my hand, to present me with power in a way I could not refuse.

In a carefully planned action early that spring, Marcellus spread a false rumor among the army that I planned to overthrow the King. Before I had even heard the tale for myself, several cohorts of Scythian recruits had risen up in arms and stormed my quarters in my support, at dawn, before I had even risen. Stepping outside my tent, barely awake, I was horrified to hear them cheering and bellowing my name, acclaiming me king. Striding out from the front ranks of the cohorts, Marcellus stepped to my side.

"By your treacherous Roman eyes, Marcellus, what have you done?" I roared, though the man could scarcely hear me over the chanting of his troops.

"Sir," he shouted back, "you once told me never to doubt your abilities. Look at these men! Here is proof of their loyalty to you, their confidence in you. Your father is mad, his invasion plan is mad, and you must take his place or risk losing everything!"

"Mad!" I spat in fury. "You are the one who is mad! I could have you flogged and executed for such words. That is treason!"

"Kill me if you want. It will not change your father's madness. Nor will it change this"—and he gestured to the crowd of soldiers chanting in ragged rhythm, all eyes intently upon us, at the argument taking place before them.

"*You* did this!" I raged. "I ignored your hints in the past, so now you compromise me, force me to choose between betraying my father and betraying my troops. You dog! Maybe faithless Romans advance their careers through such machinations, but not Pontics!"

The men began milling about us, their expressions taking on a menacing cast. Seeing the anger written on my face had set hesitation into their minds. They knew that acclaiming me king was treason, and if I did not accept the honor, then they were committing a crime, for which they would be punished. Yet Marcellus remained unperturbed.

"I haven't doubted you since you claimed leadership at the Halys River before defeating Murena. Now it is you who doubt, when I offer you leadership. Seize it, Prince! Seize it!"

Death for attempted betrayal, or overthrowing the King. This was my choice. Marcellus fully expected me to opt for over-throw, to save my own life and thereby spare the Roman exiles the certain agony of marching up the Danube to attack their homeland. I had been cleverly maneuvered. So cleverly, in fact, that the Roman exiles themselves had even stayed clear of this demonstration, thereby avoiding the compromise into which I had fallen. Yet still his words rankled. Could Father truly be mad? I shook off the thought with an almost violent reflex.

"It is not doubt that stops me," I said, "but loyalty! Have you none yourself toward your king?"

Marcellus gaped at me in astonishment. "You accuse me of disloyalty?" he roared. "You accuse *me*? You once called me disloyal for my doubts—now I am disloyal for my certainty!"

By now, the camp was in near-riot, and I stood for long moments outside my tent, imploring the men to disperse, while hurriedly scribbling a message to Father on a wax tablet, urging him to ignore any unfounded rumors of mutiny he might receive at the palace. I now understood the untenable position into which our plans to attack Rome had placed the Roman exiles: Attacking one's own mother country is impossible—men simply cannot be ordered to do it, for justice or for glory. Even mercenaries retain loyalty to their homeland.

But it was too late. Before I had even finished my note, a cohort of Father's veteran Pontic guards had arrived, forcibly dispersed the confused mob of Scythians, and placed me under arrest. Marcellus and the troops who had acclaimed me king skulked back to their quarters without resistance.

I did not languish long in prison, nor did I expect to. Within hours Father and Bituitus barged into the cell, Father's face black with rage but his voice contained to a menacing simmer.

"You are either a complete and utter traitor," he hissed, "or a complete and utter idiot for allowing traitors to operate under your command. Either way, you should be executed!"

"My life speaks for my loyalty," I said with deceptive calm. "Many times, when you were wounded or absent, I had the opportunity to seize power, and I did not."

"And yet now that my plan is about to be implemented, after all the work and preparation has been completed, your troops—*your* troops, those billeted around you in *your* camp—rise up against me! And you are to tell me this was spontaneous, without your knowledge?" He drew the long dagger from the sheath on his hip and hurled it into the packed dirt floor at his feet. The blade slammed through almost to the hilt and stood vibrating with a twanging hum. "What kind of an *imbecile* is commanding my army? And what in Hades are Marcellus and those Romans thinking? I've sponsored and sheltered those ingrate, buzzard-nosed bastards for twenty years—they'd have been long dead if I had not taken them in!"

He ranted on while I remained silent, carefully observing him for signs of the madness Marcellus claimed, wondering what was to be my fate. In the end, it was thickheaded but calm Bituitus who convinced Father of my blamelessness, Bituitus who begged the King to spare my life. His justifications were degrading in the extreme—that I should not be punished for my stupidity, for my being caught off guard by the backstabbing Romans. My only fault, he said, was in failing in the games of politics and intrigue at which we Orientals are famed to excel. In this case, the Romans had outmaneuvered their master. I listened without a word as Bituitus pleaded my case in his rough, Gallic-inflected Greek, I watched silently as my manacles and ankle chains were removed, and then I lingered pensively in the cell long after Father had stormed off. I was free to depart, for the door had been left ajar and the guards notified that my arrest had been in error. Nevertheless, I sat in the silence and the gloom for hours, pondering the events of the day, the words that had been spoken.

Indeed, I finally left only after being shoved roughly aside upon the arrival of Marcellus. The guards tossed him into the very same cell, unconscious yet still breathing shallowly, arrested and beaten for inciting the troops to mutiny. Only then did I leave the room that had been my home for those mere few hours but which had now become the entire world for Marcellus, for the remainder of his last day before his execution.

The accusations against me were false and had been proven so. Peace was restored in the camp, and Father returned to the palace. Nevertheless, his confidence in me had been destroyed, at this sign of either my potential treachery or my malleability at the hands of evil men. My star had fallen, and Father removed me from all my duties. The seeds had been planted in his mind, the seeds of insecurity and threat to his rule, the seeds of suspicion at the motives of his son. Perhaps, eventually I would be able to earn my way back into his good graces, perhaps not; but in the meantime I was suspended from active duty and ordered to surrender my sword.

Yet the botched mutiny had planted seeds elsewhere, as well. No longer was it only the Roman exiles who opposed the march west, who challenged the feasibility of the whole venture. Before his arrest, Marcellus had also raised fears among the Scythian and Pontic troops, poisoning their minds with tales of Father's insanity, of the glory-seeking nature of his enterprise, of the hopelessness of his cause. Marcellus was an officer the men trusted and respected, and in a mere few moments of whispered insinuations he had undone the decades of commitment and loyalty Father had shown his men and raised fatal doubts in their minds.

Nor was this the worst of it: My hours of pondering in the cell had given rise to my own doubts as well, that Father was toying with me, keeping me alive only temporarily as a sop to the troops, as a way to show his magnanimity even to those who opposed him. I had no doubts as to his sanity—he was as sane, or as mad, as he ever had been. Yet sane or mad, he had lost the trust of his men, and therefore the great venture he had planned was destined to be a fool's errand or, worse, a glorious suicide for all. Even in his death, Marcellus had achieved what he had set out to accomplish, when he had pinned his own mutiny on me.

Three nights after my release from prison I went to the cohorts of Roman exiles, to those who had brought me to such an impasse in the first place, and won their unhesitating support. They had already anticipated my arrival, my reversal of loyalties, and immediately sent agents and couriers throughout the army, bearing news of our impending revolt. It was to be my day of glory or my day of death, and if all went well, Father would be taking a long, well-deserved rest, to spend the rest of his life at a remote hunting lodge beyond the northern foothills. I sent word to the caretakers there to be prepared to receive a noble prisoner.

The next morning, I sent six of Marcellus' veteran Roman exiles to the palace to demand that the King surrender. Father had already been awakened by the sounds of excitement from the army camps surrounding the city, and in fact my men met on the road several messengers from the palace whom Father had sent to inquire into the cause of the tumult. My stony-faced Romans ignored the King's emissaries and continued their march, in full battle armor and drill-ground formation. Arriving at the palace, they muscled their way past the surprised eunuchs, through the protesting concubines in the city of women, and straight into the courtyard of the wing where Father had installed himself upon first arriving in Panticapaeum the year before.

The Romans found him waiting for them, he, too, in full armor, bow slung over his shoulder, curved sword strapped against his trouser-clad thigh. He had pulled himself up to his full, imposing height, huge helmet propped back on the crown of his head, mighty forearms crossed in front of his bearlike chest, legs in a wrestler's stance, as if prepared to pounce with all the catlike energy and power he still retained in his sixty-ninth year. He was flanked by Bituitus, who bore a menacing glower, and a dozen burly Pontic soldiers of his personal guard, all with hands on sword hilts, fingers twitching nervously.

Father and his men stood unmoving and scowling as the Romans entered. I had sent my men, handpicked legionaries, with the thought that their many years of service to the King would put him at his ease, afford him the confidence to accompany them quietly back to the quarters I had prepared for him outside the city, whence I could safely whisk him off to the comfortable exile I had planned. Such was not to be. Though the Roman escorts were momentarily taken aback at Father's show of defiance, they were Romans and, like all members of that crude race, utterly lacking in any of the subtlety or politesse we Asians seem to imbibe with our very mothers' milk. The centurion who was their spokesman completely discarded the eloquent demand for surrender I had carefully drafted the night before. In an astonishing display of bluff and stupidity, he lapsed into the blunt accusations and camp-speak that had been circulating among the common troops.

"Surrender, Pontics," the loutish centurion growled. "The army refuses to follow an old man ruled by eunuchs, who kills his own sons and women. The march on Italy is suicide. Prince Pharnaces demands you surrender your command and weapons to him."

At these words, Bituitus and the Pontic guards leaped forward. It was only by Father's mercy, his gratefulness for their past service, that the Romans were not killed outright. Instead, they were beaten to within an inch of their lives and allowed to stagger back to my headquarters to recount the tale. There would be no comfortable exile for Mithridates.

The Fates had made their sacrifice, and harmony and peace were the victims.

That morning I assembled my strongest legion, the core of which consisted of the three thousand veterans who had survived the terrible march through the Scythian Gates. I needed to take action while the men's resolve was still high. I mounted my horse, a magnificent war charger Father had given me the year before to celebrate my accession to the governorship of Bosporus, and marched out immediately at the head of the grim-faced troops, prepared to take the palace by force, if necessary. I gave the men only one order:

"Take the King alive. I will personally execute any man who harms him."

As I had now set my path, so Father had set his. Pulling down his helmet and donning his shield, he mounted his own warhorse and cantered out to the parade ground outside the palace doors, but still within the compound formed by the high walls ringing the sprawling complex of palace buildings. Other guards loyal to the King also seized horses and galloped up beside him, giving him a small cavalry squad of perhaps fifty men. There the furious king arrayed his men in battle formation as he turned and trotted slowly forward to the huge oaken portals of the palace walls, to parley with me as we approached.

As he moved into position, however, a group of Scythian guards in one of the watchtowers at the corner of the walls began shouting abuse down at him.

"To the crows with Mithridates! Hail King Pharnaces!" they brayed. My troops and I were still on our approach outside the palace walls, and I cursed the idiots in the blockhouse for their ill-timed challenge, which I knew would only enrage Father further. Like the Roman messengers before them, they suffered for their indiscretion. When Father heard the traitorous insults and abuse hurled at him from his own soldiers in the watchtower above, he signaled to the loyal guards arrayed at his side.

In a flash, fifty arrows streaked up from their bows into the throats of the hapless guards on the walls above, whose barricades afforded them no shelter or protection from an attack aimed at them from *within* the walls. As the legion and I watched, horrified, from outside the gates, a dozen men from the blockhouse fell dead to the ground at our feet, skewered by the missiles of the loyalist troops inside.

The palace walls erupted in pandemonium. The ramparts had been heavily fortified during the night, every corner blockhouse filled with Scythian guards, and even the battlements between each corner were patrolled by newly recruited infantry, whom Father had believed, until now, to be loyal to him. Now, however, as they saw their comrades die at Mithridates' hands and my own overwhelming forces approaching from just outside the palace, their fury erupted. Scrambling down the steep stone steps inside the walls, even leaping off the ramparts, the guards raced from their posts and down onto the parade field, two hundred of them or more, to attack the king to whom they had only so recently sworn undying allegiance.

By the time my legion had forced through the gates and entered the compound, a full-scale battle had erupted. Though heavily outnumbered, Father was still astride his warhorse, surrounded by his veteran guards. As his men fired volley after volley into the mob of Scythians, he himself charged furiously into their midst, cutting through with trampling hooves and slashing sword, then wheeling his mount and charging through again. Scythians leaped into the fray from every corner, pouring out of the palace outbuildings where the previous garrison shift had been resting, struggling into their armor, and then plunging blindly into the attack against the loyalist guards.

One by one Father's Pontics were overwhelmed, as their arrows were depleted and sword blades snapped off in thrusts between ribs and on helmets. Dozens of enraged Scythians swarmed over the Pontics, pulling down their horses by the sheer weight of their bodies, hacking at the overwhelmed defenders with daggers, and even pounding upon them with rocks, until only the King, Bituitus, and a half-dozen others were still alive, struggling mightily just to remain on their mounts and defend themselves with their heavy cavalry shields. My own men, unable to enter the palace compound because of the packed and chaotic conditions, stood clustered at the gates, straining to gain access, craning their necks to see over the heads of the men in front of them, to understand the source of the terrible cries of rage and anguish coming from inside the walls.

Suddenly Father's horse tripped, or was lamed by a Scythian blade, and his massive helmet disappeared beneath a swarm of attackers. My heart leaped into my throat and I bellowed to the troops to withdraw, to retreat, to leave the King unharmed, but I might as well have shouted to the roaring tides, for all they heard me. Scarcely had Father fallen, however, when the mound of recruits who had leaped upon him was lifted bodily into the air and Father rose like a phoenix, like a wrathful god, from beneath the vultures who had brought him down. Slashing furiously with swords in both hands, he cut through the screaming mob of soldiers like a farmer striding through wheat with his scythe; limbs, helmets, and weapons flew around him in a spray of blood. Deep gashes covered his biceps and forearms, and the right side of his helmet had been raggedly sheared off by a mighty blow from a blade. When he turned his head I saw blood sheeting down his neck and cuirass from that side, from the side of his earlier face wound.

Bellowing like a madman, he staggered through the crowd of attacking soldiers as if they were so many hounds snapping at his legs. Reaching the base of the citadel watchtower, he leaped up onto the stone steps, above his enemies, retreating onto the narrow, winding staircase inside, staving off any attackers who dared enter. Bituitus, too, and a handful of survivors from his original band of loyalists fought their way on foot to the circular tower and forced their way in.

Only then was I myself able to cut my own way through the furious crowd, dozens of whom had been killed or wounded in the chaotic mutiny, and drive them back from the tower. The undisciplined Scythians were ejected from the open courtyard howling in rage and forced to the inside perimeter. There my troops disarmed them and ordered them to crouch against the walls, where they fell into an exhausted after-battle stupor, warily watching my own veteran legionaries take up their posts on the parade ground, below the circular tower in which Father was holed up with his few loyalists.

My Roman officers led me in a daze to the stool they had hastily improvised as a throne. The Roman legion that had accompanied me from the camp would no longer wait to acclaim me king. There, in the dusty, blood-spattered courtyard, I was crowned with a roughly woven circlet of leaves from a nearby shade oak. The diadem and other crown jewels that would normally have been used were secured in the citadel with Father.

Long ago, when I was a mere boy, he had waged war against the might of Rome, at the head of the combined Greek and Asiatic forces. Hundreds of thousands of men had fought, starved, conquered, and died under his command. For decades he had been Rome's most implacable enemy, outlasting her greatest generals, defeating her mightiest armies, ultimately losing but never conquered. Driven from his ancestral home time and again, he had always returned in triumph. Even here, in this distant corner of the world, he had raised an army capable of setting the Roman world trembling again.

Yet suddenly he was no longer king. For the first time in five decades, the first time in my own life, he was no longer sovereign. And the crown of command rested instead on my head.

I felt no emotion, only a strange emptiness, an immense fatigue. Standing before the improvised throne, my sword held upright in the form of a scepter, I gazed around me as three thousand men shouted in unison, chanting my name, acclaiming me as their lord and sovereign; yet I could not bring myself to feel triumph or satisfaction. The cacophony of their acclamations seemed almost to fade, as if in the roaring of a tremendous wind, and my thoughts turned inward. As I gazed around absently, even the sides of my vision seemed to darken, slowly encroaching on my central focus until it was as if I were peering down a long tube, a papyrus scroll, and nothing else mattered, nothing else could be seen or heard, but for the single point on which my senses had focused. The sensations—the chaos and noise of that day, the bleeding and dying, Father pummeled like a wounded lion beneath jackals yet rising again to shake them off, the victory chants and acclamations—all were too much, too overwhelming, and my mind reeled. I sought solace in shutting out the chaos, the bloodshed, and the jostling. I focused on a single spot, a single face, from among that entire crowd of faces.

The face of Bituitus.

With a start, I snapped out of my reverie, and the roar of the men, the frantic waving of their pennants, the clamor of their shields pounding rhythmically on knees, rushed back at me like a wave at the shore, a crash that struck me almost physically. Yet my eyes never left his face.

He was standing in the doorway at the foot of the unguarded citadel, from which the troops' attention had been diverted by the ceremony of my crowning. With the tower at the men's backs, they had not seen him, and as further precaution he had remained prudently in the shadows behind the half-opened door, his big, familiar face peering out at me from the half-darkness, lips grim and tight-set. As soon as he saw he had caught my eye, he nodded once, quickly, and then disappeared back into the shadows, closing the door behind him.

I glanced up to the top of the circular tower, five floors above ground level, to the narrow arrow slit of a window overlooking the packed courtyard. There another face peered down, pale and distorted, mouth twisted in fury and pain, eyes filled with despair. I was so far away I could barely identify him, and he was standing away from the dark window, as if attempting to see without being seen. Still, I saw him, I did see him, and in my mind's eye I see him now, perhaps even clearer than I did then—the profile backlit by a dim lamp, fading in and out of view as men behind him passed before the single light, just as in my dreams. He turned away for a moment and then returned to his post at the window, this time holding an object in his hand, something golden—a weapon, a goblet? He so loved shiny things, things of beauty, but it was impossible to tell.

I knew instantly what I had to do. So many times I had lived this moment, practiced this occasion in my dreams, but never had I thought it would be fulfilled.

I'm coming, Father.

I stepped slowly and regally down from the makeshift dais on which I had been standing and strode into the crowd of men, who at first pounded me on the shoulders and tried to lift me above their heads in jubilation but in an instant noticed the grim expression on my face and the sword I held out stiffly in front of me, warding them off, commanding them without words to part before me. This they did, and with puzzled though still smiling expressions, they pushed back to either side, creating a narrow path upon which I strode purposefully, straight across the courtyard to the foot of the tower into which the deposed king had fled. The heavy oaken door at the base was a simple but impregnable barrier. Thick as the breadth of a man's hand, banded about with sturdy iron bars, secured from the inside by massive dead bolts augered into the very granite of the lower courses of the tower, it could not be penetrated by attackers without sustained battering or burning. The fugitives inside were going nowhere, and the legions outside were in no hurry to force the entrance.

I strode to the door and mounted the three steep steps to the threshold, which themselves had been designed precisely to impede the sort of battering that would be required to knock it down. With their narrow width, only one man at a time could stand on each step, which would not provide enough muscle to lift a ram. Standing on the top step, I turned to face the cheering legion and raised my arm. In a moment the stifling, crushing noise stopped and the men ceased their jostling and pushing against me. A tremendous sense of relief washed over me. Staring around me for a moment, at my comrades and officers, some of whom had known me since I could barely walk and who now would throw themselves into a hail of arrows at my merest word, I paused. I sought an omen, a sign, even a shouted word of advice from a low-ranking trooper. None came. All were silent. I turned my back to the men, put my hand on the handle of the thick door. As I expected, it swung open easily, and I entered.

The men behind me gaped and then roared in dismay at seeing their new king enter alone and barely armed into the enemy citadel. I had no time to lose.

Racing up the stone steps two, then three at a time, I heard the pounding footfalls behind me as my guards chased after me, shouting after me to stop my ascent. Above me, all was silence and darkness.

Climbing up the narrow steps more by feel than by sight, I burst through the doorway at the top, into the single, bare room beneath the roof, where was stored the remaining treasure of the kingdom of Bosporus, which I knew was but a pitiful amount for the administration of a realm, and where stood Father, with his small band of loyalists flanking him. Bituitus stood at attention, sword sheathed and head bowed, already in an attitude of surrender, though his men moved quickly to surround me. After seeing me enter, Father began walking, though it was in a hunched, labored motion as he paced slowly up and down the silent room. I stood in the doorway, staring, my guards behind me stopped in the darkness and balancing on the narrow steps, unable to advance forward or past me, unable to see into the room. My eyes searched Father's and Bituitus' faces for answers, and then my gaze fell to the royal sword that lay on the floor, its hilt broken off—no, not broken, but rather uncapped! With a start, I noticed the empty hollow compartment inside, a tiny *pysix*, from which the remains of the liquid it had contained dripped out and formed a tiny stain on the stone floor—brown and viscous as dried blood, dark as death, fatal as the terrible misunderstanding at its source.

I glanced up at Father, saw the grimace as he licked the residue from his lips, the wince as he clutched his belly with his right hand.

"No," I whispered, yet my voice was gone and no sound came. I stared as Father continued his pacing and Bituitus strode over to my side.

"Perhaps it is not too late," the Gaul said softly. "He drank it as you were crowned, but it is not having the effect. It has given him fire in the belly but nothing more; he is too strong. He is walking to speed the effect."

"Father, lie down!" I ordered immediately, but he merely glanced at me with a wry, twisted smile that was instantly overcome by a grimace of pain.

"You here, Pharnaces?" he gasped. "Ha! So you find this trouble is not mine alone. Do you come to commiserate? Wouldn't that be a rare bit of luck, finding another man to share your fortunes, rather than betraying him!" He leaned forward and retched, his eyes bloodshot and bulging from the pain.

"Father!" I exclaimed, appalled at his suffering and his words. "They acclaimed me king for the good of all of us, for the kingdom! Come, lie down. Papias can be summoned. You can be healed again—"

He waved off my protests and doubled over, clawing at his stomach. His men held me back while blocking the narrow stairway behind me with drawn swords to prevent my guards from entering. After a moment, the pain eased and he looked up, his one eye boring into me fiercely.

"Be sure of what I tell you, Pharnaces. You are on your own—your own arm and your own fortune—to win back your ancestors' home and city. Trust no man to help you in this task. Do not make the same mistake as I."

I struggled to escape the grip of the men who held me, but it was no use. Father watched my efforts impassively for a moment, then looked toward his guards.

"I may no longer command a kingdom," he muttered, without a trace of self-pity, "but my body is still mine to do with as I wish. Bituitus!"

The Gaul leaped forward, seizing Father's arm. He was again doubled over in pain. Two other Pontic guards stepped forward to hold my shoulders.

"Like a fool," Father gasped, "like a fool, I guarded against all the poisons a man takes with his food. Yet I didn't take measures against a far deadlier poison, within my own household. Bituitus: I've profited much from your right arm against my enemies. You may do me one last service, old friend."

Struggling with all my might against the hands that held me, I was unable to stop the Gaul. Slowly and deliberately, tears rolling down his face, Bituitus drew the dagger from the sheath at his belt and then with a quick and silent movement fulfilled his king's last request. Father dropped to his knees. Where the poison had failed to act, the Gaul's trained blade completed its work. Bituitus caught the massive head and shoulders and lowered them to the ground. The Pontic guards released my own arms and I stepped forward, clearing the doorway, and suddenly the room was filled with the shouts and cries of angry men.

The Roman troops seized Father's Pontic guards, who put up no resistance, and began leading them out of the room. By unspoken agreement they left Bituitus untouched as he knelt over his sovereign. I stepped forward and picked up the jeweled sword that lay untended on the bare flagstones, its secret cap removed and the vacant hole in the hilt winking leering death at me. Again I could feel nothing, no emotion, not even sadness—only a strange inevitability, a purposeful sense of what had to be done. Pricking the tip of the blade lightly against my finger to test its sharpness, I strode slowly to where Bituitus knelt, shoulders slumped and head hanging. Lifting my sword, I aimed the point down, toward him, and as I did so a shaft of sunlight through the narrow window slit fell on me from behind, casting my shadow over him, magnifying the trembling of the blade as it hovered in the air above his head.

For a moment, Bituitus hesitated, his eyes fixed on the sword's wavering shadow on the floor before him. Then without turning to look up at me, he reached slowly back with his hand and pulled his long white hair aside to expose his neck.

5

I did not see the condition of the body by the time it arrived in Pompey's hands, though I knew that Papias and the team of skillful embalmers he had assembled had performed their task well and quickly. Scarcely a day after Father's death, a trireme was dispatched to Sinope containing the massive corpse, as well as the half-dozen Roman exiled soldiers who had been responsible for Manlius Aquilius' execution twenty-five years before, and a small company of hostages the King had acquired over the years during his various negotiations with Rome. The body was accompanied by an official letter I hastily drafted to Pompey and the Senate, offering to serve Rome as a loyal ally and friend, provided that Rome left me in peace to rule the northern kingdom of Bosporus I had inherited from Father.

Truly, it was an extraordinary shipment, one that three generations of Rome's greatest generals had sought, and as news of Mithridates' death spread like wildfire through Roman territory, days of jubilant feasting and celebration were spontaneously declared by officials in every city and town. If the measure of a man's greatness is the degree of celebration by his enemies upon his death, then Father was surely one of the greatest men the world had seen.

Pompey was in Arabia, leading his army against the stone fortress of Petra when the Pontic heralds arrived, accompanied by Roman scouts who had wreathed their spears in laurel as is customary when reporting news of a great victory. So eager was the general to announce the news to his army that he did not even wait for the traditional tribunal to be built in the camp as the stage for a dignified, formal announcement. Rather, he simply leaped onto a heap of cavalry saddles that had been stacked for storage by the quartermaster, and shouted the tidings at the top of his lungs as the men came running to see what had possessed their commander. A great cheer rose up from the legions, and the Arabs hunkered behind Petra's massive walls were in deep consternation at what might have so aroused their enemies. They did not have long to worry. Within a day, Pompey had called off his entire invasion of Arabia, packed up the army, and commenced a rapid march back to the Black Sea.

Upon arriving at Sinope, Pompey shouldered past the dignitaries and city fathers who had hastened to the gates to meet him, ignored the throngs of well-wishers and favor-seekers lining his path, and rushed to the trireme, which had been secured at the docks under heavy guard by the local Roman garrison. I had taken care to load the vessel with a magnificent offering: bales of silks and ceremonial robes, glittering golden chalices and precious works of art, a cloak that had been owned by Alexander the Great, even the splendidly jeweled sword Father had carried by his side for decades, with the hilt still open to display the secret compartment containing the poison he had swallowed. Pompey gave only cursory glance to these items, however, demanding to see the body itself. My Pontic heralds delayed further, first bringing out for inspection Father's magnificent parade armor, a hundred pounds of solid bronze, wrought gold, and electrum, bearing an exquisite rendering of the flying horse of Pontus with bejeweled eyes, and the cauldronlike helmet, a massive work laid with seamless gold. The sword baldric alone, a magnificent specimen of polished Parthian leather adorned with inlays of gold and precious stones, was worth over four hundred talents of silver, and the royal Pontic diadem twice that again. Pompey's guards staggered under the weight of the enormous pieces, seemingly made for a Titan, though the general himself had seen Father wear them effortlessly in battle, as easily handled as the wicker and linen worn by Armenian archers.

When the coffin itself was opened, Pompey's face at first fell in disappointment as he exclaimed aloud at the incompetence of the embalmers—my expert Maeotian embalmers, so skilled at their work! But further examination and calm reassurance from the heralds restored his confidence. The linen-wrapped body was stripped and found to be intact and in fact had been perfectly preserved, down to the open wound in the chest. The body was that of an enormous man, near seventy years of age, rock-muscled yet covered with battle scars. It was the body of a man immune to disease, so strong he could only be killed by a blade, Titanic in stature, Herculean in symmetry, so heavy it took a dozen burly troopers to wield his coffin. Pompey was so amazed at the sight of this enormous cadaver that in the end he was able to ignore the fact that the face—perhaps the most celebrated face in all of Asia—had been utterly destroyed, decayed to a state that was unrecognizable, the skull crushed in transit by the rocking of the ship, rotted like a melon at the bottom of a barrel that has sat too long in the hot sun.

Despite the condition of the face, Pompey smiled as he ran his eyes in gloating triumph over the godlike body. In all the history of the world there could be only one man of such proportion and beauty, and this man he now had before him, Mithridates Eupator VI, the scourge of Rome and the terror of the seas. At last ordering the coffin closed and sealed, Pompey pronounced the end of the Mithridatic era and the beginning of a new age of peace and friendship between Rome and her client states of Pontus and Bosporus. And in a gesture of magnanimity that even I, in my careful planning, had not anticipated, Pompey then granted the remains the highest honor, paying out of his own purse for the expense of a magnificent funeral ceremony and burial in the royal mausoleum of Sinope, where lay the bodies of our ancestors. There, in that silent stone monument to the dead, each granite coffin was topped by a small box containing the jawbone and navel string of the coffin's occupant, which could be easily removed and handled for ceremonies of veneration: sixteen generations in descent from the Great King Darius of Persia, eight in descent from the first king of an independent Pontus—a kingdom that Pompey had extinguished.

And why not grant such an honor? Truly these were the remains of a great man. Pompey's physicians had carefully inspected the body, identifying it as that of Rome's ancient foe. Every inch of the corpse they had cautiously examined, from the length of the snow-white hair to the ruined and shrunken face and even the novelty of the knife sheath strapped to the penis.

Yet they had failed to note the missing little finger on the right hand.

Even in death, faithful Bituitus, bodyguard to the King and his Gallic twin, you performed one final service to your master, preventing his corpse from falling into the hands of those he abhorred, allowing him to remain forever the Last King of the Greeks.

6

These final words of my narrative I dictate in a place of which Father would have approved, on an occasion he is no doubt observing as a shade, hollow-eyed and hungry, thrust by Hades from the land of the dead to scrutinize what his life has wrought. I sit now in the tent of the general staff, on a moon-filled night bereft of sound but for the soft rustling of the guards outside my door and the murmur of the vast army surrounding me.

Yes, an army—for I have indeed become king, and not merely over the mud-citied Bosporus bequeathed to me upon Father's death but over all my hereditary lands as well. It is no longer the same kingdom as my ancestors once ruled or one that even Father would recognize were he to return. The cities they had once known and inhabited, Sinope and Amisus, have been sacked and destroyed by the Romans, burnt to the ground, and I have rebuilt them in my own fashion. The ancient clans of Persian nobles in the interior have been dispersed, driven from their ancestral estates by Roman predations. Noble families have disappeared; wealth has vanished; new immigrants have taken their place. I was once told that Jason's legendary ship, the *Argo,* still existed until recently, a thousand years after its voyage, tended by the priests of an ancient shrine to Poseidon on the Isthmus of Corinth. Whenever rot was detected in any of its timbers or tackle, it was immediately replaced; thus though the ship survived for centuries, not a single board of it was original. As the old dictum goes, "This is my grandfather's ax.

Though my father gave it a new head and I have replaced the stock, it is still my grandfather's ax." So it is for the kingdom of Pontus.

But things do not remain static for the Romans, either. Now fifteen years after Father's death, Rome's rule in Asia has weakened, Pompey himself has been killed in a fashion as foul as Father's and far less noble, and I have returned in triumph to Sinope, at the head of a pirate armada as of old, to rule the land to which I was born.

Is madness close at hand more certain than it seems from a distance? Surely Father's Roman auxiliaries had thought him mad at the time, or they would not have staged such a farce of a mutiny, one that, yes, I do call a farce, despite the fact that it left me king and sole commander. There is no explanation for their behavior other than their perception of him as mad and no explanation for my acquiescence other than that I agreed with them. Yet now, from the vantage point of many years of reflection and observation, my doubts increase daily.

There was nothing absurd about Father's plan of uniting the western barbarians—these were peoples with whom Pontus had maintained relations for decades and who had supplied our armies with thousands of mercenaries over the years. To their eyes, the old king's prestige was legendary. His planned invasion of Italy would have occurred precisely at a time when Rome was wracked by rebellion and civil war. Under such circumstances, who can dispute that Rome would have fallen at the sudden appearance of half a million Gauls and Germans, marching in disciplined formation, led by a civilized king, a veteran warrior against the Romans? Who can dispute that if I had not accepted my oak-leaf crown in a blood-soaked courtyard of a wattle-and-mud city I might now be reclining in an imperial palace in Rome—King of the World?

And now, standing outside in the doorway of my tent, which I leave open to catch the cool summer night's breeze, I have a clear view through the darkness of the vast extent of my forces, spread in perfect Roman alignment, the coals of the campfires winking cheerily across the wide plain of Zela that I know so well. Beyond the farthest line of fires I see the shadow of the trenchworks we have carefully dug, topped by the high embankment, itself defended by an impregnable palisade of sharpened stakes and spears. Passing in front of the torches ensconced in the defensive works, I see the silhouettes of the guards on their rounds, leaving nothing to escape their eyes. Nothing has been left to chance, nothing unprotected. Infiltration is impossible, betrayal from within unthinkable. The Romans have taught me well. Father would have been proud.

And it is well. For farther beyond the barricades, beyond the edge of the plain, behind the foothills and up the steeply rising mountains to their rear, beyond the edge of my own night vision, more campfires wink, these, too, in precise Roman alignment. In that enemy encampment men will also be firmly entrenched, safely palisaded, their guards watchful, and their commander brooding and wakeful, like myself. Perhaps, like myself, he may even be standing in front of his tent, staring thoughtfully into the darkness in the direction of his own enemy, whom he shall face tomorrow.

I imagine a raptor circling above, catching a rising draft—an eagle? an owl?—no, for the sake of symmetry, let us assume a hawk, the very bird with which I opened this narrative, the very epitome of ferocity and death. High in the heavens, the creature would see to either side of him the two great armies, separated by only a scant distance, behind the one, to the south and west, the coastal strongholds of Cilicia, the Mediterranean, and finally the great, corrupt, rotten and pestilential city of Rome. Behind the other, to the north, the rocky shoreline of the Black Sea, and the fickle and lovely city of Sinope, the seat of the new bastion of Greek empire and civilization in the East. Focusing his gaze more closely, the hawk will see two men, invisible one to the other but sensing each other's presence, straining to read each other's thoughts, looking to the gods to divine the minds of men. But the hawk cares nothing for these things, and swooping silently out of the night sky, he descends on his unwitting quarry. And the quarry, a small rodent or a lizard that has emerged from its hole to feed, now exposed on an open plain, will have no time to feel fear, or even pain, for the attacker's strike is swift, and death comes instantly.

Unlike the lizard, that Roman beyond my vision, the commander of that legion, feels fear. His troops are exhausted from a long forced march. They are outnumbered five to one. They are far from home, fighting on alien ground, for nonexistent plunder and surrounded by a population hostile to them. He shall perhaps comfort himself with the thought that his men are the flower of Rome and have been tested in many battles and that he himself is Rome's most acclaimed general. But that is small comfort indeed.

For he is facing King Pharnaces, son of Mithridates the Great. And tomorrow—unless we cease to believe in the gods, unless wrong is to triumph over right—tomorrow will be Rome's last day.

AUTHOR'S POSTSCRIPT

After the death of Mithridates, Pompey returned to Rome, where for the next fifteen years he was the Republic's leading citizen and military and civil commander. He was finally defeated by Julius Caesar at the battle of Pharsalus in 48 B.C. and then murdered on an Egyptian beach as he attempted to flee. Ironically, thirty years after Pompey's defeat of the pirate fleets in the Mediterranean, his own son, Sextus Pompeius, became the leader of a pirate squadron.

Pharnaces ruled quietly in Bosporus for a time, giving the Romans little cause for concern. In the same year as Pompey was defeated, however, Pharnaces seized his authority as the son of the last king of Pontus and sailed across the Black Sea with a fleet, to regain his hereditary kingdom. Though he had little money or manpower, Sinope and Amisus opened their gates to him, and the local Roman garrisons were defeated. That winter Pharnaces spent building his forces, and soon the fate of Asia was again in the balance.

Julius Caesar was not one to take such a threat lightly, however. The following summer he marched north from Egypt with three thousand Roman veterans, collecting reinforcements from the garrisons in Syria. On August 2 of the year 47 B.C. he met the Pontic army at Zela, the historic battlefield at which Mithridates had put Triarius to flight twenty years earlier. Caesar's rout of Pharnaces' forces was so overwhelming that it inspired his famously contemptuous dispatch to the Senate: *"Veni, vidi, vici"*—I came, I saw, I conquered.

Pharnaces returned defeated to Bosporus, where his rule was challenged by a local rebel. In a pitched battle on the steppe, his Scythian warriors were defeated and Pharnaces himself killed while fighting in the front ranks of his troops. He was fifty-one years of age. None of Mithridates' many other children are known to have made any mark on history.

ACKNOWLEDGMENTS

As Pharnaces notes, "History is written by the victors." This is not an original observation, of course, but it is one that applies most aptly to Mithridates, who, because he ultimately did not prevail in his lifelong struggle against Rome, has never really had his side of the story told. This is prime fodder for the historical novelist, and is a large part of the attraction of researching such an amazing character: Enough information about him survives that it is possible to construct quite a realistic environment, yet there are enough gaps in the historical record—particularly those relating to the protagonist's motives, personal relationships, and leadership methods—that the author can allow full sway to his own imagination.

Ancient writings on Mithridates are actually fairly extensive—detailed descriptions of his exploits, indeed many more than I could include in this novel, may be found in Appian's *Histories,* Plutarch's *Lives* (particularly those of Sulla, Lucullus, and Pompey), and Strabo's *Geography,* with smaller snippets scattered among the works of such other authorities as Suetonius, Cicero, Frontinus, and Vegetius. Yet the fact that these authors are all working largely from the Roman viewpoint complicates matters somewhat. Mithridates in many cases is depicted as the archetypical barbarian villain—luxury-loving, calculating, and homicidal, particularly with regard to the infamous Night of the Vespers. As horrifying as this event was, it is well for it to be taken within the context of its times. Not long after this massacre, Julius Caesar embarked on his conquest of Gaul, which resulted in the killing of well over a million noncombatants and the elimination of entire tribes, cities, and cultures. And Caesar's reasons for his campaign of destruction were arguably much shallower and more materialistic than any that motivated Mithridates. Yet Caesar was deified by Rome and is heralded to this day as one of the greatest men of all time, while Mithridates was vilified and then ultimately forgotten. So many of history's verdicts rely on the accidents of fate and one's place of birth.

The sources for my book included all of the ancient authors named above, as well as several modern ones. Indeed, on several occasions Mithridates has even enjoyed a cultural revival, of sorts. The seventeenth-century French playwright Jean Racine produced a popular five-act drama, *Mithridate,* which, though entertaining, is not to be recommended for its historical accuracy. Mozart produced an opera based upon the same theme, though it is rarely heard today. More recently, British writer Alfred Duggan produced an accessible and easily acquired biography of Mithridates entitled *King of Pontus* (1959), which is useful for readers seeking an informative and entertaining overview of the topic. The most extensive work, however, was undertaken in the late 1800s by Théodore Reinach, whose masterly *Mithridate Eupator, Roi de Pont* encompasses, I would wager, all extant information about Mithridates and his region from every known source. Unfortunately, it is a book long out of print, difficult to find, and written in a rather inaccessible, academic style of French. This, then, is the rather mixed historical and literary legacy of the man Rome feared above all other enemies.

A writer is rarely completely self-sufficient, and in my case, when working on a book, I lean quite heavily on the talents and knowledge of others. And though I owe extensive thanks to those who contributed to the writing of this book, I of course accept full responsibility for any of its shortcomings or errors. Most especially I would like to offer my appreciation to my editor, Peter Wolverton, for his critical eye and frank opinions, and for his unwavering belief in the attraction of this material to modern readers. I would also like to acknowledge the painstaking efforts of my friend and historical consultant Mark

Usher, of the University of Vermont, whose suggestions and corrections immeasurably enriched this book.

At the end of the day, however, editors and advisors can simply turn off their computers, hang up their phones, and go home, and not have to deal with an obsessive author after hours. That difficult lot falls to the author's family, and therefore the greatest credit of all is due to them, though mention of their names on an acknowledgments page seems such paltry compensation. Nevertheless, it is the best I can do, and I only trust that the reader will be able to perceive, between the lines, the impossibly deep gratitude I feel for them. Thank you, Eamon, Isa, and Marie, for your gifts of play and inquisitiveness, for your lessons on life, and for helping me to put everything into proper perspective. And thank you, Cris, for your unstinting love and support, your fine cooking, your companionship on bike rides, and your tireless editing of drafts. Through your skill and patience, you create that rarefied, nurturing, oxygen-rich environment that makes it possible to produce such a miraculous thing as a *book*. Every author should be so lucky.

Read on for an excerpt from
Michael Curtis Ford's next book

THE SWORD OF ATTILA

Available in hardcover
from St. Martin's Press!

Campi Catalaunici, Gaul, June 20, A.D. 451

The blackness of the heavens melded with the dark of the surrounding fields and woods, and the rain poured down on a scene of collective misery, the likes of which the world has rarely seen. It was as if even the gods were weeping for the fallen greatness of the empire, and for themselves.

A quarter of a million soldiers staggered in ragged formation along a dirt road whose ruts had long since turned into a quagmire. Each man's world was reduced to the tiny space around his own body—the tramping of hobnailed sandals, the dripping of water from helmet into eyes, the cold armor of the soldier in front of him, which he touched with his hand for reassurance that he was still following the right path in the darkness. As often as a soldier may train and drill with his legion, as far as he may march in close formation with a thousand comrades, as fiercely as he may fight as part of a vast body of troops, in the end, his survival depends not on his fellows or his enemies but on himself alone. No other man can endure for him the cold rain trickling down his back, the stabbing pain in his thigh where the spear point remains embedded, or the deep fear in his gut that this night, this night of agony and exhaustion, this last night, might not yield to dawn.

No light penetrated the sky, though in the distance, on the near horizon where lay the enemy camp, the sparks of a hundred thousand fires pierced the blackness like earthbound stars, as if the positions of Heaven and earth had been reversed. Close at hand, however, the only light was that which shone from the occasional pine-pitch torch stuck into the sodden earth of the ditch, or the lingering fire of an incendiary missile slowly guttering in a puddle of oily liquid. The dwindling flames seemed only to exaggerate the darkness by their infrequency, and as the column snaked slowly past, they cast quivering shadows on bloodied faces, on expressions constricted in grief and pain.

It was not the pain of physical injury, for a legionary is inured to that. A man who serves Rome by strength of his arms becomes resigned to leaving a part of himself behind in each campaign—a finger here, lopped off by a Germanic sword or a clumsy colleague's kindling hatchet; a slice of shoulder there, taken by an enemy catapult bolt or the teeth of a recalcitrant cavalry horse; an eye, the straightness of a nose, superfluous teeth, lost to brawling, or to rot, or to the ill-favored gift of a syphilitic prostitute. Yet perhaps this is only fair, to leave something behind, something personal, in exchange for the lives and treasure a soldier takes away in return. Veterans soon learn the tricks to remaining intact, for a soldier cannot survive a twenty-year hitch in the legions and continue to lose a critical appendage every year—there would be little left of a man to enjoy his meager pension if that were the case. After a few years of experience, a man learns to temper his bravery. Not to shirk his duty, of course, but to not take needless chances, either—to volunteer for safer guard postings, to lag a fraction of a moment behind the front line in a charge, to keep a weather eye out for snipers on the flanks rather than focusing solely on the enemy directly in front of him. *Eyes to the East!* the inner voice of experience cries—for in direct, man-to-man combat, a Roman can dispatch any foe by using superior skill and technique, and even an Alaman's greater strength is actually diminished by his very blood rage; but a cool, calculating sniper aiming from behind a tree can only be avoided by experience. After a man loses two or three fondly remembered body parts, second sight becomes second nature.

Yet the pain these faces expressed went far beyond the usual degree of physical suffering. The armor was blood-spattered and dented. Limbs were bandaged, or missing, or hanging at odd angles. There was no talking or singing, not even the usual litany of complaints of an army on the march.

Only the incessant tramping and squelching, of half a million feet wending their way along the vast river of mud.

This very silence was a conundrum rarely encountered. Silence among Romans, a Roman silence, is a contradiction in terms, a condition that, like bare dirt in a lush forest, or a beautiful woman traveling alone, is unstable by the very laws of nature—a vacuum begs to be filled. And as if Stentor, that forgotten God of Clamor and Din, had blearily wakened for a moment and realized his inexplicable lapse, a sound of determined voices rose suddenly to the fore. The weary troops stumbled and hesitated in their sticky trudging, wanting to stop and listen, to experience the relief of knowing life existed beyond their own individual circles of darkness and damp, but each unwilling to lose contact with the shoulder in front of him or be pushed into the mud and trampled by the unseen column of shades marching behind.

The clamorous voices became clearer, punctuated by oaths and the lusty braying of mules unhappy at the conditions under which they were being driven. A column of wooden wagons struggled along in the opposite direction from the troops, forcing its way through the weary wounded. Silently and grudgingly, by touch and by sound rather than by sight, the men stumbled into the ditch at the roadside and stood shivering in the rivulet of muddy water as the wagons passed by. Each vehicle was drawn by a pair of mules, their way lit by a field lantern mounted on a long pole arching over the animals' backs. The yellow lights glimmed weak and sickly on the faces of the auxiliaries walking beside the mules and the wagon wheels. They were young and green-looking—mere boys, hastily conscripted from a local village a few days before, lacking even the rudiments of armor and weaponry—and they stared at the exhausted soldiers they passed in wide-eyed amazement.

The leader of the wagon squadron, a burly centurion, stalked along the side of the road, whipping mules, wagon boys, and the surrounding troops indiscriminately as he worked to clear a path for his train. The weary legions, who only hours before had stood their ground against the fiercest enemies Rome had ever faced, now shrank into the darkness to avoid the sting of the leather mule strap wielded by one of their own. Every man has his job, and these troops had completed theirs. Driving a wagon train was this centurion's, and officers and common troops alike deferred to him and to his snarling whip.

As he passed, the centurion strode up and down his line of rumbling wagons shouting instructions in a clipped, military monotone.

"The truce will hold until sunrise, men! Ignore any Huns on the field—they're looking to their own wounded. And remember the general's warning—no looting! Any man I catch looting the dead, even dead Huns, will be flogged!"

With excruciating slowness the mule column strained up the short hill looming before them in the darkness. The tide of legionaries parted before them and re-formed behind them, in orderly, Roman formation. The only sounds were the exhausted veterans' soft cursing as they were forced to halt their painful progress to stand in the ditch, and the centurion's monotonous harangue.

"Just over this last hill, men. The truce will hold until sunrise. Eight hours to collect the wounded. Get those mules up to this crest. Almost there. . . . *Good God!*"

The centurion stopped as he arrived at the top of the rise and peered over it at the battlefield. He subconsciously made the sign of the cross as the column of wagons behind him slowly ground to a halt.

Below him was a scene of appalling carnage. In the dying light of the sputtering puddles left by missiles, the vast plain was littered with the black, quavering shadows of bodies. Not thousands or tens of thousands but hundreds of thousands of men and horses, lying half-sunken in the churned-up mud, rain pelting their prone forms, turning everything—mud, bodies, the very darkness itself—into a thick soup, the ground barely distinguishable from the bodies and the bodies from the darkness.

After staring for a moment, he began to perceive the individual elements of the scene. The field was not still—rather, it was a vast, writhing quagmire, slowly churning and rippling like the surface of a Saxon bog. Some of the forms crawled weakly or dragged themselves; others lifted a feeble limb as if beckoning to one another; most lay perfectly still. Wild dogs and pigs scurried stealthily among the bodies, and other groups of wagons and stretcher bearers were already hard at work, carrying the wounded and stacking the dead.

In silent horror, the young soldiers of the wagon train gathered behind the centurion and peered over his shoulder. It was a hellish sight, and the young crew froze in shock. The centurion, however, was not one for long pondering.

"Get to work! At daybreak the truce is off. I want all the wounded in by then. *All of them!* The dead we'll burn later."

With a crack of his whip and more curses from the marching legionaries forced into the ditch, the wagon train lurched forward over the crest and began its slow, careful descent down the muddy hill to the edge of the field, where the vehicles fanned out to the largest clusters of dark shapes littering the plain.

Two young Gauls, pressed into service with the Roman ambulance crew only three weeks before, picked their way slowly through the mud and moaning bodies.

"I didn't enlist with the legions to be dragging Romans out of the mud."

"Shut up. You didn't enlist at all. Father ordered us to go because the prefect ordered him to send us. What'd you expect—to get conscripted as a general?"

"No, but at least to do some fighting, kill a Hun or two. . . ."

"Shut up, I said. Help me turn this one over—"

The brothers stooped and grunted as they lifted a prone soldier to flip him onto his back. The mud grudgingly yielded its grip on the man's body with a wet, squelching sound.

"Dead. Leave him. Let's get this one over here. I saw his leg move."

Heaving the injured man onto the filthy stretcher, they trundled the load to their wagon, where the mules stood stoically in the driving rain. The wounded Roman moaned softly with the swaying of the stretcher, and the two Gauls, cursing as they tripped and stumbled through the darkness, did little to smooth his ride.

"Watch it, idiot. Can't you see his arm's almost falling off?"

"Tie it across his chest so it doesn't dangle. Do I have to do everything in this outfit?"

Laying the stretcher on the wagon's lowered tailgate, they slowly slid him off the blood-soaked canvas and onto the floorboards, settling him tightly between two others they had already picked up.

"Room for two more. Get going."

"How about that one? He's moving. . . ."

The brothers approached with their stretcher and bent down to peer at the injured man's face in the dim light.

"Nah—he's a Hun. Yellow as a sunflower, if it weren't for the mud. Half-naked, too. Huns don't even have enough sense to wear metal."

"I don't see as you have any armor yourself."

"Shut up—there's some Huns now!"

The Gauls stopped in mid-squat and stared. Several yards away, two figures strode through the field, their dark leather cuirasses gleaming wetly in the light of the scattered-fires. Each bore a six-foot spear, though no other weapons that could be seen, and they, too, bent here and there to examine a prone figure in the mud.

"Are they doing the same thing as we are?"

"Picking up wounded? Why not?"

"How're they going to carry them? They've got no stretcher or wagon."

As the Gauls watched, the Huns toed a shadowy figure on the ground to turn him over. The injured man weakly twitched an arm. One of the Huns, apparently the more senior, growled something to the other in a guttural tongue and then stalked on to investigate more movement several yards away. The other paused a moment, as if waiting for his leader to step away, then placed the tip of his pike carefully on the throat of the injured man lying at his feet, and leaned heavily onto the shaft. The injured man's arm jerked up suddenly, once, then flopped lifelessly into the mud. The Hun seized his shaft and jerked it out. He then glanced up and saw the two Gauls observing him. For a moment he stood motionless, leaning on his pike as if deep in thought, while the brothers gingerly fingered their belts, hoping they had remembered to attach their sheath knives. Then, with a grin that gleamed yellow in the firelight, the Hun nodded slightly and strode on to join his comrade, who was pointing out another injured soldier.

"Almighty God in Heaven! Did you see that? They're murderers, of their own men! Should we kill them?"

"*Kill them?* Look at their weapons, man; look at their armor—those men aren't conscripts like us; they're real soldiers."

"But . . ."

"Don't get any ideas. The centurion said no contact with the Huns. They're doing their business, and we're doing ours. Let's just get on with it."

Behind them, one of the mules snorted, and both men jumped.

"Not much more room in the wagon bed. Time we picked up a couple more and got back to camp."

As the two men again began slowly making their way through the carnage, a thin voice rose out of the darkness.

"Romans! . . . Ah, for God's sake, over here. . . ."

An arm gestured weakly from a mound of cadavers the Gauls had purposely avoided thus far, being many yards from the nearest fire, its gory details shrouded in darkness.

"There's a live one in there. Hurry . . ."

The two soldiers rushed over, seized the arm, and tugged the wounded man free of the cadavers on top of him, laying him in the mud on his back.

"I can't see a damned thing. Drag him over here."

Cursing softly as they slipped in the mud, the two bent and lifted the wounded man onto the stretcher, then slowly began carrying him away. As they passed in front of a sputtering fire, however, the elder of the two suddenly swore and dropped his burden. His brother, caught off-guard by the sudden shift, staggered backward, then released his own grip on the two poles.

"Idiot! What'd you drop him for?"

"Look at him! He's a Hun!"

The two peered at him closely in the dim light. The wounded man wore a Roman battle helmet but no armor, only a woolen camp tunic and cavalry boots.

"You're right—an old Hun, and an ugly one at that. Looted a Roman helmet from somewhere. Get him off the stretcher."

"Wait. He called out to us in Latin."

The injured man interrupted the bickering above him with a wet cough, weakly struggling to sit up between the two poles of the stretcher on which he lay.

"Romans, please . . . wait!" he gasped, in rough camp Latin. "I have information for you. . . ."

The Gauls squatted in front of him. "Information, Well, you're taking up space a Roman boy could use. Spit it out, old man, and be done with it."

"My information is for your general alone."

The Gauls stared at him incredulously.

"You expect us to take you to General Flavius Aetius? Just like that? Every Hun here would ask for the same thing."

"Huh! Beats being skewered in the throat by their own men, don't it?"

The Gauls laughed, but the wounded Hun coughed again and gripped the stretcher poles tightly with his hands to keep from being tipped out.

"Please . . . take my purse. It's on a string at my belt . . ."

One of the Gauls looked around carefully to see whether anyone was watching, then bent, groped the Hun's thin waist, and tore away a leather purse. He stood back up, stealthily peering inside.

"The centurion told us there was to be no looting."

"But the old man's got money—gold!"

"Probably looted it along with the helmet, before he took a sword in the gut himself."

The Hun spoke up again.

"Please . . . there isn't much time."

The soldiers glanced at each other and nodded. Then they bent to the stretcher, staggered back to the wagon, and roughly heaved him in. After adjusting the cargo for a moment, they stood back to appraise their work.

"What do you think—room for one more?"

"Yes—come on."

The Gauls moved off slowly to seek one more wounded Roman soldier but after several paces stopped suddenly in their tracks, listening.

Hoofbeats and baying dogs—riders were rapidly approaching. In the darkness and rain, all sense of direction was lost—the commotion could have been coming from anywhere. The two turned slowly where they stood, bewildered. They were no strangers to the sound of hoofbeats, but the baying was not that of a normal hound—it was deeper and throatier, mingled with a vicious snarling. The soldiers tensed, and again began nervously fingering their belts. Suddenly, a trio of huge northern wolves, long neck fur flaring out like manes, raced past a nearby fire, tugging at the ropes of the Hunnish handlers behind them. The Gauls stared in astonishment.

"Did you see? Are those . . . ?"

"I'd heard the Huns kept wolves, like General Aetius, but I didn't believe it. . . ."

The huge beasts leaped over bodies on the ground and then stopped, growling, at the pile of corpses from which the old Hun had just been pulled. Snorting and snuffling, they milled about angrily, confused.

A new torrent of rain burst from the sky, and just as the Gauls ducked their heads for cover, a dozen Hunnish horsemen, shouting in their harsh language, thundered out of the darkness, surrounding them with their snorting, pawing horses. Their leader, a commanding figure, loomed over the terrified boys. He wore no metal but only the grimy, worn leather battle gear they had seen on the other Hunnish soldiers. His only distinction of rank was the matted fur trim around the collar and sleeves of his tunic. He was broad-shouldered and muscular, with a controlled physical strength that belied the fury in his face. He glared down at the two cowering Gauls, eyes glittering in the torchlight, avid as a lion's when staring down at its quarry from a low branch.

The leader nodded to one of his mounted comrades, and the two of them suddenly maneuvered their animals behind the Gauls, bent down from their horses, and pressed long knives to the soldiers' necks. The conscripts froze in terror; a sudden shift by a horse, and their throats could be slashed. They stared up, motionless, the rain coursing down their faces. The commander leered as he jerked the younger Gaul's chin up and brandished his weapon before the frightened man's eyes. It was a steel blade with a finely wrought serrated edge such as the Gaul had never before seen. It reminded him of an animal's teeth, and he shuddered.

"Look lively, Roman jackals!" the leader snarled at them in perfectly accented Latin. "Did you see an old Hun pass this way earlier?"

The Gauls could barely stand on their feet for fear. The younger one opened his mouth to speak—*give away the goods; save your skin!* his inner voice cried. But before he could croak a word, the lead horseman interrupted him.

"If I find you Romans have sheltered this man in any way, then the night truce is over. Your heads will decorate my tent poles. Search their wagon."

The Huns released their grip and the two Gauls sank to their knees, weak with terror. Two other Huns in the party dismounted and began walking toward the wagon with a lit torch. Just as they approached it, an Ostrogoth horseman thundered up breathlessly out of the darkness.

"Great King!" he exclaimed breathlessly. "The wolves are baying at a fresh scent! If we hurry, we may still be able to find the old man alive!"

The two Gauls glanced at each other wide-eyed. The elder whispered to his brother out of the corner of his mouth.

" 'Great King'? It's Attila himself!"

The Hunnish commander wheeled his horse about and shouted an order in his strange tongue. The other horsemen galloped off, and the two Huns who were moving to inspect the wagon quickly remounted and raced away after them. The leader lingered a moment longer, glaring down at the two brothers, fingering his serrated blade as if in thought. Then viciously whipping his horse, he thundered off after his men.

The two overwhelmed Gauls staggered back to the wagon. There they stared at the injured old Hun, who peered back at them with rheumy eyes, as he passed in and out of consciousness. A trickle of blood glittered in the dim light as it flowed down the corner of his mouth. The soldiers stood up straighter and tried to recover their former bravado. The elder slapped the old Hun on the foot.

"Well, with all the trouble you've caused, we've got to take you back to camp now. You'd better be worth it."

One body short, they turned the mules around and began the long trek back down the road from which they had come.

Neat rows of canvas tents, each fronted by a smoldering cooking fire for the ten men who slept inside, flanked a narrow dirt path that had deteriorated into a deep-rutted river of mud. Smoke hovered low on the ground, as if pressed down by the rain, and as the weary legionaries trudged into camp and dispersed to their units, their exhausted faces were lit fleetingly by the fires and torchlight. A column of wooden wagons was lined up before a large tent, the camp's field hospital, and men moved frantically around the placid mules, shouting orders and rushing up with medical supplies. They methodically unloaded the carts of their grim burdens, and the open space in front of the hospital tent became ever more thickly filled with moaning bodies. The prone men were packed so closely that orderlies were forced to roll them onto their sides, regardless of the location of their injuries, spooning them against one another to allow room for the endless quantities of new wounded who continued to arrive. The suffering men were not even sheltered from the rain. Many were unconscious, but those who were awake groaned feebly, calling for blankets, for food, for their wives, for their mothers.

At the unloading station, the two Gauls stood arguing with their commanding centurion, who was apoplectic with rage.

"Damn you two lunkheads by all the bloody gods of Gaul! General Aetius has lost a hundred thousand men or more this day. *A hundred fucking thousand men!* And you want me to bring him a half-dead old Hun because he speaks a bit of Latin? My stable boy speaks better Latin than this old hound, and I wouldn't bring him to meet Aetius!"

The two soldiers quailed, but the elder spoke up meekly.

"I swear, sir, it was Attila himself, hunting him down! He must know something. . . ."

The centurion cursed in exasperation, at the thickheadedness of the Gauls, at the freezing rain that was pouring down his back, at the overwhelming fatigue he felt after fighting in the lines all day and now working in the dead wagons all night.

"Attila. Right. You've been hitting the grape juice again, boy. Get your sorry ass back to work. We've still got half the night left. I'll deal with the Hun now, and you two later."

The soldiers shrugged, slapped the mules, and began the hike back out to the field with the empty wagon to pick up more wounded. As they waded away, the centurion watched them with disgust, then looked down at the unconscious Hun with an expression of equal distaste.

"So what the hell am I supposed to do with you, eh?"

Bending down, he slapped both sides of the Hun's face lightly several times in an attempt to waken him.

"Speak up, Hun. I can't hear you. Ah hell."

The centurion picked up the old man as easily as if he were a sack of barley, threw him over his shoulder, and trudged off.

The tent was large, airy, and well lit, roomy and comfortable by military standards, though by any standards other than military, it was slovenly and cramped. Maps and documents were strewn on a table and spilled onto the rough plank flooring, and aides bustled in and out, shaking off water and scraping muddy boots. Rain hammered on the sodden canvas, and the wind shook the fabric so that it seemed to vibrate like the skin of a drum, forcing all inside to raise their voices to be heard. Furniture and papers had been hastily stacked in mounds, away from the seams of the fabric—for under these, at the needle holes, even liberal application of lard and wax had failed to stem the effects of the downpour, and long strings of water beads formed on every edge where two pieces of fabric were joined. A gust of wind that swelled the tent, or a clumsy shoulder brushing against the canvas wall, would send a row of cold droplets onto the heads of those sitting below, and the sound of the driving rain outside was periodically accompanied by angry curses within.

At a table and bench in the middle of the tent, General Flavius Aetius sat conferring with half a dozen of his officers. All were dressed still in the field armor they had been wearing for the past sixteen hours, and all were soaked and filthy—none had bathed or eaten since their own return from the battlefield hours before.

Their faces were grim and exhausted, but Aetius remained calm and unflappable. A tall, lean man, he had a high-bred look and patrician bearing, though without the vacant stare or excess of emotion of those who come by their position undeservedly. He exuded quiet confidence and competence, and his officers sat before him tensely as he questioned them about the army's current situation.

"What's the casualty count?"

Pellus, a veteran tribune from Dacia, squinted at a torn scrap of parchment he held in his hand, struggling to make sense of the figures he had scrawled a few moments before from the reports of his field centurions.

"General Aetius—our preliminary estimate, before darkness fell, was three hundred thousand casualties on the field. No idea how many are Huns, how many are ours. . . ."

There was a collective sucking of breath from the men present. Though every one of them was a hardened veteran, accustomed to witnessing death and sending his troops into the maw of combat, these figures were unheard of. Three hundred *thousand*? Never in history had a single battle destroyed so many lives.

A second tribune, Antony, cleared his throat and continued the summary.

"The ambulance squads are out now, sir, picking up survivors. After they return we'll have a more accurate count."

Pellus resumed the thread of his report.

"The worst of it is, sir, reports say that King Theodoric was found beneath a mound of dead Huns."

At this news, Aetius looked up in shock.

"Theodoric? What was his condition, Tribune?"

"Dead," Pellus rejoined. "Witnesses say he took an Ostrogoth javelin that knocked him off his horse. He got up fighting but in the end was overwhelmed. Wounds in all the proper places. He died bravely, that one, battling like a *primus pilus*."

Aetius shook his head in dismay. "The idiot. I have plenty of men to fight like centurions. I needed him to command like a king."

He paused for a moment, considering this latest turn.

"The Visigoths are our largest ally—that leaves them with no commander."

Antony leaned forward, dropping his voice.

"Correct, sir—all two hundred thousand of them. Even now, word is spreading through the camp. The Visigoths are confused, leaderless. Some vow vengeance under his eldest son, Thorismund, while others say they'll return to Tolosa, to prepare his funeral."

Aetius remained calm and silent, thinking. The others bore shocked expressions, the look of men who had lost everything. Finally, Pellus cleared his throat.

"General Aetius, a decision is needed," he said hesitantly. "The Visigoth king is dead. His two hundred thousand men may not fight. We have lost—"

"I heard you perfectly well the first time," Aetius stopped him. "We have lost nothing."

Sudden shouts from outside interrupted the conversation. The men pricked up their ears at the commotion and stood to investigate.

"You men are dismissed," Aetius growled as he stood up. "Antony, get a more accurate casualty count and check in again at the next watch." He shouldered past them toward the tent opening, muttering in annoyance at this new disruption. "What the hell is going on now?"

Lifting the door flap, he strode out into the rain.

In the river of mud fronting the tent, a centurion stood arguing with two of Aetius' guards, who had prevented him from approaching the general's field headquarters. The old Hun lay on the ground at the centurion's feet, wrapped in a sodden blanket, eyes half-open, shivering and gazing around in befuddlement. Aetius approached and pushed through, confronting the men in irritation.

"Centurion—what's the meaning of this? Have you nothing better to do on such a night?"

The centurion snapped to surprised attention at the appearance of the high commander himself.

"General Flavius Aetius! Greetings to you, sir, from the Tenth Legion, and all due respect. My ambulance crew encountered this Hun—" he toed the half-conscious old man, eliciting a moan of pain—"who insists on talking to you. Claims to have vital information. Sir."

Aetius glanced down curiously at the Hun, but his face registered no emotion. The injured man stared up at him, his eyes gradually focusing and widening in recognition. With difficulty, he removed his hand from the folds of the bloody, rain-soaked blanket that enveloped him like a shroud, and extended his closed fist to Aetius.

Aetius bent down and held out his own hand, and the Hun dropped something into it. The general stood and held the object to the torchlight for examination. It was a polished, yellowed fang, dangling from a plain leather thong, a common-enough talisman among the Huns. And yet it bore a *tamga*, a property mark—unusual for such a valueless thing as this. He held it closer to the light. There, he could barely make it out—a crudely carved letter "A."

The general started in surprise and stared back down at the Hun. The face—at first he had not recognized it, but now there was no mistake. That broken nose, which had healed so badly . . .

"Centurion, bring this man into the tent immediately. Guard—call a physician."

The guard sprinted away. The centurion bent and heaved the Hun again onto his shoulder, striding toward the tent opening. Aetius followed close behind.

Ducking inside the tent, the centurion deposited the Hun onto the general's cot with a grunt, then stood and saluted smartly with upraised hand. Aetius nodded to him absentmindedly and stepped toward the cot, but the centurion remained standing. The general turned to look at him a moment, at this burly veteran covered with mud and soaked to the skin, his tunic and armor streaked with blood from the wounded man he had been carrying. The centurion remained at stiff attention, eyes expressionless, staring straight ahead.

"At ease, man. What are you waiting for, a medal?"

The trooper flinched slightly, dropped his upraised hand, but remained motionless, and suddenly it dawned on Aetius why. For the first time in hours the man was out of the rain, and he was reluctant to venture back to the field again so soon.

The general's expression softened slightly. "To the guard shack with you. Tell the armorer I sent you for a cup of hot wine. I know he keeps it behind the forge."

"For the prisoner, sir?" the centurion inquired.

Aetius turned away. "The prisoner? He's barely conscious, soldier. Drink it yourself, and back out to the field!"

The centurion nodded, still expressionless, and then strode impassively out the door flap. Aetius stood for a moment listening to the splashing footsteps fade away outside. Then sighing deeply, he seized a nearby oil lamp and bent over the Hun. Though the lamplight shone close, the injured man's eyes did not even flicker.

Aetius examined the face closely, taking in the features, so familiar yet so changed with the years. Could he himself have changed as much? A man's face and body mature, then decay, becoming almost unrecognizable over time. But does his core remain fixed, as when one takes an ax, swings it at a tree, and bites all the way to a sapling that witnessed the march of Julius Caesar? This old man in front of him—was he the same man Aetius had known? Was he here out of friendship? Or something else?

A deafening burst of rain pounded on the tent canvas, like a volley of arrows striking a shield. Aetius pulled a camp stool up to the cot and sat down. He had barely settled into position when the door flap opened again, sending a spray of water into the tent.

A miserable-looking civilian stumbled in, nearly tripping over an enormous ball of fur curled up on a woven mat in the middle of the floor. The fur ball twitched in irritation, looked up with gleaming yellow eyes, and emitted a menacing growl.

"Lucilla! Hush!" Aetius ordered.

"Greetings, General Aetius," the man mumbled anxiously. "You called for a physician? With all due respect, sir, that wolf makes me nervous."

"She's tame. She hasn't eaten a doctor in days."

The man's eyes opened wide and he edged carefully around the glowering animal, who fixed a hungry stare on him. Finally putting Aetius between himself and the beast, the physician sidled over to the brazier in the middle of the tent with slow and deliberate movements, as if reestablishing his wounded dignity. He removed his felted woolen cloak, on which the droplets had settled like tiny pearls, and stretched it over the back of a chair. He then calmly removed his felt cap and ran a hand through his hair, allowing more droplets to fall onto the hot metal at the edge of the brazier, where they jumped and spat. Finally, glancing at Aetius, who eyed him coldly, he nodded his readiness and strode to the cot to venture his first look at the patient he had been called to examine. His face immediately registered distaste.

"General Aetius—this man is a Hun!"

Aetius sighed deeply. "This is news to me?"

The physician blinked in surprise, then averted his gaze. Between the yellow eyes of the wolf and the impassive stare of the general, he felt as if stage lanterns were being trained on his face. He bent down self-consciously to rummage through his medical kit, grunting and mumbling to himself, then grudgingly set to work, unwrapping the Hun's sodden blanket and cutting away the woolen tunic. As he carefully lifted away the fabric, snipping the fibers where dried blood had adhered to the man's skin, he glanced at Aetius and shook his head in dismay.

The general leaned over the physician's shoulder to see for himself and winced. He stepped back for a moment, staring at the low ceiling as if composing his thoughts. Then, edging around the hunched form of the physician, he bent down, seized the Hun's face with his hand, and turned it toward him.

"What is it? Why are you here?"

The wounded Hun started at the sound of the general's voice and his eyelids fluttered open. His eyes, however, remained unfocused and distant, and his mouth worked laboriously.

"Must tell Flavius. . . . Must . . . tell Flavius!"

"Tell me what? Old man, why have you come?!"

The physician sat back and gently removed Aetius' hand from the patient's face, respectfully but firmly shouldering him aside. The general stepped back slightly, though his eyes never left those of the old Hun. As the physician carefully adjusted a bent flange on a set of metal tongs, he conversed with Aetius, seeking both to inform him and to distract him.

"The man won't last another day, General. I would be surprised if he survived the night. If I may ask: Who is he?"

Aetius paused for a moment before responding.

"This man . . ."

At a sudden loss for words, he looked across the room, staring into space.

"This man," he continued, "he used to be a Hun."

The physician scoffed.

" 'Used to be'? They don't get more Hunnish than this specimen. So what is he now?"

Aetius looked down sadly at the dying man and held his silence. The physician observed him for a long moment, and then, fearing that his question had been forgotten or ignored, he screwed up his courage to interrupt the general's thoughts.

"General Aetius, as a matter of professional interest and . . . personal curiosity—what is this man now?"

Aetius sighed and stood up straight. Composing his face, he fixed his gaze firmly on the physician.

"Forty years, it's been. Forty years and more. No, physician, this man is no mere Hun."

"Ah. You know him then? A captured enemy officer, perhaps?"

Aetius shook his head. "No, not just an officer, though he is that, too. Keep him alive, physician, alive at all costs."

The physician's eyes gleamed at the trust the great man had placed in him.

"So this Hun, he is of quite some importance then?"

Aetius nodded and once again bent to examine the wounded man's face.

"Physician," he said, "at this moment, he may be the most important man in the Roman Empire."